THE WORLD
AROUND US

LAUREN LACEY

Trigger/Content Warning
This story contains mature themes and content that may be distressing to some readers. It includes explicit language, sexual content, and discussions of sensitive topics such as child abuse, sexual abuse, sexual violence, drug addiction, violence, parental loss, and complex family dynamics. Reader discretion is advised.

CONNECT WITH LAUREN LACEY
contact@authorlaurenlacey.com
Instagram.com/thelaurenlacey

Printed Worldwide
First Printing 2024
First Edition 2024

10 9 8 7 6 5 4 3 2 1

THE WORLD
AROUND US

Author's Note:

First, I want to thank you for reading *The World Around Us*. This love story means so much to me. I've poured so much heart, emotion, and hope into its pages. Tiffany and Mason's journey isn't just about love; it's about survival, trust, hope, family, friendship, resilience, and the beauty that can rise from the ashes of hardship.

Tiffany and Mason remind us that while life can be messy and complicated, love—in all its forms—is powerful. This is a story about appreciating the ugly yet beautiful world around us.

I know some topics in this book may be heavy or triggering. I want you to know it's okay to pause. It's okay to take breaks. And it's okay to feel all the emotions that this story might stir up. Healing isn't linear, just as love and life aren't, but there's beauty in the journey.

To anyone who's ever felt lost, hopeless, broken, or unworthy of love, this book is for you. For the fighters, the dreamers, and the survivors, this is a testament that hope can light even the darkest corners.

Thank you for trusting me with your time, your heart, and your mind. It means the world to me, and I don't take it lightly.

Welcome to Greer, Georgia. I hope you enjoy the ride. I hope you enjoy the love story of Tiffany Weathers and Mason Boom.

Prologue

Tiffany

Recurring Dream

In the frequent mist of my dream, an unclear yet piercingly vivid memory of an unsettlingly familiar voice weaves through the unfolding darkness.

"Hey, little ones. Are you ready to go home?"

It's my mother. We're engulfed in the eerie embrace of a smoky night, coughing and afraid, but my God-awful Mother calls out to us with a smile on her face – a sweet deceptiveness that cuts through the haze.

"C'mon, let's go." She lovingly says.

"But what about our –" Tiny, my big sister, cries, but Mama snaps, grabs our arms, and twists them tight.

"You heard what I said," She glares at us with disdain. "Just drink this water so you can fall fast asleep. We need to go, NOW!"

And just like that, darkness swallows the next decade of my life.

I jerk awake at this moment because when darkness entered my life, my reality turned into a living nightmare.

Over the past year, my dreams have been filled with memories of my past. Some of the memories are hauntingly unforgettable, while others are shrouded in a fog of trauma I dare not revisit. There are also some memories

I can't fully recollect. Thankfully, with the help of my family and so many others who supported me along the way, I've been able to piece together the moments that matter, which has allowed me to build a new life.

I draw strength from what I've built, brick by emotional brick. I love my career. I have friends and family who love me and a son who's the center of my universe. I'm happy — genuinely happy — and I won't allow anyone to take my joy and peace away from me.

PART 1

FIRST QUARTER NERVES

Chapter 1

Tiffany Weathers - Tiffany

My name is Tiffany Weathers, and I live in Greer, Georgia, a Southern community ripe with unprecedented growth over the years since the merger with its twin city, Beverly Mills. Greer has attracted thousands of new residents, billions of dollars in revenue, and a new professional football team, the Greer Renegades. It's a new era for the city.

My bond with this town runs deep, nurtured by memories both bitter and sweet. I'm a tried-and-true Atlanta girl, College Park, to be exact, but some of my greatest memories occurred right here in this unassuming city where I found safety, peace, happiness, and family.

Greer is also where I fell in love with Mason Boom.

The decision to move back wasn't mine alone. My family and friends pushed for it, and my son wanted it. So, I set my Atlanta-based dance studios up for success, packed our bags, and relocated back home.

Despite my initial reservations, the move was genius. I value my privacy, and the tranquility of our community has offered us more happiness than we could ever dream of.

So, here I am, back in Greer, where I've made a cozy home for me and my son. I admit that I enjoy this deep Southern escape. The 'good' side of town, Beverly Mills, sits against the beautiful oceanic backdrop, where you can find a church on every corner filled with wholesome families and friendly residents who have known one another for generations. Whereas Greer is often called the Las Vegas of the South, the 'dark' side, where morally gray values are masked behind opulent mansions, wealth, sports stadiums, a vibrant nightlife, and flashy lifestyles.

But it's so much more than that! Trauma leaves scars, and the people of Greer have been hardened to survive by any means necessary. These residents are the most cold-blooded yet kind-hearted people I've ever met.

I'm drawn to this place. It's the closest thing I've ever had to a stable home. Perhaps that's because, like Greer, there's a darkness within me — rooted in secrets and pain. The duality of my town, its shining veneer, and what lurks beneath mirrors the constant battle within myself. Maybe that's why I pour so much of myself into others — my son, my dancers, my career — hoping to create the balance for them that I can't always find within myself.

My days are filled with purpose and responsibility. As the Head Coach of the Greer Pipettes Dance Team and the owner of three dance studios, I've built a career focused on shaping others' lives. My son, who means the world to me, is my greatest priority. Yet, as fulfilling as my work and my roles are, I've started to wonder if it's time to turn some of that energy inward and focus on myself, or my heart's *greatest desire*, rather.

"Morning, Mom. You look awful." My son, Drew, nonchalantly says as he grabs his breakfast biscuit from the counter and kisses my cheek. His frankness, though blunt, is cushioned by the routine warmth of our daily interactions.

I laugh, masking the slight sting of his words, and give him a big hug. "Well, good morning to you, too, Son."

He returns my embrace and softens his tone to express his concern. "My bad. You must've had a bad dream again?"

With a note of weariness in my voice, I sigh, "Unfortunately, yes, but don't worry 'bout me. Those are just memories flooding back into my mind. The next few months are all about you. Your first game is only a month away. Fingers crossed, you'll get to start. Not to mention, it's your sweet sixteen in three months–one of the best years of your life. When your aunt Tiny and I were young, we'd watch a show called My Super Sweet 16 on tv at Aunt Dora's, where the parents would throw lavish parties for their kids. Then, we'd pretend to have our own parties. Are you sure you don't want me to throw you the 'party of the century' where I buy you a Benz and give you thousands of dollars…Monopoly money, of course."

Drew chuckles, his laughter filled with amusement and disbelief. "You better not! I'm fine with what we have. You worked hard for everything we got, and I'm gonna do the same. I don't want you to spend a bunch of money on a party, Ma. Besides, I'm a workin' man now!" He proudly declares.

I shake my head and rummage through his summer school folder, feeling a swell of pride. We may be well off now, but Drew's humility work is remarkable, and his work ethic is undeniable. Though, I do wish he'd focus more on being a kid.

"What's your schedule like today?"

"Team workout in forty minutes, Summer AP chemistry at three, lunch with Lea, football practice, then work!" Drew rattles off, barely pausing for breath.

I chuckle, shaking my head. "I was never this busy during the summer, and I still can't believe your Aunt Monica got Mase to hire you as his student intern. You're still in high school! You know he made that position up just for you, right?"

"All A's as usual, and don't be jealous." Drew snatches his schoolwork from my hands, grinning proudly.

I scoff, folding my arms with mock indignation. "Jealous of what, exactly?"

"That I get to hang out with your ex-boyfriend every day," Drew smirks, leaning against the doorway like he's got it all figured out. "I guess I'd be jealous, too, though. He's freakin' Mason Boom! He's the best, and I approve of you two dating *again*."

Who does this boy think he is?

"Keep your nose out of grown folks' business," I bite my lip to keep from laughing while shaking my head. "Now, get goin'. I know I'll only catch you for a second between your hectic schedule, but I'll see you when you get home from work."

Drew rolls his eyes dramatically and huffs, tossing his bag over his shoulder. "Alright, but seriously, who's taking me to the stadium?"

I pull him in for a quick kiss on the top of his head, my voice softening. "Aunt Mel will take you. Oh, Mase had a team shirt delivered to the house for you to wear, and I know you want to make a great impression on your first day, so I got you a new pair of pants, too."

His expression softens, and he gives me a grateful nod. "Thanks, Mom. I love you."

"I love you, too, Son." I reply, watching as he heads to summer workouts.

After Drew departs, the silence of my home envelops me, a reminder of the life I've built from the burnt ashes of my past. My house is modest compared to the grandeur of Greer's opulent mansions, but it's a fortress of my own making, a testament to the struggles I've overcome and the simple joys I cherish. It's more than I ever had growing up, and it's mine. It's ours, and I'm blessed to be a mom to a grateful son who appreciates every little bit I give him, which is every little bit I have.

Following a moment of peace, my day commences with the comforting routine of chores and check-ins with the contractors renovating my dance studio. Then, I get dressed and meet up with my three best friends, Monica, Avery, and Mel, at the coffee shop. Monica Owens-Carter owns the hottest PR firm in town, serving all the local celebrities and sports superstars. We met at Spelman's freshman orientation. She was a hot mess. To be honest, we all were, but she reminded me of my sister Tiny–abused in every way imaginable yet still so resilient. She married one of my closest friends and one of the best men I know, Rafe Boom. Avery Waylen-Owens is the city's District Attorney. She's loud, opinionated, and hilarious. The town loves her. We met through Monica back in college and have been thick as thieves ever since. She moved back to Greer with her husband and the love of her life, Deacon. Finally, there's Mel. My absolute best friend and true sister. She's an internationally known photographer, but most importantly, she's the first person who accepted me when I moved to Greer. These women are my family. And like family, they often drive me crazy.

"So," Avery dramatically announces as we sip our Caramel Macchiatos, a ritual that feels as comforting as the warm embrace of the sun on a misty Greer morning. "Since you keep deleting the dating profiles we created for you, we found you a date for the gala."

"Found?" I respond, my voice pitching to a yell. "Have y'all resorted to pickin' people off the street for me now? And damn it, I know everyone in this small town. So, who the heck is it?"

"Hey! First of all, our city's booming. We got Starbucks, Chick-fil-A, Target, two professional sports teams, and seven nightclubs. We're the new Atlanta. And Lynn Perfumery's moved back and brought a heap of businesses and jobs with them. We're *far* from a small town." Mel playfully throws her napkin in my face. "Secondly, yes, *found*! Batches of handsome, rich men are moving here nearly every week, and you've rejected every single one. So, you just gotta take what you can get at this point."

Laughter erupts among us, a welcome respite from the tension of the topic at hand – my nonexistent love life.

Monica leans in, her demeanor shifting to one of earnest concern mixed with a dash of excitement. "Tiff, you've got a great career. You're hot as all get out, smart, and successful. Not to mention, Drew's a teenager now.

I mean, my goodness, it's time! You haven't been in a relationship since —
"

"Wack ass Donny!" Mel interjects, her laughter slicing through the seriousness of Monica's monologue.

"Please, don't ever mention his name again. He was a certified snake. I'm so glad Mason stepped in."

The name alone stirs up a flood of memories—none of them good—which makes it easy to join in the laughter. Shaking my head, I can't help but recall the bitterness of my last relationship.

"Speaking of my brother-in-law, Mase is super excited to be back in Drew's life full-time. He really loves him, you know." Monica looks at me with a sincere smirk. Her words, simple yet laden with meaning, stir a complexity of emotions within me.

"I know. Drew loves him, too. Mase is such a good father figure. He's been there for him since he was a baby. Can y'all believe he's gonna be sixteen in just a few months?"

Mel shakes her head in disbelief, "Absolutely not! You practically have a grown man living in your house now. Does he know about his big gift yet?"

"Nope," I answer as my lips curl into a smile at the thought of what's to come. "He's gonna be shocked. Or, in his words, shook. He's gonna be shook! It's gonna be the greatest gift ever."

Monica's hand reaches across the table, and with her gentle touch, she reminds me of the support and love that surrounds me. "It's been a long time comin'," She then quickly switches the subject. "And your date is gonna be so excited when he sees you! He'll be waiting for you when we arrive at the Coliseum – dressed to impress and ready to sweep you off your feet."

Ugh, I'm dreading this!

My friends know damn well I have zero interest in dating anyone new. I made a vow to wait until after Drew's 16th birthday, and honestly, I barely want to date at all. Every time I try, it ends in disaster. It's like life itself is nudging me to stay single or, worse, refusing to let me be happy with the man I truly want. Maybe I should just give in to their plan. I'm almost thirty-two, and I'm in a place of peace, a peace that I wouldn't mind sharing with someone.

So, with a deep breath, I square my shoulders and look at my friends, vibrating with excitement. "You know what? I'm in. I'll go on the date. I've got nothing to lose. Well, my life, if he's a serial killer, but I'm trusting your judgment on this. But remember, this won't be anything serious. I'm not trying to move fast or settle down until —"

"After Drew's birthday!" My friends teasingly roll their eyes and say in unison.

Their exuberant cheers cut through the coffee shop's quaint ambiance, drawing curious glances from other patrons, which is my cue to exit and put the final touches on our charity gala.

Chapter 2

Flirting with Fate – Tiffany

Monica's connections span far and wide, and her heart is as big as ever. When she told me she'd host a charity gala for my dance team, I was ecstatic. Half of the donations will go to my dance team and the other half to my charity of choice–Greer Sovereign House, a haven dedicated to supporting domestic abuse survivors, recovering addicts, the homeless, and at-risk youth. Those are my people. That's all I knew growing up. Now, all I want to do is help them like so many others have helped me. Given our traumatic pasts, this aspect of the gala is important to us and adds greater meaning to what we do.

The gala is called *A Bid for a Better Tomorrow*. We needed to make a splash to garner excitement and attention from the town's wealthiest residents, so Monica convinced her very single and very sexy brothers-in-law to participate in the 'Date with A Millionaire' auction.

The Boom Brothers come from old money and impenetrable political power. They're also the most eligible bachelors in the South and three of the best athletes in the world. Once we made the auction announcement, the gala sold out in six hours! They're a complicated bunch, to say the least, but their reputation and affluence have turned our event into the talk of the town. I'm most concerned about Mason Boom, but as the co-organizer of

*A Bid for a Better Tomorro*w, I can't let my emotions jeopardize the success of our charity gala.

Mason and I are best friends, exes, and occasional enemies—but no matter what, we're always on each other's minds. He's the one I'm convinced life doesn't want me to be happy with, and maybe I understand why. We've done everything in our power to tame the intense pull between us, limiting our interactions to only what's necessary and relying on friends or family as buffers. But no matter the distance, whenever we're alone, common sense dissolves. We fall back into the "Mase and Tiff" saga like no time has passed. It's electric, comforting, and chaotic all at once.

We've been drawn to one another since the day we met. The connection we share is undeniable, a bond so intense it defies logic. Yet, it's this very same intensity that necessitates distance to safeguard us against the chaos that seems to follow our love like an ominous cloud.

He knows me, and sometimes even better than I know myself. Many people *think* we're soulmates, but the problem with knowing someone for so long is they know too much about you. Mase knows *everything* about me—my secrets, traumas, and tragedies. Our shared history, while filled with countless cherished memories, also harbors moments of heartbreak, missteps, and regret. With Mason back in Greer and now the Renegades' quarterback, keeping my emotions in check is a challenge I never quite anticipated.

But my duty is more important than my desire, so just as I've called his brothers to confirm their participation, it's time for me to call Mason.

I'd be lying if I said I wasn't nervous. And when he picks up, a familiar thrill courses through my veins, but I quickly shove my feelings aside and force myself to stay focused.

Mason's voice, a familiar yet distant melody, radiates through the phone, stirring a mix of nostalgia and unspoken sentiments within me.

"Tiff…" His tone is plain but loaded like he's holding back the words he really wants to say.

"Mase," I respond cool and composed, professional even. "I just wanted to confirm your participation for Saturday night. The gala starts at 7 p.m. at the Old Greer Coliseum."

A sigh drifts through the phone, slow and weary, but I swear I can hear a hint of a smile in it. "Well, hello to you, too, Ms. Weathers. Unfortunately, I'll be there. Monica hasn't given me much choice. I really don't feel like being around people this weekend, but it'll be nice to see you. Actually," He hesitates. "It'll be nice if I can see you tonight. Why can't you drop Drew off at the stadium? Are you avoiding me?"

His question sends a jolt through me. I'm not avoiding him, but I am avoiding my lust for him. I'm protecting him just as he's always protected me. From the magnetic pull he has on me, from everything that always manages to unravel when we're together.

"Say something, anything, Tiff. I'm starting to think you don't care about me anymore." There's a soft laugh beneath his words, but I can feel his charm coming through, subtly testing me.

"Of course, I care about you, Mase." I finally answer in a cool tone. "You'll always be my favorite weirdo. But right now, what I care about is the gala. So, please don't bail on me. The money's going to help so many dancers and people in need. Besides, this appearance will be a good look for your big comeback. It's a part of your PR strategy, right?"

Mase huffs, and I feel his frustration radiating through the speaker. "Please don't mention that. I know what to do, Tiff. Monica already told me to smile for the cameras, lightly touch on my mental health, and encourage others to take time to focus on their well-being. I know my script, okay?"

"Well, I'm glad you know what to say, Mase, but are you actually doing it?" I reply, letting a mix of concern and frustration edge into my tone. "You're not at that fancy retreat anymore. Are you taking care of yourself?"

"I'm not answering any of your questions or responding to your comments until you answer mine," He sharply cuts me off. "Will I see you tonight at the stadium? I see Drew every day but you? Every other week. I'm losing my mind over here. There's no way you haven't been thinkin' 'bout me. Not even once?"

I take a deep breath and carefully choose my words. His plea for reassurance, a simple acknowledgment of my concern for him, forces me to tread a fine line between professional obligation and personal desire. I know he wants me to crack just enough to let him in, but I can't. Not yet, not until after Drew's birthday.

"Yes, I have. I mean—I do," I admit, the words slipping out before I can stop them. "I always think about you, Mase, and it makes me both happy and sad. The last few years have been peaceful because of you. I can't thank you enough for what you've done for me, for what you've always done for me. But when we get together, it's always a mess. It's always been that way—a complete mess!"

His low chuckle hums through the phone. "We're quite the beautiful mess together, Tiffany Nicole, so I don't mind getting dirty with you again. And you're still single, which means you waited for me just like I asked. We were destined to be together, and fate never fails."

There it is—the pull, as strong as ever. We were doing so well until now. Mase breaks through my armor effortlessly, bringing my fingers to loosen around the phone while feeling a surge of emotions I can't quite contain. *Fate.* A part of me still believes it. The familiarity of our words and the ease with which we fall into old patterns belies the complexity of our relationship. His optimism and openness to love, laden with longing, tempt me to revisit the past we've shared, but I'm aware of the emotional stakes involved.

"Was it fate, Mr. Shakespeare? Or was it family and careers that brought us back to Greer?" I attempt to reject his charm. "And just so you know, I'm bringing a date to the gala this weekend. So, all this flirting you're doing right now isn't gonna fly. I don't want my new man to feel awkward around us due to your out-of-pocket behavior."

He laughs, rich and warm, like I just laid down a challenge he's all too eager to take on. But then he pauses, and I can almost hear his reluctance.

"I'm bringing a date, too…But I don't want to. I'd much rather have you by my side. Can you picture us finally together again, as we're supposed to be? The football player and his dancer, living happily ever after?"

As Mason toys with the idea of fate and destiny, his words strike a chord. Still, I'm compelled to keep my guard up for now, determined not to slip back into the chaos of a heartbreak I can't endure again. Even the mention of our dates to the gala serves as a stark reminder of the walls we've built between us, but his question still lingers, threading through my thoughts and tugging at a vision I've held onto for years – us being together.

The idea lives at the top of my mind, vivid and tantalizing, but I refuse to let him know that. "Nope! I can't picture it at all!"

He chuckles again, unphased. "I assume you'll wear a tight gold dress for me this weekend?"

He just won't give up, which further piques my interest. I roll my eyes, but I don't say no. Instead, I nod, which is understood in my silence.

"I'll see you this weekend, Mase. Mel will drop Drew off tonight. Take care of our boy, okay?"

"Always, Tiffany Nicole." His safe, assuring tone gives a warmth that has always assured me he's trustworthy, the man I could depend on, my safe space to land.

After I end my call with Mase, I allow myself the luxury of a mini-shopping spree, a rare indulgence in my otherwise disciplined life. I need a dress to wear to the gala, and I think gold would look great on me. Okay, I admit, the sheer thought of seeing the smile on Mase's face when he sees me excites me. The excitement doesn't reflect how good we look together, though we do look quite amazing. It's more about me acquiescing to his request. It's an act of forward progress, and I'm willing to take this baby step so he knows I *do* still care about him, and I'll always love him.

My Friday passes by quickly with the anticipation of tomorrow's event. Aside from a few fires here and there and rejecting interviews focused on my past, my everyday life is simple. I wake up, cook breakfast, kiss Drew goodbye, work on the renovations for my studio, coach the high school dance team, wait for Drew's practice to end, cook dinner, shower, and then sleep to do it all over again.

To most, my life may seem mundane, but for me, it's a sanctuary of peace. There's a stark difference between my past and present, and I find a sense of stability and tranquility in the simplicity of my daily routine.

Yet, beneath the contentment of my predictable existence, there's still something missing in my life, which is why I find myself marveling at my new dress. I expect to turn heads, specifically Mase's, then we'll once again be drawn to one another as if our lives were destined to be entangled together.

There's also a distinct benefit to his reemergence – my often tense, worried thoughts are replaced by sweet memories of our chaotically beautiful life together. I just wish my peaceful dreams would translate to reality, but I've come to understand that I need to take advantage of the thrill of love that life offers because as soon as I want more, it's taken away. My happy ending with Mase always seems to get taken away from me.

Every attempt we've made to recommit to one another has been thwarted, as if life itself conspires to keep us apart. I want to get who I deserve, and I want Mase to get who he deserves, and a part of me still believes we deserve each other.

The story of my life has been one of almosts and what-ifs. A series of moments teetering on the edge of fulfillment only to be snatched away. However, at this moment, I'll lie down and allow myself to bask in my sweet dreams where love is rare and protected from life's interference, where the love between me and Mason Boom is unbreakable.

Chapter 3

The Plan – Mase

Friday Night – The Eve of the Gala

Can you imagine being in love with one person your entire life? It's beautiful, right? Well, I guess that just depends on your definition of beautiful. My definition of beautiful is Tiffany Nicole Weathers.

Tiffany is one of those women you have to wear down because while I consider love a necessity, she considers love a luxury she could never afford. To her, it's a privilege reserved for individuals with time to spare and enough emotional resources to mend an inevitable broken heart. The unjust harshness of life has shaped her pragmatic mind to believe love is an aspiration rather than a fundamental need. I, however, think differently. I'm determined to show her that love, our love, isn't just a luxury but the foundation upon which we can rebuild the life we once dreamed of together.

My name is Mason Boom, and the love I have for Tiffany Weathers surpasses aspirations. It's woven into decades of laughter, tears, triumphs, and tragedies. She entered my life unexpectedly when we were just kids and danced her way into my heart as teenagers. I knew I loved Tiffany the moment I saw her, but I didn't know how much I loved her until I lost her – until we lost one another.

But what's lost can always be found, and I'm so damn grateful I found my way back to Greer, Georgia, where all that I love is here – my home, family, friends, but most importantly, my woman.

"Yo, Mase," Oh, and I can't forget my woman's amazing son, Drew, as he yells my name from across the workout room. "You ready for your big comeback?" He asks, excited to start the first day of his student internship.

"Of course, I'm ready," I warmly greet him with an embrace and pat him on the shoulder. "Or at least that's what Monica's been tellin' all the media outlets." I respond, attempting to conceal the nervous energy that simmers beneath my confident façade.

He studies my response and then asks, "So, you're nervous?"

"I guess we'll see on game day," I shrug and complete my shoulder exercises. "I'm sure I'll find my rhythm once I step on the field. I've been playing the game for so long that it's a part of me.

"Well, good 'cause I been bragging to my girlfriend about how good you are. Don't make me a liar." Drew warns.

I laugh at his boldness and his young, raging hormones. "Say what? Does your mom know about this so-called girlfriend?"

"Yes!" He shouts. "And she keeps introducing her to everyone as my 'little friend.' It's embarrassing, and she doesn't care."

"Yeah, that's ya mom. It's nice to know she hasn't changed. Just remember, always treat your girl right."

Drew chuckles. "Of course! I treat my girl just like you always treated my mom–like a queen. So, tell me, what's your plan to get her to change her mind about you?"

"Huh?" I inquire, fully understanding his question but holding my bluff.

Drew laughs under his breath. "Come on, Mase. I'm not a little kid anymore. Everyone knows you've been in love with my mom forever. So, what's the plan to win her over this time? You always have a plan."

Drew's insight into my feelings for his mom isn't just the observation of a perceptive teenager; it's a mirror reflecting my deepest desires and fears that I'm not ready to reveal.

I raise an eyebrow, but Drew is persistent and maintains his stance until I finally give in. "Okay! I may or may not have enlisted the crew to convince your mom to agree to be my 'blind date' for tomorrow night."

"What?" He smiles in disbelief. "Oh, she's gonna be pissed – happily pissed, if that makes sense."

"Promise not to say anything? She's been dodging me since I moved back. If she finds out about this, I'm pretty sure she'll run me out of town."

Drew laughs, "Bet. Your secret's safe with me. Besides, I'm Team Boom anyway. And I –" Drew's playful tone changes and reveals an earnest vulnerability. "If this works, I may finally have a dad. I'd finally get to call you Dad."

I absorb Drew's sincerity. Though he often has the emotional maturity of a well-adjusted adult, moments like this remind me he's still a child, and every child craves the presence of their parents—known and unknown. Every child wants to be loved, and the fact that he's never met his biological father haunts him.

I want a family, but I want the family that's been dangling in front of my face for sixteen years. I want Tiffany as my wife and Drew as my son.

I hug Drew and assure him, "We'll always be family. I love you, Drew. And I don't love you like a son. I love you because you are my son, no matter what."

He tightens his hold around me, and I hold back my tears from the pain of a devastating past with hopes of moving toward a healing future with the only love I've ever known—the love Tiffany's given me and the blessing of allowing me to be Drew's father figure no matter where she and I stood throughout the years.

When we release our grips, Drew clears his eyes and asks, "Alright, now it's time to put me to work, but first, you gotta introduce me to your teammates."

I introduce Drew to my coach and teammates, show him around the facilities, and share stories from my time in the NFL. As I bring him into my world, I reflect on the trials that have tested us and how, despite everything, we've come out stronger. Tiffany and I share a history marked by pain and loss, yet it stands as proof of our resilience and our ability to weather any storm. Missing Tiffany meant missing Drew too, and this weekend feels like a chance to rebuild what we've lost and take the first steps toward becoming a family again.

We've endured the pain of our past, but now it's time to embrace the present and create the future we've always dreamed of.

Chapter 4

The Setup – Tiffany

Today's the big event! This is my chance to get to know the who's who of the city, potentially unlocking a wellspring of donations for causes close to my heart. I'm so excited, but not as excited as my girls as we jam out to Ciara and prepare to get dressed to attend the gala.

With my back against the mirror, I observe the diamonds on my arms, neck, and ears. "Y'all, this is too much!" I say, feigning protest as they add the final sparkling touches. The expensive jewels on my body make me feel royal, a luxury I never thought I'd experience growing up.

"Oh, hush!" Mel laughs, playfully scolding me as she adjusts a necklace that likely costs more than my home. "You got money now, Tiff. Embrace it for once! It's about time you stop being so sporty all the time. You look so damn good right now!"

I cross my arms and wait, half-exhausted from their pampering, half-skeptical about all the fuss. "Damn, y'all must think I'm ugly or somethin'. It's literally just clothes, jewelry, and makeup! I doubt I look that –"

But then, the girls spin me around to face the mirror. My words vanish into silence. I barely recognize myself. My gold and white gown clings to my curves with deliberate precision. The fabric glides over my body with an elegance I never knew was possible. A line of diamonds glimmers down my neckline, leading to a high slit that feels as bold as it does daring. This isn't just a dress - it's a masterpiece, a work of art that showcases my sophistication, power, and sensuality. A thrill runs through me, warming my skin as I take in my image. I don't just look sexy; I feel it, too.

My girls exchange proud glances at their skilled handiwork then Mel completes my look by spritzing my signature vanilla fragrance; a concoction my sister Tiny created when we were kids to remind us of the beautiful, sweet smell of our mother.

"Tiff, you're so beautiful. You're always beautiful, but wow! I'm contemplating leaving Rafe for you right now." Monica jokes, her eyes reflecting genuine admiration.

"I'd definitely leave Deacon for you right now. I'd go back to him, of course, but you're looking like sexy, freaky deaky wifey material right now."

Mel laughs at Avery. "She's right. The bob, the body, and the dark makeup, girl! You're oozing sexy, single and ready to mingle."

"Tiff, you're 'bout to pull all the fine, rich men tonight, especially your date." Monica nods in agreement, "Y'all are a match made in heaven! Good luck keeping your goodies in the jar!"

While they joke about the attention I'll receive, I can only think about one man. I've been thinking about him since yesterday's call. I've been thinking about him since he moved back to Greer. His image, his goodness, his essence, his presence, *him*. Mason Boom has been on my mind and in my heart nearly my entire life.

"Wow, Mom! You look amazing." Drew's entrance and his awe at my transformation bring a lightness to the room.

I throw my hands in the air and shout, "Okay, c'mon now! I couldn't have looked *that* bad."

They laugh as Mel adds, "No, you just didn't look *this* good."

"Seriously, Ma, your date's gonna go crazy. I can't wait to see his face," Drew's excitement quickly disappears as if he accidentally revealed details I shouldn't know. "Oh crap, my bad!" He blurts out.

His slip of the tongue piques my curiosity.

Monica places her arm around Drew's shoulder and clarifies, "What he means is your date's going to lose his mind when he sees you for the first time. Isn't that right, y'all?"

Their tight-lipped smiles and nods aren't convincing. I know they're up to something. "Well, I hate to break it to you, but this new guy is in competition with," I look at Drew and gently nudge him away. "Go finish getting ready. I'm 'bout to have girl talk."

"Appreciate the heads up." Drew leaves the room so I can have a serious conversation with my girls.

"As I was saying, I don't think I'll be able to focus on my date tonight. Not when the strongest connection I ever felt will be in the room with me."

Their eyes soften at my vulnerability, and Monica grabs my hand to offer assurance. "I have no doubt you'll be able to focus on the fine hunk of a man we picked out for you. So, don't worry about Mase. He'll be in there with a beautiful woman of his own. Just have some fun tonight. You deserve it. We're such slackers. Mel's been running around with some secret hot tamale while Monica and I have been so busy with the kids that we've barely helped you organize anything. You've done everything on your own. Still the same Tiff from our college days–strong enough to do it all."

Monica's reminder of my independence and strength is both a comfort and a burden. Independent, determined, and strong. That's me.

"That's the problem, Monica!" I exclaim with frustration. "I don't feel like being strong right now. Having to be strong without any breaks is exhausting. I want to be vulnerable. I want someone I can lean on. I'm tired of holding myself up. I want to be held. I don't want to recite any more affirmations. I want to be someone's answered prayers. I want...I *only* want—"

"Mase." Mel interrupts, "You only want Mason Boom."

Mel echoes my deepest desires, laying bare the truth of my heart. I want Mason not just as a temporary presence in my life but as a forever partner.

A tear pricks the back of my eye as I finally admit, "I do. I want Mase so bad, but every time I think I can finally get what I want, something pulls us apart. Should I just give up? Is my heart forcing something that was never meant to be?"

Avery's gaze holds a mixture of understanding and encouragement. "Like my mother-in-law always says, 'Love isn't worth it, if you don't fight for it.' And it looks like you're fighting for it right now, especially with that high split showing every bit of your leg. Who knows, life has a funny way of bringing people back together when the time is right. Maybe that time is tonight."

Her words resonate with me as I realize every moment Mase and I have experienced over the years was during some of the most chaotic struggles of my life. The timing was never right, but time heals, and so have the scars on my heart and the pain of my past. Perhaps, this time, our love really can last.

"You heard Aves. Tonight, and the days and weeks to follow will be the beginning of the greatest days of your life. Just try to focus on the gala and your date…not Mase! You know that color on you drives him crazy. I got five bucks you're gonna let him cop a little feel." Mel jokes.

The room vibrates with the collective energy of our laughter and tears. It's the kind of pure, unadulterated joy that comes from the depths of enduring friendship. My girls are right. I'll see Mase tonight for the first time in a very long time, and be it friendship or relationship, this will be a new beginning for both of us.

~ ~ ~

When our car pulls up to the Old Greer Coliseum, Drew rushes out to meet up with his 'little friend,' a.k.a. his girlfriend, who also happens to be one of my star dancers on the Greer High Pipettes Dance Team. My best friends and I look around in amazement at the parking lot full of cars and the long valet line of Rolls Royce's, Bentley's, and Lamborghini's!

Avery confidently approaches the imposing steel door, where her husband, Deacon, stands, ready to escort her inside and commence the evening's festivities. "I smell money, which means there will be a lot of empty pockets and checkbooks by tonight's end. I'll see y'all inside."

Mel surprises us by flirtatiously swaying over to Jay Boom, the young athlete most notorious for breaking women's hearts.

"Mel!" I gasp with my eyes wide open.

"Girl, I'm the Mistress of Ceremony, and I needed a hot date at the last minute, that's all. Ain't nobody checkin' for Jay!"

But the fond placement of Jay's hand on the nape of her back and her warm reaction to his touch says otherwise.

Then there's Rafe, Monica's fiercely protective yet gentle and kind husband. She sashays to him and for a moment, I feel a tinge of sadness but also a glimmer of hope as he wraps his arms around her waist. If Monica could find everything she deserves after everything she's endured, then surely, I can too.

"And then there was one." I mutter under my breath as I stand alone, nervous as hell with my right hand tightly clutching my side.

I walk through the Coliseum admiring the elegant drapery and carefully arranged floral displays from Waylen's House of Flowers'. There's an ambiance of sophistication, a testament to the meticulous planning and effort I put into organizing tonight's event. I can't help but feel a swell of pride, knowing that I, Tiffany Weathers, a poor rough-around-the-edges girl from College Park, accomplished all of this.

As quickly as the awe of the décor commands my attention, it leaves when I'm captivated by the statuesque, dark chocolate man standing before me. It takes a moment for my brain to process who my eyes see—Mason. The love of my life, wearing a black tuxedo with gold accents that perfectly complement my dress. In his hand is a white rose and on his face is the most handsome smile.

My son and friends surround him while admiring the flush of emotions on my face.

"And then there were two." Monica turns to me with a mischievous glint in her eyes.

Mason, ever the charmer turned social recluse, smoothly kisses the top of my hand and formally addresses me. "Good evening, Ms. Weathers. It's been a while, as in seven days, two hours, and four minutes, since I last saw your beautiful face. So, please allow me to reintroduce myself. I'm Mason Boom, your blind date for the evening."

We stare into each other's eyes until the commotion fades, and the music becomes a distant melody as our magnetic energy grows. A second ago, his lips were on the top of my hand, and now we stand, his chest to my breast, caught in a silent exchange that speaks volumes of our screaming desire to be together.

Life sure does have a funny way of bringing people back together when the time is right. Tonight is that time, and this time, I'm ready. It's my time to be happy, and it's our time to embrace the love we always shared. A love that's worth one in a million, a love that's solely meant to be between me and Mason Boom. In this moment, there's an appreciation of our past and a renewed confidence in our future.

Chapter 5

The Gala – Mason

My palms are sweaty, my legs are shaking, my mind is racing, and I'm nervous as hell. I have no idea how Tiffany's going to receive me when she sees me or if she'll receive me at all. She wants me to stay away from her because she thinks we're too consumed with each other but I'd rather be consumed by her love than void of it.

"Aye, man, you got this." Rafe, my brother, pats me on the back and attempts to calm my nerves.

"We'll go out and escort the ladies inside first," Deacon outlines the plan with a coolness I only wish I could adopt. "Tiff will walk in steel-faced, feeling a bit nervous and probably lonely without her girls. We'll set you up for the big surprise."

"And BOOM! Tiff sees you lookin' all fly with ya pants all crisp, and she melts and falls in love all over again," Rafe shouts in his usual optimistic tone as he snaps his fingers. "Just like that!"

While I appreciate their enthusiasm, skepticism sweeps through me. "Bruh, this is Tiff. You know that ain't happening."

Rafe shrugs, "Well, I guess we'll see 'cause the ladies just pulled up."

As Rafe, Jay, and Deacon exit to greet their dates, Drew enters and stands next to me in excitement while I anxiously wait for my future to unfold.

Tiffany's entrance is a moment suspended in time. A scene charged with emotions that renders me momentarily paralyzed. I'm confused about which emotion to act on – desire, fondness, anxiousness, or fear. The slight smirk on her face and twinkle of amazement in her eyes embolden me to step forward and reclaim who I've always known to be mine.

I gently kiss the top of her hand and look directly into her eyes. "Good evening, Ms. Weathers. It's been a while, so please allow me to reintroduce myself. I'm Mason Boom, your blind date for the evening."

She stares into my eyes, and I into hers. If we said nothing for the rest of the night, I'd be satisfied because our concentration sparks hope, the flirtatious dance of our eyes saying it all.

It will always be me, Tiffany, and the world around us.

"Mr. Boom, it's nice to meet you. I take it the rose is for me?" Her velvet voice carries a sensual edge that I've missed more than anything.

I nod and gently pin the white rose behind her ear. "Beautiful. Everything about you is beautiful."

For a moment, we forget our friends and family surround us, but Tiffany quickly gathers herself.

"Alright, y'all got me good, you dang on liars! And you, Drew? You been keepin' this secret from me? You aren't allowed to come home tonight, young man!" She jokes.

Our friends and family laugh and part ways to enjoy the gala.

Then, she looks at me in admonishment and shakes her head. "Mase, if this weren't my big night, I'd cuss yo ass out!" She smiles, but she's serious.

Tiffany's a bulldog, and I love it. I respond with a mixture of jest and truth, seizing the moment to remind her of our undeniable chemistry.

"That's exactly why I surprised you. You can't deny me in front of all these people."

"You're right, I can't, which is why I'm gonna enjoy auctioning you off tonight."

"Please don't remind me," I extend my hand for her to take. "Actually, no more talk of selling me off to any desperate housewives. You're the star of the show, and my job is to be your arm candy."

She takes her hand in mine, and I take a deep whiff of her intoxicating vanilla, magnolia, and honeysuckle scent.

Unable to control myself, I softly whisper in her ear, "You smell delicious, by the way."

She chuckles and nearly blushes as I try to break down her steel walls.

"You've been saying the same thing since we were kids."

"And you've been smelling delicious since we were kids."

We share intimate glances and small chit-chat between hugs and handshakes, but nothing is sweeter than being introduced as her date.

Doting Guest #1: "Ms. Weathers, you have to tell me the story of how you and the infamous Mason Boom met. What a beautiful reunion."

Doting Guest #2: "Ms. Weathers, you and the Mason Boom again?"

Doting Guest #3: "You look so good together! May I take a picture of the two of you?"

Doting Guest #4: "You're glowing, Ms. Weathers! Love sure does look good on you. Your love story–hell, your life together had the entire world in tears!"

To each guest comment, Tiffany, the queen of putting on a show, replies, "Thank you. Mase and I have been close ever since I could remember, even when I couldn't remember. He always believed in us, in who we were to one another. He's quite amazing. So, don't forget to bid on him tonight. I'm only lending him out for the evening."

I watch her schmooze and receive monetary commitments from dozens of guests. Her adeptness at navigating the attention we draw only heightens my admiration for her, even as the attendees' questions begin to probe too deeply into subjects we would rather not entertain tonight.

Silly Question: "Mr. Boom, are you ready for your big comeback? Can you really compete with the youngins'?"

Intrusive Question: "How are you really doing? You've been hit with revelation after revelation over the years, have you had enough time to grieve?"

Dumb Question: "So, which woman did you love more, Kira or Tiffany?"

They crowd around us like vultures, questioning me about the upcoming season, my well-being, my injury, and my emotional outburst during the trial. They question me about...everything.

My anxiety worsens by the minute. I've been out of the spotlight for a year, for good reason, and right now, I'm pushing down my anxiety because my desire to be with Tiff is heavier than my pain. I may be able to hold my poker face steady for the guests but I can't hide from Tiff, and with each invasive question, she senses my growing discomfort.

"Hey," With our hands clasped tightly together, she whispers in a gentle, caring tone. "You wanna sit down for a minute?"

"Am I that obvious?" I ask, my voice laced with nervousness and shame. "I used to be the charmer in front of the cameras, but I see that's all you now, and I must say, the spotlight suits you. Just let me know when I start embarrassing you."

She shakes her head reassuringly, "You're doing great, Mase. I just happen to know you better than anyone in this room. You'll get used to being in front of the cameras again, especially when the season starts. You're Mason Boom, the Golden Boy. C'mon, let's take a break."

Her reassurance, her understanding of me, and her ability to sense my discomfort and know when I'm nearing my limit make me love her deeper than I knew was possible. Tiffany's realness calms me, her touch soothes my nerves, and her smile warms my heart. More than anything, she grounds me.

Saved by her perceptiveness, we walk to our table, and Tiffany releases a sigh of relief. "Whew, my feet are killing me! I can't wear heels like I used to."

I laugh as she rubs her feet, "I remember those days. You were the sexiest majorette on the field." I wink.

"And you were the thirstiest baller chasin' after me." She teases.

"Hell, I still am!"

My laughter subsides when her smile fades as she speaks with a hint of seriousness. "We've both chased after each other, Mase, and it didn't work every time. Aren't you tired of chasing?" She asks.

As her question lingers in the air, I find myself imprisoned by attraction. My gaze inadvertently drifts to the long slit in her dress that reveals her sexy, toned thigh. My eyes continue to travel from her silky-smooth legs to her perfectly plump breasts, her full lips, mesmerizing eyes, and sleek shoulder-length haircut.

I sigh, "I'll stop chasing you when you give yourself to me for good, forever. I didn't come back home just to play football. I came back home for you. I want you back, Tiffany Nicole, and I won't stop chasing until I call you my wife." I caress her face and lean in closer. "So, you finally gonna give me a chance to prove that we're meant to be together?"

Our lips are less than an inch apart, and I'd do anything to taste her again, but I'll settle for the closeness, which is just as titillating. As we contemplate revealing our truths, the time between us freezes, with only our desires drawing us closer to one another.

"I'm yours, Tiffany," I declare. "Tell me you're still mine. Tell me I'm still your first and only. Tell me you still want me." She subtly rubs her leg against mine while my hand inconspicuously sneaks into the split of her dress and grazes the inside of her thigh.

Caught in the thrill of the moment, she closes her eyes and moans, "Mase."

So close to the place my fingers crave to wander, I move a little higher and insist, "Say it, Tiff. I've been watching horny men stare at what's mine for the past hour. I wanna hear you say it. Tell me who you still belong to."

Her composure falters, and I feel a warm wetness on the tip of my fingers. I'm hypnotized by her sweet scent, captivated by her beauty, and paralyzed by her sensual whimpers.

"Mase, I do want you, and I'm sti –" She moans again but the electrified air between us is abruptly diffused by the untimely voice of loud-mouth Melody Baker!

"Alright, ladies and gentlemen! You know we can't continue having a grand 'ole time without thanking the owner of Good News PR, Monica Owens-Boom and Greer's beloved dance extraordinaire, Tiffany Weathers. Come on up here and say a few words."

All eyes turn to us. Tiffany quickly regains her composure, fixes herself up in a panic, and then hits me with her clutch, but she can't hide her flushed face or the brief but much-appreciated moment of vulnerability.

"Dammit Boom! You almost embarrassed me in front of everyone! What was your plan, huh? Give me an orgasm out in the open? Ugh, you're so annoying!"

I laugh in response to her feigned annoyance and shrug. "Hey, you said it yourself? I'm a thirsty man."

Then Mel, from the podium, eggs us on, "Whoops, it looks like we interrupted a little lovey-dovey time between the two old flames. Copping a feel, huh?"

"Absolutely not, Melody Baker!" Tiffany loudly retorts from the crowd. "Mr. Boom's 'feels' are reserved for tonight's lucky bidder!" The crowd cheerfully reacts to her quick-witted, playful response as I escort her to the stage.

Handing over the microphone, Mel steps back and allows Tiffany the spotlight she commands so naturally. It reminds me of back in college when she'd captivate the crowd with her moves. Everyone falls into a respectful silence as she gathers her thoughts, takes a deep breath, and then confidently addresses the crowd.

"Good evening, everyone. I'll keep this as brief as possible. I'd like to thank all of you for your pledges, donations, and support. I'd also like to thank Monica for trusting me to curate an amazing event to benefit the incredible dancers of Greer High and so many families in need. I'm sure you've read the headlines about me over the past year or so, which is why it's no surprise as to why I'd like to thank you, Mason Boom. You bulldozed your way into my dark life, and now I can't get rid of the sunshine. Thank you for everything."

'Oohs' and 'ahhs' encompass the room, but between the two of us, there's a deep fondness that transcends words. Her thank you means more than appreciation. It's laced with love.

"Okay, y'all, that's enough mushy stuff!" She dismisses the crowd's coos. "I'm shutting up now because it's time to spend money on these handsome men!"

The crowd cheers, and Mel takes over, "Alright, let's get this party started! Who wants to go on a date with a Boom?"

Tiffany assembles me and my brothers, Grumpy Ass Bash, who recently won his second NBA championship, and Playboy Jay, who's undoubtedly the greatest soccer player in the MLS, on stage.

Bash nudges my back, lowering his voice to a whisper. "Look down, bro. Why the hell would you flirt with Tiff before you have to go on stage? You know you can't control yourself around her. Get your shit together."

And just in time, Mel bellows into the mic, "Ooh, you see that ladies...*and fellas*? The Boom Brothers' rumors must be true. You better bid high."

Damn, I look down to cover as much of my erection as I can, then look at Tiffany, whose reveling in my embarrassment.

Jay says aloud to the crowd, "That's right! The rumors *are* true. We Booms are *very* blessed." Jay playfully winks, specifically at Mel who scoffs in return.

With the three of us on stage, Mel captures everyone's attention to begin the bidding. "Okay, ladies and gents! As you know, all proceeds will go to the Greer High School Pipettes Dance team and the Greer Sovereign House. If you win the bid, you'll be treated to an exclusive night out with one of the most eligible, wealthiest bachelors in the South. So, let's begin!"

Before she continues, a mysterious woman drenched in diamonds raises a provocative question that sends whispers cascading through the room. "And what if we want more than a night? What if we want an entire day?"

"*With who*?" Tiffany unintentionally blurts out before quickly placing her hand over her mouth.

The woman responds with a raised brow, "I want the one and only Mason Boom."

Though she'd never admit it, Tiffany's territorial over me, and it fills me with a satisfaction that's hard to conceal. It's the woman's explicit interest in me that escalates the situation.

"Excuse me?" Mel's surprised and irritated reaction momentarily interrupts the elegant evening. "Uh, I mean...hmm. Mason, it's up to you. Would you mind spending an entire day with the highest bidder?"

Mel squints her eyes and gives me the *'You better not'* look, then I look at Tiffany's beautifully concerned face.

My response weighs in the balance, but I hide my fear with a charming, "Hey, it's for a good cause, right?"

The crowd cheers, but Tiffany's displeasure is as clear as the distance she puts between us. I hate to upset her, but everything happens for a reason.

Grumpy Ass Bash then whispers in my ear, "I know that woman, Mase. You can't have her. She's mine."

I dismiss his insistence with a shrug. "But she clearly wants me. Well, for an evening, at least." I wink to piss him off.

He angrily grumbles, "Damn it, Mase. I swear –"

Mel's voice overpowers his when she begins the bidding. "First up is Mason Boom. Hmm, let's start out at $10,000. Do we have any bidders for $10,000 for a day with the one and only Mason Boom?"

Immediately, hands raise around the room, and the bidding quickly kicks off. The atmosphere is charged with excitement, each bid fueling the next. I steal glances at Tiffany, who tries hard not to reveal her anger, but I see the tension in her posture and the worry in the slight clench of her jaw.

"$50,000!" The mysterious woman shouts, silencing the room. Her voice is confident, and her eyes are locked on me with an intriguing and intimidating intensity.

I hear Bash muttering curses under his breath, but my focus is on Tiffany. I see the annoyance on her face. She's clearly unhappy with the turn of events, but there's a hint of mischief in her eyes, too.

"$65,000!" Shouts another voice from the back. With each raise, Tiffany's expression grows weary, a storm of emotions playing out on her face.

The bidding war escalates, and the mysterious woman raises her challenge until she reaches the $100,000 mark. It seems she's won.

However, Mel yells, "Oh, is that someone in the back raising their hand? It's Avery and Deacon Owens!"

What the hell is Mel up to? Why are our friends raising their hands?

"$125,000!" Avery yells. The crowd gasps, but I follow Avery's eyes to Tiffany, who winks at her. I knew she wasn't gonna let me get snatched up so easily.

Mel rejoices and quickly exclaims, "Whoa! Mason's got a fan club. I think we should wrap this up. $125,000, going once, going twice..."

A resounding bid echoes from the crowd, "$250,000!" The mysterious woman says.

Utterly surprised expressions fill the room, and a loud applause erupts. Tiffany and Mel look to Avery and Deacon, who shake their heads in defeat.

Mel, forced to continue, slowly announces, "$250,000 going once, twice, and sold! To the shady lady in diamonds!"

The crowd applauds, and the woman stands up, flashing a triumphant smile as she makes her way to meet me offstage.

Tiffany, who had been silently scheming throughout the bidding, approaches us but doesn't even bother to greet the winner, which means it's time for me to face the consequences of what just happened.

She glares at me with a look of hurt, then warns, "You better make sure it's just one day, Mase."

I nod, understanding her underlying message. Yet, I wouldn't be myself if I didn't piss her off even further.

"But what if I want more than a day? What if I want forever?" I ask.

Her mouth drops, and before she can cuss me out, the mysterious woman who won the bid says, "Good evening, Ms. Weathers. You're just the person I'm looking for. Do you have a moment to speak with me?"

"Well, I'm surprised you want to speak to me and not the man you blew all that money on." Tiffany looks the beautiful young woman up and down, angrily glaring back and forth between us.

Observing Tiffany's jealousy is getting me all hot and bothered. *Damn, my woman is sexy.* Despite her frustration, there's an unmistakable possessiveness in her voice. It's impossible for her to hide her feelings for me.

The bidder graciously smiles, then sharply teases, "Well, it's all for a great cause, right? I actually have a question. Would it be possible to gift my date to someone else?"

Confused, Tiffany responds, "Uh, I mean, I guess. As long as your check clears, you can gift Mason to the Pope for all I care."

The woman laughs. "Well, I'd only like to gift my date to one person, and that's you."

Tiffany's eyes widen and she looks at both of us. She places her hand on her hip until her fuse blows. "What the hell is going on?"

Okay, the fun and games are over now, and I'll likely be on Tiff's shit list for good. So, I clear my throat and reveal the truth. "Tiff, this is Lottie Daniels, the co-owner of the Greer Devils and Bash's new boss. I asked Lottie to bid on me tonight."

Angry, Tiffany yells, "You did what? Mason Boom, I'm gonna kill you!"

Lottie interrupts, "I think that's my cue to leave. I have another Boom brother to wrangle anyway."

Lottie walks away to accompany my jealous brother Bash and leaves me to suffer Tiffany's wrath. Tiff stands in front of me with a lit fuse and a mouth full of cuss words. Yet, I find it difficult to subdue my growing bulge.

She casts her gaze downward, her frustration intensifying upon the sight. "Oh, this is turning you on, huh? I don't even know what to say to you right now!" She exclaims, visibly more irritated. Yet, beneath her vexation, there's an underlying relief. The realization that I'm unequivocally hers brings a complex mix of emotions to the surface. She's at a loss for words, not out of anger alone but because she's comforted by the control she has over me.

"Okay, before you yell, let me explain. I didn't want my first date in forever to be with a stranger. I wanted it to be with my soulmate. I want you or no one at all, Tiff." My words are sincere, an attempt to express the depth of my feelings and the seriousness of my intentions.

Tiffany's initial stiffness melts away, replaced by a tentative openness as she processes my confession. Seizing the moment, I gently grab her hand and pull her closer to me. My gesture, though simple, is an invitation to close the emotional distance between us, to acknowledge the bond we share and the future I envision for us together.

"Let me go, Mase," She protests with a hint of playfulness, pushing against me yet not moving away. "You've got to stop with all these elaborate stunts and games. And that woman, she's gorgeous. You had me covertly messaging the crew to outbid her! How do you even know her?" Her voice carries a mix of jest and genuine concern, highlighting the absurdity and intensity of the situation.

I can't help but laugh and wrap my arms securely around her waist with my hands finding a comfortable resting place at the small of her back.

"But why were you jealous, Tiff? Why didn't you want me to go on a date with her?" It's a playful yet poignant question aimed at uncovering the layers of her feelings.

Now backstage, secluded from the curious eyes of the world, I tenderly caress her face. She leans into my touch, and her defenses melt away under the warmth of my palm. It's a moment of vulnerability and connection. It's a moment we've shared hundreds of times throughout our lives.

"Mase, please." She implores in a soft beseeching voice. "I don't want to have this conversation. Not here. Not now." Her plea is a mix of desperation and sincerity as a reprieve from the emotional intensity of our connection.

"Then when? Where?" I press, my smile gentle but persistent. "You said it yourself back in Seattle, we've already let too much time slip by. And let's not forget," I add with a playful grin, "I just shelled out $250,000 to spend a day with you. So, you gonna leave my money on the table or let me take you on a date?" The question hangs between us with anticipation and hope.

Tiffany's beautiful brown eyes meet my gaze, and after a moment's hesitation, she drifts into deep thought until a reluctant smile breaks through. "Dammit, Mason Boom. I guess it's for a good cause, right?"

A wave of relief washes over me, and I pull her into a tight embrace. Like always, we communicate in silence as our breaths sync, and we inhale each other's comforting aroma. This is what I need–to feel the warmth and familiarity of the love that still exists between us.

Whispering close to her ear, I affirm, "This is our time, Tiff. We're both back home, exactly where we belong—with each other. I'll always be your first and only, and you'll always be my first and forever." It's a declaration of our readiness to reclaim what was once lost and embrace the promise of a shared future.

She pulls back and gives me a look that's both tender and exasperated. "You drive me insane, Mase. But you're right. We're home, and it's finally our time." My heart leaps at her words, sparking deep hope within me, a fervent belief in our potential for happiness together.

"So, is that a yes to the date?"

"Yes, but no more surprises, okay? Your schemes and bad ideas always end up making me mad." Her playful warning is a reminder of our tumultuous past, yet it's tinged with a willingness to move forward.

My laughter fills the space, a sound of pure joy. "Bet. I'll *try* my best to behave." I solemnly swear with my hand placed over my chest.

"*And...,*" She emphasizes. "You have to promise, if it doesn't work out, if life gets in the way again, we'll stop chasing after one another and seek happiness elsewhere." She states, setting the terms for our new beginning.

I nod as the gravity of her words sinks in. "I promise. No more chasing if it doesn't work out."

It's a vow I easily make, not because I anticipate failure, but because I'm confident in our future together. I believe in us — our resilience, our history, our triumphs, our bond, our destiny. I'm winning my woman back, and I'm ready to prove to her that we belong together.

Chapter 6

Talk of the Town – Tiffany

Three months ago, Mason Boom yet again bulldozed his way back into my life. I just can't seem to escape him, and now I have to go on a date with him. Well, I don't *have* to, but it'd be wrong not to fulfill my commitment. Okay, okay! I *want* to go on a date with him.

But if I weren't still in love with him, I wouldn't be so worried right now. Am I going to be able to control my pent-up sexual frustration while spending a whole day with the only man I ever loved? Probably not.

As I spin around in my chair and mull over my impending date, Monica breezes into my dance studio office and interrupts my dizzy spell.

"I know you aren't still stressing out about that damn date! Tiff, you're so dramatic. Didn't you agree to wait until *after* Drew's 16th birthday, which means it's nearly two months away! Stop freakin' out. Where's my go-with-the-flow roommate from college, huh?" Monica playfully teases, attempting to subdue my misery.

"I was never that girl, Monica. You know that."

"Oh, yeah! I forgot," She laughs. "But you are the confident woman in my life who instilled confidence in me. If it weren't for you, Mel, and Avery, I wouldn't be married to the most amazing man in the world which brings me to a topic you've heard over and over. I know I've apologized for setting you up like 50-leven times now, but you and Boom are a hit! There are pictures of y'all everywhere, just like back in the day, except the headlines are much more positive this time. And donations are still pouring in!"

I finally stop moping to reluctantly glance at the headlines plastering our past for us all to see. She's right. My name is everywhere, which is exactly what I didn't want. I left my old life with Mase back in Atlanta. Yet, every headline is connected to our past.

Headline #1: Mason Boom Reunites with His Long-Lost Love

Headline #2: The Deep History Between Mase Boom and Tiffany Weathers

Headline #3: Mason Boom and Tiffany Weathers – Together at Last

Headline #4: Boom's Good Luck Charm Returns – He'll Need It.

Even more annoyed than before, I groan, "Ugh! I don't want to read this. Not when the broken puzzle pieces of my past are finally being put back together. I don't want my life to be torn apart again. Mase and I deserve privacy."

"Fine," Monica gives in and stops swooning. "Ignore the headlines, but at least look at the tracker. That'll make you smile."

I search our donation site and view the processed payments, then gasp in disbelief. "Oh, my goodness! Six million dollars? This can't be real."

Her grin is as genuine as her enthusiasm. "It's all real, Tiff. See, I told you. Your life story? Your love story? Your reunion? It isn't just tabloid gossip; it's a fundraising powerhouse. Everyone loves a beautiful romance, especially one as special as you and Mason's."

I chuckle and dismiss her claim. "If you call what Mason and I have a beautiful romance, then my goodness, you're as delusional as everyone else in this town."

"Okay, don't believe me then. Just keep torturing yourself by denying true happiness. In the meantime, I'm gonna go pick the baby up from my mom's house. I'll see you at Drew's game tonight. Will Mase be there, too?"

With a deep exhale, I reply, "Drew would be devastated if Mase didn't come. So yes, he'll be there."

"Great! That means even more donations! Cheer up, Tiff. You know you're excited to see your man. Besides, I 'accidentally' peeked at Rafe's group chat, and Mason's so excited about your date. He said you're both planning it?"

"Unfortunately, yes!" I lament. "He's planning most of it, but he's making me plan the end. I have no idea what to do! What is wrong with this man?"

She chuckles, "He's a hopeless romantic – the exact opposite of you."

"I'm a realist, Monica." I counter, trying to sound stern but failing to hide my affection for Mason's antics.

"Well, realists need love, too." She adds with a hint of concern. "Actually, after Drew's birthday, I think you should take some time off."

Monica's suggestion catches me off guard, and the thought of the stressful consequences of abandoning my surmounting responsibilities sends me into a panic.

"What? I don't have time to take off. Football season is underway. Drew has two a day practices. I've been teaching the Pipettes all-new choreography that they've yet to hit. Not to mention, this construction zone of a dance studio is one permit away from not opening on time. And after Drew's birthday, you *know* how busy we're going to be. I just can't!"

"Tiff, slow down, relax, and breathe." Monica pleas empathetically. "I got everything under control. Yes, Drew's big day is tomorrow, but it'll be yours as well. You run yourself ragged and never enjoy the fruits of your labor. Take time off, rest, and spend time with your family. You deserve it."

Monica's right. I have so much on my plate right now, and tomorrow is a momentous occasion for Drew and my family.

With resignation and gratitude, I concede. "Okay, but only for a few weeks! That'll give me enough time to celebrate Drew's birthday and get settled into what'll be the next chapter of our lives together as a family."

"Good, I'm so happy for you, Tiffany. You'll always be an inspiration to me."

Monica's pride and affectionate words wrap around me like a warm embrace, a reminder of the unwavering support we have for one another.

"Aww, I love you, too, Mons. Now, let me get back to work. If I'm gonna take time off from adulting, I need to send my friends and family a ten page handover." I joke.

"You can write a whole novel for all I care, but just know, I'm not gonna read it!" She playfully quips.

"Monica!" I laugh.

"Just kidding. I'll make sure the renovations move along as planned. I'll see you at the game. Avery, Deac, and Rafe are home making Drew's signs now. We're so excited to cheer him on!"

After I leave the studio, I head home to prepare for Drew's first game as starting quarterback. Mase has been training him since he was a little boy and increasingly more since we've all moved back to Greer. So, of course, Mase was the first person he called when his coach informed him he'd be starting in this week's game. Football is huge in the South, and Greer High School has the best football program in the state. Recruiters already have their eyes on him. This kid is my life, and it's unbelievable that my baby boy has grown up so fast. It's even crazier that he's walking in his father figure's shoes.

Speaking of Drew...

Son: Hey Ma, are you at the school yet? I stopped by the dance room to say good luck but didn't see you.

Tiffany: Oh really? You stopped by to see me or your little friend?

Son: ...both ☺ Anyway...I was wondering if a few friends can come over after the game? I figured you'd say yes if I invited them instead of me hanging out late.

Tiffany: And you figured right! Of course they can come over. I'll order pizza.

Son: Thanks, and will Mason be there, too? Everyone's excited to meet him. Please?

Tiffany: I'll see what I can do, but I don't want you to get the wrong impression about us, and I don't want to flaunt a man around who may or may not stay.

Son: But you've never done that before. I only met lame Donny, but Mase has always been in my life. I wanna flex a little lol

Tiffany: Ugh, okay! I'll invite him over.

Inviting Mase over is a terrible idea – a huge leap into familiar yet treacherous waters. I already know how the night is going to go. Mase will come over, talk about his glory days in football, take a few selfies, then he'll plop right down on my couch and take full control of my remote until we both fall asleep to our favorite movies. I miss those days, but we also don't need to fall back into old habits. Nevertheless, against my better judgment and mental protests, I dial his number.

"Ooh, I wasn't expecting a call from you. My day just got a whole lot better." Mason's unguarded delightful tone instantly warms my heart…and other areas, too.

"Hello to you, too, Mr. Boom. What're you up to?" I manage to casually inquire despite the rapid drumming of my heart.

"Hmm, I'm just tallying up the countless times we've spoken on the phone since the gala. Let's see we've had twenty-three thirty minute phone conversations, you and the ladies have visited my home four times, and you attended three of my home games. Oh, and I'm finalizing the last details of our date." Mason playfully replies.

"Mason Boom, we've only been talking so much because of Drew's birthday and you know it! I appreciate all of your last minute help, that's all. Your new house was looking like a sad bachelor pad so the girls and I had to fix it. And why wouldn't I go see a pro football team play in my own city? I assure you, my attendance had nothing to do with you." I lie, well-aware he doesn't believe me. "And seriously, I hope you're not planning anything elaborate for our date. You're a pro at embarrassing me, Mase. Let's just do something simple like dinner and a movie."

"Simple? I don't even know how to spell simple. And you love my grand gestures just like back in the day."

"I hated them!" I laugh. "Case in point, it was literally my first month working at the club and what the heck do you do?"

"Who doesn't love a serenaded spotlight grind to a Pretty Ricky medley." He laughs as he reminisces on his foolishness.

"Uh, me! I literally hid behind the bar. Like, c'mon, you could've at least played some Neyo. You may have even gotten some that night."

"Damn, if only I would've known then what I know now." He jokes.

"Oh goodness, I don't know what I'm gonna do with you. Just take me to Saturday Night Skating. I wouldn't mind swervin' circles around you for a bit."

"Look at you, plannin' for our future. Skating it is for date #2, Tiffany Nicole."

"You just love saying my name, don't you? You're like that annoying brother that keeps poking until you get a reaction."

There's a pause, the line going silent for a moment. "You know damn well you don't see me as a brother!"

I can't resist teasing him, "I sure do. You're the Theo Huxtable to my Vanessa."

"You know what? I'm hanging up." I feel his infectious smile through the phone.

"Then, bye." I playfully challenge him. He folds.

"Damn, woman. You just gonna let me go that easy, huh? I do have to go, though. I'm studying some plays. Then, I gotta pick up Bash and Jay so we can head to Drew's game." Mason replies, his tone casual yet filled with underlying excitement.

Bringing one, let alone three major athletes, to a high school football game is a recipe for disaster. I have to put a stop to this right now!

"You're bringing your brothers, too? It's gonna be a media circus. I want Drew to live a normal life, not be a popular, entitled rich kid with connections like you were in high school."

Damn, that hurts. You gotta get over that. He's a future football star. It's just gonna get worse from here, and you know I can't stop my brothers from seeing him play. They love their nephew, and my mom is gonna be there an hour before the game starts. She and Crystal are excited to watch him play. You know they've been calling me every day since the news dropped about *us*."

"Fake news! There is no *us*. We're not even dating, and I don't know why they want us together so bad." I exclaim.

With the utmost sincerity, he quickly responds, "Because we're like magnets. We're naturally drawn to each other, and that's special. We're special together."

"Oh, Mase, your charm is attractive, but your persistence is exhausting." He laughs, but I proceed. "Anyway, I was calling you because Drew wants you to come over after the game. He wants to show you off to his friends. Can you stop by?"

"Of course, you wanna hang out afterward? Watch movies?" He asks in a hopeful tone.

Textbook Mason Boom, resorting to our predictable patterns. And despite knowing better, I find myself agreeing.

"Sure, why not?"

My answer even surprises him. "You serious? Uh, okay. Classics?"

"Of course, Brown Sugar."

"Cool. Then, Love & Basketball. But here comes the tricky third choice, Poetic Justice?" He challenges.

I laugh and playfully retort, "What, you're trippin'. I'll raise your Poetic Justice to a Love Jones."

"Damn, that's a good one. Deal. But, then The Wood afterward."

"Or…we can watch The Best Man," I counter, reveling in our exchange.

"Tiffany Nicole Weathers, you're killin' me! Fine, you'll be asleep in my arms by the time the second movie's done anyway." He teases.

"You're probably right about that! So, be prepared to hear me snore."

"The snoring I can deal with. It's your slobbering I can't handle." He jokes.

"I do not slobber!" I laugh in protest. "I gotta get up and get ready. Don't forget to tell the Bakery that Drew's cake needs to be finished by noon. The party starts at 3 p.m. I'll see you at the game."

"I know, Ms. Worrisome. See you soon." Even his warm goodbye makes me smile.

When I hang up the phone, a sense of ease washes over me. Our conversations are always so effortless and filled with laughter. Every interaction with Mase reminds me of the good times we've shared.

Leaving my studio, I dash over to the school to prep my dancers and cheer Drew on. Drew is my pride and joy, and though he's young, he's stepping into his own spotlight. And then there's Mase, a man who has always been a significant part of our lives, reentering the scene in a way I hadn't anticipated. So many life changes are happening all at once, and I have to make a mental note to embrace the unknown future and allow myself the chance to rediscover joy and maybe even love again. I remind myself that life has proven itself to be unpredictable, but sometimes, the most unexpected paths can lead to the most fulfilling destinations, and I'm determined my last stop will be happiness.

Chapter 7

Game Time – Tiffany

I t's just a few hours before game time when I pull into the parking lot of the school's new stadium. Greer High School is the most expensive public school in the area with regular donors being the wealthiest in the city. Every after-school program costs a fortune to participate in, but they also have the best STEM program in the South. So, when Drew begged me to send him here, I agreed to enroll him because we needed a fresh start and he deserves the best.

Everything has seemed to fall into place. Drew's a budding superstar, and is even dating now. But most importantly, Mase is back in his life. I think the latter blessing brings him the most peace.

I used to feel guilty for making Mase an 'instant dad,' but he accepted a responsibility that he didn't have to, and he's never acted as if it's an obligation. He truly does love my son, and every part of me wishes I could change the "my" to "our."

I have to stop thinking about shoulda, coulda, woulda's when I see dozens of reporters and paparazzi waiting like vultures, ready to invade my life again. And when I try to move past them, they bombard me with dozens of suffocating questions.

Reporter #1: *"Ms. Weathers, is it true you've rekindled your relationship* *with Mason Boom?"*

Reporter #2: *"Can you guarantee you won't be a distraction for him?"*

Reporter #3: *"Are you ever gonna admit you cheated on him, or is Mason Boom actually your son's father?"*

I hide my face, ignore them, and keep walking. I just have a few more steps until I reach the gym, but the questions become more invasive and just downright disrespectful.

The final straw that pierces through my defenses is when someone asks, *"How's your sister doing?"*

The panic I've been keeping at bay threatens to break free as I whirl around and yell, "stop it! Just —"

Before the floodgates open, the Boom brothers, Jay and Bash, step in like guardian angels.

"Leave her the hell alone!" The smoldering Bash warns. "Or do I need to get all your names so my team can dig up every dirty deed you've ever done and bury you with it?"

Mase sneaks beside me and tightly clasps his hand with mine, "My brothers will handle this. C'mon, you got dancers to prep and we gotta go watch our boy play."

Mase's presence calms me and allows me to put aside my fear of Drew's big night being ruined by outsiders who will never understand our lives and all we've endured.

We arrive right on time for Drew to spot us before he begins warm-ups. He'll probably get in trouble, but he rushes to the sideline to greet us.

"Mom, what're you doing over here?" Drew says in worry. "The entire band's about to come out. How's Lea lookin'? Is she nervous? I tried textin' her but I figured you told the girls to put away their phones."

"I needed to see you before kick-off, and I'm glad I did because the last thing you need to be doing right now is thinking about a girl! It's your first game as starting quarterback. Focus!"

While I fuss, Mase just laughs and swings his arm around my shoulder. "Chill out, Tiff. I was the same way when I was Drew's age."

Trying not to smile, I quickly reply, "Exactly! Easily distracted by a cute face and long legs."

Mase attempts to whisper. "We both know you're way more than a cute face and," He looks down in awe. "And those damn legs..." He shakes his head.

I get caught up in his antics until Drew brings us back to reality.

"Ew, is this how old people flirt?"

"Boy, hush!" I playfully wave him off. "Good luck out there, okay. You have a section full of family rooting for you. And I don't want you looking out in the stands at your little friend."

Drew rolls his eyes and embraces us then I head back to the gym to prep the Pipettes for their intro.

"Alright, ladies! Now, y'all have practiced your butts off learning new music, new cadences, new moves – the works. You killed it last year, but this season you're becoming legends. You aren't just dancers. You aren't just majorettes. You're Greer High Pipettes. Now, get in formation and let's kill it tonight."

My girls line up between the band and drill team, prepared to lock in as the horns blow. Their sequins catch the stadium lights, and the steady rhythm of the drums from the band behind them pulse through the air. Like every performance, the Pipettes effortlessly execute my choreography. I step back, proud and confident in my girls as they infuse adrenaline and excitement into the Greer High football team.

After the opening introduction, I sit behind the team, accompanied by my friends and family in the stands. Mason's stepmom, former Governor Sherri Carter, Greer's wealthiest resident Crystal Lynn, and all of our friends are here. This is the family we found. This is the family that helped me raise that amazing young man on the field.

"Wow, Tiff!" Sherri praises. "You sure did get those girls in shape! That's the best this town's seen the Pipettes in years."

"Thanks, Sherri! They're a talented bunch, that's for sure. Nearly half of them are already slated for scholarships." I reveal then instantly get nervous when I spot Drew on the field. "Oh God, y'all! Here we go!" I cry out but Mase transfers his calming energy to me.

"He's gonna do great!"

I hope so. The pride I feel for him is immeasurable, but so is my anxiety. A jolt of fear sweeps through my body and manifests in my tightened grip on Mason's hand. It's the first play of the game, and the tension in the air is palpable as Drew takes his position on the field. He looks focused and determined, with the weight of this moment resting on his shoulders. While my heart races with excitement, my worry overwhelms me more.

As the ball snaps and Drew drops back to pass, he's blindsided by a defensive lineman twice his size. The impact echoes through the entire stadium. A collective gasp springs from the crowd, and my grip on Mason's hand tightens even more.

I yell as loud as I can, "C'mon offense! Protect the quarterback!"

Mase, with a steady and confident voice, reassures me, "He's okay, Tiff. He's tough."

I nod, trying to steady my racing heart. Drew slowly gets up and shakes off the hit. The team lines up again, and this time, Drew's fired up and ready for his get back.

When the ball snaps again, Drew steps back, scans the field, and in a moment that feels like minutes, he finds his receiver and launches a perfect spiral throw. We all jump from our seats and scream wildly.

"Go, go, go, go!"

The player dodges tackle after tackle and sprints towards the end zone until we all scream, "Touchdown!"

The crowd erupts as our friends and family hug and exchange high-fives. My fear and anxiety dissipate into pure joy. Mason's arms are still around me, but now we're both jumping up and down, caught up in the moment's excitement.

"Did you see that? My baby threw that ball!" I shout, tears of pride welling in my eyes.

Mason laughs, his own excitement matching mine. "He's incredible, Tiff! What a play!"

Drew's teammates surround him, pat him on the back, and celebrate the amazing start to the game. And it doesn't stop there. As the game continues, Drew throws one perfect spiral after the next, sneak handoffs, and impresses the crowd with his run game. We're all thinking the same thing, he's a sight to watch.

"Drew's so amazing." Sherri fondly observes. "This reminds me of when we all used to attend your games back in the day, Mase. And is one of your majorettes his girlfriend, Tiff? I'm pretty sure he just blew her a kiss. Aww, this is Tiffany and Mason all over again!" She gushes.

"Oh goodness, I hope not! Yes, that's Drew's friend." I reply, trying to downplay the relationship.

Monica and Mel laugh. "Stop calling her that. He's old enough to date now."

I sigh and roll my eyes. "I know. I'm just not ready to accept it. Next thing you know, he's getting married and then having kids. It's just too much! Then what about me? What will I have?"

"A life." Rafe jokes.

Monica elbows him and adds, "what he means is you'll have time to enjoy life by yourself or with that man sitting next to you."

"Thank you," Sherri exclaims with relief. "I'm glad someone said it. These two here sure know how to stress us mothers out. Isn't that right, Crys?"

We all laugh as Crystal Lynn coyly adds, "well, as y'all already know, I'm one patient mother, so I'll hold out hope for the two of you to fall in love for as long as I can. You were meant to be, you know?"

I smile at Crystal Lynn, the sweetest, most kind-hearted woman I've ever met, then quickly slide beside her to speak more intimately.

"Are you flying out tonight?"

Gently squeezing my hand, she nods. "Yes, I have a business meeting in Texas, but Terry and I will be back tomorrow afternoon. Tomorrow is the second happiest day of our lives. We promise we won't be late."

I feel like a giddy little girl. "Good because everything changes tomorrow."

"For the better." She says while hugging me tight.

Sherri and Crystal get up to leave for the evening, but not without Crystal saying, "I love you, Tiffany Nicole."

Sherri also bids her goodbye, "We'll see everyone at the birthday party. Please tell Drew we're so proud of him. Love you, ladies!"

Mase, Rafe, Jay, and Bash all whine to the same tune. "Well dang, Ma, what about us?"

She rolls her eyes and playfully scoffs, "love you, too, boys!"

Briefly lost in my thoughts around family and reclaiming what was once lost, Mase breaks my concentration.

"You and Crystal are like two peas in a pod."

"We are, aren't we?" I smile in full appreciation. "But I wouldn't even have her in my life if it weren't for you. You changed my life, Mase."

We consider the shared history between his family, The Lynns, and me. The mysterious Greer house fires ruined so many lives. Crystal lost her daughters. Mase's mom died, and so did Rafe's dad. I couldn't imagine losing Drew. I lie my head on Mase's shoulder to console my dark thoughts, holding back my tears.

"Not as much as you changed mine," Mase admits with a gentle caress on my cheek. "I knew you were the one for me from first glance but you definitely stole my heart when the Sunday school teacher told you to sing your favorite song." A smile creeps on his face.

"Oh my God, Mase! I was like fourteen years old! It's not my fault I wasn't raised to be a bible-thumpin' hillbilly like you. How long are you gonna hold that over my head?" I laugh.

"Until I find another person bold enough to sing Musiq Soulchild's Love in church!" He teases.

I laugh, "I stand behind my mistakes. Besides, it was a great song," Then, with a look of admiration, I adjust my tone. "Seriously Mase, thank you. You've stuck beside me all these years."

"Well, when you love someone with all your heart, it's impossible to let go," he says while grabbing my hand to convey the numerous meanings behind his words. "I'll never let go of the people I love because every moment is precious, and life isn't guaranteed. We can both testify to that."

His words resonate with me, echoing my own thoughts. I observe my friends and glance at the field where Drew plays, feeling a surge of deep, protective love.

When the game ends, we make our way to the field to congratulate Drew. His smile is wide and bright and fills me with indescribable joy. What matters is this moment, and when I look down, my hand has found Mason's yet again. His words ringing true in my head – never let go of the people we love because every moment is precious. And right now, I'm going to make the most of each moment with Drew, Mason, and all the people I ever loved – Tiny included.

~ ~ ~

Back at the house, Drew and his friends listen to Mason's stories from his glory days on the field and take selfies for social media. Then, they kick him out so they can return to being cool, unimpressed teenagers. Mason exits with a laugh, leaving the boys to their devices and conversations with girls.

Meanwhile, I shower and set up my living room for the ultimate movie night. Fuzzy socks, check. Blanket, check. Popcorn, check. Fresh breath, check. Wine, check. Nervous about being so intimately close to Mase again, check.

When he enters my living room, he comes to an abrupt halt as his eyes lock onto mine with an intensity that sends a shiver down my spine. Panic flutters in my chest as I wonder what's wrong. Is he having second thoughts? Do I look okay? Do I smell okay? Why is he looking at me like I'm an alien or something?

Mason's intense gaze holds mine for what feels like forever until his eyes soften, and a small, affectionate smile plays on his face. "Tiffany, are you purposely wearing my old shirt?"

Completely aloof, I look down and read Morehouse Football. Oh crap, I sleep in this all the time. I sleep in Mase's old college shirts almost every night.

"You tryin' to tempt me?" He asks in low, dark admiration.

I'm overcome with a flutter of excitement. "I have a drawer full of your clothes! I haven't had a chance to throw them away yet." He smirks.

"It's been a decade. How long do you need to get me out of your system? You know exactly what you're doin' to me, Tiffany Nicole." He playfully teases.

I roll my eyes and scoff. "Are you ready for this movie marathon or not?"

"I am, but not if I gotta look at you wearing those short shorts and rockin' my old football tee. And you know how intoxicating your smell is to me. It's gonna be hard not to touch you." We both look down to notice his long, thick-hanging bulge.

I chuckle, "oops." Mason shakes his head, but I continue. "By the way, who said you couldn't touch me?"

His face lights up with a blend of surprise and delight at the brazen invitation he happily accepts with a leap on my couch and a raised brow. "Do I get to hold you, too?"

"Yes, you can hold me as tight as you possibly can," I'm probably more excited to say it than he is to hear it. "But if, and only if, you promise to bake your homemade biscuits for me in the morning. Your biscuits are my favorite, and I've been deprived for far too long!"

Mase smiles at my subtle invitation to spend the night. "Biscuits in the A.M. it is, then." He replies while comfortably settling on the couch.

I nestle my body in his lap. "Umm, that shower did you well 'cause you were smelling like grass and sweat, Mr. Boom."

He laughs. "I was thinkin' the same about you. I'm glad I don't have to hold my breath all night."

I playfully hit his chest, then replace my hand with my head as he holds me in his arms and we watch beautiful black romances while reveling in our own.

"Sometimes," Mase whispers. "When I dream about us, it's like watching a movie."

"I don't want to watch any movie that doesn't have a happy ending." My words hang between us, laden with hope and shared longing for a future that mends past hurts and fulfills deferred dreams.

Mase turns to me, his gaze intense and tender, then gently lifts my chin with his finger. "Hey, our story isn't done yet. Not only will we have a happy ending, but you'll regain all that was lost and receive everything your heart ever desired."

My eyes soften, and I feel our hearts magnetically pulling us toward each other. Caught in the moment's sincerity, my heart guides my next words.

"Could it begin now? Our happy ending?"

Mason smiles, leans in, "*Our?*"

I smile and nod, sharing the understanding that the greatest happiness we've ever experienced has been with each other.

Our lips hover in the space between, desperately desiring to be pressed together. We move closer. So close that I feel his warm breath mingling with mine, only leaving a slight anticipation of being reunited once again. Mase, with all his self-control, presses his forehead against mine instead.

"It's taking everything in me not to kiss you, Tiff." He says with a soft caress to my cheek.

"It's taking everything in me not to let you," I confess, our gazes still locked. "Maybe…we can just exchange a light peck. Just a small kiss, for old times' sake?" I foolishly suggest as if I could control myself.

"Yeah, I mean, we could do that. Just a little peck, right?" Mase agrees with my bad idea.

In a panting breath, I utter, "Umm hmm, sure. Just a peck."

We both smile, slowly moving closer, our lips meeting with a gentle graze. Our kiss is soft and tender. A delicate reacquaintance of two souls that desperately hoped for this moment. It deepens with every moan, driven by years of suppressed emotions and unreleased desire. As our tongues rediscover one another, our hands roam and rekindle a fire I thought would never be lit again. I'm burning for more. I've been needing more ever since the day I walked away. Mason, the life we built and everything in it is all I ever needed.

What was supposed to be a peck on the lips quickly escalated to Mason's hands all over my body and my tongue tied with his.

I haven't felt like this in a year. I haven't felt this good since the last time Mase touched me, and I feel myself sinking into his addictive grasp. His lips move to my neck. I know we have to stop, but my heart takes over.

"I missed you, Mase. Please don't stop!"

But he does. He abruptly stops touching me, which instantly makes my heart drop.

"I'm sorry, Tiff, but we can't," he says between heavy breaths. "I don't want to distract you from your big day. I want you, I swear I do, but nothing is more important than tomorrow. It'll be a fresh start for your family." He warmly smiles.

Mason's gentle refusal is grounded in consideration for the importance of tomorrow. It speaks volumes of his character and his commitment to ensuring that this time there will be no more distractions on our path to happiness.

With heavy sighs, we pull away, our eyes meeting one more time, reflecting a mixture of joy, love, hope, and unadulterated desire.

Mason brushes a strand of hair away from my face and gently caresses my cheek. "Please tell me tonight isn't a one-time thing." He whispers, his voice barely above a breath.

"It doesn't have to be. After tomorrow, this can be an everyday thing, if you want." I propose with calming resolve.

He smiles. "I want that and so much more, Tiffany Nicole."

As I settle back into my position cradled in Mason's arms, the movie continues but for us, the sequel to our story is just beginning. A story of second chances, healing, endurance, and resilience. We've evolved. We've grown. We've overcome the pain that would've torn us apart if we remained together when our minds were too immature, our emotions were too damaged, and our hearts were too broken. We may not be whole, but we're healthier.

As my eyelids fall heavy, our laughter and flirtation dying down, I have one final question.

"Do you think my family's gonna be okay? I feel like my dreams are finally coming true, but what if tomorrow turns out to be a disaster? I hate being in the spotlight, Mase. What if our family secrets come out, including —"

With his hands massaging my scalp, he calms my fears, "Tomorrow will be the best day of your life. The truth about what happened that night stays within our family. I'll always protect you. It's what I was born to do – to protect and love you forever. It's me, you, and the world around us."

My eyes close for the evening, and the last touch I feel is Mason's lips on my forehead. I haven't complained about sleeping alone for years because my only desire was peace and stability, but being enclosed in the warmth of Mason's arms reminds me there's nothing wrong with being alone, but there's even greater satisfaction in being held safely in the arms of someone who loves you as equally as they love themselves. Mason loves me in spite of myself. I love him for his unwavering presence and strength in my life.

And tomorrow, I'll need Mason's strength once again because Drew's Sweet Sixteen will be a momentous occasion of long-awaited healing, incomparable joy, and familial restoration. Tomorrow will be the first day of the rest of our lives together as a family.

Chapter 8

Sweet Sixteen – Tiffany

I can't believe I overslept! It was the wine. It *had* to be the wine. Or maybe it was the cuddling? Mason cuddled me into a sleep coma last night, and we woke up on my couch with our bodies entangled. What makes matters worse is Drew saw us, but we ate a family breakfast, where Mase cooked his famous homemade biscuits, my favorite. We were all so happy this morning, especially Drew, but I don't want him to get the wrong idea. So, I sent Mase packing immediately after breakfast. With a lingering hug to comfort him, of course.

I just don't want to fall back into the same pattern of loving a man life won't let me have, though I desperately want to give it a try.

And speaking of dating, Drew's *little friend* is in my house right now helping me set up for his sixteenth birthday party while Jay and Bash with a shopping spree in one of Jay's flashy sports cars.

"Coach Weathers, should I put the Bluetooth speaker in the backyard? Drew likes to blast his music so loud the neighborhood hears." Lea asks.

I respond in a sweet yet firm tone, "Well, Drew isn't paying my mortgage or HOA fees now, is he?"

"No, ma'am, he sure isn't!" She cheerfully agrees. "I'll control the volume and make sure everything stays under control."

"Thanks, Lea. I must admit, you've really grown on me."

She chuckles, then playfully replies, "You're kind of growing on me, too, Coach. So does that mean I'm being upgraded from little friend to girlfriend?"

I laugh. "Don't push it."

Time flies by fast. In the middle of decorating, I receive an emergency text in the group chat.

My Forever Family

Monica: I got bad news, and I need an assist. Rafe and I are running behind. I won't be able to pick up the surprise.

Tiffany: Are you serious? Can anyone else help?

Avery: I'm sorry, sis. I'm still stuck in Beverly Mills. Deac is still at work, and the babysitter isn't here, so I'm useless until the party.

Mel: Crap! I wish I could but I'm at a photoshoot trying to wrap up before the party.

Mason: I'll do it.

Tiffany: You're already bringing the food and cake. It'd be too much.

Mason: It's fine. Food and cake are taken care of. I volunteered to pick up the gifts first anyway, but that was back when you were dodging me. Now that we're good again, I'm resuming what should've been my role in the first place.

Tiffany: Aww thanks Mase ☺

Rafe: Are y'all flirting in the group chat?

Monica: They certainly are!

Jay: Oh goodness. Mase and Tiffany are in love again.

Bash: This is annoying. Take me out the chat. I want no parts of this saga.

Deacon: Well, maybe we'll finally hear some wedding bells.

Jay: Wedding bells? If these two ever get married, yall know what song they're gonna walk down the aisle to?

Mel: Sam Cooke. Lol. Been a Long Time Comin'

Rafe: Nah! I'm thinkin' Jagged Edge Let's Get Married.

Avery: Lol. There won't even be a wedding! They just need to skip to the honeymoon.

Mason: I'm blocking everybody.

Tiffany: Seriously! Yall are beyond petty. Mase and I are in a good place. We're friends, and that's the official story. Now, I'll see everyone in less than three hours.

Lea and I finish decorating in the nick of time. I proudly admire my handiwork and appreciate how sweet Drew is to allow me to exercise my corny, limited decorating skills for his big day. We designed my foyer to resemble a football stadium tunnel, complete with LED lights and fog machines. As the guests enter, they'll be greeted by holographic images of Drew in quarterback action. In one corner of our living room is the photo booth with virtual football and science lab backgrounds. In the other corner is the Virtual Reality Science Zone.

The backyard is a teenager oasis with loud music, a drone racing course, and a space for young folks to do whatever version of clean dancing they have. I may be going overboard, but I have the most amazing son in the world, and perhaps I do want to vicariously live through him for a moment. I think it looks amazing, but I didn't have much growing up, so anything impresses me.

"You think this is too much?" I ask, aware she has the inside scoop on Drew's likes and dislikes.

She shakes her head. "Not at all, Coach. Drew's gonna love it, especially the food."

Oh, the food and cake! That damn Mason. He's so extra, but I don't mind. I told him to order some pizza, but he sent an entire team of caterers to organize an array of choices – chicken fingers, a taco bar, sliders, crinkle and steak fries – all of Drew's favorites. And the cake – wow is all I can say! Mason went above and beyond. The bottom tier resembles a football field. The middle tier represents his love for science and technology with edible coding symbols and lab tools. However, I think I love the top the most. It's small but meaningful. The saying 'Me, you, and the world around us' is etched on the side with an edible sculpture of me and Drew when he was a baby on top.

A concerned Lea passes me a tissue, "Coach, you're crying. Is everything okay?"

I dab my eyes and reply, "Oh, I'm fine, Lea. It's just – it's an emotional day, that's all."

There are some things I can't explain, not yet, but I will. While this is my season to finally be loved, it's also my season to be unburdened by secrets and freed by the truth. It all begins today.

I wipe away my tears and give her a grateful nod for her concern, then we usher in the guests. The entire football team arrives, dozens of school friends, and my friends turned family are here.

Bash texts me to inform me they're in route with Drew, but Mason is nowhere to be found.

My Forever Family

Tiffany: Uh Mase where the heck are you? Everyone's here and Drew will be here in 10 minutes

Mason: Traffic is crazy. Pulling up in 40.

Tiffany: 40 minutes?

Mason: Calm down, Tiff. I'll text you when I'm outside. Just be ready to present his gift. Don't stress, okay? This will be the happiest day of his life ...and yours too.

Tiffany: Thank you, Mase...But hurry up and get your ass here now! Lol.

My worry temporarily fades as I gather the guests to prepare for Drew's arrival.

"Okay, everyone," I loudly announce. "It's time!"

My hands are shaking. I throw a party for him every year, but this is different because after today, everything changes, and I hope it's for the best.

As I scan the room, I see the excited faces of his friends, the proud expressions of our family, and the anticipation in everyone's eyes. The energy is high, and joy fills the air.

When we hear Jay's car pull in, signaling Drew's arrival, I whisper, "Everyone, get ready!"

The room instantly hushes, echoing only the sound of shuffling feet and ill-contained giggles.

The front door opens, and Drew steps through the threshold, where he's greeted with fog. Then, the house erupts into a loud, joyful "Happy Birthday!"

The look of surprise and joy on Drew's face is priceless. He looks across the room to take in the faces of his friends, teammates, and family. Then, his gaze finally lands on me. His smile widens, and he gives me a huge hug.

"Ma, this is amazing!" He exclaims, still in shock and awe. "I told you I wanted something small. Did you seriously do all this?" He asks in disbelief.

"Well, I had some help…from your girlfriend." My eyes move to Lea, who stands nearby in a lovestruck gaze.

Drew smiles, and for a moment, he even looks emotional.

I place my hand on his shoulder and ask, "you okay, Drew?"

He nods, "I'm good. Thank you, Mom. You're the best. I love you so much."

I smile. "I love you too, Son."

Drew hugs me one more time before he makes his way to his girlfriend and friends to celebrate his big day.

With the party now in full gear with bangin' music, loud laughter, delicious food, fun games, and good times, a profound sense of contentment washes over me. However, when I receive the text I've been waiting for, my contentment elevates to an overabundance of excitement.

Mason: You've been worried about everything and everyone else all day. Are you okay, Tiff? Are you ready for this?

I think about his question and decide to answer honestly. If anyone can calm my nerves, it's Mason.

Tiffany: I don't know. I'm nervous but so excited. It's been a long time comin'.

Mason: It has and you can only go up from here. Now bring your sexy ass outside. And round up our boy, too.

I don't know why, but the way he speaks to me makes me smile.

Ready to unveil Drew's gift, I enter the backyard to interrupt the sports debate between him and his friends. "Okay, kids, listen, I'll settle this right now. Lebron is the GOAT!"

"See! My mom knows best, y'all! Case closed." Drew points at me and his friends laugh.

"That's right. Now, Drew, you ready to open your gift?"

Confused, he asks, "Gift? Isn't this party my gift?"

"Not in the slightest. C'mon everyone, follow me!"

We make our way from the backyard to the front of the house. Drew stands next to me with our family surrounding us as we walk through the front door. He freezes when he sees the brand-new black Jeep Gladiator RUBICON parked in the driveway.

His friends marvel in excitement, and Avery comments, "dang, Deac. It's time to upgrade our mini-van."

"Mom, you got me a car?" He enthusiastically asks as he approaches the gorgeous ride.

"Actually," I say as Mase reveals himself by opening the driver's door. "Mase, bought you the car. I told him not to, but he said you've been obsessing over this car for years."

Drew wraps his arms around Mase. "Thank you! This is awesome! It's the best gift ever."

"You're welcome, son. But you might wanna hold that thought. Your mom's gift is next. Well, it's a gift for the both of you."

Mase signals me to stand next to Drew while he walks over to the passenger side to open the door.

The most beautiful, young yet aged through hardship, woman slowly steps out of the vehicle. Mason's right. It's a gift for the both of us – a gift I was expecting yet still shocked to receive.

Me and Drew's eyes are filled with tears as we see the woman we love the most, the woman who sacrificed everything for us. The woman who endured years of torture for my comfort stands before us.

"Tiny." I whisper.

Her face is overwhelmed with tears, but she manages to whisper back, "Tiffany."

Too much time has passed for me to stand still, so I run to her and wrap my arms around her once fragile but now whole body. We embrace one another with loud cries – sounds we're used to hearing, except now, these are joyful tears laced with hope and anticipation for our future.

"You smell so good." She says as she inhales our special fragrance. "It must be a special occasion." She tearfully jokes.

"Of course – it's me, you, and the world around us, remember?"

We release from our embrace and then turn to a tearful Drew, who looks nervous and perhaps even afraid. Then, I look at Tiny, whose expression is the same.

She stares then mutters under her breath, "He's perfect."

My hands are clasped with hers and gently, I whisper, "Re-introduce yourself."

With her lips quivering, voice wavering, tears flowing, and nose sniffling, she struggles to speak clearly but utters, "Uh, hi – my name is –"

But Drew cuts her off and runs to her with his arms wrapped tightly around her body and says, "Mom. Your name is Mom!"

Our cries grow louder. Tiny unclasps her hand from mine and returns his embrace, then nods. "It's nice to meet you, Son."

Mason slowly walks beside me and wraps his arms around my waist as we watch my sister Tiny reunited with my biological nephew – Drew Weathers, her son.

Drew looks at me, Tiny, and Mason. "This is the happiest day of my life. Our family is finally complete."

And indeed, we are. The four of us embrace each other with all the love we have.

Tiny saved me time and time again, and if it weren't for her, I wouldn't be happy. I certainly wouldn't be here. She gave me confidence, freedom, protection, and motherhood. Now it's my turn to give her the life that was taken away from her when we were just kids. No one should ever have to experience so much hardship and torture, especially at the hands of our parents.

We made a vow that I would raise our son and give him the best because we only ever had the worst. I'll continue to keep my promise, but now it's extended to Tiny, too. It's what she deserves – nothing but the best, and I promise to make up for what she never received—love, safety, healing, peace, and family.

Today marks a new beginning, the start of an unfolding story of our intertwined lives. Mason and I were bound by fate from a young age, and to understand our destined forever, we need to go back to where it all began—the past, where each piece falls into place, bringing our world together again. And so, the fated love story of Tiffany Weathers and Mason Boom begins now.

PART 2

SECOND QUARTER SETBACKS

Chapter 9

The Beginning of it All – Tiffany

As I stand here today on my son's sixteenth birthday, surrounded by my sister, Mase, and loved ones, I find myself reflecting on the moments that shaped me—pieces of my life I've rarely shared, let alone remembered. To understand who I am now, I need to go back, back to where my earliest memories began weaving together the story of the woman I was always meant to be and the love I was always meant to have.

My earliest memory traces back to when I was four, a memory so vivid that it became a recurring dream. It's more of a scene than a memory—filled with smells and sounds, the sweetness of love mixed with tormented cries. Our mother, Shirley Weathers, once so loving and kind, shuffled us from city to city, but our origin story began in Savannah, Georgia. Mama held on to countless photos of herself pregnant with us, but none of the three of us together. Despite those photos, the memory that stands out is fleeing Savannah. That night marked the first of many terrible memories and became the nightmare I still relive. That night is where my love story truly begins.

~ ~ ~

Four Years Old – When My Life Burned to Flames

Enveloped in darkness and choking on thick smoke, I find myself staggering, coughing, and crying out in a voice strained with terror and desperation. "Mommy! Daddy! Where are you? Help!" Each word is a battle, fought between gasps for air and the overwhelming fear of death gripping my heart.

Clutching my vanilla scented baby blanket for comfort, I stumble through the haze until I feel the reassuring grip of my sister's hand. "I'm here, Nicole. We'll find them together." She declares in a tone that serves as a beacon of hope amidst the chaos.

For a moment, her words soothe me, but fear overpowers even her bold hopefulness. As we navigate the labyrinth of our massive home, we scald our hands turning each doorknob, searching room to room, for someone to help us. The smoke invades our lungs, and the thick air is laced with a pungent taste of despair while the sting in our eyes feels like a cruelly relentless punishment.

Overcome with the terror of our doom, I sob to my sister, "We're gonna die, aren't we?" My words are a whisper – a fragile thread of fear that threatens to unravel me completely but she envelops me in a fierce embrace, her presence a fortress against the encroaching flames.

She whispers back in a tear-filled voice of determination. "No, I'll never let that happen, and neither will Mommy and Daddy."

Her conviction shelters me from our circumstance, but the illusion shatters all too quickly when the direness of our situation drags us back to a reality fraught with danger. The fire rises taller, the smoke grows darker, and panic begins to claw at my insides like a relentless tide until the sudden appearance of our mother's hand piercing through the fog anchors us back to hope.

Her voice, muddled yet gentle, cuts through our fear, "C'mon girls, let's go." Like a guiding light, she leads us through the inferno and into the safety of the night through our back door. We escape the immediate threat, but she cautions us to avoid the chaos of screams and cries that lurk at the front entrance.

Under the moonlight, we finally see our mother, but Tiny and I halt with our feet pressing deep into the dirt. We grasp each other's hands as tight as possible. Then, with my voice trembling, I ask, "Where are we going?"

Mama's response is a mixture of exhaustion and urgency, with her labored breaths emphasizing her frustration.

"C'mon, I said we gotta go!" She snaps as her eyes dart back and forth, and her body twitches with nervous energy.

"But what about our –" Tiny cries, but Mama tightens her grip on our arms and adds a subtle twist to demand our obedience.

"You heard what I said," She glares at us with disdain. "Just drink this water so you can fall fast asleep. We need to go. NOW!"

I reach for the water bottle, but she quickly pulls it away alarmed by voices, which prompts us to make a hasty retreat. "Shit. C'mon, girls. The car is over here." She points and ushers us forward with a sense of urgency that leaves no room for debate.

I settle into the backseat of the car with a desert-dry throat and a brutal cough wracking my lungs. Desperation creeps within me; the need for relief is overwhelming, but the sight of the water bottle gives me hope.

Thankfully, Mama eventually hears us then offers a sip.

"Stop the damn coughing, please. Drink this. It'll put you to sleep." She says in faux concern.

The bottle glistens in her hand, and I take it, but in the shadowy confines of the car's backseat, my older sister leans close, her voice hushed and tinged with fear.

"Don't drink it." She warns, her eyes wide with apprehension as she glances towards the front seat. "She's crazy."

Mama catches her whisper and snaps at her without even turning around. "I heard that, little girl. Drink the damn water, or else you're gonna be coughing for days. Don't play with me, Tiny!"

The reference sparks an angry protest within my sister. "Don't call me that! That's not my name."

"Fine, we'll just have to do this the hard way." With swift movements, she reaches back and presses a washcloth against Tiny's face. Her screams briefly pierce my ears until her struggle ceases, her eyes flutter closed, and she succumbs to a forced sleep.

Turning her attention to me, Mama's expression softens. "Now, you're my good daughter," She coos with a deceptive warmth. "You don't have all that mouth like your sister. Are you gonna drink your water, or do I have to put you to sleep, too?"

Fearful and without options, I nod and drink. The water tastes bitter, but it's better than the lingering smoke in my pained throat. Moments later, I, too, drift into a reluctant sleep.

~ ~ ~

It's been three Christmases since our home burned down. We've lived a bit of everywhere, but we never stay anywhere long enough to go to school or make friends.

My blanket still has a faint smell of vanilla and honey suckle and the words *Nicole and Taylor – It's me, you, and the world around us* written in permanent marker. It's a reminder of when Mama wasn't so mean. The mother from my memories is so different than the mother I've come to both hate and fear. When we aren't on the move, we're sleep. We wake up early, drink Mama's special water then by the time we awake, it's nighttime again.

I lost count of the days, weeks, and months a long time ago but I don't lose count of the minutes I go without eating.

That is, until one morning, dawn interrupts our sleep, and we awaken to a new reality, our first home, in Macon, Georgia.

"Wake up." Tiny says in a weary voice.

"I'm so hungry," I complain as hunger tortures my stomach. "We haven't eaten in days, and we don't have any more water left."

Tiny offers her comfort. "I know. Don't worry. I'll make sure we eat."

"We're hungry, Martha! Or is it Kayla? What's your name this time?" Tiny challenges our mother with a boldness that belies her size. "Are we ever gonna eat, or are you just gonna keep torturing us?"

Despite her small stature, Tiny's spirit is huge. However, while Tiny is a warrior, Mama is a monster.

"Tiny, can you just be quiet? I'll feed both of you if you just shut up. You get food when you obey. You don't get food when you fight me."

"Okay," I murmur, my voice small but determined. We're used to bargaining for food – our silence in exchange for sustenance. "I'll do it. I'll be quiet and listen."

For a moment, Tiny's defiance holds steady but wavers only when my hunger turns to voice-breaking tears, "Please, just listen to her. I'm so hungry, Tiny."

With a heavy sigh, Tiny unfolds her arms in defeat and agrees to comply. "Okay, fine. I'll shut up and listen, too. But why do you always get to change your name, and we can't?"

With a sinister curve of her lips, she rebuts, "Because I'm the boss! Your only job is to listen and obey. And it's your fault we even have to move again. You keep messing up your names! Now, hands out." Mama pulls a belt from the glove compartment then wraps it tight around her hand.

Our eyes widen and fill with tears at the sight of our worst enemy— Mama's thick, brown belt, hanging ominously in her hand. It's strange how quickly we forget the sting of its bite, the sharp pain that lingers long after the strike. Sometimes, I hate how easily we push those memories away, how we've learned to tuck the hurt into the corners of our minds. Tiny and I are so used to holding each other up, finding comfort in shared whispers and hugs, that we bury the bad times deep, pretending they don't exist. But the belt is always there to drag us back, to remind us of the mistakes we make and the hell with Mama we can't escape. It's a cruel cycle—comfort and pain, hope and fear—and we're trapped in it, clinging to each other as our only refuge.

"Please, no not again!" I scream with tears streaming down my face, my voice cracking under the weight of desperation.

"Hands out, now!" Mama's voice slices through the cries, cold and unyielding. "If I say it again, it'll be twice the pain."

Her strength in withstanding this torment, week after week, without breaking is both heartbreaking and awe-inspiring, but it makes Mama hate her even more.

"Say it." Mama commands.

"My name is Tiffany. Tiffany Nicole Weathers. My name is Tiffany. Tiffany Nicole Weathers." I repeatedly stammer between sharp whips. My swollen, throbbing hands twitch involuntarily, and every word feels like a plea for mercy that won't come.

Our punishment ends at the first sight of the blood. I cry and try my hardest to be as strong as Tiny, but I can't nor will she allow me to suffer alone. I collapse and cry into Tiny's arms.

"It hurts, Tiny. I can't bend my hands."

Tiny, in just as much pain, holds me tight. "I know, Tiff. but it's okay. We'll heal. We always do."

"Cheer up girls. I barely made you bleed. I bet you forget who you are now…or until the next punishment. Your name is Tiny Weathers. And you, sweet girl," She says, touching my face in a gesture that makes me recoil. "Your name is Tiffany Weathers. My new name is Shirley, but of course, you call me Mama. You hear me?"

Swallowing hard, I feebly utter, "Okay."

"Wrong answer, *Tiffany!*" Mama's tone shifts from sugary sweet to venomous in an instant. "Every answer needs to end with Mama. The more you say it, the happier I am. And the happier I am, the more you'll get to eat. Now, do you hear me?"

"Yes, Mama."

After submitting to the rules, she rewards us with water. It's fresh, completely different than the water that puts me to sleep. We drink so fast that the water is gone in nearly one gulp.

"Thank you, Mama." We say in unison with hopes of receiving more.

"May we have something to eat? Please, Mama."

We sense her smile from the backseat. She doesn't respond, but shortly afterward, we finally stop at a gas station.

"I'm going inside the store to get you a snack. The childproof lock is on. So, you can't get out and don't you dare look at or talk to strangers. I'll be right back."

When Mama exits the car, Tiny, with bruised and bloody hands, slowly unbuckles her seat belt. I can't take a second punishment in one day. The last time that happened, it took three weeks for the bruises to heal.

But Tiny is determined to save us. She searches everywhere – the glove compartment, console, and under the seats, but finds nothing.

"What're you looking for?" I helplessly ask.

Tiny shrugs and frantically moves about the car. "I don't know. Keys, maybe. We gotta get outta here. She's been getting worse and worse," Tiny's desperation prompts her to bang on the window and scream as loud as she can. "Help! Somebody, please!"

"Tiny." I attempt to coax her back to the seat to behave, but she pulls away.

"That's not my name. It's not what's on our blanket. You don't have to do what she says. I think she's dangerous. I don't even think she's –"

Tiny's cut off by Mama's sharp voice. "Tiny Weathers! What the hell are you doing?"

She tries to lock the door and scream some more, but Mama unlocks it, hurries in the car, and quickly speeds off. The sudden motion causes Tiny to fall and hit her head on the glove compartment.

I scream, "Taylor!" The name I call Tiny in secret, the name from our blanket.

As my sister cries, Mama scowls at me, "You got blood on my window. You tryna get me arrested? You want you and your sister to be separated? And you, Tiff!" She looks at me. "I leave you alone for a few minutes, and she's already rubbing off on you, huh?" She tsks, then holds up a pack of crackers. "I was feeling so generous, but you take my goodness for granted. I guess you'll just have to wait 'til tomorrow to eat."

I look at Tiny, who mouths, 'I'm sorry,' while rubbing her head. I lift my blanket, inviting her to cuddle with me so we can inhale the ragged yet comforting scent. This time, we drift to sleep naturally to avoid our hunger and dream about the life we miss.

"I love you, Sis," I whisper in Tiny's ear. "It's me, you, and the world around us."

~ ~ ~

"We're here!" Mama's haunting voice awakes us from our sleep. "Eat these crackers. I bet you're hungry, huh?"

Tiny, who doesn't look so well, mumbles, "Please." She fights to keep her eyes open. Her skin looks grey, and she's in and out of consciousness.

"What's wrong? Tiny, please wake up. Are you okay?" I shake her.

"Shit! I probably been dosin' y'all too much, and that bump on your head ain't lookin' too good," My mother grimaces. "Tiny, here baby, drink some water and eat. We're gonna visit Mommy's friend and get you all bandaged up, okay? Help your sister, Tiff."

Tiny slowly opens her mouth, and I stuff it with crackers and sips of water.

"My head hurts, Nicole. Am I dreaming? Please tell me this is just a bad dream."

Mama scoffs. "So damn ungrateful. If you were dreaming, could you feel this?" She places her hand on Tiny's thigh and proceeds to pinch her skin.

"Ow, ow, ow! Please! Please let go! It hurts so bad." She begs as she wildly moves her body to break loose from our mother's brutal hold.

"What's the magic word, Daughter?" She smiles sinisterly.

"Just say, Mama. Please, Tiny. I don't want you to cry anymore." I plea.

A sense of helplessness washes over me as Mama tortures Tiny. She's so strong, and she always looks out for me, which makes it easy to forget that she's just a kid, too. We're both vulnerable and in pain caused by the woman who should offer us sanctuary, not suffering.

In a low, nearly incoherent voice, a sobbing Tiny utters, "Ma- Mama. Please let go of me, Mama."

"Oh baby," She quickly releases her grip and caresses Tiny's face as if her cruelty was a figment of our imaginations. "Of course. I love you girls so much," Mama rubs Tiny's thigh, and then playfully laughs. "All that crying, and I didn't even break your skin. You're so dramatic, Tiny."

I observe my sister as my mother teases her. Tiny's skin may not be broken, but her spirit certainly is.

"Now listen up. If you keep misbehaving, I'll have to call CPS, and they're gonna take y'all away and separate you forever. Do you want that? Do you want to be alone for the rest of your life? You wanna never see your sister again? It'll be all your fault, Tiny."

"Okay, Mama," She responds through her cries. "I swear I'll behave. Just don't separate us. Please, Mama." She begs.

Mama nods. Despite her cruelty, we're thankful because she's our only way to survive. After devouring an entire box of crackers, Tiny and I find momentary solace. With full bellies and half-smiles, the car stops in front of a huge house. For the first time in a long time, we have hope. Maybe hot water, a comfy bed, clothes, and a home. I may not know where we are, but anything is better than sleeping in a car.

"Whoa, this is nearly as big as our old house. Is this our new home?" I ask in the open air with the hope Mama will respond.

"You wish! Your days of living a privileged life are long gone and are never returning. Children who live in excess grow up to become untrustworthy, weak adults. I have to course-correct you girls. Tiny's a disrespectful little brat. A terrible little girl, aren't you? Ugly and undeserving of love." She directs her attention to my sister, who lowers her head in shame.

As we approach the home, Mama reminds us to remember our names and only speak when spoken to. "I need to pick up a few things so we can start our new lives together. Remember, when I'm happy, you'll be happy, too. So, don't make me look bad."

We trail behind her up the steep hill. While waiting for someone to answer, I look up to see my mother, who, over the last few days, has looked different. She looks fragile. Shaky and sweaty. Maybe she's hungry. Or maybe she's sick. When me and Tiny are sick, we often get the sweats, too."

"Remember, be on your best behavior. You're Tiffany, and you're Tiny. If you behave, I'll get you something even better than crackers. Will you be on your best behavior for Mama?"

We nod and reply in unison, "Yes, Mama."

When the door swings open, a woman wearing a flowy yellow dress greets us. She looks like she's wearing sunshine. A stark difference from the three of us.

"Wow, she's beautiful." Tiny whispers loud enough for me to agree.

"Kayla, what the hell? I haven't seen you since you were pregnant, and I haven't heard from you since your last stint in rehab. Your family – they said you were dead," She looks confused, but her gaze softens momentarily when she notices us, a brief acknowledgment of our existence before her resolve hardens once more. "They're absolutely beautiful, but you gotta get the hell away from me. I've been clean for four years, and you don't even look like it's been four hours. I got a family now. The most I can do is get you a first-aid kit, some clean clothes, and a room for the night. The girls can eat a decent meal and take a warm bath," She wrinkles her nose at the sight of us. "It looks like you could all use one."

My mother rolls her eyes. "Don't look at us like that. You think you're better than me now, huh? Don't forget where you came from. Don't make me tell your rich husband about our glory days – trickin' and schemin'. I'm sure he knows nothin' 'bout what you're willing to do for a quick fix. I just came for money; that's all I want."

The woman's face becomes wrought with concern and fear, prompting her to briefly step away. When she returns, she extends an envelope filled with cash towards my mother. As Mama reaches for it, the woman's grip tightens. "Please don't put it all up your nose," She then shakes her head. "Or in your arm."

With her patience running thin, Mama snatches the envelope and turns away, nearly dragging us behind her.

"Don't come back, Kayla!" The woman yells. "Or I'll call the police. We both know you don't want that to happen! This isn't Greer. Your rich parents and friends can't hide your dirty deeds here!" Her words force Mama to increase her pace.

"C'mon, girls. I got what I need." She happily informs us.

This is the first time in a very long time my mother has genuinely smiled. Her look of excitement as she clutches the cash tightly in her hand is priceless.

"So," She says with her foot pressed to the pedal. "Who wants a cheeseburger?"

"We do!" I happily scream.

Mama laughs. "Two cheeseburgers, comin' right up! But first, I need to make a quick stop."

It's been months since we had a cheeseburger so it's impossible to hide our excitement. This feels like the best day of our lives.

As we revel in anticipation, I whisper to Tiny, "What if we get fries, too?"

Her face lights up, "Ooh, and with ketchup?"

"And an orange Hi-C?"

Tiny clasps my hand and reminds me, "I'm gonna be on my best behavior. I swear I won't get us in trouble anymore, okay? I'll try not to be so terrible. I'll even call you Tiffany, but never forget who you are, *Nicole*." She winks.

I gently squeeze her hand in solidarity. "I'll never forget, *Taylor*." I whisper softly.

My sister and I smile, finding comfort in our mutual support and understanding of how to *play the game* as Mama's obedient, chameleon-like daughters.

But *playing the game* doesn't always mean we'll win. We figured a stop would only take a few minutes. However, a few minutes translates to hours of riding around from corner to corner into the dark night. It's been hours since Mama promised us those cheeseburgers, but we remain patient as each hour passes.

"Dammit!" She hits the steering. "I know this is Baptist country, but someone's gotta have some smack. I'm dying here!"

"Mama, do you need a doctor?" Tiny asks.

"Huh?"

I interject, "You said you're dying. What's wrong?"

"Oh," She blankly says. "Mama's sick, but it's only because I ran out of my medicine. I just need to find a doctor, and I'll be back to one hundred percent. Then, we'll eat, okay? I'm so proud of how well-behaved you are."

We proudly smile. However, when Mama finally makes her 'quick stop,' I notice the medicine man doesn't look like a doctor. In fact, the doctor's office she walks into looks like an old, run-down house.

"There's somethin' weird about Mama's doctor." Tiny unwraps her arms from around my body and rushes to the front seat.

"Hey, what're you doin'? Don't get out of the car. Please don't leave me alone." I beg.

She looks back at me and shakes her head, "I'd never leave you by yourself, especially with that woman. I'm just locking the doors to keep us safe."

I sigh in relief. "How long is it gonna take to get her medicine?" I ask as my stomach roars.

Tiny sighs. "I don't know, but let's just think about that cheeseburger. It's gonna be yummy. I can taste it now."

"Umm, you're right!" I sigh.

Tiny and I distract ourselves with somewhat recognizable memories of beach days, church services, and breakfast biscuits. Mama says we're liars with big imaginations, but our memories feel more real than the lives we actually live.

"Truth or not, never forget, okay? We have to promise never to forget who we are or where we came from."

I lift my pinky finger and reply, "I promise."

She wraps her finger around mine, and we make a secret pact. However, it's hard to keep a promise at only seven years old. It's even harder to remember who we are when our minds are on one thing and one thing only – survival.

We fall asleep and dream of a belly full of the cheeseburgers we never ate.

Chapter 10

Grief – Mason

Six Years Old

Over a year ago, tragedy shattered our lives. My mother, two of my best friends, and my other best friend Rafe's dad, were all cruelly taken from us. Now, it's just me, my two younger brothers, and my dad—my heartbroken dad.

Thankfully, Rafe and his mom, Sherri, have been here every day. The loss we've endured has intertwined our families' fates and bound us together in shared mourning. We don't know how the fires started, but we do know our lives were ruined, and we'll never be the same.

I'm Mason Boom, son of the ambitious and young Assistant District Attorney Charles Boom, godson to millionaire activists Terry and Crystal Lynn, and now the surrogate son to Councilwoman Sherri Carter. Our families are Greer, Georgia royalty, often labeled the 'good ones' in a town where wealth and corruption go hand in hand. Greer is a place where every good deed seems to invite twice the trouble, making my parents' mission to revitalize our town a constant uphill battle. As each day passes, I find myself questioning why they strive to be different in a town that rewards those who embrace its darker side.

I'd never felt so much unyielding pain until I lost it all. The weight of the sorrow I bear is too heavy, even for an adult. Childhood has slipped through my fingers, replaced by a premature ascent into adulthood, dictated by the cruel hands of fate.

"Dad," I whisper, slowly stepping into my father's dark bedroom. There, he lies on the bed, clutching a pillow close to his chest and staring at a wallet-sized photo of my mom. "Um, are you hungry? Rafe and I are gonna make some breakfast. Want some?"

Sniffles. His reply is a series of sniffles and wordless expressions of his deep sorrow. I lower my head and quietly close the door. Across the hall, Rafe also closes the door to our guest bedroom, sealing away the sound of his mother's sobs.

We look at each other and nod, understanding that sometimes parents hurt too, and it's okay if they can't always be the nurturers we need. Together, Rafe and I proceed to make breakfast, as we've done for the last year.

We push the dining room chairs up to the stove and make a mess of the kitchen as usual. Though broken eggshells decorate the floor and pancake batter often lies wasted on the counters, the food is usually edible *enough*.

"Burnt pancakes, again?" Bash groans, a stark reminder that we have no idea what we're doing. "You're a terrible cook, Mase, and the sausages are still frozen, Rafe!"

Okay, so maybe our cooking isn't all that edible, but we're trying.

"Stop complaining and eat your food." I admonish, invoking my dad's firm voice with the hope of injecting some semblance of normalcy into our imbalanced lives.

"How 'bout I heat up the food a little longer? I bet it'll taste better." Rafe tries to temper Bash's mood, but his grief erupts into a tantrum.

"I don't want my food hot!" He screams in a fit of tears. "I just want my food cooked by Mommy, and you aren't my mommy. And you aren't Daddy, Mase. I want Mommy back, and I want Daddy and Aunt Sherri to stop crying every day. I want everything to go back to what it used to be!"

Rafe and I stop pretending to be parents and be the kids we are. I miss my mom so much, and Rafe misses his dad. We miss everyone, and we wish the parents we have left had the strength to help us understand how to deal with the pain we're experiencing while dealing with their own. Soon we're all crying. We know our parents are hurting, but we still need them because we're hurting, too.

Rafe, Bash, and I hug, releasing our frustrated and confused tears, but we're interrupted when we hear our front door open and see Uncle Terry and Aunt Crystal walk in.

"Boys, where are your parents? What –" She sniffs, then her eyes dart to the stove, and she panics. "Oh no, not again!"

Uncle Terry and Aunt Crystal rush to the kitchen to put out the small fire Rafe and I didn't know we started.

I fearfully shake my head and mumble, "I'm sorry, Aunt Crystal. We're just –"

"So hungry." Rafe tearfully interjects while rubbing his belly.

Amid our sadness, the Lynns offer us warmth and peace. They gently wipe away their own tears before turning to dry ours. In their vanilla orchard, magnolia, and honeysuckle-scented embrace, lies the love we've been missing and the comfort we need.

"Terry," Aunt Crystal says with an endearing voice yet bittersweet smile. "How 'bout you make the boys some of your famous homemade biscuits? The girls love your biscuits," She pauses as she catches herself referring to the twins in the present tense, a torturous reminder of the joy that once inhabited her life. "Well, they used to. Our girls *used* to love those biscuits."

Uncle Terry, with a tenderness that surpasses his grief, rubs her shoulder, then plants a kiss on her cheek. "Okay, boys, Aunt Crystal's gonna go get your parents, and I'm gonna make a good ole' Lynn family breakfast. You wanna help?"

He flashes the biggest smile and I don't even care if it's fake; it's the first smile we've seen in months. He's being the father that mine can't be right now, and I'm grateful. I'm grateful that our families, although utterly destroyed, still manage to show up when needed.

Uncle Terry shows us how to make his biscuits and clean up after ourselves.

"You know, I've learned a thing or two about being in a house full of girls." He says playfully.

"Oh yeah, what'd you learn, Unc?" Rafe asks as he loads the dishwasher.

"That we gotta learn how to take care of ourselves and take good care of them because they need help, too. So, from now on, when you cook, you also clean. Just like when you use the bathroom, you...?" He leads.

"Flush and lower the toilet seat!" I answer.

He smiles, "Exactly. You boys are gonna be alright." He high-fives us, then pulls out a picture of our families during a beach weekend in Beverly Mills.

"We lost nearly every photo in the fire except our beach day photos. This puts a smile on my face every time I see it. Here, keep it." Uncle Terry hands me the photo. "Everyone deserves to smile. So, when you're struggling, just look at this picture and remember what a beautiful family we had. Then, be thankful for the beautiful family we *still* have."

I look at the picture, and though I'm devastated over the loss of four loved ones, a smile still forms across my face at the sight of my mom, Rafe's dad, and the Lynn twins.

Nearly half an hour later, Aunt Crystal returns with my dad and Rafe's mom, slowly leading them into the dining room. She's leading them back to a reality where they can grieve and still be present for the loved ones they have left.

My dad always carried himself with a profound sense of pride. He was proud to be Black. Proud to be a Morehouse grad. Proud to be a prosecutor. He was proud to be a father, but most importantly, he was so proud to be my mom's husband. Now that she's gone, there's a piece of him missing. And that once proud man now stands before me, dragging his feet and fighting within himself to hold on to the shred of pride he has left.

Amid her sea of grief, Aunt Crystal, somehow lends dad and Aunt Sherri the remaining bit of her strength. "See, all isn't lost. Look at these beautiful boys y'all have. They need you. They love you. And together, you can comfort each other."

Her words, though heavy with sorrow, carry a promise of healing and love. Aunt Sherri embraces Rafe while dad scoops me and Bash into his arms.

"Hi, boys." Dad's voice breaks. "I'm sorry I haven't been the dad I should be, but I'm gonna do better, okay? I'm gonna get some help. We all are."

It's a promise, a first step toward mending our family's fractures. My dad carries us to the playpen where Jay screams at the top of his lungs.

"All he does is cry, Daddy. Eat, poop, and cry." Bash complains.

Dad laughs softly, "Well, I think I know what he wants," He picks up Jay, smells his diaper, and makes a funny face. "Yep, he's a stinker, boys."

Dad changes Jay's diaper, then Aunt Sherri straps him into the highchair while the Lynns set the table.

"Ahem," Aunt Crystal clears her throat to politely steer everyone's attention to the dining room. "I think it's a fitting morning for a family breakfast. Don't you think?"

We all gather around the table and soak in the warm aura of grace, gratitude, and closeness. As we sit together, the smiles around the table and the peacefulness in baby Jay's demeanor signal a much-needed pause in our shared sorrow. Our parents don't speak, but they don't need to. The silence and togetherness soother the pain that's torn us apart.

"Hey Boys, how 'bout y'all go upstairs and play while the parents talk about a bunch of boring stuff?" Uncle Terry suggests after we eat.

"Ugh, do we have to, Uncle Terry?" I ask.

"You heard him." My dad firmly interjects. "As a matter of fact, if you go upstairs and behave, we'll watch your favorite movies when we're done."

Rafe's face lights up. "The Three Ninjas?"

"You bet!" Aunt Sherri confirms.

"And Mortal Kombat, afterward?" I ask with hopeful eyes.

They both nod, then we get up and clear our plates from the table.

Once we're out of sight, we march loud and long enough in the hallway to appear as if we've left but peek our heads around the corner and listen.

"Thank you," Aunt Sherri expresses her gratitude to the Lynns. "We needed this. I haven't been able to go to that shell of a new home we moved to. It isn't the home I built Rafe Sr. and I built. I've barely been a mom to Rafe Jr. It's just been so hard, but that's no excuse. Not when you and Terry—" Sherri pauses, and Crystal nods, understanding Aunt Sherri's aching all too well.

However, the resolve in the Lynn's eyes breaks the grief stricken atmosphere.

"The pain we feel is immeasurable, but so is our anger, which is why we're here." Uncle Terry declares as he reveals a folder. "The investigation's been closed for six months, but the girls' remains still haven't been found. They're alive, y'all. Sherri and I are positive that our daughters are alive."

Aunt Sherri sighs then gently places her hand over Aunt Crystal's, "I know you're hurting, but we've all read the report. Bodies *were* found." She says in a soft but firm tone.

Aunt Crystal subtly pulls away and rejects her claims. "Bodies we didn't see! This entire investigation was botched, and y'all have been too distracted to notice. Look!" She urges, nodding towards Terry, who spreads the documents across the table like a map to the truth.

"We hired a private investigator. Please, just hear us out." Uncle Terry implores.

Though hesitant, my dad and Aunt Sherri agree and listen intently.

Uncle Terry takes a deep breath before he delves in. "So, at first, we thought the Battalion Chief led the investigation due to our high profiles, right?"

"Sure, it's not uncommon." My dad shrugs.

"Well, is it uncommon to be asked to recuse yourself nearly three times?"

As Uncle Terry continues to unveil the findings, my dad looks stunned by a mugshot, or maybe just caught off guard, until Aunt Sherri intervenes. "Charles," She begins, carefully extracting the document from his grasp. "That's –"

"Ricky Preston, the fire chief's cousin," Dad murmurs. "Nearly every crooked police and fire crew member has waged war against me ever since I convicted Slick Boy Rick." Dad's visibly shaken as the pieces click into place.

"Not to mention the formal investigation into the Chief of Police." Aunt Sherri adds.

"And let's not forget that Ricky was also Kayla Drexler's drug dealing pimp." Aunt Crystal reveals. "Don't you see what's happened? We were all at my house for family dinner that night. We were targeted."

Their faces are a canvas of shock and horror. The Lynns possess the affluence and wealth that placed my dad and Sherri in positions of power. Aunt Sherri and my dad were the political machines behind 'cleaning up the streets' and exposing the top of the brass. Collectively, their actions made them heroes to most but enemies to a powerful many.

The fire wasn't just a tragedy, it was a message. A declaration of war from the from the dark shadows of evil that have overpowered our families' light. My heart aches knowing that in their quest to embody good, they may have unintentionally invited evil, a darkness that has destroyed everyone we love. Now, as we navigate grief, our families must also confront the irreparable damage they caused.

"Do y'all see it now?" Uncle Terry asks. "They killed your wife, Charles. They murdered your husband, Sherri. And –"

An emotional Aunt Crystal interlocks her hand with Uncle Terry's, "And our deranged surrogate, Kayla Drexler, abducted our daughters."

Their assertion hangs in the air, shattering the resignation that once settled over us. This isn't just about coping with loss anymore. This is about accepting a stark reality: trauma hardens the heart, being 'good' doesn't always yield justice, and most haunting of all, the Lynn twins, Taylor and Nicole, are still alive.

Chapter 11

The Weather Girls – Tiffany

Life with Mama ain't been easy, that's for sure. We relive our fragmented memories through old photos at the beach, church, and playground, but those fun images of being surrounded by other kids and happy adults are getting harder and harder to remember.

In the beginning, it was difficult to forget – names, memories, the people we *thought* we were, but with practice and her 'special water' each night, we've come to accept that Mama is here to stay, and any dreams and delusions we may have experienced in the past are long gone – figments of our imagination just like my frequent nightmare of fleeing our home that burned down in flames.

When we moved to Macon, Georgia, we jumped from motel to motel until Mama found a room to rent in a little house owned by an old lady named Harriett. She was our guardian angel, watching over Tiny and me while Mama disappeared for *work* or after she got *medicine* from her doctor. We'd go days without seeing her, but life is much better when she isn't around. Ms. Harriett cooks actual meals for us, and we take baths almost every day! She even gets our hair done, and Mama hates it, calling us 'spoiled' and 'still ugly.' She says eating, bathing, and pampering are luxuries we have to earn, but Ms. Harriet willingly provides them for us.

Ms. Harriet also homeschools us, which is better than nothing. Before homeschooling, "Gullah Gullah Island" and "Barney" taught us nearly everything we knew, which wasn't much because Ms. Harriet was shocked when she realized I was seven and Tiny was eight, and we still didn't know how to read. We're getting there, thanks to her efforts and encouragement.

Mama's harsh words, though, still cut deep. They have a way of sticking to us, branding us with labels we fight hard not to believe. Mama always calls us stupid and even calls Tiny retarded, but for each insult Mama throws our way, Ms. Harriet is around to affirm our worth and teach us that we're more than her cruel words.

"The only stupid person is the one who takes you two angels for granted."

When Mama isn't around, we go to the library and ice cream shops. One day Ms. Harriet let us pick out not one but two books! Then, she let us get two scoops of ice cream.

"Ms. Harriet, this is the best day ever!" Tiny exclaims while wrapping her in a tight hug.

With wide ice cream mustaches, we sit down to tackle our reading lesson, but we both stumble and trip up on words as usual.

Tiny's frustration boils over. "I'm so dumb! I bet every kid knows how to read and write. We'll always be the stupid Weather Girls, just like Mama says we are."

"I'll let you get by with all that foul mouth cussin', but there's no way I'm gonna let you two girls believe your mama's lies. You're the smartest set of sisters I know. You take really good care of yourselves and each other. And I've never met a dummy able to do that. You can't listen to her. She's sick. She's a drug add —" Ms. Harriet abruptly stops speaking and then sighs as she considers her next words. "She just needs help, okay? But don't y'all worry. You've come such a long way, and I be dang if I let you give up now. C'mon, let's read the story together."

With patience, she guides us through our reading, turning our self-doubt into budding confidence. Ms. Harriett helps us pronounce each word until we begin to read each sentence with very few interruptions or confusion. We read chapter after chapter, reading more boldly with each flip of the page. By the time we finish our ice cream, we nearly finish the entire story.

"See, told ya, the smartest sisters I know." Ms. Harriet winks and shelters us in her embrace.

Her belief in us, her conviction that we're capable of greatness, is a lifeline in the murky waters of our existence. This moment marks the first time I've ever felt proud.

Tiny exhibits relief, and her eyes shimmer with unshed tears as she whispers, "So, I'm not stupid like Mama says I am?"

Ms. Harriet smiles and swiftly affirms, "Nope, not the Weathers girls. The Weathers Girls are geniuses. The Weather Girls are strong. The Weather Girls are *nothing* like their mother. Now, let's get back home before she finds out."

The drive home is quiet, and Tiny just stares out the window.

"You okay, sis?" I ask.

She shrugs. Her expression remains lifeless. My sister and I share the same dreams, dreams that are often so much better than our reality. These vibrant and detailed dreams are our refuge, a place where the impossibilities of the life we want melt away into a realm of endless possibilities.

We often dream we have different names, a different mom, and even a dad. We dream of living in a big house and having best friends—three boys and an annoying baby brother. We dream of the smell of vanilla orchard, magnolia, and honeysuckle—the smell that used to radiate off the dirty blanket we sleep with at night. Our dreams are heavenly, but they also make our reality feel like hell.

"Hey," I whisper, breaking her concentration. "You feel like dreamin'?" I ask.

Finally, Tiny smiles.

"Okie dokie, Taylor. What would you like to eat for lunch today?" I playfully ask, pretending to be a chef.

"Hmm," Tiny ponders. "How 'bout some of those delicious homemade biscuits."

"Homemade biscuits, comin' right up!" I reply.

"Thank you, Chef Nicole." Tiny happily responds.

Ms. Harriett watches us from the mirror. However, she scrunches her nose and asks, "Girls, what's up with the names Taylor and Nicole? Why not one of those names of the shows y'all like to watch? Topanga, Tia, Moesha, or Helga, for goodness' sake!"

We laugh but opt not to respond, knowing we've already said too much. A few hours later, Tiny and I are finishing schoolwork in our small bedroom when Ms. Harriet enters. She observes Mama's maternity photos and some papers on the nightstand before she addresses us.

"Hello, Weathers girls. What're you ladies up to?"

Tiny shrugs, "Oh, nothin' much. We're just learnin'! I think I have a favorite subject, Ms. Harriet. Science!"

Ms. Harriet playfully gasps, "My, oh my! Is that right? You know, Tiny? I think you'd be a great scientist. You always ask great questions, and you always find the right answers. Speaking of, I have a few questions for you girls, and somethin' tells me you might have the answers."

I excitedly ask, "Ooh, is this a game?"

"Sure, let's call it a game." Ms. Harriet shrugs and then sits on the floor next to the mat Tiny and I sleep on every night. "Can you girls remind me where you're from again?"

I laugh and reply, "That's so random, Ms. Harriet. We're from Savannah, Georgia, silly. Mama says so. Look at that picture of me and Tiny on the beach." I point to the toddler photo of us that we no longer remember.

Ms. Harriet nods, "Are you sure that isn't Beverly Mills Beach? You sure you've never been to a place called Greer, Georgia?"

"We ain't never been to Greer. And before here, all we did was dream of having a different life. That's our Mama up there. That's all we know, and what she says is the truth." Tiny declares while pointing to the picture of Mama pregnant with one of us.

A look of sadness washes over Ms. Harriet's face as she shakes her head. "Oh, you beautiful little brainwashed girls. I've always had a feeling somethin' wasn't right."

After her weird comment, Ms. Harriet stands up and extends her hands to us. We place our hands in hers, and she lifts us up to follow her to her bedroom, where we notice a suitcase.

"Okay, I think I have everything. We just gotta get the heck outta here before Shirley shows up." She grabs her keys and purse then walks towards the door, but Tiny's eyes are glued to Ms. Harriet's tv screen.

We stand still and watch the woman on the television. She looks so sad, so familiar, but so perfect. Emotions stir within us. We feel the connection through the screen. We smell vanilla orchard, honeysuckle, and magnolia.

Tiny and I clasp one another's hand in shock, "Tiffany, do you see her? That's the woman –"

"From our dreams." I tearfully finish her sentence.

Ms. Harriet caresses Tiny's face. "It's okay, girls. Don't be afraid. That woman just misses her daughters. That woman is your mo –"

Before Ms. Harriet can finish her sentence, we hear Mama's loud voice through the house. "Tiny! Tiffany! We need to leave. Now!"

Mama runs up the stairs but quickly stops when she sees the three of us in front of the tv.

"Ms. Harriet," Mama cautiously steps towards us. "What're you doing with my girls? What lies are you tellin' them?" She asks angrily.

Ms. Harriet holds on to us protectively and then scoffs at our mother. "Your girls, huh? How far apart are they again? You look the same in all your maternity photos, as if you were pregnant with twins. Can you explain why they call each other Taylor and Nicole?"

Mama glares at us. "You two did this, didn't you? You stupid little girls! This is all your fault. We have to leave because you disobeyed me!" She screams and yanks our arms, pulling us away.

The thought of leaving Ms. Harriet plunges us into a state of desperation.

"We're not going anywhere with you! We aren't leaving Ms. Harriet. She loves us."

Mama laughs, "Love? Oh my God, Tiny, when're you gonna grow up? Ms. Harriet doesn't love you. I pay her to act like it! Everything in life is transactional."

Ms. Harriet shakes her head and denies Mama's claims, but she continues, "Deny it, Harriet." She challenges.

"Just because you pay me to babysit doesn't mean I don't love these girls. Do the right thing. Turn yourself in. They need their mo –"

Mama belts out a wild, scary scream, "I *am* their mother! Get downstairs, girls! It's time to leave." She lunges towards Ms. Harriet, and we run out of the room to avoid the ensuing violence.

"Please!" We hear Mr. Harriet scream. "You don't have to do this."

My mom, disoriented and manic as usual, replies, "I'm sorry, but…I do."

She slams the door shut while Tiny and I stand at the top of the stairs in fear of what Mama's about to do to Ms. Harriet. The first and only person in the real world to ever love us.

"Damn, ya mama wasn't lying, you Weathers girls sure are pretty." Our silent mourning is interrupted by the deep, disturbing voice. His words washing over us like an uncomfortable wave.

Tiny tightens her grip around my hand, and I inch closer to her for protection.

"Who are you?" Tiny asks.

The tall, dark man smiles with a toothpick hanging from the side of his mouth.

He chuckles, "My name's Pop."

Tiny whispers, "Goes the weasel."

I accidentally laugh at her joke, which causes his slimy smile to turn into a frightening scowl.

"And you must be Tiny," He says while licking his lips. "Your moms told me 'bout you, and that smart mouth. I got plans for you, big plans."

Tiny closes her mouth, and this time, it's her who buckles under my protection.

The man walks up the stairs, brushing his body past Tiny. "My car's running. Get in. Your mom and I will be right out. Then, Daddy's takin' y'all to your new home."

We hurry downstairs to avoid any more conversation with the stranger. But when we exit Ms. Harriet's home, we hesitate to get in the blue BMW.

Tiny anxiously looks around. "Okay, we're in the clear. Let's run away, Tiff. We gotta get the heck outta here. I don't like that man. I hate the way he looks at me. Maybe we can find that lady from tv—the one from our dreams."

"And say what, Tiny? Hey nice lady, we been dreamin' 'bout you. Will you be our mommy? You think bein' lost is gonna be any better?"

"Anything is better than this! Anyone is better than her. Please, Sis. We always got a bad feeling about Mama, but I got a really bad feeling 'bout this guy."

I sigh and consider our options. Mama's resourceful. We know she does everything possible to hurt us, but at least she ensures we have a place to sleep. If we run away, we have no idea where to go or who to trust. We can't risk getting caught by the police or CPS. They'd separate us.

"We can't, Tiny. As long as we have each other, we'll be safe. We'll protect one another. Maybe, in the new city, we'll find another Ms. Harriet to love and take care of us."

Tiny releases a sigh. "Why do we have to find people to love us? Why can't we just be loved by our mom like every other kid?" She cries.

I hug my sister. "Well, I love you. That's gotta mean somethin', right?"

Tiny smiles and tightens her embrace. "It means everything, absolutely everything. It's just me, you, and the world around us. Remember that."

We wait for nearly an hour for Mama and Pop to return. When we spot him rushing out of the house with our luggage and Ms. Harriet's jewelry box, we close our eyes and pretend to be asleep. My body leans against the door, and Tiny lays against me with the hope we can get through the ride without being spoken to or forced to sleep by Mama's 'special water.'

We sense pop's eyes roaming our little bodies as we fake sleep in our nightgowns. He slowly brushes his finger along the side of Tiny's thighs, prompting her to gasp in horror and tuck her trembling body deeper into mine.

"Oh, Tiny, you beautiful girl. You have no idea what's in store for you. I'm gonna treat you real good."

I feel Tiny's silent tears drop on my gown. She was right. We should've run away. We should've searched for the lady in our dreams. I wrap my arms around her to repel Pop's touch until Mama rushes into the car, frazzled, discombobulated, and in panic.

"Is it done?" Pop asks.

Mama shakes her head, "I got all I could. Let's just get the hell out of here before we get caught."

"Dammit, Kay," Pop says. "You can't pull this shit again. We ain't in Greer no more. We gotta keep a clean sheet. Our folks pulled a lot of strings to get us the hell out of dodge."

"Shh," Mama says. "Don't call me Kay 'round the girls. *Kayla* died, remember? It's Shirley now."

He laughs, "That's an old lady name."

Mama nods, "That's right, it's old, unassuming, and it ain't mine, *Slick Boy Rick.*"

Pop chuckles, but his expression turns dark as he swiftly grabs Mama by the neck.

"Watch it, Kayla. You may not be one of my girls anymore, but if you want this," He pulls out a tiny bag and dangles it in her face, "You better show me some respect."

She nods, "I'm sorry, Pop. I won't ever disrespect you again."

Pop extends the baggie to Mama, and she anxiously snatches it away. She looks back, but I close my eyes and hope she doesn't catch me watching. She lights a pipe and inhales while Tiny and I instantly begin to cough as the smoke and distinct smell of chemicals and burnt plastic fill our noses. This must be her medicine. This is what helps her calm down.

Pop rolls down the window, and Mama tries to cover us even more with our blanket, but not before we hear the sirens. Firetrucks speed past, rushing toward the home we had come to know so well, now engulfed in flames. It seems that everything Mama touches ultimately burns to ashes.

"Mama," I softly call out.

Barely coherent and conscious, she mumbles, "I knew you weren't sleeping, pretty girl. What do you want?"

"Um, will Ms. Harriet be okay?"

Mama crushes up pills and pours them into our water. "Don't worry about Ms. Harriet. She tried to take what was mine, and she got what she deserved. Now here, drink your water." She says before dozing off to sleep.

Ms. Harriet's determination to shield and fight for us was a beacon of hope in Mama's relentless darkness. Yet, her determination to help us may have just cost her everything. She was so good to us, but the price of being good is far too high. Now, we find ourselves on the brink of leaving behind yet another familiar life and embarking on a new chapter in our lives with Mama and Pop, a chapter filled with uncertainty, fear, and pure evil.

Chapter 12

Greer, Georgia – Tiffany

Nine Years Old

The older Tiny and I have gotten, the more we've come to learn about the type of person Mama is – a liar, a thief, a crackhead, and possibly a murderer, too.

Liar – where do I even start? Before settling for Shirley Weathers, I've heard my mama be called Martha, Kayla, Daisy, Lisa, and Kerry. She's been called everything but honest. She's worn more names than she has shoes. And don't bother asking me where I'm from because sometimes she says Savannah, but other times she says Atlanta, and on one occasion, she mentioned a city I never even heard of – Greer, Georgia.

Thief – Did I mention she steals? I don't know why because Pop has a good job or else he couldn't afford all those silk shirts. Granted, we live in a dump where the carpet nails are exposed, and the roaches are territorial, but he stays dressed up, wearing gold rings. So, why the heck did Mama steal and pawn the new Walkman and jewelry Pop bought Tiny? And wait for it…cars. My mom stole a car.

Crackhead – I've watched enough of Pop's favorite movies—Dead Presidents, Menace to Society, and New Jack City to know what a crackhead is, and my mama is one. I used to think she was sick because she constantly needed her *doctor*, but I quickly learned her medicine was nothing but a pipe that Pop frequently supplies her with. Her medicine has become her greatest downfall. Everybody knows who Mama is. She's the Bankhead Crackhead, College Park Scammer, the Old National Highway Hoe.

Murderer – I know Mama killed Ms. Harriet. It took some time to figure out why we left Macon, but the more Mama says, *'Try me. Do you wanna end up like Ms. Harriet?'* the more I'm sure that sweet old lady is dead and gone.

Despite my mother's foolishness and Pop's questionable career, our neighbors love and protect me and Tiny, especially Ms. Dora. I refuse to allow Mama to do to Mr. Dora what she did to Ms. Harriet. I don't think she can either because Ms. Dora and that cane of hers can hold their own. Mama learned that on the day she stole her car.

"Shirley!" Ms. Dora's voice thundered across the neighborhood. "Get your crackhead ass back here with my car before I call the police!"

All the neighbors laughed and snickered.

"That's Crackhead Shirley for you. I feel so sorry for those pretty girls." A neighbor shook their head.

Even the teenagers joined in. "Shirley always actin' crazy."

Now, Shirley. Imma say this one time and one time only. Give me my keys, and don't touch my shit ever again!" Ms. Dora warned, her finger pointed stiff and firm.

As a matter of fact, Mama, unfazed and flipping her hair with a sly grin, had the audacity to barter.

"Oh, Shirley hush! Now, I'll be happy to give you your keys back, and I might even throw in my pocket knife if you gimme $20."

It was humiliating, but Mama doesn't care about what people think. She only cares about Pop and her next high, leaving Tiny and me to fend for ourselves. Thankfully, our College Park family, especially Ms. Dora, has stepped in to fill in the gaps, giving us a sense of love and worth we'd otherwise go without.

"Now, if I gotta tell you to do your homework one more time, Imma hit you with this spoon, little girl" Ms. Dora fusses while taking a pan of lasagna out of the oven.

"Ugh, but Ms. Dora! I hate science. I can finish it later when Tiny gets here. She's the future scientist, anyway." I grumble, snapping my textbook shut.

Ms. Dora softens a bit. "Alright. Where is Tiny? I don't like you girls wandering around like you do! And if I have to tell you to stop selling candy at school one more time, I'm tappin' butts! If you need anything, just ask me or the neighbors."

"But we had to, Ms. Dora!" I laugh. "We felt bad for asking you for money all the time. Tiny's staying after school to work on a new project. Did you know she placed second in the science fair? Thanks to you buying the supplies she asked for. I don't know why Pop wouldn't; he buys her everything else. I hate that he likes her so much and treats me like I'm invisible."

Ms. Dora sighs and steps away from the stove to comfort me. "Oh, sweet child, trust me when I say you don't want his type of kindness. If I had a say, I wouldn't leave him alone with either one of you girls for two seconds. If I weren't gettin' old and didn't have the dance studio, I'd take you girls far away to my hometown of Greer."

"Greer? I heard Mama talkin' about that place on speakerphone one time. She was cryin' and tellin' some lady she wanted to go back, but the lady said she should've never chose drugs and thugs over their family."

"Hmm, really?" Ms. Dora muses. "That's interesting. I thought you Weathers' were from Savannah. I'm gonna ask around about Shirley. Everybody's gotta story, and I'm gonna get the scoop on hers when I go visit."

"Ooh, we going on a field trip?" I ask, barely able to contain my excitement.

She chuckles. "Calm down, little girl! *We* aren't going anywhere. I'm going to see family."

"But…I thought I was your family." I murmur, feeling a pang of sadness.

"Oh, Tiff, you are, but you know how your parents are. They let everybody take care of y'all but don't let you go anywhere. And quite frankly, I don't feel like whoopin' they ass when they come at me with their nonsense. So, you're stayin' put. All the neighbors know I'll be gone, and they know to watch out for you and Tiny. You'll sleep over at Mrs. Wilkins' house. If Tiny stays late after school with Mrs. Wilkins on that Friday, then you know what to do, right?"

With a playful, proud salute, I confirm. "Yes, ma'am. Go straight to Mrs. Jenkins' house. Her key is under the mat. Don't go home and never be alone with Pop or Mama."

"That's my girl," Ms. Dora smiles while setting my plate of lasagna in front of me.

Ms. Dora's the best. She's the mother, grandmother, and aunt that Tiny and I always wished for. She helped Tiny pursue her passion for science. She's one of those STEM nerds now. She's even a part of the Feldwood Elementary Science Club. She's going to make us rich one day.

My grades are fine, but I'm not a genius like Tiny, and Pop buys her all the nice clothes. She's cool, and the girls in class don't talk to me unless she's around. *In the words of Pop, 'I ain't nothing special. I ain't never gonna be no Tiny.'* I just exist, but as long as I have Tiny, existing is enough.

I am, however, a great dancer. One day, Ms. Dora caught me 'shaking my behind' to one of my favorite songs and spanked my butt but immediately followed up with, *"I'm gonna teach you how to dance for real."* I take classes at her studio for free now. I'm good, but one day, I'm going to be great.

After dinner, I set my textbooks aside and lose myself in practicing pirouettes in the living room. Soon, the front door swings open, and in bursts Tiny and her Science teacher, Mrs. Wilkins, full of energy and smiles that light up the room.

"Tiffany! I'm home!' Tiny exclaims, eyes sparkling with excitement. Ms. Dora interrupts with a chuckle. "Well, good afternoon to you too, child." She says, and Tiny laughs, giving her a big hug.

Mrs. Wilkins takes in the smell from the kitchen. "Ooh, Ms. Dora, is that your famous lasagna?"

Like most teachers at Feldwood Elementary, Mrs. Wilkins is from College Park and even used to be one of Ms. Dora's dance students. If Mama did anything right, it was moving us here, where we have people like Ms. Dora and Mrs. Wilkins to look out for us.

Ms. Dora hands Mrs. Wilkins a packed plate. "Now you go on home and let that husband of yours rub your feet!" She teases.

Mrs. Wilkins laughs and turns to us. "Great job today, Tiny! I'm so lucky to be your teacher. And I see you, Tiff. Your turns are looking sharp." She winks and heads for the door but nearly bumps into Mama, who's stumbling in with Pop, his arm possessively around her.

"Oh, Shirley," Mrs. Wilkins greets, "I didn't hear you coming up the steps. And I'm sorry, Mr. Weathers." She trails off, looking at Pop, who grins, 'Just call me Pop, Miss Thang.'

Mama's face turns sour. 'Will you stop looking at my husband, Kendra? It's bad enough you wish my daughters were yours. You want my man, too?' Mrs. Wilkins, calm but firm, retorts, "Oh, shut up, Shirley. Everyone knows you don't deserve those precious girls. Now, don't forget to sign their permission slips. I'd hate for them to miss *another* field trip."

When Pop enters Ms. Dora's home, he makes a beeline past me and straight to Tiny. He picks her up and twirls her around as if she's his most prized possession. I'd love for Pop to treat me that way. I really wish one of my parents would love me. I see snippets of love when Pop showers Tiny with affection and adoration. Then, I see what a daughter needs to do to earn love.

I only saw it once when Tiny and I were playing hide-and-seek. I was in the closet when Pop snuck into the room and gave Tiny a beautiful necklace that she later gave me. I don't think I'm strong enough to earn Pop's love yet. To be so small and have his body on top of mine? I know it hurt because she cried and initially said stop, but Pop asked if she needed Mama's medicine again or if she wanted him to love me instead.

She screamed, "No, please, not Tiffany! I don't want her to cry. I don't want her to hurt. I'll be quiet and be loved." She cried so hard in silence. It looked painful, harsh, and every bit of wrong, but she must have gotten used to it because the gifts, attention, and love kept coming.

But one day, Mama happened to wake up from her stupor and interrupted them. Oh, was she mad! She yelled and called Tiny a hoe, then whipped her until her back bled. We stayed in the house for days until her body healed. That was when we started staying with Ms. Dora after school. We are NOT allowed to be alone with him.

"How's Daddy's favorite girl doin'?" Pop asks, still twirling her around.

Ms. Dora quickly yells, "Get your hands off her!" while Mama simultaneously yells, "Get your fast tail off him!"

Tiny's excitement immediately dissipates, but Ms. Dora admonishes Mama, "*She* isn't the one you should be worried about. What do y'all want anyway? This is a drug-free zone."

"Aww, c'mon, Dora. I been off the rock for four months! Besides, ain't nobody out here smoking that stuff no mo'." Mama says while wiping the remnants of the white powder from under her nose.

Ms. Dora shakes her head. "There are some things children should never see or know. I'm sure you're just stopping by to ask for help, and it's already done. I called my friend over at Fulton County Utility. Your water will be back on tomorrow morning. In the meantime, I got the girls. Now, go ahead and go to 'work.'"

Every day with Ms. Dora is a relief, and bedtime is even better because it's just me and Tiny. Ms. Dora bought us big twin beds for her house, but Tiny and I prefer to sleep together. Be it on the floor, in cars, in motels, or on a couch, we just belong together. We always have, and we'll always be together. And tonight is no different.

"You think life will be easier for us one day? Like, will Mama ever get clean? Will we ever live in a house that ain't fallin' apart? Will I ever have friends? Do you think – Or…will I ever get to call Pop Daddy? You think he'll ever love me like he loves you?"

Tiny chuckles, "Oh, Tiff. Pop does love you. Just keep being nice and sweet. That's what he likes. And if he ain't nice to you, don't worry. If he don't love you then maybe that's a good thing 'cause his love hurts. Sometimes, I wonder if it's really love at all 'cause my love for you never hurts. I promise I'll love you more than anyone, and it'll be enough to make you never miss the love we never had. When we grow up, I'm gonna be a scientist and get a job at Lynn Perfumery. And you're gonna be a famous dancer. We're gonna be rich, Tiffany. We're gonna be so happy, safe, loved, and rich."

Tiny and I fall asleep to her last words, which are etched in the only reminder we have of a time when life smelled beautiful–our vanilla-scented blanket.

"I love you, Tiff. Always remember, it's me, you, and the world around us."

~~~

Today, I'm going out of town! That's right, I'm visiting Ms. Dora's hometown of Greer, Georgia. It's my very first vacation. Sure, it's not Disneyworld, but it beats home. I just wish Tiny could be here, but Tiny's staying with Mrs. Wilkins this weekend to work on her experiment for the Lynn Perfumery Contest.

"Ms. Dora, how much longer we got?" I press, shifting in my seat as Greer comes into view. "And how old is your niece's daughter? You think she'll like me? I don't have any friends other than Tiny, and she doesn't count 'cause she's my sister!"

"We're right on the outskirts, Tiffany. Stop being so antsy." Ms. Dora instructs, glancing at me with amusement. "And what'd I tell you about your broken English? My great-niece's name is Mel, and she's your age, so I'm sure you'll get along just fine. They just moved back here not too long ago, too. My niece got out in the 80s just in time for college before the crack epidemic hit. You always hear about L.A. and New York, but it hit the South real bad."

"Were people here like my mama and Pop?" I ask curiously.

"Oh, yeah!" Ms. Dora nods. "Crime, corruption, and violence ran rampant. After I left, a fire rocked this town and took the lives of Crystal and Terry Lynn's little girls. They own the Lynn Perfumery and runnin' the contest Tiny's in."

I gasp. "How old were they?"

"Hmm, toddlers, maybe." Ms. Dora sighs, her voice heavy. "You know, I'm not one to gossip. *However*, there's a rumor that those girls were kidnapped. But anyway, what was my point? Don't worry about whether any of these people like you or not, and don't be fooled by the big houses you see out here. Nobody's perfect. Everyone's got problems, and you're just as worthy, if not worthier, than those broken souls behind glass doors, you understand?"

Ms. Dora's crazy idioms are often confusing, but I do understand this one. Friends or no friends, I *am* worthy, and I have Ms. Dora and Tiny to remind me of that every day.

However, that life lesson quickly goes out the window the moment we arrive in Greer. If this is what corruption looks like, then call me crooked because this place is beautiful. You can fit four of my houses into one out here.

"Whoa! Ms. Dora, that house looks like a castle! And so does the next one! And the next one! They look like Monopoly houses!"

She laughs. "Girl, did you hear anything I just said? Wait a few minutes, you'll see that everything that glitters ain't gold."

And she's right. Five minutes later, when we depart from the beautiful, affluent Greer neighborhoods, we enter the heart of the town, where it's wrought with homelessness, abandoned homes that look like mine, and businesses with boarded-up windows.

"Oh, no, Ms. Dora. What happened here?" I ask, in shock by the stark contrast between the Monopoly neighborhood and the inner city.

"Just what I explained, but thankfully, my niece, Callie, is the campaign manager for one of Greer's honest politicians, Sherri Carter. She, along with that handsome hot shot ADA Boom, has really turned things around. They're local heroes, campaigning for change and doing good. They got rocked by the fire too but kept fighting," Ms. Dora explains in a prideful tone over the resilience of her hometown residents.

As we pull into a parking lot beside a football field, my eyes widen in disbelief.

"Ms. Dora, we're goin' to a football game?"

"Are you impressed by every little thing, Tiff?" She laughs. "We won't be here long. C'mon, I wanna show you somethin'."

We step out into the chaos of a local football game. I've never seen anything like it. Ms. Dora leads me toward the bleachers, where I notice a group of older girls dancing. Their movements are sharp, soulful, and filled with energy.

"Ms. Dora? What is *that*? I wanna learn that type of dancing?"

"That's majorette dancing. The Greer Pipettes, one of the best dance teams in the South. Thought you might like it."

"Is that Dora Reign? The legendary founder of the Greer Pipettes, the *best* and the *baddest* majorettes in the nation?" A woman with a whistle and a track outfit asks.

"That is me, and I is she! Dora Reign, founder of the Greer Pipettes and former Alcorn State College Golden Girl!"

"Wow, it's so good to see you back here, Coach Dora!"

"When I heard one of my former students was the new coach of my Pipettes, I just had to drive down to City Scrimmage day. My family's moved back to town, so you might be seeing a whole lot of me and this young lady right here." Ms. Dora places a surprising spotlight on me. "Coach Dawson, this is Tiffany Weathers, my little protégé. The girl can move!"

"Wow!" The coach says. "I look forward to seeing you dance at the Battle of the Bands one day or maybe even the Bayou Classic!"

"That's right!" Ms. Dora brings me in close. "This little girl is the future of majorette dance."

No one's ever spoken about me in such a way, and I had no idea Ms. Dora believed in me so much.

As the football game unfolds, the energy of the crowd is infectious. The buzz focuses solely on the young quarterback commanding the field. I'm captivated by him—his speed, precision, and small but powerful authority.

One of the locals must notice the awe in my eyes because she leans closer. "See that kid? That's Mason Boom. He's our Golden Boy. Mase is gonna be the first Greer to go to the NFL and get out of this God-forsaken town."

However, as the game continues, the conversation on the bleachers takes a sharp turn.

"That's ADA Charles Boom's boy," Another spectator adds, her voice dropping to a whisper. "You know, there's talk that Charles and Sherri Carter, well... they've been a bit close ever since the fire. Some people say they were havin' an affair. They might've even lit the match themselves so they could be together. Scandalous, ain't it?"

Ms. Dora intervenes, "Enough of that now! Charles and Sherri have been nothing but good to the people of Greer. We're not here to spread any salacious rumors. Now, shut your mouths and watch the game." She scolds, and the group of women immediately falls into silence.

Ms. Dora then excuses herself to speak with the new coach, leaving me to soak in the atmosphere. My attention returns to the field to Greer's Golden Boy. I don't know this Mason kid, but there's something familiar about him, something compelling, something magnetic. He must feel it, too, because when he gets ready to throw the ball, he turns his head in my direction and stops, and the longer he stares, the faster my heart beats.

"What's he doing? Is Boom coming over here?" The friendly spectator curiously asks.

I sit frozen, watching the Golden Boy dash towards me, but Ms. Dora blocks my view and extends her hand. "Let's head out, Tiffany. We've got more places to see and people to meet."

Dang it. It's like she cut the movie off right before it got good. I cast one last glance over my shoulder, but he can't see me. I think he was looking for me because now he looks disappointed. I don't know why, but my heart feels unexpectedly full as I look back, trying to understand what felt so familiar about him—the unexplainable connection in the way his gaze held mine, as if we'd met in another life or shared a memory just out of reach. I want to know him, to understand why my heart is still racing. But Ms. Dora is already pulling me away, leaving my questions—and whatever strange connection just sparked between us—hanging in the air.

A few hours later, after visiting a few of Ms. Dora's old friends, we finally arrive at Ms. Dora's relatives' house.

"So, your niece is one of the rich ones in town, huh? What kind of jobs do they have?" I ask Ms. Dora while eyeing the beautiful home.

Ms. Dora laughs. "My nephew-in-law is Greer High's principal, and my niece is one of those Political Strategists– always on those news stations yellin' at folks. You'll meet little Mel if she's in a good mood. There's no tellin' with that one. She ain't all there in the head."

As soon as Ms. Dora gives me the scoop on her family, their door swings open, and I'm greeted by a stunning girl with a smile like my sister Tiny. chaptThis is the girl Ms. Dora said ain't right in the head? If that's what 'ain't right' looks like, then sign me up! Because she looks as happy as can be.

"Aunt Dora!" Mel greets her. "I haven't seen you in years. You're an old lady now."

I accidentally laugh. No one ever talks to Ms. Dora like that.

"Old my butt. And if you don't watch your mouth, I'm gonna spank you," she laughs. "Now, where's your mom and dad?"

Mel opens the door wide so we can enter.

"Right here, Aunt Dora!" Mel's mom calls from inside. She's standing in the doorway of what looks like a dining room, her arms wide open, smile as bright as Mel's. "Come in, come in! We were just setting the table for dinner."

As we step into the dining room, the warmth of a family envelops me. The walls have family photos, paintings, and shelves full of books. The table is filled with more food than I've seen at any meal back home. There's laughter as everyone takes their seats, with Mel pulling me down next to her.

"You'll sit here! Next to me. We're gonna be best friends, I just know it!" She beams.

"Aunt Dora tells us you're quite the dancer, Tiffany," Mel's dad says as he flashes a welcoming smile. "We're excited to have you join us for dinner."

I can't help but smile, feeling the warmth spread through me. Dinner passes with easy conversation. They talk about my life in Atlanta, and I tread lightly, focusing instead on Ms. Dora's kindness and Tiny's brilliance at school. Ms. Dora shares stories of Greer, painting a picture of the town's history and the community's resilience.

"So, Tiffany, I gotta tell you about my friends, Rafe Carter and Mason Boom. They're kind of famous around here," Mel's eyes light up as she talks. "Mason's amazing at football. And Rafe's super smart. They're cool, even if they're just dumb boys." She shrugs.

I laugh, my voice mingling with the clinks of cutlery and soft music playing in the background. "They sound interesting. I think I saw Mason earlier. Didn't I, Ms. Dora?"

Ms. Dora nods. "You sure did. The entire town was raving about their little Golden Boy."

Mel gasps. "You were at the game?"

I shrug. "Well, we left early, right after he ran towards me like a weirdo."

Ms. Dora laughs. "Oh, hush, child. That boy didn't run towards you."

"He did, Ms. Dora! He was staring at me the whole time." I explain.

Mel laughs. "So, you're the ghost, huh? Mason's a little loony. He goes to therapy more than me! He's been staring at a family picture for years, and he thought for sure he saw a Lynn twin. You sure you're ain't from Greer? It'd be somethin' if you *were* one of those billionaire babies." She jokes.

"Mel, that's enough," Mel's dad interrupts. "No dark discussions at the dinner table."

As the evening winds down, I help Mel clear the table while her parents prepare a movie. This is what a family feels like.

"Hey, Tiffany," Mel says as we stack the dishwasher. "Forget what the old folks said. If my best friend said he saw Nicole Lynn then I believe him. Fate never fails." She winks.

Her words, simple and sincere, make me smile. Sure, she may be a bit loony, but she also might be the first girl outside of Tiny to ever be nice to me. We all watch a movie together. This might even be the first time I watched a movie without cussing, murder, or sex. This feels so good, and I think I'm falling in love with Greer, Georgia.

"Here," Mel throws me a pair of pajamas when we enter her room and prepare for bed. "You can finally take off that Little House on the Prairie dress." She playfully teases.

"Dang it! I told Ms. Dora this dress was hideous. Everyone's probably been laughing at me all day."

Mel playful waves me off with a smile. "Girl, you're fine. No, correction, you are FOINE! You're a literal head-turner. I mean, Mason dang near broke neck his running after you."

We both laugh, and the warmth of her words makes me feel a little more at ease. Before we fall asleep, I notice Mel has a cordless phone on her nightstand, something I've only seen on tv shows where kids have everything.

"Uh, Mel. Do you mind if I call my sister Tiny?" I ask, my voice hopeful.

"Sure, but only if you promise to bring her next time you visit." Mel bargains with a grin.

I dial Mrs. Wilkins's number and hold my breath as I wait for Tiny to pick up. We've never been separated before.

"Tiffany, it's about time you called!" She answers the phone. "Mrs. Wilkins has been trying to reach Ms. Dora on that new cellphone of hers."

I sigh, "You know Ms. Dora and technology don't mix. Is everything okay? Is something wrong? Are you hurt?" I panic.

Tiny's tone is light, almost dismissive. "Yeah, it's all good. There was an issue, but Mr. and Mrs. Wilkins sorted it out. Pop tried to get me to come home for the night, but they shut that down fast."

A shiver of worry runs through me, and I quickly glance at Mel then turn my body to discreetly whisper into the phone. "Tiny, you know the rules. We don't stay at home without each other or Ms. Dora nearby."

"I know, I know," Tiny reassures me quickly. "I told you. It's handled. Don't worry. Just hurry up and get back. I miss you, and I hate being away from you."

I sigh, "Same here. But no matter where we are, it's always gonna be – "

"Me, you, and the world around us." I feel her smile through the phone.

"I love you, Tiny. I'll be back tomorrow. Get some sleep." After speaking to my sister, a sense of relief washes over me, but as I hang up, I notice Mel watching me.

"Everything okay?" She asks.

I nod, forcing a smile. "Yeah, just family stuff. Thanks for letting me use your phone."

Mel's expression softens. "Anytime. You know? My life ain't all roses and rainbows either, so you don't gotta pretend with me. I always hear my dad tell my mom he's her safe space to land, so as your new best friend, I'll be your landing strip."

As we climb into our respective beds, Mel's words echo in my mind, wrapping around me like a warm blanket. She offers me a "safe space to land," a phrase that feels too mature for our age yet so fitting. For the first time in a long while, I feel peace. For the first time in a while, I feel a semblance of peace, a far cry from the chaos that usually surrounds my life. It's like I've stepped into a different world, one where the shadows of hardship and struggle are held at bay by the light of kindness and understanding.

Then, my thoughts drift to Tiny. I can't wait to bring her here, to show her that there's a life different from what we've known, one filled with hope and possibilities. This town is a glimpse of a future where we can escape uncertainty and neglect. We deserve stability, happiness, and safety, and I'm determined to make it our reality. I'm determined to make Greer our home someday.

The next morning, the aroma of breakfast and the sound of lively conversation pull me from my dreams. Callie cheerfully announces, "Wake up, sleepyheads! It's time for church!"

"Crap, I didn't pack any of Tiny's nice clothes." I mumble under my breath, but Mel overhears.

Mel's bubbly voice rings in my ears. "Don't worry. I got enough ugly frilly dresses for the both of us." She tosses an overly decorated dress on the bed, and oddly enough, I don't feel embarrassed by Mel's offer. "You know," She says with an innocent smile. "Mason Boom's gonna be at church today."

Why is she telling me this? And why is she smiling as if I'm supposed to smile back? After breakfast, Ms. Dora and I follow Mel's family to church.

"So, what'd you think of my family? You enjoying yourself, Tiff? I know this ain't some vacation to brag about at school, but I hope you've had fun. You seem to have hit it off with Mel."

"It's been the best weekend ever, Ms. Dora. I've never eaten so much food and worn such pretty clothes. I just wish Tiny was here with us," Then, I remember our phone conversation. "Oh! I forgot to tell you, I called Tiny last night and she said Mrs. Wilkins has been trying to contact you. Pop tried taking Tiny –"

Before I could explain further, Ms. Dora speeds into the church parking lot and yells, "Pop did what to Tiny?!" She asks, worried out of her mind.

I've never seen Ms. Dora in such a panic. She quickly pulls out her phone to call Mrs. Wilkins.

"Aunt Dora," Mel knocks on the window. "Is everything okay?"

Ms. Dora forces a smile. "Yes, sweetheart, just gotta make a quick phone call. Why don't you take Tiffany inside? I'll catch up with you girls in just a few minutes."

I reluctantly step out of the car. Mel grabs my hand and gives me a reassuring squeeze as we walk up the church steps, the hum of soft hymns flowing around us. Mel leads me to a pew where two boys are already seated. The church's vibrant chatter dims as I slide into the pew next to Mel, who's already bubbling with excitement. The stained-glass windows scatter light across our faces, painting us in colors that feel too bright for my somber mood.

"Hey, guys. I want you to meet my new best friend. I've been telling her all about you idiots." Mel announces.

Rafe, with a playful smirk, responds, "A new friend? We're your only friends, Mel!" His comment sparks laughter, but it fades when my gaze falls on Mason Boom—the same boy who dazzled on the football field yesterday. Now, he's just an arm's length away, watching me with an intensity that sends a frightening shiver down my spine. Why is he staring through me, and why aren't I trying to stop him?

"You smell delicious." He says out of nowhere.

Startled, I find myself taken aback. "Um... thank you... I think...weirdo," I blurt out, my voice tinged with confusion and a hint of amusement. His forwardness pushes me to slightly edge away, wary of his boldness.

Mason seems to sense my discomfort and scoots closer, eager to explain. "Sorry, Nicole." He blurts out.

Confusion tightens my brow as I snap back, "Boy, I don't know who you think you're talking to, but my name is Tiffany Weathers, *not* Nicole."

He leans in, lowering his voice, "But you smell like a Nicole."

His words make me uneasy, prompting me to glance around, half-expecting Ms. Dora to appear and save me from this conversation. But she's nowhere to be found, which makes me think nothing is fine and Tiny's in trouble.

"Where the heck is Ms. Dora?" I mutter, more to myself than to him, as I stand up.

Mason's plea is soft, almost desperate. "Please, don't go."

Before I can respond, the youth pastor's voice echoes through the church. "Mason Boom, you're up!" As he hesitates, Rafe and Mel exchange worried glances, trying to usher him forward.

As Mason reluctantly goes to the pulpit, his eyes linger on me, filled with a mix of confusion and fascination. Half of me is worried about my sister and the other half is worried about who Mason Boom thinks I am and why. I need to leave. I need to find Ms. Dora, and I need to get back home to my sister.

I exit the sanctuary, but the abruptness of his shout stops me in my tracks. He proceeds to exit the pulpit and sprint towards me. Mel and Rafe are close behind, but I see Ms. Dora—distraught and worried.

"Nicole, wait!" Mason calls out as I reach the vestibule.

"Tiffany, who is this little boy?' She asks in a maternal tone.

"I don't know, Ms. Dora, just some boy who thinks I'm a girl he used to know." I try to play it cool.

Suddenly, Mason closes the distance between us. Before I can step back, his arms wrap around me in an eager embrace. My body accepts his embrace so naturally as if its yet another safe space to land.

His whisper is urgent against my ear, "You're not just some girl I used to know. It's me, you, and the world around us. Remember that."

How in the world does he know me and Tiny's phrase? Before I can gather my thoughts or respond, Ms. Dora's commanding voice cuts through the charged moment, "C'mon, Tiffany. We got a long drive back to Atlanta, and Tiny needs us!"

She gently pulls me away from the moment, away from Mason Boom. There's so much I want to ask him, so much I want to say, but all I can manage to do is smile and mutter, "Goodbye, Weirdo."

And it's just enough for him to smile back.

I hope he remembers me. I hope he savors my smile like I do his because today smiles are worth more than life itself because life, after today, life changes forever.

Chapter 13

Fate Never Fails – Mason

Nine Years Old

My mom died when I was only five years old. I thought my life was over, but thankfully, with the support of the Lynns and Sherri Carter, we've stitched together a semblance of happiness from the remnants of our sorrow. We're not the family we once were—there are spaces now, gaps where laughter once filled the air from people who once held my heart, but we're finding our way and holding on to faint but beautiful memories that propel us forward.

After the fire, Dad took a year off work but returned with renewed determination. Now, he's campaigning to be the next District Attorney of Greer. His pain fuels his quest for justice, turning personal loss into public service. The Lynns continue their search for Taylor and Nicole. They've done at least a dozen interviews and public pleas for information, and despite years without a lead, their hope remains unshaken—a beacon for my own belief that they're still out there.

Sherri's running for Congresswoman. She's become one of those people on the news always fussing about change, yelling back and forth with people on the tv screen. And now, she's going to be yelling even more because her political career is ascending to new heights. It's interesting that this town once hated our families, but after the tragedy, they loved us.

The Lynns, Carters, and Booms nearly eradicated all the corruption in the town. We should be relieved, but the cost to get here—losing the people we loved the most and thus hardening our hearts—overshadows our victory. For the Lynns, their job isn't finished until they uncover the conspiracy behind their daughters' disappearances. For my dad and Sherri, they've found peace in believing it's all over. And now, their shared peace has transformed into something else.

Recently, Rafe and his mom moved next door, but they might as well have moved in with us, considering how often they're here. Every morning, they join us for breakfast, and then Sherri or Dad drives us to school. Seeing Dad so happy is something new, something good. He can't seem to stop smiling, especially when he tries to sneak in personal time with Sherri.

"So, what does your schedule look like today? Think you can squeeze me in for lunch?" Dad asks Sherri in a hopeful whisper, trying to sound casual.

Sherri chuckles, "I'm not eating lunch with you again, Charles. Remember last time?" She teases. "I enjoyed the laughs, but I missed two important meetings!"

Their smiles are so frequent these days, a stark contrast to the years of darkness that settled in our hearts. It's both strange and wonderful to feel the spirit of happiness in our lives again.

"Oh c'mon," Dad playfully nudges her. "The future Congresswoman needs to let loose a bit, especially before the big election."

"Uh…Mom?" Rafe interrupts their intense gaze to remind them we're still around.

Realizing they've been caught up in each other's allure in front of us, they hastily separate from one another and turn their attention to getting us ready for school. At morning drop-off, Sherri turns to us with a smile that fills the vacant space in my heart.

"Y'all have a good day at school, okay? Your dad will pick you up and take you to practice and I'm making tacos for dinner! I love you boys! See you at home." She says, looking at Rafe, me, Bash, and Jay.

Sherri's lingering words fill me with warmth, but also stir a pang of both guilt and sadness as I think about my mother. My memories of her are etched in my mind but admittedly slowly fading away. Her absence still hurts and what hurts even more is that I desperately want to tell Sherri, *"I love you, too...Mom."*

At school, Melody Baker tags along and complains, as usual, about being the only girl in our gang. "You guys suck! I can't wait for more girls to join the crew. I think I'm gonna hold friend auditions."

Mel's cool. Her energy is infectious, even on her tough days. She's like one of the boys, but she really does believe we suck. We're forced to hang together because her mom is Sherri's campaign manager. Mrs. Callie's the sweetest person in the world, but rumor has it that she knows how to make people disappear, and Mel's dad is Greer High School's principal, so I kind of have to be nice to her. Mel brings the fun – well, most of the time. She can either be the life of the party or the end of it. She has these moments where she can hardly function, and she'll stay in bed, refusing to leave the house, but our therapist helps her feel better just like she does for me.

Mel, like me and Rafe, is no stranger to pain. We're a group of kids who've all experienced loss way too soon. But when we're all together, we somehow manage to become whole again.

"You know, Mel, if the Lynn twins were still around, you wouldn't be on your own," I tell her while flashing the beach picture Terry Lynn gave me. I think about Nicole and Taylor as much as I do my mom, but I'm ashamed to admit that I have to look at this picture more often because it's getting difficult to picture their faces without the reminder.

Rafe playfully pats me on the back and teases, "Dang, Mase. You gonna be obsessed with the twins your entire life? Excuse me," He clears his throat, "I mean Nicole."

I chuckle. "How could I have been obsessed back then, huh? We were toddlers, practically babies."

"And Mom said you used to stare at her like a goo-goo gaga baby!" He teases.

I smile while shaking my head. "You're gonna be angry at yourself a few years from now when I find them. They're still alive, Rafe. I can feel it." I try to convince him yet again.

Rafe rolls his eyes and opts not to respond, nor do I push the issue further. We all have different beliefs as it pertains to the aftermath of the Greer House Fires, and Rafe has accepted that everyone who died that night is gone forever, especially his dad. Everyone sees Rafe as the 'look on the bright side' type of kid, but I hear his cries. I see his pain. His grief still sits in the deepest pits of his heart.

"Hey," I place my hand on his shoulder. "My bad. I keep forgetting what Dr. Lee said. I need to stop obsessing over permanent pasts and focus on the here and now."

Rafe forces a smile. Then, Mel immediately lightens the mood.

"Mase, I'll be so glad when you actually take Dr. Lee's advice. You can't chase ghosts all your life. My goodness, you're nearly ten years old – practically a teenager!"

Even Rafe's sadness can't overpower Mel's dramatic humor. "Uh, we're not even close to being teens, Mel."

She dismisses him with a wave. "Oh, hush, Rafe. Mase, if these girls are still alive like you so passionately believe, then they'll come back. You don't gotta stop livin', though. Just trust in fate. Fate never fails."

"Fate?" I question, completely lost in her philosophical lingo.

"Yep, fate!" Mel adds in dramatic flair, throwing her hands in the air as if casting a spell. "My parents say it's so powerful that it can connect people no matter where they are in the world. It's like magic, but real."

She may be goofy and over the top, but she's right. Fate must be at work because I constantly feel an unseen connection—a connection that seems tied to something bigger than me.

Even as the school day passes in a blur of classes and lunchtime jokes, I always seem to carry an unshakable weight inside me—a constant feeling that Nicole and Taylor are still out there, just like the Lynns believe. Some people think the Lynns are clinging to false hope, calling them crazy for holding on so tightly to the belief that their daughters are still alive. But they're not crazy; they just seem to be parents who can't rest until they know for sure that their children are gone, parents whose love knows no bounds. I feel that same certainty deep within me too.

When we arrive at practice, I try to shift my focus. The field is where I feel most at home, where I can run away in my dreams and temporarily forget the nightmares that often keep me awake at night. Here, each sprint and tackle is a release, each play is a small victory in the battle to keep my worries at bay.

While my brothers and Rafe run to their teams' practice fields, I move slower because my mind is too heavy for my body to move with time. I think because I'm the oldest and remember more than my brothers, I'm often more reflective about life. I wish I could shake my heavy sorrows and idealized dreams, but I can't. I will always crave the people who should've never been taken away from me.

"Hey, you ready for the city scrimmage today? It's your first one, and I see you overthinkin' Mase. You're gonna do great. We're all here to cheer you on." My dad assures me.

I'm not thinking about football, performing my best, or the people cheering me on. I'm thinking about the people who brought the best out of me – Mom, Rafe's dad, and the Lynn twins.

Nevertheless, I suit up for practice, and as soon as I'm on the field, the familiar smell of turf and sweat fill my senses. Dad's rooting me on. The town's chanting my name. Coach is barking orders as usual, and I'm in the zone. The City Scrimmage is one of the biggest football days of the year because everyone in town comes out to watch us play. Football is life down here in the South. We eat, breathe, and sleep with our spikes in the ground, and today's my time to shine.

"Alright, Boom! Show the folks what you got! Let 'em see that arm." My Coach encourages me.

After I practice my warm-up throws, my team lines up. I feel the weight of expectation heavy on my shoulders, and the stands are a sea of familiar faces, all eager to catch a glimpse of the superstar my coaches and dad keep talking about. I tighten my grip on the football and feel the laces bite into my skin, a reassuring pain that grounds me to the moment.

"Set! Hut!" I call out as the scrimmage begins.

My teammates execute their routes with precision, just like we've practiced dozens of times before. As I drop back, my eyes scan for my receiver, Rafe. He darts down the field, and just as I cock my arm back, ready to unleash the pass that I've thrown nearly every day for the past year, a mesmerizing flicker of movement catches my eye in the stands.

Beautiful brown skin. Dark eyes. Tight, curly hair…It's *her*.

Our eyes meet, and it's as if time stops, everything fading away until it's just me, her, and the world around us.

I've stared at the picture of the Lynn twins every day for the nearly five years. I remember what they looked like, and every day I imagine how they look now. And that girl is a replica of my imagination. *That* girl is Nicole Lynn.

"Heads up, Mase!" Rafe's sharp voice snaps me out of my haze quickly enough to evade a tackle and release the ball for a perfect pass, but as soon as I'm clear, my gaze drifts back to the girl. She's still there, still watching, still staring, and slightly flashing the most beautiful smile I've ever seen. It's Nicole. It has to be.

But then again…where's Taylor?

"Timeout!" I suddenly yell aloud, a bit louder than I intended, but nevertheless, everyone stops and awaits my next command.

But I don't speak. Instead, I rush towards the stands, desperate to reach her and confirm what my imagination and heart know to be true.

But before I can reach her, a woman takes her by the hand and leads her away. I quickly run across the field and try to find them, but they've disappeared from view, and now I'm left standing here with my heart pounding in both frustration and elation.

"Mase! Get over here!" I hear my coach yell from a distance, but all I can think about is Nicole.

Until a gentle hand touches my shoulder. It's my dad keeling over to catch his breath. "What's wrong, Son? What's going on? Is everything okay?" He frantically asks through labored breaths.

Still trying to decipher reality from my imagination, I slowly open my mouth to utter, "Nicole. I saw her."

My dad releases an exasperated sigh, "Really, Mase? Did you really run off during your debut to chase a ghost? I thought Dr. Lee was making progress. Nicole's gone, Son, and so is Taylor. So is your mom. I know it's hard, but you gotta come back to reality, okay?" Dad hugs me tightly, but it doesn't feel nearly as warm as the sight of the girl from the stands.

He wants me to accept reality. I try my hardest to live in it, but the image I store in my head of everyone I lost is what keeps me sane.

When Dad and I return to the field, I avoid the confused looks and murmurs, solely focused on football despite Nicole's face consuming my thoughts.

"That's right, Boom! Shake em'!" The parents cheer from the sidelines as I execute each play, setting my teammates up for touchdown after touchdown until the fourth quarter buzzer rings.

"Y'all see that? Those are my boys! Mase and Rafe, the future of the NFL!" My dad, so loving and proud, boasts to the parents and residents of Greer.

He embraces both of us, and we're soon engulfed even tighter in his warmth when we also feel Sherri's love hovering over us.

"That's right. Y'all did so great out there." Sherri says, still hugging us tight with my brothers next to her. My dad's warmth shifts from his embrace to his eyes as soon as he sees Sherri.

"Hey, you," He whispers in a low, raspy voice. "I didn't think you'd make it."

"And miss our boys' first scrimmage? ADA Boom, you should know me better than that." She winks.

Rafe snickers and whispers, "They're doing it again, Mase. My mom. Your dad." He admires.

However, while Rafe admires their connection, I lament it. My dad is looking at Sherri the way he used to look at my mom. This is so wrong, and I think they know it because his gaze quickly averts at the sight of one of our gossiping neighbors. Dad and Sherri quickly separate, flashing curt nods and tight smiles. Then, we scurry home in separate, awkward silence.

After dinner, the tension from the field still lingers, and Dad and Sherri exchange an unspoken look.

In a strained voice, he suggests, "Boys, why don't you head upstairs and take showers?" Rafe and I pretend to comply, but we quietly linger at the top of the stairs to eavesdrop.

"Charles, we need to talk," Sherri says softly, with eyes filled with a mixture of fear, forbidden desire, and pain.

"I know," Dad replies. "Sherri, I know this is complicated. Hell, it's wrong, isn't it? Our families... My wife. Your husband. Us..." His words drift off.

"I know, Charles. We were all so close," Sherri interjects, her voice trembling. "I feel guilty every time I look at you because I know this is wrong. I know you miss your wife, and I damn sure miss my husband. I know you still hurt, and I'm still in pain, but being with you makes me hurt a little less every day." Sherri begins to cry.

Their whispered conversation confirms what I've suspected. They're drawn to each other, not just by shared history but by a real affection that has slowly knitted our fractured families back together.

Dad reaches out and wipes her tears. "Being with you makes me hurt less too. We may not be healed but at least we aren't hurting like we used to. I don't give a damn what the town is saying. I only care about how you're feeling. Tell me how you feel, Sherri. Tell me whatever this is between us could be something more. Please?" My dad says in a pleading whisper.

Sherri looks so broken as she shakes her head. "We can't," She cries in my dad's arms. "You called Rafe your boy, and I called the boys my sons. This isn't right."

For a moment, I forget Rafe is next to me until he tearfully whispers, "But it is." He grabs my hand and says, "I miss my dad, and I love your dad for being the dad I no longer have. It feels right, doesn't it Mase?"

A part of me agrees with Rafe. It does feel right. Dad and Sherri fill some of the emptiness left by the fire. But it's also confusing. It feels like a betrayal to Mom and Rafe's dad. I don't know how to reconcile these feelings. I don't understand how I can be happy and sad at the same time.

Dad and Sherri deserve happiness. We've all been through so much pain, but together, we've been hurting a whole lot less. Maybe this is what healing looks like—messy, complicated, and sometimes, a little bit wrong but also right.

Rafe and I reconcile our emotions while our parents surrender to theirs. Our parents sit there, holding each other, not saying anything. Sherri rests her head on Dad's shoulder, and he gently strokes her hair. It's a moment that I almost feel like I shouldn't be watching, but I can't help but admire the way my dad loves, and I'm sure I'll love just as passionate and intense one day too.

"Sherri, we've been through so much together. You make me smile. You make me feel alive."

Sherri sniffs and shakes her head. "You make me feel alive too. But I don't know how this could work."

Dad leans in closer, their foreheads touching. "We'll figure it out together."

The conversation is interrupted by a phone call. A wide smile forms when he sees the caller ID.

"It's Crys and Terry." He announces. "Hey, Terry. Hey, Crystal," They greet them, and Dad puts the call on speaker phone.

"Charles, Sherri! We just knew y'all would be together. How'd the boys do today?" Terry's voice booms.

Sherri playfully gasps, "We haven't heard from you two in a whole month, and the first question you ask is about the boys? Well, hello to you, too!" She laughs.

Terry laughs and replies, "Yep! Now, how'd they play?"

Sherri and Dad exchange an excited glance as if their previous conversation never occurred.

"They were amazing!" Sherri exclaims. "It was Mason's first scrimmage as quarterback, and he was unstoppable."

"Rafe was right there with him, cuttin' and scoring." Dad adds with a proud smile spreading across his face. Dad and Sherri stare at each other with locked eyes.

"Uh…are y'all there?" Terry interrupts, bringing them back to reality.

Sherri laughs, her voice a bit shaky, "Uh, yeah. Sorry, we, uh, got carried away, I guess."

Crystal slowly laughs, "Carried away, huh?"

Sherri shakes her head. "Crys, don't start. I feel your sarcasm through the phone."

"And we see your smiles through the phone." Crystal rebuts.

"So, what's really going on between you two?" Terry sternly asks.

Dad and Sherri exchange a glance but say nothing.

Crystal sighs and breaks the tension. "Silence equals shame, and there's nothing to be ashamed of. This is where we are in life – finding sanity and comfort in the most unexpected places. For us, it's relentlessly searching for our daughters. For you two, it's building a bridge to happiness and walking across it together."

Dad squeezes Sherri's hand, and her smile softens.

"Be it friendship or more, y'all have our blessing. Be happy again. You deserve that." Crystal declares.

Our parents smile, and Dad replies, "You two deserve to be happy also, you know?"

"Oh, we will," Terry confidently says. "As soon as we find the twins."

Our parents' eyes are sad, reflecting the hope they lost years ago. But I wish I could speak up and let Crystal and Terry know that it's their turn to be happy, too, because I found Nicole today, and I'm going to find her again.

As I look at my dad and Sherri, I think of Nicole's coincidental reemergence. Maybe fate is real, and it's leading us somewhere new, somewhere hopeful, somewhere happiness awaits. Maybe Mel is right — fate never fails.

~ ~ ~

Weekends in Greer are all about football, but there's a sacred time of day that even football can't compete with—Sunday morning church service at Greer Baptist.

Today is one of those Sundays where the air is charged with devotion and solidarity, and the pews of Greer Baptist are packed as the church buzzes with the energy of a town gathered in worship. Here, I've found peace over the last few years. In this place, I'm surrounded by folks who radiate kindness. However, today, my nerves are as taut as the strings on Minister James' old guitar, even with Rafe trying to lighten the mood.

Rafe gently nudges me, "What's up, man? You nervous?"

I force a smirk and brush him off. "Of course not. I know the Ten Commandments like the back of my hand." I boast.

"Ten? I thought there were eleven!" Rafe's eyes widen, sending me into a panic.

I blurt out, "Holy crap! Eleven commandments?!"

Mel scoots in the pew and bursts into laughter. "Relax, Mase. It's ten. Rafe's just messing with you. Besides, you're everyone's Golden Boy. The church will pretend there are eleven commandments just to make you feel good. You're gonna do fine."

"Thanks, Mel," I mumble, trying to focus back on my notes.

"Hey, guys. I have a friend that I want you to meet." Mel says.

Rafe teases. "A new friend? We're your only friends, Mel!"

While those two tease one another as usual, an unexpected yet familiar scent drifts through the air—honeysuckle and vanilla. It's overpowering, all-consuming, and pulls me out of my reverie. I lift my head to search for the source, and that's when I see her. The girl from the field, the girl from my dreams, the much older but same girl from my picture, Nicole Lynn. It's fate.

She walks in like sunlight slicing through clouds and sits in the empty space between me and Mel.

My brain goes haywire, and my materialized thoughts slip out without thinking. "You smell delicious."

She turns to me with her eyebrows raised and clearly taken aback. "Um... thank you... I think...weirdo."

"Sorry, Nicole."

"Boy, I don't know who you think you're talking to, but my name is Tiffany Weathers, *not* Nicole."

I lean in and lower my voice. "But you smell like a Nicole."

"Where the heck is Mrs. Dora?" She mumbles under her breath and stands up.

I quietly beg, not wanting her to walk away. "Please, don't go,"

Just then, my youth pastor calls out, "Mason Boom, you're up!"

Rafe nudges me and tries to snap me back to reality while Mel looks worried. "Come on, Mase, focus." She whispers.

Rafe's eyes dart back and forth between me and the *Tiffany* girl. How can he not see what I see? My legs feel like they're made of something much flimsier than flesh and bone, but nevertheless, I stand up, take a deep breath, and try not to look at the glimmer of fate sitting in the pew.

"C'mon, Mase. Snap out of it." I mutter to myself, then face the congregation and find that same confidence I had just moments before Nicole's unexpected arrival.

"Alright, young Boom. Show us what you've been learning in Sunday school."

I got this, I think. "Uh," I mumble into the mic. "Thou shall not…"

The confusion on my dad's face is just as poignant as the confusion in my mind.

"Mase," He whispers from the front row. "You okay, Son?"

But my eyes stay fixed on Nicole as she stands up to leave with the woman. I can feel the eyes of the congregation on me, but nothing matters—not the worried furrows in my father's brow, not the snickers from my friends, not the muffled whispers snaking through the pews. Only her. Only Nicole.

"Nicole, wait!" I yell into the mic.

The words burst from me, loud enough to echo against the stained-glass windows. Rafe and Mel chase behind me while I chase Nicole. She stops right outside the sanctuary doors, but the woman accompanying her turns around with a puzzled glare.

"Tiffany, who is this little boy?' She asks.

Tiffany—no, Nicole—no, Tiffany, whoever she is, shrugs. "I don't know, Ms. Dora, just some boy who thinks I'm a girl he used to know."

I close the distance between us, ignore Rafe and Mel's murmurs, and hug my long-lost friend as tight as I can. "You're not just some girl I used to know. You're the girl I always knew. It's me, you, and the world around us. Remember that."

Suddenly, her stiff body relaxes in my arms. Our honeysuckle and vanilla-scented hug feels long-awaited. It feels like home.

"C'mon, Tiffany. We got a long drive back to Atlanta, and Tiny needs us." The woman gently tugs her away, breaking our embrace.

She leaves me with a subtle wave and a surprisingly warm "Goodbye, Weirdo."

A smile spreads across my face despite the bittersweet pang in my heart. Rafe startles me with a slap on my shoulder, pulling me back to reality.

"It was her, wasn't it? It was the Lynn twin." Rafe says in disbelief.

"That's my new friend I was telling you about—Tiffany. Are you telling me that's the girl in the photo you stare at every day?"

I gaze in the path of Nicole's direction, still shocked by her re-emergence.

"I swear that's her y'all. I found her. I found Nicole Lynn."

Then, Mel, my serendipitous sidekick, leans in close with a soft whisper that carries more hope than volume.

"I told you, Mase. Fate never fails."

Chapter 14

Suffering – Tiffany

Our three-hour drive back to Atlanta was tense, nearly paralyzing us with worry. Finally, overwhelmed by the silence and dread, I ask, "Is Tiny okay?"

Ms. Dora doesn't respond immediately. Her grip is tight on the steering wheel, and her eyes are focused on the road ahead. The silence stretches, filling the car with a heavy, expectant air. When she finally speaks, her voice is thick with emotion she tries to mask.

"No," She says, the weight of that single word pressing down on us both. "And she probably won't be for a very long time."

My heart sinks, the fears that had been whispering at the back of my mind now screaming loud and clear.

"What happened?" I ask, my voice barely above a whisper, fearing the answer yet needing to know.

Ms. Dora takes a deep breath. Her next words are deliberate and heavy, with a pain that mirrors my own. "Tiny...she's suffered through something terrible, something no child, no woman, or man should ever have to face. Right now, the only thing we can do is protect her, so she has the peace of mind to continue on."

The car feels smaller somehow. "Your body is your own, Tiffany. Your mind is your own. Don't let anyone take that away. People may try to hurt you. They may even break you, but what's broken can be fixed, and what's hurt can be healed. No one can destroy you. Be there for Tiny to remind her of this." She says, while tears stream down her face.

Her words settle and I lean back against the seat, the fabric of the car familiar and oddly comforting as I process her words and soak in her tears. Protecting Tiny, protecting her peace — it's a responsibility I accept wholeheartedly.

As we continue the drive, the scenery blurring past the windows becomes a backdrop to my thoughts, and when I drift to sleep, I think about Greer and me and Tiny's clean slate.

But first, I have to get us through this hell hole of a reality because now, we're home and approaching Mrs. Wilkins' front door.

The Wilkins' house looms before us. The front door is open, inviting us into the crowded living room of familiar faces. The kinder adults from the neighborhood who've often looked out for Tiny and me are here, their expressions a mix of sadness and defeat. Amongst the crowd, I spot Mama—her posture defiant, her head held high. She stands oddly proud amidst the whispers.

The room quiets as we enter. Ms. Dora's presence commands immediate attention. She nods to Mrs. Wilkins, who begins to explain what happened with a shaky voice. "Alex had to work the night shift," She starts, her hands nervously twisting a tissue. "Pop must've seen his car leave because a few hours later when Tiny and I were asleep, he broke in and took her home. I didn't know she was missing until this morning," Mrs. Wilkins continues, her eyes darting towards Mama, who remains silent. "That's when I called you, Ms. Dora. Alex and a few other men immediately went and got her back this morning. Pop wasn't there and hasn't returned since. Shirley was in the bed passed out with a needle in her arm, oblivious and…"

Mrs. Wilkins' voice fades as she wipes her tears while observing my bruised and nearly unconscious sister.

What did Pop do to Tiny? She looks like Mama, bruised, broken, and high. Pop couldn't have done this. He loves her. She loves him. He lets her call him Daddy. He does everything for her. I – It doesn't make any sense.

The adults talk amongst themselves while I sit next to Tiny, placing my arms around her shoulders. "Tiny, it's me, Tiff. I'm so sorry for leaving. I'll never do it again, okay? I'm so sorry for leavin'. You're gonna be okay."

She groans in pain but laughs. "Of course, I'll be okay. Daddy's gonna give me some more medicine so I can feel better. He said I did so good. I did so much better than the other times. He still wants to love you too, but I made him promise not to ever love you, Tiff. You gonna be okay as long as I let him keep lovin' me. I just gotta keep lovin' all those men, too. It's worth keepin' you safe."

Tiny drifts off to sleep, but the atmosphere is charged with simmering anger and uncontrollable cries and whimpers.

Now I see Mama, head no longer held high, "He promised not to do it again, not yet, at least." She shakes her head and mumbles under her breath.

Ms. Dora, in a volume I've never heard her speak, yells, "Again? What kind of mother are you? You and that pimp of yours are going to jail. Someone call the police. Now!"

Mama tries to break away from the neighbors who cornered her as she melts into a pleading mess. "Please, don't call the police," She begs. "I uh, I – I can give Tiffany and Tiny away—to a good family, I swear. I – I know someone...famous billionaires who'd love to have two daughters. Just let me give them back. I – I mean away to a new family."

Her plea hangs heavy in the air, tainted with the stench of empty promises.

"They can have the life they always deserved," She continues, her eyes darting, searching Ms. Dora's face. "Just don't call the cops. Things will get so much worse for everyone, including the girls. They'll be put in the system and separated."

Ms. Dora scoffs, the sound harsh and unforgiving. "You think you can barter with their lives like you do your drugs? You're gonna get what you deserve, Shirley. You're gonna be locked away for a long time."

Amid the chaos, Mama turns to me, her gaze sharp. "You hear that, Tiff? Ms. Dora doesn't love y'all. She's gonna separate you from your sister. Then, you'll have no one. Absolutely no one."

The words hit me like a physical blow, knocking the air from my lungs. Panic rises within me like a tight, suffocating fear. "Is that true?" I ask Ms. Dora, my voice trembling. "Will they separate me and Tiny?"

Ms. Dora's face softens as she looks at me, her expression a mix of anger toward Mama and deep concern for me. "Your mom doesn't know what she's talking about, Tiffany. It's not guaranteed—"

"But it's still possible?" I interrupt, my eyes welling up with tears. The thought of being separated from Tiny is unbearable. "Please, Ms. Dora," I beg, my voice barely a whisper. "Don't call the police. Me and Tiny need each other. We can't be separated. She's all I got. It's just me and her. We need each other, Ms. Dora. Please don't call the police! Don't take my sister away from me. Please, please, please!" I tearfully express.

But Mrs. Wilkins says, "It's already done. We called them right before you arrived. They'll be here any minute now."

The room falls silent, everyone's eyes are on us. I can feel the weight of their stares, the gravity of the moment pressing down on us. Ms. Dora looks at me, then at the neighbors as everyone contemplates the consequences of the decision they made for me and my sister.

Ms. Dora steps closer, her presence a warmth that feels like a promise. "Listen to me, child," She says in a firm yet gentle tone. "I'm not gonna let anyone tear you and Tiny apart. I don't know what's gonna happen, but I do know that what's been happening is never gonna happen again. You girls deserve so much better."

Her words offer a glimmer of hope in the storm of my fears. I nod and replace my fear with trust in Ms. Dora's fierce love, protection, and promise to keep me and Tiny safe, but the sense of relief is quickly interrupted by the knock on the door.

Suddenly, Mama nicks one of the neighbors with her pocketknife and breaks loose from the corner they hold her in.

"Dammit, Shirley!" Our neighbor yells and attempts to chase after her, but she's quick. Mama disappears through the back door and into the shadows of the street corners where she belongs.

Just before she escapes, she turns to look at me, her eyes wet with something that looks like regret or maybe just desperation.

"I tried, Tiffany. I really did try to be a mom," She calls out, her voice strained. "Greer, go to Greer. Your happiness is in Greer, Georgia." Then, she's gone.

The second knock on the door jerks everyone back to reality. Mr. Wilkins opens the door to reveal the police, accompanied by EMS and a Child Protective Services worker. The world shifts into a blur—flashing lights beam through the windows, voices murmur, and there's a sudden urgency in the air. It overwhelms me. This moment feels like a tragic play where I'm both the audience and the unwilling star.

The medics rush to Tiny, whispering medical terms I barely understand. "Narcan," I overhear, my stomach clenching at the implication. Tiny's fate is worse than we all feared. A seemingly kind but professional CPS worker approaches me and gently takes my hand while Ms. Dora and Mrs. Wilkins speak to the police, with their words punctuated by gestures of distress and insistence.

"Everything's going to be okay now, Tiffany." The CPS worker says softly.

But is it? How could I believe life would ever be okay when, apparently, all this time, what was happening to Tiny wasn't? Mama's special water, Pop's frequent visits to her room, and my desire to have that with him, too, someday. None of it was ever okay, and I'm wracked with guilt for not realizing it, for not stopping it, for not saving my sister.

How could I be so stupid and naïve? How could I be so selfish to leave Tiny alone? I'll never allow anyone to hurt Tiny again. But it may be too late because the only words uttering from her mouth are, *"Where's Daddy? Tell him I'm sorry. I didn't mean to get him in trouble."*

She cares more about the loss of his 'love' rather than losing herself. My sister is going to need a whole lot more help, healing, and protection than what I can offer.

As the weeks and months drag by, so do Tiny's withdrawals. Her desire to see pop again, to be *loved*, still persists. But he and Mama are on the run while Tiny and I are in Greenbriar Group Home for Girls. Waiting. Hoping to be placed with a family that's willing to foster us both.

Here is where I dream. I dream of a life where struggling is strange, and happiness is easy. I dream of Greer, the place that felt like home, the place that perhaps holds the key to a new beginning, a safe haven for the Weathers Girls.

Chapter 15

The Way Out – Tiffany

Fourteen Years Old

"Keep your form tight. Turn, and turn, and turn! Good Job, Tiffany! Keep going!" Ms. Dora says, critiquing my angles before the end-of-season Grand Slam Championship. "And....deathdrop!" She yells, and I instantaneously react on command, throwing my body to the ground to complete my final stand battle set.

This dance studio has become my safe haven. With every practice, every competition, and every trophy, I'm more determined to use this gift to get me and my sister out of South Atlanta.

We don't live on the streets, but life under state care is a far cry from the freedom Tiny and I once dreamed of. The first six months in Greenbriar were tough. Tiny would get into fights with the older girls, which means I got into fights too. We built up quite the *don't mess with us* rep because we know how to scrap.

After three strikes, we were kicked out. Then, came three more homes where instead of fighting being the issue, Tiny breaking curfew was. We were even placed in a few foster homes here and there, but let's just say there are a lot of Pops in this world, and I be damned if I allow any of them to touch me or my sister.

In our new home, however, there are strict rules we must abide by – school, approved after-school activities only, then home. But Tiny barely goes to school anymore. She quit everything science-related and tells anyone who will listen that she has *no home, no hope, no nothing*.

Our newest foster mom allows me to spend time with Ms. Dora every weekend. While I believe Ms. Dora and Mrs. Wilkins saved us, Tiny believes the opposite. It's like she has amnesia because she thinks they ruined our lives when they only want the best for us. Mrs. Wilkins even transferred to Tiny's school to keep an eye on her. She tried to continue cultivating her love for science, but Tiny only cares about the attention she receives from older boys.

Tiny now veers towards self-destruction. Her dreams of being a scientist are replaced by the thrill of boys and money. I've heard the rumors about her, and I've even seen the truth—sneaking out our bedroom window, entertaining the slick hot boys in Impalas posted up at every club from College Park to Union City to East Point. It's no secret she's one of the prettiest girls to come on the Southside. At fifteen her body is more developed than most, and she's even playing grown-woman games. Every weekend, she drops by with a new hairdo, fancy clothes, and expensive jewelry–absolutely nothing a teenager can afford but everything a working girl can. She told me I needed to learn how to use what I got to get what I wanted, but all I want is safety, stability, and peace for the both of us.

When Tiny and I were taken away from Mama, we were expected to just carry on like normal kids. How were we supposed to act normal if we never had a normal life? When I asked our group home leader if we could go to therapy like that girl Mel from Greer had mentioned, she laughed. She just looked at me and laughed. Life has only become harder, and I can't work through my confusion by myself. I can't even fix me and Tiny's relationship anymore.

"You're supposed to be the smart one, but all you're doing is making stupid decisions. We're never going to get adopted by a good family because of you!" I yell, but her laughter is bitter and tinged with cynicism.

"Wake up, Tiffany! I'm the only one making sure we survive. I'm making sure we have a future. It's just me, you, and this shitty world around us! Don't you get it?"

She hides the money she made for the week underneath my mattress. Dance is my way out, but Tiny thinks her body is the only exit. She looks back and forth between me and the window as if she's waiting for someone— as if someone controls her every move. She's ansty and paranoid. I'm all familiar with her erratic movements. I know when someone is using.

With a single tear flowing down my face, I grab Tiny's hand to steady her angst.

"You've become just like Mama, you know? It doesn't end well. You gotta stop. Who is he, Tiny? Who's supplying you with drugs? Who's making you do all these things? I can help you. It won't be like before. I'm stronger now. I can protect you. Just like you protected me. Please." I beg.

Tiny shrugs off my concerns with a cold laugh. "I'm not Mama, Tiffany. And no one's *making* me do anything. You are so damn dramatic! I know how to play the game, okay? Hell, you think I can't control my high at this point? I call the shots. I give myself to who I want when I want, and I'm actually getting somethin' out of it. Money for us to get away someday. Pop is teaching me every—"

I gasp, and Tiny freezes at the realization that she revealed the truth.

Pop is back and in control. He's always been in control. He groomed Tiny since we were babies. He defined what love is to her. He presents a false sense of safety, and I find myself unsurprised that he's reentered her life and implemented the sadistic plans he had for her all along.

I tighten my grip on Tiny's shoulders, the urgency in my voice barely hiding my desperation. "Teaching you? Tiny, I'm calling the police. You can't go back to him. He's a dangerous pervert. He hurt you! He rap –"

"Shut up!" She yanks away and silences me with a scream. "That never happened. It never fucking happened, Tiff! Just stop it. Pop never touched me in any way I didn't want. He gave me too much drugs on accident. He was just tryin' to help with the pain. He apologized, and everything I do is on my terms now. I've forgiven him. If it weren't for Pop, we'd be living out of cars, motels, and boarding houses forever. He saved us from Mama."

My heart races, a mix of anger and fear in my stomach. "He's worse than Mama! That man is evil. Look what he's done to you, what he's done to us. He doesn't love you. This is wrong!"

Tiny rolls her eyes and releases an exasperated sigh. "Oh, Tiffany, you'll never understand. Love is complicated, okay? And besides, he wasn't our real father anyway. Look, I've gotta go. Just...keep this money safe. I'll see you in the morning. Please, don't tell anyone. I'm doing this for us. We're gonna get the hell away from here soon. Maybe, we'll even go to that small town you're always talkin' about. Just trust me, okay? It'll always be me, you, and the world around us."

As she heads for the bedroom window, she pauses and turns, a hint of the sisterly bond we once shared flickers in her eyes. "Hey, you need to stop worrying about me and focus on dancin' your ass off at the championship. I'm sorry I haven't been around much, but I promise I'll be there to cheer you on."

I manage a small smile and cling to her promise. "You better be," I say, trying to mask my worry. "Just...be safe, okay?"

She doesn't respond because neither one of us believes in safety anymore, just survival. Tiny smiles then she leaves me alone with my swirling thoughts and the heavy weight of a promise that feels increasingly empty.

~ ~ ~

Weeks have passed, and every time I see Tiny, she looks and behaves differently. Her change is swift, likely because it doesn't take much time to destroy a child who's already damaged.

But today is the final competition of the season before summer break. It's my time to shine. The dance floor is where I can release all my frustration and disappointments and just be me. I'm ready to showcase my hard work, and I'm ready to win the Grand Slam Championship trophy. My team needs me to nail every step, every formation change, every pose, and I intend to deliver.

As the battle heats up, the energy in the gym is electric. Teams from all over have come to compete, but none of them bring the heat like Ms. Dora's College Park Diamonds. I'm at the front, in the captain's spot, calling the counts and leading the charge. "Five, six, seven, eight!" My voice cuts through the music as we launch into a high-energy sequence.

"Sharp arms, Tiffany! Hit those marks! Let's go, Diamonds!" Ms. Dora's voice is both a beacon and a blade, pushing me to excel. As we hit the final pose, the gym erupts in applause. We nailed it, and I scan the crowd for Tiny, hoping she's there to see that *this* is our way out. But she isn't.

While the judges tally the scores, I step outside for a breath of fresh air, trying to shake off the disappointment. That's when I hear catcalls from a group of older boys leaning against the wall.

"Yo, Tiff! You were killing it in there! Shaking that ass, doing those splits. You badder than a dime, almost as bad as Tiny. Bet you're just as talented as your fine-ass sister, too, huh?" One of them leers, stepping closer.

Anger flares within me, sharp and hot. "Get off me, Slim," I snap, my voice colder than I intended.

Another boy laughs and rakes his eyes over me while licking his lips. "Come on, Tiff, don't be like that. We're just appreciating your talent."

"Appreciating? Is that what you call it?" I retort, then turn to the boy who hasn't moved. I try to move past him, but he stands firm, so with all the strength my dance-trained legs can muster, I knee him in the balls.

He kneels over in pain, and I smile. "I guess I'm not the only talented one. Who's doing splits now?" I spit out, my voice laced with venom.

I hate men, and I hate that I hate men because I know they aren't all bad, but unfortunately, bad is all I've ever met.

Back inside, the awards ceremony starts. Third place, Clayton County Starlettes. Second place, Bankhead Barbs. Then, there's a slow pause as I interlock hands with my teammates and Ms. Dora.

"Coming in first place, led by the legendary, Dora Reign, is the illest junior dance line in the land, The College Park Diamonds."

Hundreds of fans cheer in the stands, 'Diamonds! Diamonds!' with everyone smiling and in awe of our talent. I'm proud. I'm humbled. I'm excited. I'm wondering where Tiny is. She's still nowhere to be found. Her absence cuts deeper than my accolades can soothe.

"You were spectacular out there, Tiff. I know life hasn't treated you and your sister fair but the magic you're able to create out of lemons is beautiful. You're a true champion." Ms. Dora says during the car ride home.

Ms. Dora's pride and admiration warm my heart, but I can't seem to stop thinking about Tiny. Why didn't she come today? Why haven't I seen her in nearly two weeks? Why'd she have to walk in Mama's footsteps? Why hasn't anyone saved us from this hellhole of a life?

"Thanks, Ms. Dora. Too bad Tiny wasn't around to see me tonight. Too bad she's never around anymore."

"Hmm, about that. What's up with Tiny? She hasn't been to school. She's completely pushed Mrs. Wilkins away. We've tried our hardest to get custody of you girls, but the system doesn't always seem to pan out for us folk. We're still trying to find you both a happy, stable home. But..." Ms. Dora hesitates. "But we can't do that if all the rumors about Tiny are true. You gotta tell me the truth. Do I need to alert the police? Is Pop back?"

I'm too wrapped up in my disappointment to consider my promise to Tiny to keep quiet. So, I just shrug and allow the truth to roll off my tongue.

"Whatever you've heard about Tiny, it's true, Ms. Dora. Believe everything you hear and even everything you don't." My voice is a whisper as tears trace down my face.

Ms. Dora's presence is the only comfort I've come to rely on. She squeezes my hand tight and wipes away my tears.

"You keep sayin' you're tryin', but why haven't we been adopted yet? Are we that unlovable? Are we so damaged that no one wants to waste their time?" I ask, pulling away slightly to look up at her.

She sighs, "Now, you know that ain't the case. You also know adoptive parents prefer younger children. You and Tiny will be aged out in just a few years, which means most families won't have time to build the connection they want with their child. *However,* I was hoping Tiny would be here tonight so I could share the good news.

"Ms. Dora, what're you up to now?"

She chuckles, "Well, you remember those nice politicians I was telling you about years ago? Congresswoman Sherri Carter and her fiancée, District Attorney Boom, from Greer? Well, they were able to pull some strings on your behalf. There's a family interested in long-term fostering you and Tiny."

Relief and a surge of hope wash over me. "Really? Me *and* Tiny? Someone's gonna take us in? They're actually gonna let us live with them for good? They're gonna love us?" I breathe, a smile breaking through my tears.

"Yes, I know this family personally, and they're going to love the both of you with their hearts," Ms. Dora confirms, squeezing my shoulders. "It's gonna happen, Tiffany. As soon as I get home, I'm gonna call everybody I know who can help us get your sister away from that sick bastard. You *and* Tiny are going to get everything you ever wanted, a mom and dad who truly love you."

During our drive back, my mind races with dreams of a new life, a real family with a mother to love me, and all I can say under my breath is, "Finally."

Days after the competition, there's a scrape at the window piercing my ears. It's Tiny. She slips through, looking like a spectacle of her harsh past, a disillusioned present, and a daunting, consequential future.

She's dressed in an expensive jumpsuit, and her hair is neatly styled into a long ponytail, all out of place for the worn look in her eyes. What's even worse is her bruised eye. The makeup doesn't do it justice, and neither does the fake smile on her face. It's clear she's been out, living a life so far removed from the innocence of her age.

"Tiny," I rush to help get her settled on her feet. Then, I immediately hug her, completely forgetting about the absence between us. "Oh, thank God you're okay! I've been worried out of my mind."

Tiny laughs and dismisses my concern. "Chill out, Tiff. I swear we just saw each other a few days ago. So, you ready for competition day?" Tiny asks with a forced cheerfulness. "I can't wait to cheer you on!"

In shock, I look deeper into her weary eyes and bruised skin. She's energetic. She's antsy, unnerved, and anxious...just like Mama used to be. I stare at her, noting the disconnect between her appearance and her demeanor. I've seen enough around town and growing up with Mama to know that Tiny's gone–my Tiny is completely gone.

"Tiny, the competition was days ago. You missed it." I explain, hoping not to break her further than she already is.

Confusion clouds her face before she dismissively shakes her head, allowing a curt laugh to escape. "Oh, yeah. You're right...I knew that. I was uh...just testing you!" Her attempt at humor doesn't hide the tremble in her voice or the lost glint in her eyes. She then begins hitting herself in the head. "Fuck, I'm so stupid. I'm so damn stupid." She mumbles under her breath.

Sitting down beside her on the bed, I grab her hands and transfer my warmth to her cold, sweaty skin. Ms. Harriet, Mrs. Wilkins, Ms. Dora…they worked so hard to undo what Mama did to us, only for Pop to reverse engineer her mental and emotional fortitude.

"Tiny, now you know you're far from stupid. You're the smartest girl I know. Where have you been? And what happened to your eye?"

She pulls her hands away to avoid my gaze. "I fell is all. I'm so damn clumsy nowadays. Pop keeps telling me I need glasses. I'm always bumpin' my head and bruisin' up myself. But I've just been around town meeting so many rich people. That's why I missed your competition. I'm taking care of us, just like I promised, Tiff."

Tiny peps up, then pulls out a wad of crinkled cash, dirty money. "Look!" She proudly says. "I know it ain't as much as I've stashed before, but Pop says the cost to live has gone up, which means he's been taking more of my cut to pay for all these pretty clothes and my medicine." She sniffs and then wipes her irritated nose.

Silence fills the room as my heart breaks for my big sister. I close her dollar-billed palm and smile. "Keep it, Tiny. You can keep any money you ever make from now on because you don't need to keep doing this anymore. It's over."

The struggle is over. The pain is over. The fight for survival is over. Tiny's sacrifice is over. But her reaction doesn't match mine as she looks down at the half-packed suitcase.

She stands abruptly, "Over? You're leaving me, aren't you, Tiff?"

Before I can get a word in, she launches into an angry rant, pacing back and forth. "I knew it! Pop told me not to trust you. He said you'd betray me just like Ms. Dora and Mrs. Wilkins. He said you'd leave me, just like Mama! He told me not to come. I got this black eye tryna get over here only for you to leave me behind! How could you do this to me?!"

I wrap my frantic sister tight in my arms. "Tiny, calm down, please!"

I hold her as still as I can. She fights against me, but I stand my ground until she manages to calm down.

"I'll never leave you, you hear me? Never." I whisper, my voice thick with desperation. "This suitcase is for us. Ms. Dora did it. We're going to meet our new family this week – a different city, a fresh start. This is what we always wanted. Everything's going to be okay, Tiny. We're going to be okay."

My excitement is dampened by Tiny's tears on my shoulder. Why is she quiet? Why isn't she excited? Why isn't she reciprocating my embrace?

Her whisper's so fragile it might shatter. "But I'll never be okay, Tiff. I can't go with you. There's still hope for you, not for me. If I go with you, you'll never have the peace you've always dreamed of. You'll never be happy. I'm too broken. Wherever we go, whatever new start Ms. Dora has planned for us, it won't work. Not with me dragging you down."

"Tiny, listen to me," I implore. "What's broken can be fixed. What's hurt can be healed. And what's lost can be found. A good family found us, and we *both* deserve to be safe, happy, and loved."

Tiny scoffs. Her laugh is hollow and betrayed by the stream of tears flowing down her face. "I'm not a cracked vase. You can't just patch me up and put me on a shelf. I'm...sick. I'm sick just like Mama was, just like she is. I'm fifteen and been with twice as many men as my age. This is it for me. I only say I'm saving up money for us to get away to make me feel better, but I ain't goin' nowhere. You got a future with a family, and I have Pop."

I shake my head. "You got a future, too, Tiny! And it doesn't involve Pop. We gotta get you away from him. We need to be somewhere he can't reach you, somewhere he can't twist your mind. You're a gem, Tiny, not dirt, and I won't let him walk on you anymore."

"You think I haven't tried? You think I want this life?" Her mask falters, and her tears have now changed to heavy cries. Her words spilling out like venom. "Pop is everywhere, Tiff! I can't escape him. He's in every shadow, around every corner! I hate him and love him all at once, and I just want it to stop. I wish we never met him but I need him. I don't have school. I don't have science. I don't even have you. I'm nothing. I'll never be nothin', but you still have time. Be free without me. Please let me go."

I've never seen Tiny cry so hard in our entire lives. Though what's broken can be fixed, I don't even know where to begin, so I hold her broken-down body in my arms. No one deserves to have their voice taken away. No one deserves to have their choice taken away. No child deserves what she has endured. And if anyone deserves a better life, it's Tiny.

"Everything changes tomorrow, Sis. We're going to a real home to be with a real family. We'll never be separated again. It's me, you, and the world around us, Tiny Weathers."

I wrap her in our childhood blanket, and we drift to sleep on the bedroom floor. But before I close my eyes for the evening, I slide Tiny's cell phone out of her pocket and text pop.

Tiny: Tiny is moving away. She's leaving with me, and you'll never be able to hurt her ever again. Sincerely, FUCK YOU!

My Love (Pop): Lol. Well hello Tiffany. My girl is well trained and she'll always come back to me. I'm her home and you're a reminder of everything she'll never be. Enjoy tonight because I'll make sure you never see her again...unless you wanna pay for it ;)

Tiny: I'm calling the police but if they don't get to you before I do then I'm gonna kill you. Might not be tomorrow, or next week, but one day I'm going to do the world a favor and end you. Goodbye you son of a bitch.

I slip the phone back into Tiny's jacket and fall asleep, content for the first time in... forever. Tomorrow is the beginning of our happily ever after together.

But as dawn stretches, I wake to silence, and the fresh scent of vanilla, magnolia, and honeysuckle replaces the body that kept me warm through the night. Clutched in my trembling hands, I find a small bottle of fragrance and a note, each word etched with the finality of a long goodbye:

My Sweet Tiffany Nicole,

It's time for you to outshine our darkness. I'm leaving—not because I don't love you, but because you deserve a chance at a real life, a life without me and the damage I'd cause.

I never finished that fragrance challenge by Lynn Perfumery...but I remembered enough. I mixed vanilla orchard, magnolia, and honeysuckle—our favorite. It's for you. Whenever you smell it, think of our dreams of the mother who'd cradle us in her arms and the dad who'd cook us biscuits every morning. Our dreams are finally coming true. Live in them and be happy.

Always remember, it's me, you, and the world around us.

Love you always,

Your big sis Tiny Weathers

Today, I'm about to meet the family eager to welcome me into their lives, my heart is heavy with a bittersweet realization. We, Weathers girls, have weathered many storms together, dreaming of a shared escape that now, cruelly, diverges—mine toward a promise of love and stability, hers back into constant torment she believes she can't escape.

Soon, there's a knock at the door—Ms. Dora, my CPS worker, and the advocate from the agency are all waiting to escort me to my new life. I gather my few belongings: a suitcase with just seven outfits and the precious bottle of perfume—crafted by all the love Tiny has to give and distilled into the essence of what's meant to keep us connected.

As they discuss the logistics surrounding Tiny's absence, Ms. Dora catches the worry etched deep in my eyes and mouths, "Where's Tiny?"

I shake my head slowly; the finality of the gesture says it all: She's gone. Understanding the depth of my grief, Ms. Dora whispers, "We'll find her, Tiffany. And we'll make sure he pays."

The CPS worker gently pulls me back to the present. "So, Tiffany, it's time to meet your new family. They've been waiting for you. Are you ready to start your new life?" She asks, her tone soft yet encouraging.

The reality of my new life unfurls before me, hopeful and promising, but the ache for Tiny gnaws at my soul. Clutching the fragrance bottle, I tighten my grip as if I'm holding on to her spirit—understanding that it's a bridge between what was and what could be. I'll find her. I'll bring her into this new life where love isn't perverted and trust isn't laced with fear, where kindness isn't drenched in manipulation, and where being cared for is the norm and love is abundant.

I'm ready to live a normal life. It's a late start, but I'm ready to be a kid.

So…Greer, Georgia, here I come.

Chapter 16

Love at First Sight – Mason

Fourteen Years Old

W e're gonna be brothers! Can you believe it, Mase?" Rafe heartily pats me on the back. His eyes shine excitedly as we stand side by side in front of the mirror.

Today's the day! The beginning of a monumental chapter in our lives. My dad and Rafe's mom are getting married. It took them a while to tie the knot, they began quietly dating when I was ten. Two years later, we moved into our new home together. Year three, Dad took the entire family on a trip to Paris, where he proposed under the twinkling city lights. And here we are in year four – officially starting a blank slate for all of us as a blended family.

"Nope, I still can't believe it," I echo Rafe's sentiment. "You've always been my brother, but today it's official."

With a contagious grin, Rafe drapes his arm around my shoulder. "Yep, I'm officially your big brother!"

I playfully nudge him off. "Chill out, bro. You've only got me by two months."

Bash cuts in from the corner of the room, "It doesn't matter how old you two dummies are, I'm the most mature."

Jay, my ten-year-old brother, twirls into the room. "Don't I look good? Mel's gonna faint when she sees me!" His fun and carefree laughter fills the room.

Jay's first crush would be Mel, of all people! Rafe's curiosity pulls us back to the matter at hand. "Speaking of Mel, where is she?"

Jay grins, proud of his insider knowledge. "When I called her to say good morning, she said they'll be late."

Rafe rolls his eyes but laughs. "Bro, you're such a stalker. Stop drooling over her and get real. You're ten, and she's fourteen."

Undeterred, Jay pops his tuxedo collar. "I might be ten, but I got the mind of a man."

"A man who just stopped peeing the bed a few years ago." Bash adds with a sarcastic grin.

Jay furrows his brows and sneers, "Dang, why you gotta put me on blast like that?"

I burst into laughter. "Your pisscapades ain't a secret, Jay, even Mel knows, so keep dreamin'. But anyway, she messaged me the other night about her new sister. Sounds like she's had it rough but is a cool person. Mel thinks I'll like her. Says she's my type, whatever that means. I'm just glad she's made a friend. I sometimes forget she's even a girl."

"We need some more girls in our lives. And your type means sun-kissed, ocean twilight skin like Nia Long." Jay explains.

Then Rafe adds, "Curly hair."

Bash chimes in, "With lips like Meagan Good."

"And she has to have absolutely zero interest in Mase. I bet ten bucks Mase is gonna fall in love at first sight when he meets Mel's new sister." Jay wagers.

Bash eagerly chimes in. "I need to join in on this bet."

Rafe counters, "Well, who are we betting against because we all know Mase is gonna fall hard and fast. He's a hopeless romantic."

"What? Why would y'all even think that?" I protest, though a part of me wonders if they're right. "I'm fourteen. I haven't even had a girlfriend yet! My only focus is football."

"And music," Rafe adds, rolling his eyes. "You've ignored every 8th grade baddie that's asked you out, yet you're the R&B king. If you burn one more Chris Brown or Neyo CD, I'm gonna lose my mind. Lord, please send Mase his first girlfriend. I'm so sick of love songs, no pun intended."

While we all joke amongst ourselves, our laughter is cut short as the door swings open, revealing the bride and groom.

"Dad! You can't see the bride before the wedding, it's bad luck!" Bash exclaims, half-serious.

Dad laughs in unmistakable joy. "Oh, Bash, you and your superstitions! I'm the luckiest man in the world—four awesome sons and an amazing wife-to-be." He smiles gratefully. His eyes meet Sherri's, and it's clear he believes every word.

Jay darts over to Sherri and hugs her. "Hey, Mom," His voice is filled with genuine affection.

Sherri is the only mother Jay and Bash really know and the only one that I can remember.

"Hey, Son," Sherri returns his embrace, then turns to address us all. "We just wanted to check on y'all. Today's a big day and I know how anxious you boys get."

Sherri's loving warmth fills the room. Then, the mood shifts as she and Dad kneel to our level, their expressions serious yet kind.

"Anyone feeling nervous? I know we've been talking about this day non-stop for nearly a year. But how're y'all feeling? Are you sure you're okay with us getting married?"

"Of course," I quickly respond, as resolute as ever. "We've always been a family. This wedding is just a reminder."

Sherri's smile is warm as she reaches into her beaded bag, pulling out four small, carefully wrapped gifts. She hands one to each of us.

"That's right, Mase. And because we've always been a family, I wanted to give you all a special gift as a reminder." She says thoughtfully.

I unwrap the gift to find a restored wallet-sized picture, one I haven't seen in years. I used to stare at it all the time when I once believed in what wasn't real. It's a snapshot of our families—The Booms, Carters, and Lynns, on the beach. The sun is set behind us, casting an orange glow that seems to highlight each person with a warm embrace. My younger self and Bash are in dad's arms, and Rafe is mid-laugh with his father. But it's the faces in the background that catch my attention. My mother is holding Jay, smiling, her joy immortalized. Beside her, are the Lynns with their twin daughters playing at their feet. On the back of the photos is the shared phrase our families always used to say, 'It's me, you, and the world around us.'

Sherri's voice brings me back, "It's important to remember all the parts of our family, those here and those who are with us in spirit."

Her words flow softly, each one wrapped in the weight of memory and the strength of continuance. She leans closer and gently squeezes my shoulder as she points to my mother in the photo.

"Your mother's love, her kindness—it's a part of you, Mase. And though she's not here physically, her influence, along with the love of Rafe's dad and the goodness of the Lynn twins guide us. What a beautiful family we have."

We come together for a group hug. The connection between us is reinforced not just by her words but by the tangible presence of those we carry in our hearts. I love Sherri Carter, and I'm so grateful to call her my mom.

The picture in my hand is more than a memory; it's a bridge linking past to present, a reminder that every joy and tragedy I experienced at such a young age has shaped me into the young man I'm becoming.

Dad's voice breaks through my reflections. He looks at each of us and tenderly says, "I love you, Sons."

Sherri's eyes gleam with tears that don't quite fall, but Jay's voice halts our deep current of emotion and lightens the mood. "Alright, it's time to get this show on the road! The sooner y'all tie the knot, the sooner we can hit the dance floor!"

As we proceed to line up for the ceremony, my heart is filled with joy. Dad and Sherri stand at the altar and stare into one another's eyes mirroring a reflection of mutual adoration and a shared future.

"Ladies and gentlemen, we're gathered here today to witness the union of Charles Boom and Sherri Carter." The pastor announces, his voice echoing around the decorated backyard of our estate. "Two hearts who found their way to each other through paths paved with both joy and sorrow. Today, they choose to blend their lives together, honoring not only each other but also those they've loved and lost."

"Sherri, with this ring, I give you my heart. I stand here today, humbled by our journey and blessed by our future. You've shown me that from loss can come strength, from sorrow can come joy, and from grief can come a new beginning. I love you and I promise to cherish our family, to honor our past, and to build a future filled with love and laughter."

"Charles, our union is an ode to memories of love past, the warmth of love present, and the promise of love yet to come. I honor the love I carry for you in my heart, the love I share with you, and the love we'll nurture together. Our love has healed the painful wounds of the past, and our family has beautifully mended my broken heart. I promise to love you forever. It's me, you, and the beautiful family around us." She says as she slips the band onto my dad's finger.

"May these rings forever remind you of your commitment to each other, and may your love continue to flourish in the light of understanding and mutual respect. With the power vested in me, Charles Boom, you may now kiss your wife Sherri Carter-Boom." The officiant concludes the ceremony.

As Dad and Sherri seal their vows with a kiss, applause fills the air—cheering for a love both renewed and remembered.

The reception begins on the other side of our estate. The festive air sweeps us up in its tide of laughter and music, pulling everyone into a whirlwind of celebration.

In the midst of celebrating, Aunt Crystal pulls me aside. Her embrace is warm, and she smells of honeysuckle and vanilla, always centering me in a state of peace.

"Mase, we're leaving a bit early tonight," She whispers, her usual sadness tinged with resolve. "There's a new lead on the girls. We're gonna go to Atlanta and do some investigating. It's a long shot, but we have to try."

I nod and take one more inhale of her scent. "I know you'll find them, Aunt Crystal."

She and Uncle Terry share one last round of hugs with everyone, but minutes after they leave, the subtle trail of vanilla still lingers in the air. Suddenly, Mel bursts through the crowd in a whirlwind of apologies and explanations. Her wild energy is a stark contrast to the Lynn's sad goodbye. I turn around with my frustration on full display as I realize she's missed the entire ceremony.

"I already know what you're gonna say, Mase! And I'm sorry! I'm so bummed we missed the wedding, but you know these past few weeks have been a whirlwind—adjusting to our new family dynamic. I promise I'll make it up to you." She pledges with her left hand in the air and her right across her heart.

I roll my eyes and wait in anticipation. "How exactly are you gonna make up for missing your best friend's wedding?"

Mel's expression shifts to mischief. "Oh, Mase! You're so dramatic. It's your *parents'* wedding, not yours. But here's how!" Her excitement is palpable as she steps aside to reveal a familiar face. "I'd like to *formally* introduce you to someone. Mason Boom, meet Tiffany *Nicole* Weathers, my new sister."

The air shifts as the scent of vanilla grows stronger, and the lingering smell that Crystal Lynn left behind fills the space between us.

There she stands—the girl from four years ago, the girl from the church, the girl from the football field, the girl from my distant memories, the girl from the photo at the beach, the girl forever etched in my mind.

"Nicole." Her name quietly forces its way through my lips.

Her expression shifts to one of annoyance as she recognizes me and breaks the silence with the suck of her teeth and scrunches her face in disgust.

"Oh God, not you, again. You're that kid from church a few years back! Mel, is this some kind of prank? You said you wanted to introduce me to my future best friends. Look at how he's staring at me. He gives me the creeps!" She whines.

I should be offended by her reaction. I should be angered by her insults. I should be pissed off that she wants nothing to do with me, but how can I be mad when I'm too captivated by her beauty–deep brown skin perfectly kissed by the sun with curly natural hair that frames her face like a halo. And I think she just might be mean as hell. She's got this alluring aura that draws me in, even when she's pushing me away.

Jay elbows me, pulling me back from my daze. "Look who's drooling now?" He teases with a wide grin.

I clear my throat, try to compose myself, and deepen my voice in mock seriousness, which only makes Mel stifle a laugh.

The air buzzes with nervous excitement as I prepare to introduce myself to Tiffany Nicole Weathers, but my overconfidence takes the reins. "Tiffany Nicole Weathers," I start, puffing out my chest and extending my hand with a flourish. "I'm Mason Boom, future NFL star, the most popular incoming freshman at Greer High, and yes, the most handsome man you'll ever meet. If you ever need anything, just let me know. I'm all you need."

Laughter erupts from my brothers, and my face heats up as embarrassment floods in. *Holy crap. Did I actually say that out loud? Could I be any more ridiculous?*

Mel rolls her eyes and whispers just loud enough for me to hear, "Dang Mase, you're layin' it on thick, don't you think?"

Tiffany's frown turns into a puzzled look, obviously not sure what to make of my over-the-top, embarrassing intro.

"I see you're still the same weirdo from the church pews." She raises an eyebrow, her tone dripping with both amusement and skepticism.

"Weirdo? Well, I guess that's better than creep," I laugh nervously. "But seriously, it's really nice to meet, officially. I mean, isn't it crazy that we're here again, in front of each other? And you still smell…so delicious." I blurt out in my attempt to sound cool.

Damn it, not again! Why can't I just keep it cool?

She immediately recoils and I back away until her expression softens and a hint of a smile tugs at the corners of her mouth, offering me a brief moment of assurance.

"You've gotten weird again, but it's nice to meet you too, Mr. Future NFL Star." She cautiously observes me and then looks for Mel, who's drifted off into the crowd.

Desperate to change the subject, I dive into a torrent of questions. "So, tell me about yourself. Where are you from? What do you like to do for fun? How does it feel to have such a crazy sister? You must have some stories to tell already, huh?"

Suddenly, our fun back and forth stops with Tiffany's sharp head snap. Her entire mood changes.

"My sister?" She calls out frantically. "How do you know Tiny? Don't you dare talk about my sister!" She yells aloud. Her cracked voice attracts the attention of guests.

The atmosphere instantly shifts. An onslaught of tears streams down her face and wash away the cool facade she had previously maintained. My earlier embarrassment is forgotten in the face of her distress. Her trembling hand is tightly clenched against her thigh, her body nearly paralyzed in fear, but I rush to her side.

"Why the hell did I think I could start a new life? I'm not normal. I don't belong here." She cries to herself, completely oblivious to her surroundings.

My brothers' feet are stuck to the floor, but I step closer and closer until my finger cautiously touches her shoulder.

Tiffany jerks away, recoiling as if my touch burns. "Don't touch me!" she snaps, her voice sharp and defensive.

I take a step back, giving her space, but I keep my hands extended—open, patient, and unwavering. I wait, watching the walls around her crack ever so slightly until she trusts me enough to place her guarded, trembling hands in mine.

"Hey, it's okay. Just breath," I assure her, rubbing my thumb over the top of her hands and taking a deep exhale. "You belong here. You're a Greer kid now which means we got you. It's me, you, and the world around us."

Tiffany gasps and lifts her head as her breathing slows. "Where'd you hear that from?"

Before I can explain, Mel reappears out of breath and apologetic as ever. "Oh, no! I'm so sorry, Tiff. I just stepped away for a minute. I didn't mean to leave you alone. I'll never leave you again."

It's as if she's suddenly grounded back to reality and aware of her surroundings.

"Oh, crap!" A disappointed Tiffany mutters under her breath while releasing her hands from mine. "I've barely been in public for twenty minutes, and I embarrassed you already, didn't I, Mel? I embarrassed your entire family. Y'all should just send me back to Atlanta. I tried my hardest to be perfect and happy-go-lucky, but I'm not."

Rafe interrupts with warm, inviting laughter, "Perfect? Trust me when I say we're far from that. Quite frankly, I prefer your mini breakdown over perfect any day. Isn't that right, Mel?"

Mel smiles and nods. "Got that right, Rafe."

Mel hugs Tiffany and says, "I told you these guys are the best. You're one of us now, Tiffany Weathers. You ready to start your new life?"

Tiffany nods. "I am." Then, she surprises me with a gentle gaze and a slight smile. "Thank you, Mason 'Weirdo' Boom."

I return her gratitude with a nod and come to the resolve that I *am* a hopeless romantic, and my brothers were right. I definitely just fell in love at first sight with Tiffany Nicole Weathers.

PART 3

THIRD QUARTER COMEBACKS

Chapter 17

Captains – Tiffany

High School

"Dr. Lee, thank you for seeing me at such short notice...and so early in the morning." I say as I settle into the comforting space of her office.

She greets me with a warm smile, the kind that always puts me at ease. "Well, don't tell anyone, but you're one of my favorites, Tiffany. I've really enjoyed watching you blossom—from a scarred, traumatized girl to an outgoing, confident young woman. So, tell me, what brings you here at six a.m.?"

I hesitate, the words tangling up a bit as I speak. "I—I've developed feelings... strong feelings... for Mason."

Dr. Lee chuckles softly, her voice soothing. "And that scares you, doesn't it?"

My cheeks flush with embarrassment. "It feels silly, and I'm sorry for wasting your time with this."

She leans forward, her expression earnest. "Oh, Tiff, you're not wasting my time at all. It's completely normal to feel apprehensive about these new emotions and even the physical thoughts you might have. Just like it took time for you to understand what a healthy father-daughter relationship looks like with Mr. Baker, it'll take time for you to adjust to what a healthy romantic relationship feels like. Building a sense of safety with others will come gradually. It's okay to like someone as more than just as a friend."

I fidget with the hem of my sleeve, still unsure. "I know, I'm just scared. Tiny trusted Pop and probably every man who offered her love only to be deceived and taken advantage of."

Dr. Lee offers a reassuring smile. "Your feelings are perfectly valid, Tiffany, but her experiences won't necessarily be yours. It's important to set boundaries that make you feel safe. Learning to trust and accept love on your terms doesn't need to be rushed."

"Does this mean I shouldn't be afraid to, you know, *like* like Mase? He's been nothing but kind to me. He's charming, honest, attentive, and makes me laugh. I love watching him play football, and he loves watching me dance. And we go to Beverly Mills Beach whenever we have an off day. I can talk to him about anything, Dr. Lee. And he's... he's really handsome." I admit a little more enthusiastically than intended.

Dr. Lee laughs again. "It sounds like you've got quite the first crush, Tiffany. Mason seems to be a supportive friend and he appreciates you just being you. That doesn't require rushing into anything. Allow yourself to feel appreciated and respected—it's what you deserve. So, yes, it's okay to *like* like him."

Feeling a little lighter, I stand up, ready to face the day. "Thank you, Dr. Lee. I think I needed to hear that."

"You're welcome, Tiffany," she replies warmly. "Now, go to school and enjoy being a teenager. And don't stop journaling!"

Leaving her office, Mr. Baker is waiting for me outside with Mel. Seeing his familiar, caring face, I can't help but hug him. "The session went great. Thank you for everything." I say with a genuine smile, feeling more open and trusting than ever as we head to school.

I've created a new identity for myself here. No one knows I was poor, or my mom was a drug addict. No one knows what happened to my sister. No one even knows I have a sister. Well, Mel does. She was expecting two sisters when I arrived, but she only got one. She got me, and her family has loved me unconditionally, turning my dreams into an *almost* reality.

Now, I can *act* like a normal kid, but not a day goes by when I don't think about Tiny. How she's doing, what she's doing, and where she's been. Aunt Dora visits Greer monthly now, giving me updates on her whereabouts, her recent stint in rehab, her relapse…Aunt Dora's been there for her. I wish I could be too. Then maybe her circumstances would be different; maybe her life would be like mine.

When I was taken in by the Bakers nearly three years ago, it took months to adjust. I mean, who wouldn't struggle? I was nervous, mean, a hard-headed mess, thrown into a household of wealth, warmth, and security. It was everything I ever wanted, but nothing I was ever prepared for.

They loved me through my breakdowns, through my nightmares, angry outbursts, and endless nights of crying Tiny's name. They also loved me through therapy sessions that helped me understand a girl like me *deserves* to be loved, protected, and to feel safe at all times. The Bakers are a family any girl would love to be a part of, and they're the family I'm proud to call my own.

~~~

Team captains are leaders. They're motivators. They're tough yet inspiring. And today, I stand at a threshold I never imagined crossing. Today, I find out if I've been named captain of the Greer High Pipettes. I can't believe it! Who would've thought I'd be able to lead anything, let alone an entire squad of girls but I can, and I hope I will. Because I've worked hard to create my identity. I've worked hard to become normal.

"Tiffany Nicole! You ready for your big day?" Mel's voice cuts through my nerves as we stride towards the auditorium. "You're about to make history! The first 11th grader to be captain of the dance team. You're officially the SHIT!"

Rafe weaves through us with a grin. "Hold on, now! Don't forget about Mase. He's gonna be named captain of the Varsity football team. That's history, too."

Mel tosses a playful look between us. "What a coincidence, huh? Two of the hottest 11th graders, potentially leading the dance and football teams? Sounds like a match made in heaven to me!"

"Absolutely not!" I assert, stepping away from Rafe's casual embrace. "Mase is a player, a borderline stalker, and just plain weird! I'm not interested, and he needs to quit telling everyone I'm off limits."

"But you are…" A deep, familiar voice chimes in from behind us. I know that voice. I know that voice from anywhere, it's Mason.

Okay, pause. I *do* like Mason Boom—despite my best intentions not to. After everything with Tiny, I was convinced I'd never let any guy close to me, but Mason, with his persistence and disarming smile, has managed to wedge himself into my life.

Not only has he worn me down and convinced me he's a good person, but he's also become a great friend. They all have – Melody Baker and the Boom Boys. Everyone has accepted me with open arms, and though it was rough in the beginning, my life has completely changed.

Mason, despite his privileged background, is as humble as they come. He's sweet and mindful, unlike the older boys who used to hit on me and Tiny or the old men who'd lick their lips and wink at us. Well, Mase stares at me but not in a perverted way. He looks at me in admiration rather than desire, which scares the hell out of me because kindness and respect aren't common where I'm from. In fact, I think the Booms are the only boys I've ever felt comfortable around. They offer reassurance that not all men are the same, and perhaps, some can even be trusted.

As we reach the auditorium, Mel's teasing breaks my self-reflection. "Back off, Mase! My sister is only off-limits if she says she is. So, Tiff, are you fair game for these *foine* ass 11th grade boys, or will you allow Mason to claim you for himself?"

Mason catches up with us, and before I can answer, says, "Hey, that's not fair! Of course, Tiff's gonna say the exact opposite of what I want to hear. She keeps playing hard to get."

Our laughter fills the hallway, but my reply is swift and firm. "First of all, I can speak for myself, Mase. And for the record, I don't like anyone, especially you! I like to dance, and that is it. When're you gonna give up the chase, huh?"

"When you stop running, Tiffany Nicole." His response is immediate with a playful wink.

Something about him grinds my gears, but I can't help but smile, even when I don't want to. "Stop saying my middle name all the time!"

I definitely gave myself that middle name. I chose it because it felt right. Nicole feels natural to me, and there's a distorted memory in my head of being called Nicole once. So, when I moved to Greer, the name became a part of my new identity, which, for some reason, excites Mase. That's fine, though; I'll be anyone to him as long as it's not the poor girl from College Park.

"Ugh, stop flirting!" Rafe interrupts.

Mel nods in agreement, then throws a curveball. "Mase, aren't you dating that cheerleader Bree now, anyway?"

The name hits me like a cold splash of water. My head immediately turns as feelings of shock and annoyance rise up within me. "Bree? The senior?! You're dating *her*?" My voice escalates slightly, a mix of surprise and irritation threading through my words.

My mind races—*Fawwwk! My B cups can't compete with Big Titty Bree!* Not that it matters. Not that I care. Because Mase and I are just friends. *Just friends.* But damn, why does he have to look so good in his practice uniform? He looks so…delicious.

Ugh, snap out of it, Tiffany.

Mase catches the frown that I can't quite mask and brushes against me with a playful nudge. "Aww, is the girl who claims she doesn't like me actually jealous?"

"Boy, bye! Ain't nobody thinkin' 'bout you." I wave him off with a dismissive hand. "As a matter of fact, I think you and Bree make a cute couple, the absolute cutest." I add, laying the sarcasm on thick.

Our friends erupt into laughter, even Mase.

"Cute? That word isn't even in your vocabulary, Miss Grumpy-stiltskin." Mel chimes in, always ready to stir the pot. "Can y'all cut the act and just admit how madly in love you are? We don't need all the hot and sexy gazes or riddled language, especially not before our road trip to Atlanta next weekend. No one wants to be suffocated by your sexual tension!"

"Ew!" I shoot back, cringing at the thought. "Don't ever mention me, sex, and Mase in the same sentence, okay?"

Mase rolls his eyes and plays along. "Yup, what she said. Besides, it's my birthday trip, so I've decided to invite Bree. She keeps begging to hang out with us and…" He trails off and glances my way with a mischievous glint in his eye. "I need to show her that there's nothing going on between me and Tiff."

Rafe and Mel burst out laughing. "But there is!" Rafe teases.

As we approach the gym, I put an end to the teasing. "Alright, that's enough, you two. Seriously, there's nothing going on between us. Bree is more than welcome to join us, Mase."

Mase looks taken aback by my firmness. "Really? You sure? If it bothers you, you know I won't bring her. I want you to feel comfortable at all times."

The disappointment in his voice echoes the pang in my heart. Of course, I'd like to enjoy his 17th birthday together – just me, Mase and our closest friends, but this trip to Atlanta is about more than his birthday for me. I have other plans; I'm going to visit Tiny.

I haven't seen my sister in years, and next weekend is the perfect opportunity to reunite with her. I know Aunt Dora's updates are watered down because she only tells me what she thinks I can handle. Tiny's not doing well, and I need to see her with my own eyes.

I force a smile, and my heart sinks with each word I speak. "Yeah, Mase, I'm sure. Bring Bree. It'll be fun." The taste of my lie lingers, but I push through. "She should be there to celebrate with you. After all, it's your birthday, and you should have everyone you care about there."

Mase studies my face, searching for feelings I hope he doesn't find. The intensity of his gaze is almost too much, but I manage to hold his stare.

Finally, he nods, and a slow grin spreads across his face. "Alright then, it's settled. Bree's coming with us. Hey, good luck today. I've got no doubt you're going to make captain. I'll peek inside during my ten-minute break."

I blush. "Thanks, Mase. And I've got no doubt you're gonna be named captain, too. You're Mason Boom, future NFL star, remember?" I tease, recalling the confident way he introduced himself when we first met, which always brings a light moment between us.

His laughter at the memory eases some of the tension, and I feel a brief respite from the emotional chaos swirling inside me.

As he heads off to join Rafe, he glances back and calls out, "Catch you later, Tiff! I look forward to celebrating us tonight, Captain."

The complexity of my emotions about Mason Boom, our friendship, and the impending road trip to Atlanta twirls inside me like a dance routine I've yet to master.

Before I can make sense of it all, Mel loops her arm through mine, giving me a squeeze as we step into the gym. "Inviting Bree? What the heck are you up to, Tiffany Weathers?" She whispers, her voice a soft murmur meant only for me.

"I'll clue you in later, Mel. Let's just focus on practice, okay?"

When we step into the gym, I resolve to focus on practice and hopefully hear my name announced as this year's captain. I want this so bad!

Dance means everything to me. When I moved to Greer, Aunt Dora could no longer be my dance teacher, but Coach Dawson was the next best thing. She trains me in ballet, jazz, tap, and hip hop, but most importantly, she bucks. And she bucks hard! She breathes majorette dance, and so do I.

I settle near the front, ready to warm up then Coach Dawson approaches with an encouraging nod. "You're here early, Tiff. That's exactly what I expect from a leader. You ready for today?"

"Absolutely. I even whipped up a new routine and sent it over last night. Did you get a chance to look at it?" I ask, a mix of eagerness and nerves threading my words.

She gives me a cryptic smile, sparking a flutter of anxiety in my stomach. "Oh, I saw it alright." She responds, her tone unreadable.

A pang of worry hits me. Did I push too hard? It's in my nature to throw my whole self into dance—every beat feels like it courses through my veins, urging me to move and express myself. Dance is how I interpret the world around me, and sometimes, I fear my intensity might be overwhelming.

"Is it terrible?" I ask, my voice teeming with passion while explaining the intricate fusion in my routine. "I was inspired by Southern U's Dancing Dolls—their movements are like poetry. They embody a grace that makes every motion art, particularly in their port de bras and body rolls."

I pause, my hands animated as I describe my dance. "Then there's the raw energy of the Jackson State J-Settes. Their style is bold and sexy, with movements that command attention. It's not just dance; it's an expression, almost a challenge thrown right at the beat of the drum."

Feeling a rush of excitement, I continue, "I tried to weave both styles into one performance. I wanted to capture the Dolls' fluidity and the J-

Settes' boldness. The choreography celebrates the entire spectrum of black majorette dance. Do you think it works, or is it too ambitious? Am I doing too much?"

Coach Dawson's unreadable expression transforms into a smile of approval, igniting a spark of confidence within me. "Tiffany, you've got a fire in you that's rare. Don't ever dampen your flame. Your routine? Yes, it's ambitious, sultry, exhilarating, and buck-tastic. It's going to challenge you and the team in the best ways possible. Ms. Dora said you were special years ago, and you've proven her to be right."

The warmth of her reassurance washes over me, bolstering my confidence. As I tie up my sneakers and get ready to own the dance floor, I can feel a thrum of excitement pulsing through my veins.

"Get warmed up because not only are you going to perform your new routine for your teammates," Coach continues, her voice imbued with a conspiratorial tone that piques my interest. "We're also going to showcase new choreography at homecoming, and after what I just saw, I think your new set would be perfect."

Mel, who's been quietly observing, lets out a surprised gasp. Meanwhile, I'm momentarily speechless with the thrill of the opportunity sinking in. Leading the band and dance team at homecoming isn't just a display of my skill; it's a moment to truly shine and make my mark in front of the entire school. Hell, in front of the entire town! In front of Ms. Dora. And...in front of Mason.

When the doors burst open, the sounds of sneakers squeaking and rhythmic beats fill the gym, and my teammates stream in with chatter echoing off the walls. But the noise dies down almost instantly when Coach claps her hands and calls everyone to attention.

"Welcome to a new school year, Pipettes!" Coach Dawson beams, her eyes sweeping over us with an intensity that fuels my nerves. "Let's cut to the chase. I've got some big news to start off the dance season."

Mel squeezes my hand and then whispers, "Holy crap, Tiff! I think it's happening!" Her excitement is contagious, and my heart pounds against my chest in anticipation.

Is Coach Dawson seriously gonna drop the bomb now?

"And now, the moment you've all been waiting for," Coach Dawson continues, her voice rising above our anxious murmurs. "I'm proud to announce that the captain of The Greer High School Pipettes is none other than Tiffany Weathers!"

My teammates erupt in cheers! Even the senior dancers clap and whistle. Their approval warms me from the inside out as I'm swept into hugs, high fives, and congratulations.

Just a few seconds later, a different kind of commotion catches everyone's attention—the entire football team, led by Mase, charges through the door, whooping and hollering. "That's my girl!" Mase yells to purposely embarrass me.

Ooh, I'm gonna get him back good. Everyone laughs and swoons a little at his public display of support.

Coach Dawson, however, rolls her eyes, though the corners of her lips twitch in amusement. "Mason! Get your team out of my gym and back onto that field! C'mon, out you go." She chides, pointing towards the exit. Then, Mase throws me a wink before following his teammates out.

Once the football team leaves, Coach Dawson turns to me with a serious but supportive expression. "Tiffany, you're captain now. So, take the lead. Get everyone warmed up and stretched."

Practice is intense and invigorating. I lead my team through new routines, feeling every beat and step resonate through me as I proudly build on the legacy of Greer's majorette history.

Afterwards, Mel and I decide to catch the tail end of Mase's practice arriving just in time to hear the head coach announce, "Your new captain is none other than the quarterback who led us to last year's state championship for the first time in 15 years—Mason Boom. Your co-captain, all-time Greer High leading scorer, Rafe Carter-Boom!"

I cheer the loudest and even throw in a "That's my Mase!" His teammates tease him, but his gaze finds mine across the field filled with pride—until Bree, shrieks, "Mase! What the hell?"

Mel bursts into laughter beside me. "You're so wrong for that, girl. You know exactly what you're doing."

"Who me? I'm just cheering on a friend." I try to feign innocence, but Mel doesn't buy it.

On our way home, I find myself thinking about my new life, feeling optimistic and guilty.

"It's strange, you know? Being normal," I confess to Mel as we near our house. "Sometimes, I forget this is all real—that I'm not just pretending. That maybe, just maybe, I can really have this life without it all falling apart."

Mel picks up on my somber tone and glances over with a frown. "You're thinking about Tiny, aren't you?"

I nod. "I feel so shitty for being happy and safe knowing she isn't."

"Hey, why don't we visit her next weekend when we go to Atlanta? We'll see how she's doing. I know Aunt Dora thinks we're too young to know the truth, but sometimes the truth is what we need. Knowing the truth creates change, and maybe we can help change Tiny's life. Mom and Dad said she'll always have a home here with us when she's ready."

I swear the Bakers are a different type of family, one out of a storybook. Their acceptance and pure love are everything me and Tiny need.

"Uh, actually, I was planning to visit by myself. I didn't want to drag you and our friends into my mess."

Mel reaches over to squeeze my hand. "Tiff, we're sisters now. Your past isn't a burden—it's part of what made you who you are. It's part of my life now, too, and our parents. No matter what, I've got your back, no judgment, just love and support."

Gratitude washes over me as we turn into the driveway. The lights inside the house spill out onto the porch, painting it in warm, inviting tones. Mel glances over with her expression, a mix of excitement and curiosity.

"So, you ready for a celebration?" She teases, her eyes twinkling with secrets.

I nod, but my thoughts are still tangled with images of Tiny. We open the car doors and step into the mild evening air, the faint sound of laughter and music greeting us as we approach the front door. When I swing the door open, I'm met with a chorus of *"Surprise!"*

The living room is a riot of color, with balloons bobbing against the ceiling and streamers draped across the walls. In the middle of it all stands my foster parents, Maurice and Callie Baker, along with Aunt Dora, each holding a balloon that reads, "Congratulations, Tiffany!" with their faces filled with pride.

My heart swells, their love and support anchoring the swirling emotions of the day. Maurice steps forward, his usual reserved demeanor replaced by a beaming smile. "As principal of Greer High and as a dad, I want to say we're so proud of you, Tiffany. Congratulations on making captain!"

Callie wraps me in a hug. "You've brought so much joy into this house, Tiffany. We just wanted to celebrate that, celebrate you." She whispers, her voice thick with emotion.

Aunt Dora's tears glisten in her eyes, and she joins the hug. Her presence comforts me, reminding me of all the bridges I've crossed to get here. With every ounce of laughter and each memory of the last few years, the Bakers weave me deeper into the fabric of their family.

As the night winds down, I sneak away to my room to text Mase.

Mase: So...did they go all out for you tonight?

Tiffany: You know it! Balloons, over-the-top dinner, stories about how hard-headed I was when I first came here. Aunt Dora even drove down to see me.

Mase: Lol. Well, you deserve it. I hope they talked about how mean you were too. ;)

Tiffany: Oh hush! You deserved my wrath. You still do. Btw did I get you in trouble with your gf Big Titty Bree?

Mase: LMAO! Yo, Tiff. You really are jealous, huh? She ain't my girl. We're just talking. I'm saving that title for someone else.

Holy crap! Mase is flirting...like flirting, flirting.

Mase: Uh...you gonna ask me who I'm saving that title for? Her name rhymes with Shiffany Micole Tethers.

Why is he like this?!

Tiffany: Mase! Leave me alone. I'll never be your girl. Now go to sleep, Captain.

Mase: FINE! But I'm gonna wear you down one day woman...maybe next weekend when we're alone at my folks lakehouse ;) Goodnight Tiffany Nicole

Tiffany: Goodnight Mason Boom

With that resolve, I drift off to sleep to revel in my dreams with my blessing of a new sister, my best friend, and my little bit of everything in between, Mase.

Chapter 18

Road Trippin' – Tiffany

"**O**h my goodness! It's your first road trip!" Mrs. Sherri exclaims, wrapping Rafe and Mase in a tight hug. She turns to her husband with a nostalgic smile, "Charles, remember ours? All of us were inseparable. Oh, the adventures we had!"

Rafe and Mase laugh. The Boom family is an interesting blend of love born from the flames of tragedy. Maybe that's why I feel so close to them. It reminds me of the flames and loss of my own past.

"Your mom and I grew up in the 80s. We were wild, but you kids have access to all kinds of foolishness. So, don't try it 'cause we got trackers and hidden video cameras…" Mr. Charles says half-joking, half-serious.

"EVERYWHERE," Sherri emphasizes with a pointed look. "And don't go out sticking your nose where it don't belong. Atlanta ain't all big buildings and bright lights. You may think you're tough, but y'all are *suburban* children. You aren't street-smart and don't know anything about the inner city. Don't get got out there!"

Mama Baker chimes in with a lighter touch. "Ahh, Sherri! The kids will be fine! Besides, Aunt Dora's gonna check on them." She turns to us with a sweet expression on her face. "Mel, Tiffany, you girls have fun. No clubs. No alcohol. And no boys! Well, besides the Booms, but not in that way…if that makes sense. And Mel, please remember to take your vitamins. You *need* to take them."

Our parents exchange nervous expressions. They're more anxious about us driving off without them than we are.

"Happy Birthday, Son!" Mr. Boom tries to lighten the mood. "What's that word y'all say nowadays? Turn up!" His attempt at sounding cool falls flat, but his intention doesn't.

Without meaning to interrupt their sentimental moment, I realize we're missing a person. "Hey, Mase, where's Bree?"

Caught off guard, Mase stumbles over his words. "Uh, Bree?"

His dad looks puzzled, "Bree? Who's that?"

"Just one of Mase's flavors of the week," Rafe dismisses with a roll of his eyes.

I can't hide my irritation, recalling how close they seemed. "Seems like more than that from how cozy you two were at your locker yesterday." I retort, folding my arms defensively.

Mase, as if it's just me and him around, gently caresses my cheek. "You know that's not true, Tiff. She was all over me because you came around. She wanted to make you jealous. I uninvited her because of it."

Surprise and relief wash over me. "Really, Mase? Because of me?"

"Uh, are we missing something?" Mrs. Sherri murmurs to Mama Callie.

Mr. Baker throws his hands in the air. "Crap! We're officially old! We can't even recognize when our kids are crushing on each other."

"Yep, a road trip is officially canceled!" Mr. Boom jokes. "I'm not tryna be a granddaddy any time soon."

"Dad!" Mase yells, embarrassed. "We're just friends! Now, stop playin'. Y'all are just procrastinating at this point."

We share one last round of hugs before piling into Mase's BMW to head to Atlanta.

The reality of the adventure hits me—I'm embarking on a road trip, a normal teenage milestone. Well, a normal milestone by Greer's standards. I can't believe I'm going on a road trip. We're just teenagers! Rich Greer kids are used to this but not me. I can't believe this is my life. Beneath the surface, I grapple with disbelief; this normalcy still feels foreign after all I've endured.

Barely ten minutes into the drive, the mood shifts as Rafe amps up the excitement, "Ready to get fucked up this weekend? I'm talkin' 'bout legendary 'Hangover' shit!"

Mel immediately replies, "You know it! Did you get the cards?" She asks Rafe.

Rafe pulls out a set of I.D.s "Yep! Sure did. This weekend is gonna be EPIC!"

"Whoa! Fake I.D.s?" I ask in shock. "Do y'all know how much trouble we're gonna get into? We're gonna get caught!" The sight of my new alias, Nicole Anderson, sends a jolt of anxiety through me. "Nicole! You could've at least chosen a name people don't know me by!"

The thought of jeopardizing my new life terrifies me. The last three years of my life have been nearly perfect. What if my fairy tale comes to an end? What if I go to jail? What if I get tossed on the street? What if I end up like Tiny?

"Uh, oh!" Mase says as he eyes me from the front mirror. "Check out Tiff's face. She's thinking the worst...again"

"Am not!" I rebut. *But I am!* "Listen, I don't come from money and power like y'all. I don't have the luxury to be reckless. Not everyone can live carefree."

The car falls silent for a moment, allowing my insecurities to permeate through my privileged friends minds. Then, with a reassuring smile, Rafe adds, "But you can!"

"He's right," Mel laughs. "You're a Baker now. We do what we want. Dad's the principal, Mom's got serious connections. Not to mention

Sherri's bound for the governor's mansion, and Mr. Boom pretty much decides who goes to jail. We're untouchable. You've got to embrace this life, Tiffany."

I can't help but roll my eyes, attempting to mask the smirk on my face. "You make us sound like spoiled little shits!"

"Relax, Tiff. We appreciate the life we have, but we also know how to have a good time. And so should you. You deserve it. Besides, this weekend is special. It's my birthday, and I'm spending it with my brother, best friend, and the girl of my dreams." Mase's confession comes with a mischievous wink that sends my heart racing.

Mel gasps. "Whoa, Mase! Are you officially putting in your bid to date my sister?!"

Rafe claps his hands, grinning wide. "That's what I'm talking about. Express yourself, bro."

Mase meets my gaze in the rearview mirror. His eyes are soft but intense, and I'm momentarily lost for words until I'm saved only by Rafe's song choice—Pretty Ricky 'Shorty Be Mine'—coming through the speakers.

The laughter that follows lightens the atmosphere, and before we know it, we're pulling up to the Boom's lake house—a masterpiece that looks like it's been lifted straight from HGTV. It's a vacation paradise.

"Whoa! This place looks like it came right out of a magazine!"

"Because it did," Mase replies, a touch of pride in his voice. "Dad bought this as an anniversary gift. Mom had a stack of magazines and worked with a designer to recreate what she liked best. Someday, it'll be a vacation spot for me, my brothers, and our families."

"But until then, it's our bachelor pad." Rafe pops open a bottle of champagne with a flourish. "Toast, anyone?"

"Just one sip, Tiff!" Mel urges, handing me a glass. "I don't understand how you can be the boldest dancer on the floor, but as soon as you step off, you turn into Tiffany the Nun. Let's have some fun! It's a celebration—our first weekend away from the parents, *and* you're back home in Atlanta."

This ain't the Atlanta I'm used to. Nevertheless, I raise my glass and the unfamiliar feeling of liberation tingles through my veins.

"To best friends and family!" Mel announces.

I take a huge gulp, downing it all in one sip. The champagne is strong. It burns and tickles the back of my throat, but I kind of like it! So much so that I pour another glass, and another, then one more.

Mel and I turn on the music and make dance videos while the guys watch football. As the night unfolds with music blaring and laughter echoing through the house, I find myself swept up in the atmosphere, dancing, and drinking champagne without a care in the world. Every now and then, I even throw in a sexy move, or at least I try to, to catch Mason's eye.

After a while, Mel and Rafe head to the hot tub while I flop down next to Mase on the couch.

"You're adorable when you're tipsy, you know that, right?" Mase chuckles while I scoot as close as I possibly can to him.

"I'm not tipsy, Mase!" I slur. "I'm just…tipsy!" I giggle.

Mase wraps an arm around me and pulls me closer. Only the air can fit between us. He takes a deep whiff of my scent and exhales a contented sigh.

"I can never get enough of you, Tiffany Weathers." He admits. "But no more drinking for you. You're a lightweight. A cute lightweight."

I mock salute him. "Aye, aye, captain!" But as the buzz of champagne fades, a sobering thought crosses my mind. "This isn't like me, you know? I never drink. Drinking can be addictive, and Lord knows I got enough addicts in my family–my mama, my sister, hell, I don't think anyone would be surprised if I become one too."

"Sister? Tiff, I didn't know…" Mase's expression shifts to one of surprise and concern.

"Yeah, not many people do." I admit.

"But I want to know. I want to know everything about you. We're friends." He hesitates. "I'd like to think we're *more* than friends."

I sigh and lay my head on his chest. "Until I moved here, every man I've ever met was vile. I'm still learning to trust again, Mase. Learning not to instinctively believe men have ulterior motives. Just bear with me a little longer, okay?"

Mase kisses my forehead, then switches the football game to one of our favorite movies, Brown Sugar.

As I drift off to sleep in his arms, he whispers, "I'll wait for you, Tiffany Nicole. I'll wait for as long as I have to because you're worth it."

~ ~ ~

Saturday morning hits me like a freight train—my head throbs with the echoes of last night's laughter and champagne. I don't even remember getting in bed. After I brush my teeth, I tie my curls up in a bun and ease my way into the busy kitchen mid-conversation.

"I don't know," Mase frets, his brow furrowed in genuine concern. "UGA is great and all, but I'd most likely be second string QB until Jackson Sands graduates. Not to mention, I'll barely see any of my friends."

"You mean you'll barely see Tiff." Mel's voice floats in, laced with a tease, as she saunters out of the room with a smirk.

I can't help but laugh, rubbing my temples. "Mase, if you're aiming for the NFL then UGA is your golden ticket. Seriously, just commit. Who in their right mind would turn down a full ride to the best football school in the country?"

"Me. For the right reasons. For the right person." He caresses my hand while his intense gaze seers through me. His words linger in the air, his fingertip tracing idle circles on the back of my hand.

"What's that yummy smell?" I ask, my stomach rumbling in anticipation.

Mase grins and heads towards the oven to pull out a tray of biscuits. "It's our Uncle Terry's homemade biscuits." He announces with a proud grin. He carefully tears off a small piece and blows to cool it down.

Watching him, I can't help but admire how the morning light catches his smile—how effortlessly handsome he looks all the time.

"Open up." He says, his voice warm. The buttery richness explodes with flavor as Mase feeds me the biscuit, and I moan aloud at the taste.

"Hold up, uncle?" I ask, pausing mid-chew.

Rafe leans against the counter, joining the conversation. "We aren't related by blood. They're like family, though. Our parents grew up together—been through it all."

Rafe's voice fades as he gets lost in his thoughts. He's the joy of the group but not right now–not as he thinks about the death of his biological father and friends.

I squeeze his hand. "Why don't they ever visit Greer? Why don't y'all ever talk about them?" I probe further.

Mase's expression darkens. "Living in a town where people know the truth but won't tell you? They'd just be relieving their pain every day, especially since they still believe the girls are alive. There's a void still inside them. It was in me, too, until a few years ago."

I lean in. "What happened a few years ago?"

Mase, with a serious expression, says, "I met a mysterious girl who got fostered by a dope ass family in town. She not only filled the void in my heart but all I felt was missing was found."

Rafe and Mel swoon, but I'm caught off guard by his admission. "Hold on, you talkin' bout me? You're so weird, Mase." I try to mask my melted heart with mock rejection.

"You know you feel it, Tiff. Our connection is undeniable."

"Ugh, teenage hormones. Get a room, you two. This is a birthday weekend, not a freakin' weekend." Rafe breaks the tension with humor.

"Crap, your birthday! I almost forgot!" Caught up in the moment, I remember why today is special. I dash to my suitcase and pull out a carefully wrapped gift. "Happy Birthday, Mase!" It isn't much, but it's genuine—it's my way of expressing myself as he so often does with his words.

"Um, it's two patches I designed of a football player and a dancer," I explain while he quietly reads the stitched inscription, "It's me, you, and the world around us."

Nervous as all get out, I hold my breath and wait for him to speak. His silence lasts longer than expected so I fill the space with rambling.

"I know it's not anything expensive or fancy, but it's just my way of assuring you that a void was filled within me too." Still, no response. "Do– Do you like it?"

Finally, he flashes a tender smile, then pulls me closer and wraps me in his big arms. "I love it, Tiff. I'm gonna get it sewn onto every jersey I ever wear. It'll always be me, you, and the world around us."

I think he gets it. I think he understands that I'm learning to trust my heart and accept love when it's pure and real.

After breakfast, we all get changed and go into town. The plan is for Mel and me to shop for a sexy club dress while the guys go the movies. However, I need to figure out a way to find Tiny.

"Alright, let's meet back here in two hours." Mel instructs as we head out.

Rafe, too distracted by his phone, dismisses us with a wave. "Don't worry about us. We're gonna be busy picking up girls, anyway."

Mase laughs but catches my eye. "Don't listen to him. That's definitely not happening."

Mel laughs. "Of course, it isn't 'cause Rafe ain't got no game."

As soon as the guys enter the theater, Mel dangles Mase's car keys in front of my face. "Ready for Operation Find Tiny?" She smiles.

"Oh, Mel, you're seriously somethin' else!" I hug her and wrap my arms tight around her neck.

"I'd do anything for you, Sis. I've been waiting to meet my other sister, so let's go find her."

Mel and I head down 75 South, a whopping thirty-minute drive. We drive all around town looking for Tiny–Greenbriar Mall, Cascade Skating Rank, Old National Highway, and Hapeville. We check every corner, but Tiny's nowhere to be found. So, we go to the one place where we know we'll get some answers.

"Aunt Dora! Open up!" We say in unison, banging on her door.

Mel cautiously looks around the neighborhood. It's obvious she's never stepped foot in the hood before.

"Girl, it's broad daylight. Ain't nobody 'bout to rob you!" I tease.

She sighs in embarrassment. "Don't make me seem like I'm out of touch. I'm just – out of my element, that's all. Our parents were right. I don't know anything 'bout the hood." Mel feels ashamed. Her cheeks redden, but I can't help but laugh.

Aunt Dora's door swings open, and there she stands, not the least bit surprised by our appearance on her doorstep. "Well, I've been waiting for you two hard-headed girls to stop by. I don't know why Callie thought I was gonna drive my hind parts all the way to some lake. Black people don't go to no lakes. Now, what do y'all want?"

"Aunt Dora, why do you live here and not in some big house out in the suburbs like we do? You're rich, aren't you? Mama said you paid her college tuition." Mel asks.

I'm taken aback by her revelation. "Rich? Aunt Dora, let me find out you could've moved me and Tiny away from this place a decade ago! What the heck?"

"Oh, hush, child," Aunt Dora chides gently but firmly. "My dance studio is here. We were hit hard back in the 80s and 90s, but the community is coming back together. And I ain't going nowhere. All my money goes back into the neighborhood." She pauses, eyeing us both. "Now, I assume y'all came lookin' for Tiny, huh?"

I nod, swallowing the lump in my throat. "Just shoot it to me straight, Aunt Dora. Where is she? I need to see her. It's time to bring her home where she belongs."

With a soft expression, Aunt Dora sighs. "Oh, you girls are so sweet and naïve. Why don't you just enjoy being teenagers? Tiny ain't goin' nowhere with y'all. She–" She starts, but I cut her off, my irritation spiking.

"Is she okay? Is she locked up again? Is she in rehab? Is she still trickin'? Is she with *him?*" My frantic questions tumble out.

Aunt Dora relents under my barrage of questions. "I don't have many answers, Tiffany. The last I saw Tiny was a few months back when I picked her up from county jail. Me and Mrs. Wilkins brought her here to my house. We laid out a plan for her to get her G.E.D. and even had a job interview lined up, but after a few days, she was antsy and lookin' out my window too much. After I fussed at her for missing her NA appointment, she pushed me down and stole my wallet. My hip's been sore ever since. I know she's been through hell, but I gotta look out for me, too. Mr. and Mrs. Wilkins found her strung out on the street, then dropped her off to a women's shelter." She hesitates, her voice cracking slightly. "I wanted her to stay with me, but I'm getting too old, Tiff. I can't have a drug addict and the trouble they bring in my house—it's too dangerous."

We nod, understanding.

"Word on the street is that Tiny hangs out at a club called Lure," Aunt Dora continues. "It's some fancy schmancy nightclub where all the celebrities, ballers, and big execs go. It's 18 and over, so I better not find out y'all tried to get in."

Mel and I exchange an innocent look and agree, but Aunt Dora's skeptical. "Umm hmm. Alright, y'all. Get on out of here and enjoy the rest of your weekend."

Mel and I drive back to the lake house, grinning at each other. She smirks and says with a playful tone, "Club Lure, here we come!"

Chapter 19

In the Club – Tiffany

"I'm used to wearing leotards and shimmery get-ups when I'm performing at school. What I'm not used to wearing are skin-tight dresses that mold to my curves like plaster and four-inch heels that give the illusion that I'm some leggy model. I'd like to think my style is more vintage tomboy mixed with a dash of femininity, but this is giving something more. Something darker, risqué, and something all too familiar; I look exactly like Tiny.

Nevertheless, my brown skin glows under the room's soft lighting, and the smell of my vanilla fragrance permeates the atmosphere. Mel pinned my curls up so elegantly, and my makeup has added years to my teenage face. The mirror reflects a version of me that's uncomfortably mature, a stark reminder of Tiny being forced to live a harsh life way too young, way too fast.

"Tonight, we have fun, but most importantly, we find your sister." Mel reassures me, her voice firm yet kind.

She knows exactly what to say when I get lost in my fear and worry. I must admit, I lost an amazing sister in Tiny years ago when Pop stole her life away, but I've gained Mel, who almost seems too perfect to be real.

Stepping out of the room, I'm caught off guard by Mase, standing right there, dressed in Gucci pants and Mr. Boom's Rolex, eyes wide with admiration.

"Wow, Tiff, you look..." Mase stammers. "You smell…" He inhales. "You're…perfect."

His compliment leaves me speechless, and my heart uncontrollably flutters. I'm as in awe with him as he is with me. Mason Boom is the finest boy I've ever seen. He extends his hand to me, and we head to Club Lure, my stomach churning with nerves. At the door, I hand over our fake I.D.s, trembling.

The bouncer looks back and forth between our cards and faces. Then, he glides his tongue over his teeth and smirks, looking me and Mel up and down like a piece of well-done steak.

His lingering gaze makes my skin crawl. "Take a picture, it'll last longer, creep."

Mel laughs beside me and then whispers. "Tiff, just smile and be nice!"

"Being nice will get you into trouble out here. Be firm."

The bouncer chuckles under his breath and shakes his head but slips VIP bracelets onto our wrists and announces, "Fresh baddies comin' up! We got a feisty one, too!"

Ugh, douche. My discomfort grows, but Mel's excitement is stamped all over her face. Inside, the club's vibrant energy buzzes around us, a stark contrast to the unease knotting in my stomach. Tonight, I'm out of my element, but for Tiny, I'd navigate any world, including hers.

There are hundreds of people here, men and women, who are on the prowl. College students looking to get away from the stress of schoolwork. Pro athletes are ready to be praised, and wealthy businessmen are looking to flash their money. Tiny's gotta be somewhere in the mix, but it's hard to tell amongst the hundreds of people who all want to be lured into any other world outside of their reality—even Mase, who grabs my hand and leads me to the dance floor.

"We're gonna go get drinks!" I hear Mel and Rafe's faint voices in the background, but my attention is solely on Mase.

"Dance with me." He says.

If we were back at home, I'd immediately push him away, but this isn't reality, so I'm willing to engage in the fantasy of following my heart's desire.

I wrap my arms around his neck, and we dance like grown folks. For a moment, I get so consumed in his presence that I forget the reason why I'm here.

"Tiff," Mase whispers. "So, you're telling me you want me to go to UGA and give all this up?"

I giggle. "Mase, I want you to be happy."

"Well, if you really want me to be happy, then you'll be my girlfriend."

I stop dancing, and we look each other in the eyes. Mase has asked me to be his girl a million times over but never with this level of earnestness in his voice. And never with this amount of seriousness on his face.

I want to say yes. I want my first boyfriend. I want Mase, but I don't want him to know the damaged parts of me.

"We can't. We're too busy. We'll distract each other, and we always butt heads. We're just friends!" By the end of my rant, I'm panting and hoping I've convinced Mase to abandon the idea of us being together.

Instead, he cups my face, his thumb gently brushing across my cheek. Then, he lifts my hands—once bruised and now rough with calluses—and soothes them with a soft kiss.

"We're more than friends, Tiffany Nicole. And I'm standing here in front of you asking you to be mine because I know we're right for each other. I know we're meant to be together." His gaze holds mine, unwavering and sure, and every word is weighted with an intensity that's hard to deny.

My heart races, and a part of me—the part that's been longing to be with him—wants to leap forward.

"Mase, it's not that simple." I murmur, my voice a blend of longing and fear.

He smiles softly, still cupping my face gently. "I know you've dealt with pain. Even through your gorgeous smile, I know you're still hurting. I want to know it all. I want to help you through it all. And I want to be there when the pain goes away. I want to be yours and yours only. Tell me you want the same."

In the midst of my protest, I attempt to pull away, but the music changes, a slower, more intimate song. Mase pulls me closer, and for a moment, the club's noise fades, and the flashing lights blur into the background.

His whisper tickles my ear. "Let me be a part of your healing, not just a bystander. We're young, but I know how to love. Let me love you, Tiff."

As I look into his eyes, seeing the honesty and vulnerability, I realize that maybe, just maybe, I can let Mase in. Maybe his love will overshadow the trauma that has suffocated me for so long.

The beat of the song deepens, matching the pulse in my veins. Mase's grip tightens, and I feel the barriers within me start to crumble until I finally lean into his embrace, allowing the music and his presence to cocoon me from my wild thoughts. "Okay." I whisper back.

His smile broadens, lighting up his features. "Okay, what?" He slightly pulls back, looking deep into my eyes as if he's trying to communicate without saying another word.

My apprehension transforms into a slow smile. "Okay, Mason Boom. I'll be your girlfriend!"

Mason's eyes light up, and before I know it, he scoops me up and swings me around in a dizzying twirl. Laughter bubbles up from my throat. When he finally sets me down, my heart races from the feeling of pure contentment, anxiousness, and love.

"Okay, boyfriend," I say, my voice a mix of boldness and nerves. "Are you going to give me my first kiss?"

My question catches him off guard, and his smile falters for a split second as he processes my request.

"Of course," He whispers. "I'll be your first kiss. I'll be your first everything, Tiffany."

"But I'm not *your* first everything." I chuckle.

Mason rubs his thumb across his lips and then looks directly into my eyes. "You may not be my first kiss or first girlfriend, but you're definitely my first love and the only girl I want to spend forever with." His voice is thick with sincerity and passion, solidifying his words as a promise.

Then, in the swirling chaos of the club, Mason leans in. The world slows down, the noise fades, and all I can see are his brown eyes. His lips meet mine in a sweet kiss that seals his vow. It's tender, careful, and passionate. It's everything I imagined it would be. It's perfect—a kiss that's not just a mere meeting of lips but a connection that conveys all the words we've left unspoken and all the promises we're yet to keep. As our kiss deepens, I feel a warmth that melts away the last remnants of doubt and fear clinging to my heart. Though I've known Mase for just a few years, I feel like I've known him my entire life. I want to experience the way he makes me feel for the rest of my life.

The euphoria from Mason's kiss evaporates as quickly as it arrived when the most stunning woman I've ever seen enters the club. It's Tiny. She looks completely different—healthy, wealthy, safe, and happy. This is the girl Ms. Dora said was strung out on drugs?

Mase notices the shift in my gaze, and soon, Mel and Rafe gather around. Everyone waits for me to explain.

"Damn, who is she?" Rafe blurts out. He squints, "Hey, y'all kind of look alike, except she's ten times finer."

Mel playfully elbows him. "And you aren't fine enough to get either one." Her expression softens as she turns to me, "Is that her, Tiff? Is she—"

"My sister." I manage through the tears that trickle down my face. "That's Tiny. That's my sister."

"Sister? You have a sister?" Rafe echoes.

My thoughts overpower Rafe's voice. I need to see Tiny. I need her to see me. I need to be complete again, with her by my side. Ignoring the knot of emotions welling inside me, I push through the crowd. Despite her being just across the room, she feels worlds away. Every step feels like a mile, and my heart races as I try to bridge the distance between our past and my hopes for our future.

"Tiny," I scream to no avail against the thumping music. "Tiny Weathers!" I try one more time then, as if she faintly heard a whisper, she looks into the crowd but doesn't see me. She trudges up the VIP stairs with an older man who has his hand on the nape of her back.

Mel yells, "Tiff, the bracelet!" Then flashes the VIP bracelet the bouncer gave us. I clutch the bracelet around my wrist and dash through the crowd with a burst of desperation and adrenaline.

I had no idea Mase was trailing behind me until he calls out, "Tiff, wait!" Mel and Rafe are also right on my heels.

Reaching the base of the stairs, I flash the bracelet at the guard, who steps aside and lets Mel and me through with a nod. However, the guys are stopped immediately.

"No bracelet. No entry." He declares stoically.

"Do you know who our parents are? I'm sure you've seen DA Boom and Sherri Carter-Boom, the future governor, on your TV screen. I'd hate for her to make a call to the mayor about rumors of illegal activity taking place. Happy to keep my mouth shut if you just let us through."

With a grumble, the guard steps aside, muttering under his breath, as he opens the rope allowing Rafe and Mase to enter.

The dimly lit lounge spreads out like a world of its own, bathed with colorful lights that cast long shadows across the faces of Atlanta's elite.

"I'm starting to think this was a bad idea." Mel says while pointing out the lines of cocaine on each VIP table.

"I know addicts, Mel. You saw Tiny. Does she look like an addict?" I dismiss her concern. "There she is!" I announce, pointing at Tiny, who's sitting at the far side of the room, surrounded by three men who can't keep their hands off her.

"Uh, I think we should leave." Mase suggests.

"Tiny!" I yell, waving my hand in the air. She looks towards me with squinted eyes. Her initial expression is confusion, then shock as she finally recognizes me.

Tiny playfully slaps the two men's hands away from her body, then gets up and quickly paces over to me. I can't tell whether she's excited, disappointed, or angry to see me. Either way, I feel myself coming full circle.

Tiny's energy captivates everyone as she strides toward us. Her laughter, mixed with tears, fills the space between us as she envelops me in a tight hug.

"Tiffany! What the hell?" Her voice quivers with emotion. "What are you doing here? How'd you find me? Oh my God, you look so good, little sis!"

I've imagined this reunion countless times, playing out different scenarios in my mind, but now that it's happening, I'm overwhelmed.

All I manage to say is a timid, "Hi."

We both break into laughter, the kind that heals old wounds, as we wipe away our tears. Standing there, wrapped in her familiar scent, I feel a restoration of something I feared was lost and could never be found.

When Tiny releases me from her embrace, her gaze sweeps over to my friends, who've been standing awkwardly on the sidelines. I forgot they were even here. Tiny has that effect on me–to believe that it's just me, her, and the world around us.

"And these must be your friends. Have y'all been taking care of my sister?" Her voice is playful yet pointed.

There's a stark contrast between the Tiny of my memories and this vibrant woman. She's happy, just like me. We finally got out of the miserable life Mama and Pop gave us. It's a joy to see her so full of life and so far removed from the past.

Rafe is dang near drooling, while Mel stands there, shocked and silent. Mase, on the other hand, stays cautious—that's just the protective friend in him. Well, *boyfriend* now.

Clearing my throat to break the momentary pause, I gesture towards my friends. "Guys, introduce yourselves."

Mel, seizing the moment as Tiny extends a friendly hand, envelops her in a bear hug that nearly lifts her off her feet. "I can't believe I have two sisters now! You're everything Tiffany described and more. You're perfect, big sis!"

Tiny hugs her back and then chuckles. "And you must be Melody Baker. Ms. Dora told me so much about you. I love your energy. I'll have whatever happy pills you're on."

Mel's eyes go wide. Her expression goes from joy to embarrassment. "I don't take any medication; they're just vitamins!" She hastily clarifies, her tone edged with alarm.

"Whatever you say, Mel. Your secret's safe with me." Tiny winks.

Rafe steps in and drapes an arm around her to ease Mel's discomfort.

I gesture towards Rafe. "This is Rafe" Tiny takes his hand, shaking it with a firm grip.

Then she turns to Mase with a knowing smile, "And you, you must be..."

"Mason Boom. I'm—"

"The future of the NFL. The Golden Boy of the South. *And*, let me guess, my sister's first boyfriend." She flashes a mischievous smile.

Mase and I exchange a look, and Tiny chuckles. "I have a knack for reading people. And I can smell young love from across the room."

Finding comfort in Mase's familiarity, I weave my fingers through his. "We just made it official tonight." I confess, the warmth of the moment coloring my cheeks.

Tiny observes us with a nod of approval. Her simple acknowledgment sends a wave of happiness through me.

"We'll give you two a moment," Mel offers, nodding towards Mase and Rafe. "Let's grab a drink from the bar."

As Mel leads them away, Tiny and I settle into a tall round table nearby. Despite being only a year older, Tiny exudes a maturity and presence that almost demands I straighten up and mirror her poise. She glances back, signaling to the older men behind her that she'll return soon. Their expressions are a mix of annoyance and anger.

Tiny manages a weak smile as she dismisses them, her laughter is a practiced art, almost second nature. But the longer I watch her, the clearer she becomes to me.

The glitz of the nightclub can't mask the exhaustion in her eyes—a silent testimony to countless days and nights spent trying to numb her pain. But I can help her. I can turn the façade she's hiding behind into something real. I can protect her now like how she once protected me.

I reach for her hand, "Tiny, come back to Greer with me. We can start fresh. You don't have to put on a show anymore. It's everything we thought it'd be. You'll be loved, genuinely loved, the right way."

Her smile fades, and a hardened, almost cynical laugh escapes through her pursed lips. "Greer? Tiff, that's your happy ending, not mine. You think I can just walk away from all this?" She gestures to the chaos around us, her glamorous façade barely concealing the prison it's become.

"Yes, 'cause it's not just me anymore. We won't be alone. Mel, Rafe, Mase—they're family now. And the Bakers. They love me, and they'll love you the same."

Tiny shakes her head, pulling her hand away. "Love? If you haven't noticed, I'm not very easy to love. Besides, Pop... he's not just going to let me walk away. The last time I tried, I ended up worse off. *You* think this is bad, but I don't. I'm nothing without him." Her voice breaks, a whisper of vulnerability showing through. "This is nothing compared to where I've been."

My heart aches as I see the fear lurking behind her gaze. "We're not kids anymore, Tiny. I'm not letting you suffer alone. I've got connections. The Booms will put Pop away for good. They could even find Mama and arrest her if we want. I can protect you now."

She scoffs, her laughter tinged with bitterness. "Protect me? This ain't no fairy tale. This is the real world, Tiffany. Ain't nobody give a damn 'bout no middle school educated hoe with a rap sheet."

The tension between us thickens, her refusal intertwining with my desperation. "I'm not asking you to believe in fairy tales, Tiny. I'm asking you to believe in me, in the chance for a better life. I can finally help you just like you've always helped me."

Her eyes soften, and for a moment, it seems like she might relent. But then she stiffens, and a mask of contentment slides back over her face. "I really gotta go, Tiff. They're waiting. And you... you need to go enjoy that beautiful life of yours. Forget about me. We're just too different now."

On the brink of tears, I beg her once more. "We'll always be the same. We share the same dreams, remember? Come with me. Life will be so much better for you. We'll be together. Please, Tiny. Please." My tears blur my vision, and my pleas evoke a waterfall down her face.

She sniffles and searches through her clutch for something to clean herself up. She doesn't bother to acknowledge the drugs falling out of her bag, but she does observe the small fragrance bottle, which makes her cry even harder.

"Broken dreams—that's all my life's ever been. Here," she reaches out. "Take this bottle, I'm sure you're running out."

She hands me her signature fragrance, which I'm sure is a painful reminder of when she once believed she had a chance at a normal life.

"Tiny, at least give me your number. I'll call you every day. I'll text you every minute. We can arrange to see one another on weekends. Please?" I plead, my voice almost lost in the cacophony.

She hesitates, "Tiff, I can't. I just...can't." Her voice is a whisper, defeated and fearful.

"Why not?" I press, my desperation mounting. "Not even a number? Please, why don't you want me in your life?"

Tiny shakes her head and releases a rage-filled scream that forces me to slightly back away. "Because you're finally safe! Okay?" Her frustration garners the attention of nearly everyone on the balcony. "You may have been damaged, but I'm destroyed. You can be fixed, but I can't. Now, please, go and be happy. Be loved. And stay safe. My job is done. And I'm done with you. So, please, leave me alone!"

Her words cut deep, and her rejection feels like a door slamming shut on a future I envisioned for us together. I hastily scribble my number on a napkin and push it towards her. "You deserve to be safe, happy, and loved, too."

She picks up the napkin, her fingers trembling slightly as she wipes away a tear. With a final, heart-wrenching hug, she turns and walks back to her seat, leaving me standing in my broken-hearted misery.

When we were kids, Tiny was my shield. She protected me and preserved my innocence while having hers taken away. The realization of lost years hits me. While I've been sheltered and nurtured into a life of safety and love, Tiny's been out here, weathering storm after storm alone. Guilt claws at my conscience. The fact that Tiny might never know the safety and peace I've found feels like a betrayal. I'm here, on the other side of suffering, while she continues to exist within its grasp.

Mase pulls me back from my thoughts. His presence is my silent strength as he gently wipes the tears from my eyes. I bury my face in his chest, seeking refuge in his warmth. He doesn't press for an explanation, and I don't volunteer one. His quiet support is my anchor as we leave the club and head back to the lake house.

In the sanctuary of the bathroom, I let the shower's hot stream mingle with my tears. As I later lie in bed wrapped in desolation, Mase knocks softly on the door.

"Just checking in. You okay?" I pat the space next to me, and as he settles beside me, I lean into his embrace.

It's time Mase knows where I came from. The truth about who I am and the things Tiny and I endured. As I speak, a weight seems to lift from my shoulders, and a determined resolve anchors within me. I refuse to let go of the hope that one day, I'll give Tiny safety, happiness, and love because if anyone deserves it, she does.

"So, do you pity me? Do you think any less of me? Do you see me differently now?"

Mase's eyes lock with mine, his response immediate. "Of course, I see you differently, Tiff. I see you for the strong, caring person you are, which only makes me admire you more. I'm never gonna leave you, and as far I'm concerned, your mission to help your sister is mine now, too. I love you, Tiffany Weathers."

His love washes over me, uncovering the truth I somehow knew from the moment we met. "I love you, too, Mason Boom."

Chapter 20

Senior Year – Mason

"You're in high school, Mase! You're not in love!" Mom insists while flipping pancakes.

"Aww, c'mon, Sherri. The kids have been together for over a year now." Dad interjects, offering me a supportive wink across the breakfast table.

"See! Dad gets it!" I exclaim, exchanging a conspiratorial grin with Rafe.

"Ma, didn't you fall in love with my dad in high school?" Rafe teases, leaning back in his chair with a smirk.

Mom pauses, the spatula frozen mid-air as she searches for a reply. "That was different!"

Dad chuckles. "How so, exactly? I'd get in trouble for breaking curfew every night with Tandy. And you and Rafe Sr. dressed up as a bride and groom for Halloween." He reminisces with a twinkle in his eye as he teases her.

Laughter erupts around the table. "Hmm, hypocrisy much, mom?" I challenge, playfully raising an eyebrow.

"Charles!" Mom exclaims, swatting at Dad with her dishtowel before turning her attention back to the stove. "All I'm saying is, Mase and Tiffany are so inseparable that he's making life-changing decisions based on their relationship rather than what's best for him."

Dad sighs and sets his coffee cup down on the table. "Your mom's got a point, Son. You should've committed to UGA months ago. What's going on?"

I scramble for an excuse, anything to avoid the truth that would solidify my mom's worries. "I'm just taking my time, that's all. Why rush to commit if I'm gonna be second or third string? I'd rather attend a school where I have a chance at starting."

"He's waiting on Tiffany to receive her dance scholarship. He's going wherever she's going." My brother Bash casually reveals with a mischievous grin.

"Bruh! Did you really just snitch on him?" Jay groans, throwing a balled-up paper towel at Bash. "I know not to tell you nothin'."

"Dang, Bash. Just couldn't help yourself, huh?" I shake my head, more amused than annoyed.

"Okay, boys, that's enough!" Mom grabs her purse and heads for the door. "Charles, please talk some sense into him. I have to head out. I've got the CNN interview this morning and then MoneyTalks this afternoon. I better not get another call about girls fighting over you, Jay. Bash, please don't fight anyone today. And Mase, no more PDA in the hall with Tiff, please. And dang it, Rafe, you better not name-drop me again as an excuse to get out of class. You better be glad Mr. Baker's the principal, or else you'd be expelled by now. I'm the governor now. I need y'all to behave."

Dad supports Mom with a stern nod. "That's right, boys. You heard your mama."

"You too, Charles!" Mom adds with a grin.

Dad looks stunned. "Huh, what'd I do?"

Mom places her hand on her hip and then squints her eyes. "I need you to stop commenting on every picture you see of me on social media! No more heart emojis, okay?" She throws a meaningful glance at us.

Dad sighs. "Fine, no more emojis. There's just somethin' about seeing you in a pantsuit that turns me on. Ooh, and don't get me started on your knee-length dresses."

My brothers and I laugh while mom struggles to hold hers in. "You see? This is where the boys get it from. Have a good day. I love y'all! Oh, and Mase, make the right choice!"

As soon as Mom leaves, I turn to Dad. "Alright, be real with me. I know you loved my mom, and I know you love Sherri with all your heart. What would you do if you were me? What would you do for the woman you loved?"

Dad's expression turns thoughtful, his eyes reflect pride and concern. "Son, your future is important. You need to focus. You're the most talked about high school recruit in the nation, and it's time to make a choice. You understand?"

I nod in disappointment. "Yes, sir. I understand."

Then a slow smile creeps on his face. "*But*, to answer your question, if I were you, I'd follow the woman I love to the ends of the earth because the right choice is the choice that makes you happy." He winks.

"Thanks, Dad. I knew you'd understand."

I've always admired the way my dad treats the women in his life. From the bits I remember about my birth mom, he didn't just love her; he adored her, respected her, and valued her. With my stepmom, Sherri, he's just as devoted. It's not just the big gestures but the everyday acts of kindness that really show his love. He cooks her favorite meals, calls her out of the blue just to hear her voice, sneaks up and wraps his arms around her, and always makes sure her bath is ready after a long day. *"My priorities are God, my wife, the kids, then everything else."* He doesn't just say it, he lives it. That's how I want to be with Tiffany—always loving her completely, wholly, and unconditionally.

～～～

During lunch period, I review one scholarship offer after the next until the abrupt noise of trays landing on the table startles me back to reality. Rafe, Mel, and Tiffany completely break my focus. Tiff, looking fine as hell in my letterman jacket, slides onto my lap and presses a sweet kiss to my cheek, sending a ripple of warmth through me.

"So, have you decided what school you're going to yet?" She probes.

"I don't know, have you?"

Flashing a victorious smile, she pulls out an envelope emblazoned with Spelman's crest. "As a matter of fact...," She says, handing it to me. I quickly scan the letter, and my heart swells with pride.

"We are pleased to inform you that you have been accepted..." My voice trails off, and I pull her closer into the warmth of my chest. "I'm so proud of you, Tiff," I whisper in her ear.

Her happiness is infectious. "Thanks, Babe. I'm so excited! The dance coach has high expectations, so I just hope I can bring it. Going to college is a dream come true! But enough about me; you've got every SEC school knocking on your door, and signing day is less than a month away. You've got to make a choice, Mase."

"Easy. My choice is you. I'll follow you to the ends of the earth." I say without hesitation, then she excitedly wraps her arms tightly around my neck.

"You know your parents are gonna blame me, right?" She half-jokes.

"Mom will come around," I assert. "I'm going to officially tell her I'm joining Rafe at Morehouse in a few weeks." I lean in, lowering my voice to a husky whisper. "I can't wait to watch you dance for me on the field in your uniform. Every football player needs his dancer."

Our exchange culminates in a passionate kiss right in the middle of the lunchroom, drawing playful jeers and whistles from our classmates. No one can tell me I'm not the luckiest guy in the world.

"Isn't that somethin'? We're all heading to Atlanta! Are y'all ready?" An excited Mel chimes in.

"Hell, yeah!" Rafe exclaims. "Especially with my favorite quarterback throwing the ball to me on the field. I'm gonna be head down scoring, head down in my studies, and head down in somethin' else, if you know what I mean."

"Boy, ain't nobody givin' you the time of day," Mel says before turning her attention to Tiff. "What about you, Tiff? Are *you* ready to go back to Atlanta?"

"I'm fine." She insists, though her voice lacks conviction, and her eyes flicker with fear.

"You know you don't have to *act* around us anymore. We're family." I gently remind her.

She sighs then intertwines her fingers with mine. "You're right. So, the truth is, I got a text from an unsaved number two days ago. It was Tiny."

Curious, Mel leans over. "Okay, and?"

"I didn't know what to say. Y'all know how broken I was after last year."

She hands me the phone and I read the messages aloud.

Unknown: Hey.
Tiffany: New phone. Who dis?
Unknown: Hi, Sis. It's Tiny.

"Babe, this was two days ago. You need to respond now. If she reached out, she needs you. You can't turn her away. You can put your guard with any and everyone but not her, Tiff. You love your sister. I know you were hurt, but just imagine how much pain she's been in."

Her resistance crumbles, and slowly, she reconnects with the core of who she is—the sister who vowed to save Tiny no matter what. She pushes aside the sting of rejection, her pain overshadowed by the hope of giving Tiny the life she deserves, and we help her craft a reply with the hope that Tiny responds.

After my football practice, I watch Tiff dance, admiring her every move and the subtle glances she throws my way. But when practice ends, her angst returns.

"Oh my God, Mase. She texted back!"

Tiny: I'm sorry it took so long to reach out to you, but I need you, Tiffany.

That evening, everyone meets at my house to devise a plan to save Tiny. A heavy weight of responsibility settles on us, but especially on Tiffany, who now holds her sister's future in her hands.

"Alright, Captain. Walk us through the master plan." Tiffany tells me.

I begin. "Okay, during dinner, we'll tell the parents we want to go to the lake house for the weekend. Then, we'll go pick up Tiny and bring her back to the house. Greer Coastal Rehab is expecting her arrival on Monday morning. Then, we'll prep one of my parents' rental properties for her to stay at afterward. Simple as that." It *sounds* simple, but it's much easier to plan how to save a life than it is to actually do it.

The following Saturday, we drive up to the lake house. The ride is quiet, somewhat dark and brooding. Each one of us is lost in our thoughts. I think we just realized that perhaps we're in over our heads, but it's too late to turn back now. In the great room of the lake house, the magnitude of the moment finally boils over.

"So, am I the only one having second thoughts?" Rafe surveys our expressions.

Mel admits. "Actually, I'm having second, third, fourth, and fifth thoughts."

Sensing everyone's fears and even Tiffany's apprehension, I try to hide my doubts as well. My parents have always instilled in me the importance of taking action and being a man of integrity.

"Y'all can stay here and hold down the fort. Tiffany and I will bring Tiny back. What we're doing is dangerous, and there's honestly no telling what could go wrong. We'll check in with each other every step of the way. If we don't call you every fifteen minutes, something's gone wrong, and you need to tell the parents everything."

Tiffany sidles up next to me, her hand finding mine. "Thank you," she murmurs. "For everything."

I squeeze her hand and offer a reassuring smile. "We're in this together."

Rafe runs a hand through his hair and releases a deep breath. "Alright, man. Just...be careful, okay?"

I nod, and Tiffany and I get ready to leave. But as soon as we open the front door, we're met by my parents, the Bakers, and Ms. Dora standing on the doorstep, bags in hand.

"Surprise!" They say in unison.

"Uh, Mom, Dad? What're y'all doing here?" I manage to ask, my voice laced with surprise.

Mom beams at us. "We've been so wrapped up in the election over the past few months that we dropped the ball in spending time with our babies, who will be out of the house in just a few months. So, we thought we'd surprise y'all by hanging out this weekend! Besides, I needed to stop by the Governor's Mansion to check out the renovations anyway."

"I'm just here for the nice view and some free food." Ms. Dora adds.

They step inside to place their bags down, but our parents notice the collective dismay on our faces.

"Hmm, it seems we ruined the kids' plans?" Mom says, only half joking.

Rafe forces a smile. "No, of course not. We were just...surprised, is all. We're happy to see you."

While the parents settle in, we huddle in my room. "Okay, time to pivot," I whisper. "We'll have to book a hotel on my card. Mel and Rafe find a nearby hotel where Tiny can check in for the night. Tomorrow, we'll just have to drive back to Greer earlier than planned. But act normal. They can smell a lie from a mile away."

Later, Tiffany and I approach our parents, putting on our best, most innocent teenage faces.

"We wanted to go on a date tonight. You know? Get some alone time," I say. "Atlanta is special to us. It's where Tiff finally said yes to being my girlfriend. Is it okay if we head out for a few hours?"

"Of course, Son. You two enjoy your evening."

Tiffany quickly texts Tiny, updating her on the change of plans.

Tiffany: Something came up. Mase and I will pick you up at 7 pm. Will you be okay to wait a few more hours?

Tiffany's worry deepens with each silent minute. "We've been texting for weeks. She always replies right away." She murmurs while checking her phone.

"It's ok, baby. Everything's gonna be okay."

Dressed for our supposed date, we drive to the address Tiny gave us. Tiffany calls her repeatedly, but each call goes unanswered. The tension between us is thick, and my attempts at reassurance do little to soothe her growing fear.

The house that greets us is a stark contrast to the safety of our lake house retreat. It's dilapidated, with peeling paint, broken windows, and an overgrown yard that screams neglect. So, I retrieve a baseball bat from the backseat as a necessary precaution. As we approach, the sinking feeling in my stomach grows.

I slowly walk up each step with Tiffany closely behind me.

"You sure this is the right address?" I ask.

"This wasn't the original address. This is the one she texted me late last night." She informs me.

"Somethin' ain't right. Text the crew for help." I add, tightening the grip on my bat.

"I'm scared, Mase. I'm really scared." Tiffany admits, clinging to the back of my shirt.

I knock. No answer.

And when I knock again, the door ominously creaks open, revealing a pitch-black interior and a staunch smell. We step inside and use our phone flashlights to cut through the darkness.

"Tiny?" Tiffany calls out, her voice echoing through the empty halls.

After checking each room, we finally hear a whimper from the back room.

"Tiny!" Tiffany tries to run past me, but I stop her just in time before she collides with a tall, older man with a gun pointing straight at us.

With a crooked smile, he says, "Hello, daughter. Long time, no see."

Tiffany's frozen in place. This must be the sick piece of shit who tried to ruin the Weathers girls' lives. I know tonight's mission was to save a life, but I think we'll have to take one instead.

Chapter 21

House of Horrors – Tiffany

I should've predicted that our plan to rescue Tiny wouldn't unfold smoothly, but I'm not the same naïve, scared girl I once was. Even with the barrel of Pop's gun staring down my face, fear isn't the word to describe how I feel. I feel determined, frozen in survival mode, trying to figure out how the hell I can kill this man.

"Drop the bat, young blood." Pop has aged, but he still looks young, and his voice is slick with venom as he motions us forward. "Walk slowly, both of you."

With his gun pointed directly at us, he leads Mase and me into the room, where I see Tiny tied up, body battered, bruised, and bloody.

"Tiny!" Completely abandoning Pop's instructions, I rush to my sister's side. "What'd you do to her? She's been clean for months."

Pop's sadistic laugh rings through my ears. "She's an addict. All they do is lie. Still a stupid little girl, I see, but damn, you've sure grown up. I could use a fresh girl like you to put to work."

"Hey," Mase, flaring up in anger, calls out. "You better watch it."

Pop smirks and turns his attention to Mase. "And who are you? The boyfriend? I heard my daughter's *protected* now. Rich family, politically connected, nice house, nice cars. Still a virgin, I assume? Unless you've had a taste already?" He observes Mase's clinched jaw and balled fist. "Oh, I see it all over your face. You're each other's firsts, huh? Be careful. These damn Weathers girls are hard to resist. Trust me, I know firsthand." He winks at my sister. "Which is why, for the life of me, I can't figure out why my number one girl, would try to leave me! I didn't want to hurt you, Tiny. I hate it when I have to discipline you, especially now, with that precious baby boy in the other room."

A dazed and confused Tiny murmurs, "Drew. Please don't hurt my baby."

Baby boy? Their words cut through the chaos in the room. Tiny has a son. This revelation explains everything—the urgency of her messages, her attempts at sobriety, her desperate desire to escape. Tiny isn't just trying to save herself; she's trying to save her son. She's trying to save my nephew. Now, more than ever, Mase and I have to follow through with our plans to do whatever it takes to save Tiny and her baby.

"Where is he, Tiny? Where's Drew?" I ask.

She groans, barely able to open her mouth. "The other room. Please help him."

"Alright, that's enough!" Pop shoves us towards the wall, his gun waving menacingly in the dimly lit room. "Time to say your goodbyes," he sneers, pushing us to face the grimy, peeling paint. "But first, say goodbye to Tiny, Daddy's sweet girl."

As Mase and I stand there, my heart painfully thuds against my ribs. The room feels colder, and the air thinner. The anticipation of death suffocates me, and I struggle to draw a full breath.

"It's gonna be okay, Tiff. I love you." Mase whispers.

Just then, Mase's phone vibrates loudly against the silence.

Pop's eyes narrow. "Who's that?" He asks.

"It's our friends checking in. If I don't answer, then you'll have a problem. A big problem." He slowly pulls the phone from his pocket, then answers the call on speaker phone.

"Yo, Rafe!" He says.

"Hey, Captain. Got Tiff's text. Just checking in. How's the playbook looking over there?" Rafe's voice comes through, coded in coolness.

Mase glances at Pop, his eyes flicker with a spark of defiance. "Tell the head coaches the game plan. We need to switch to a full defense. The offense is getting tricky, and we might have to run an unexpected blitz."

"Got it, Cap! Extend the play for as long as you can. Full blitz on the way."

Pop's face contorts in confusion, and he grows angry. "Cut the shit, kid! Hang up the damn phone."

Mase hangs up but doesn't waver. "Look, I should let you know, my mom is Governor Sherri Carter, and my dad is soon-to-be Judge Charles Boom. They're tracking my phone. They know where I am. If you don't let us go, you're not just facing local police. You're looking at federal time. Although prison might be your safest option. My parents might just make you disappear."

For a moment, Pop hesitates, his grip on the gun loosening slightly. Then, with a smirk, he reveals, "Life sure is funny, huh? If you make it out of here alive, which you won't, tell Sherri and Charles their old friend Slick Boy Rick says hello. They'll know exactly who I am. It's a shame the Weathers girls will never know the truth."

Mase and I exchange a look of confusion, but before we can process his words, Mase launches a swift attack. He jerks his head back to collide with Pop's face.

"Shit!" Pop yells and tries to subdue Mase, but he's quicker and stronger. Mase tackles pop, sending the gun clattering across the floor and at my feet.

Amid the chaos, I hear baby Drew's cries pierce my ears. I'm so overwhelmed. I want to drown out the noise, but I can't. I want to fast-forward to a brighter day, but I can't. I have to get through this moment. Pushing through my fear, I force myself to move. Mase pins down Pop zip ties his wrists and ankles while I grab Tiny and Drew's belongings.

"Can you stand?" I ask Tiny, and she nods.

"She'll be back." Pop talks trash while still pinned to the ground. "And when I come to get her, I'm gonna take you with me, Tiffany *Nicole*. I'm gonna turn you out just like I did your mama and just like I did your sister. I'll rip you to shreds, you uppity bitch."

Mase twists his wrists tighter and tells him to shut up, but he doesn't. He just keeps going and going, replaying the years of abuse and torment he inflicted on my sister since she was a little girl. I just want him to stop. I need him to stop talking. It takes everything in me to refrain from killing him. It takes everything in me, which means there's nothing left to hold me back.

"I know hundreds of men who'd want you, but I think I'll take you first and then –"

Bang! Bang!

Pop has nothing else to say because nothing can be said after I pick up the gun and pull the trigger, shooting him once in the chest and once in the head. Mase stares at his dead body in shock.

I see the smoke still blowing from the gun, but I can't manage to move until Tiny stands and slowly removes the gun from my outstretched arms. She goes to the other room at the sound of her son's cry while I stand still, tears flowing down. Mase runs to me.

"Oh my God, what'd I just do? I just – I just. I killed him!" I shout into the air.

"Tiffany!" Mase envelops me in his arms, his voice a soothing balm as I tremble uncontrollably. "It's okay, baby. You did the right thing. You ended it."

Tears blur my vision, and the consciousness of my actions crushes me. "I'm a murderer, Mase. I killed him. I just wanted him to stop talking. I wanted to hurt him for hurting Tiny." My voice breaks. "I'm so sorry, Mase. I didn't mean to kill him. I – I don't know why I did it. I just –"

"You just saved me, Tiffany. You saved us." Tiny weakly interjects, limping into the room with her baby cradled in her arms. Her voice is frail but determined. "If you didn't do it, he would've found a way to kill all of us. He had to die, Tiffany. I'm sorry I couldn't do it myself. I'm so sorry I dragged you all into this."

Tiny begs us for forgiveness as if apologizing is a reflex. I'm torn between relief and sorrow, but also, in this moment, I see freedom reflecting in Tiny's eyes. Then, I see that beautiful baby boy, who has yet to be tainted, in her arms.

"You just gave him a chance, Tiff." Her gaze drops to him. "My son has a chance to be safe, happy, and loved. And he will have his aunt in his life."

I dry my tears, and then Mase and I exchange a confused look.

"I killed Pop." Tiny insists. "I shot him. Okay?" She nods.

I vehemently shake my head. "No! I'm not gonna lie. No, Tiny! I'm not letting you do this. I'm not letting you take the fall. You've been through too much. I can't let you go to jail. I did this. I can't ruin your life."

"Oh, Tiff." She cries. "What life? Jail is much better than this hell. I prayed to die until I got pregnant. Then, I prayed to just survive until you answered my text. You're my miracle, Tiffany. God finally answered one of my prayers, the only one that ever mattered. And now I can live."

I protest, still unconvinced to lie. "Behind bars? You deserve so much more, Tiny. I can't let you take the fall."

Tiny looks to Mase for support, and his hand finds my shoulder. "Please, Tiff. Let her do this for you. I'll get my mom to help her."

The injustice Tiny's endured burns through me. "Why should Tiny have to continue to suffer? She's a mom. Her son needs her."

With a bittersweet smile, Tiny responds, "He's three months old, and he hasn't eaten in a day. My son needs a healthy, stable family who can take care of him. He doesn't need me – not now, not when I'm like this. I know you're gonna live a great life. Will y'all take care of him? Will you promise to give him a life we never had?"

Resigned, I slowly nod. "Yes, I promise. I'll love him like my own."

Tiny and I embrace while Mase takes charge and coordinates our stories before his parents and the bakers arrive, making it convincing enough not to raise any suspicions.

"Are you sure this'll work?" I ask nervously, afraid of being caught in the biggest lie of my life.

"No," Mase admits. "My mom will know the truth right away, but she won't push us. She and Callie will go into clean-up mode. They'll fix it, and I'll do anything to protect you and your family. I love you, Tiffany."

I lean my forehead against his and reply, "I love you, too, Mase."

He seals our vow with a kiss, but before we can savor the moment, Mel and Rafe burst into the room. Behind them, our parents emerge, their expressions turning to horror as they take in the scene. Mel screams, and Rafe takes her outside, where our parents urge them to get back in the car. Sherri and Charles stand frozen, bewildered by the body lying in a puddle of blood.

Mrs. Sherri gasps. "Charles, is that –"

Mr. Charles nods. "Ricky Preston."

Mrs. Sherri looks back and forth between Tiny and me. For a moment, it's as if she's seen a ghost. Then she asks, "I had no idea you had a sister, Tiffany. This man is your stepfather? How? When?" Her questions tumble out, urgent and unsteady.

"Dad?" Mase interjects.

But Mr. Boom sharply cuts him off. "Not now, Son! Don't you say a word."

Mrs. Sherri's attention turns to Tiny, her expression softening with concern, "The baby? Is it his?"

Overwhelmed, Tiny shrugs. "I really don't know, ma'am. I don't know much of nothin'."

"Oh, you poor girl," Mrs. Sherri murmurs, her voice cracking as she calls out, "Callie!"

I see a different side of Mrs. Baker, one who is likely used to cleaning up messes. Mrs. Baker calmly kneels down before us and offers reassurance.

"Everything's gonna be okay. Now, tell me what happened," she firmly instructs. "I don't care if it's the truth or a lie. We can make it stick. We'll sweep as much as possible under the rug, but someone's gonna have to take the fall for pulling the trigger. Gunshots were already reported."

We recount the rehearsed story, our voices steady despite the chaos swirling within. Our parents listen, nod in agreement, and then instruct Mase and me to head to the car, where Mr. Baker waits to drive us back to the lake house.

As we make our way to the front room, Aunt Dora meets us. Mase and I tend to Drew while Tiny rushes into Ms. Dora's arms.

"I'm so sorry, Ms. Dora!" Tiny sobs.

Ms. Dora consoles her. "It's okay, Tiny. You know you ain't got nothin' to apologize for. I'm so sorry for leaving you. I should've never turned you away. Now, I hear there's a baby to welcome to the family."

Tiny manages a weak smile as she introduces her son. "Yes, ma'am. He was born prematurely. This is Drew. He's perfect, ain't he?"

"Just like his mama," Ms. Dora affirms. "I won't let him get put in the system. I couldn't get y'all when I tried, but I got the Booms on my side now. We're gonna take good care of him—and you, Tiny."

Tiny nods and I hug my sister as tight as I can. "I'm so sorry, Tiny. I'm so, so sorry. You've always protected me, even now." I whisper in her ear.

"There's nothing I could ever do to repay you for what you did for me today. I love you, Sis. Take care of our boy. And thank you, Mase."

With a final kiss on my nephew's forehead, we exit the house. I don't know what's going to happen. I don't know how this situation can be rectified or covered up, but I do know that I just single-handedly decided Tiny's fate. I did what so many others have done to her – I dictated her future. I took away her chance at happiness. I took away her freedom, and possibly for good this time.

During the car ride back to the lake house, Mase looks ahead in frightening silence with hands his hands clenched tight.

Rafe murmurs, almost to himself, "What have we done? Are we gonna go to jail? Our lives are over."

Mel looks at Mr. Baker with tears streaming down her face. "Dad, what's going to happen to us?"

Mr. Baker glances between us. His voice is steady, but his eyes show his concern. "Everything's gonna be okay. Your mom's gonna take care of everything. You've got nothin' to worry about." He repeats as if trying to convince himself as much as us.

The reality of what I've done to everyone sinks deeper with every mile we put between ourselves and that house of horror.

I find myself replaying every moment that led us here. I could've saved her without *sacrificing* her. I didn't *have* to kill him. The truth is, I *wanted* to kill him. I wanted him dead. But I shouldn't have let my desire for vengeance cost Tiny her freedom.

As we pull into the driveway of the lake house, we retreat to our individual rooms without even a glance at each other. I turn on the shower and let the tears slow. I cry for the irreversible decision I made, for the grim future awaiting Tiny, for the scars I've inflicted on my friends, and for the end of the blissful ignorance that has enveloped the last four years of my life. I need to leave. While I can't erase everyone's memories, I can remove myself from their lives to avoid causing further damage.

Afterward, I find Mr. Baker and my friends gathered in the living room, all emotionally spent.

"You might not believe this right now, but you're all great kids, and you're going to grow into even better adults." Mr. Baker reassures us while glancing back at Mel, who fiddles nervously with her vitamins. *Vitamins*, which are actually antidepressants and mood stabilizers, she's sorting in an attempt to ease the break she's experiencing because of me.

Later that evening, Callie, Sherri, Aunt Dora, and Charles Boom return to the lake house with weary expressions on their faces. Mr. Baker immediately rushes to his wife, who accepts his embrace with a sigh of relief. Sherri and Charles, visibly exhausted, retreat to the master bedroom without a word to us. As the door closes behind them, the muffled sound of a heated discussion filters through.

From the other side of the door, Charles' voice rises. "We need to call Crystal and Terry. This can't just be a coincidence."

"And make them relive hell all over again? And give them hope that their girls are alive? Crystal just tried to kill herself, *again*! We can't do this to them. I got rid of Kayla and Rick's entire family. It doesn't make sense, Charles. They're not the twins."

"Please, Sherri. You saw those girls together. Look, I get it. You're practical. You carry on as a coping mechanism, but I don't. I hold on to possibilities, always have, and so does Mase. That's why he's so connected to her. His heart knows that Tiffany is—"

Sherri interrupts, her voice breaking. "Stop it, Charles! Please! We can't put them through that pain again. Those girls have memories, a history that has nothing to do with Greer, or Crystal, or Terry. Let it be. We need to focus on our sons and those girls out there. Hold it together, please."

We all pretend we aren't eavesdropping when the door opens again, and they beckon Mase and me into the room.

Mr. Charles starts, "Everything will be okay, but Tiny's going to be gone for a long time. We told her not to say anything, but she confessed. With her record and open warrants, there isn't much we can do without raising suspicions."

"But – but what about my nephew?"

Mrs. Sherri answers, weary but firm, "We're working on it. For now, he's in temporary foster care until the investigation wraps up."

I become hysterical at the thought. Tears stream down my face, and Mrs. Callie steps in. "I have connections, Tiffany. We'll get him placed with Aunt Dora until we find a suitable family for him."

"But *I'm* his family," I protest, my voice breaking. "I promised Tiny I'd take care of him."

The parents exchange exhausted glances. Then, Mase grabs my hand. "We'll get him back, Tiff. I promise."

Mrs. Sherri snaps. "No, you will not!" She declares with stress and frustration overpowering the room. "This obsession, this... whatever this is between you two, it ends tonight!"

"This little relationship is over. You could've lost everything, son. Including your life." Mr. Charles gently adds.

Mase pleads. "But I didn't, Dad." Mr. Boom still shakes his head. "You said when you find happiness, you go to the ends of the earth. Remember? Tiffany is my happiness."

Tears well up in Mrs. Sherri's eyes, but her voice remains adamant. "It's over!"

Defeated, I sob harder, and my voice breaks as I apologize. "I'm so sorry, Mase. I'm sorry, Mr. and Mrs. Boom. I'm so sorry, Mr. and Mrs. Baker. I should've never come here and messed up your families."

Callie and Maurice pull me into a warm embrace and whisper, "You have nothing to be sorry for. We love you, Tiffany. But the Booms are right. After today, nothing will ever be like it was."

I nod and look back at Mase, who tries to reach out to me, but I reluctantly pull away and join Mel to pack my bags to return to Greer and finish my senior year alone, leaving behind the joy and family I had found.

~ ~ ~

Despite my efforts to distance myself when we return home, Mase's attempts to connect are relentless. He calls, DMs, leaves letters on my desk at school, and even resorts to communicating through Mel, who's now in therapy twice a week, thanks to me.

"You know, I'm not one to give bad advice, but you either need to talk to Mase or give him a reason not to want to talk to you. He's losing his mind at school. Everyone knows y'all aren't together anymore, and every time a guy mentions your name, he freaks. It's his third fight in weeks. Dad can't keep letting him slide. You need to talk to him, and you will today because he's here. Right now."

My eyes widen in shock and disbelief. "Mase is here? Mel, how could you?"

She raises her hand, stopping my protest. "Rafe and I are guarding this door until you two sort this out. Our lives haven't been the same since that day, and pretending everything is normal isn't working, especially for you, Tiffany. We can't end high school like this, and we definitely can't start college together like this. Talk to him. Give him—and yourself—some peace."

Mel exits my room, leaving me face-to-face with Mase.

As he steps closer, I back away, but his gaze slowly dismantles the walls I've built around myself. It doesn't take long before I find myself collapsing into his embrace, our arms wrapping around each other with an intensity that speaks volumes.

He buries his face in my curls and inhales. "I've missed you."

"I've missed you too," I admit, my voice trembling as I slightly pull back to look at him.

The exhaustion etched deep in his eyes hits me hard. I can tell he isn't sleeping, and I know he isn't Greer's carefree Golden Boy anymore. I ruined that. I ruined him.

"Oh, Mase, look at what I've done to you," I whisper. "I've tainted your good with my bad, and I love you too much to bring you down."

Mase cups my face with a gentleness that almost breaks me. "No, Tiffany. I love you too much for you not to know that you're the best thing that ever happened to me."

Tears flow as he leans in to kiss me, a kiss that's both a promise and a farewell. This moment helps me realize that I can't lose anyone else. I've lost enough.

"Maybe," I whisper, apprehensive to continue. "Maybe space is good. Maybe we can try again in the fall when we start school." I suggest.

Mase looks at me with regret in his eyes. "I'm not going to Morehouse." His voice is steady despite the emotion I see swirling in his deep brown eyes.

"Tomorrow, I'm announcing my late commitment to UGA. I'll be leaving in three weeks."

The reality of his news crashes over me like a wave, and I cry harder than I ever have before. My body shakes with sobs. "So, you're leaving me?"

He pulls me closer into his arms, holding me tightly, his voice cracking as he whispers, "I don't want to. I'll follow you to the ends of the earth, Tiff. If you tell me to stay, I will."

I shake my head, tears streaming down my face. "I won't do that," I whisper, my voice trembling. After a deep breath, I exhale. "I don't want to hold you back. Maybe this is how it's supposed to be. Just know, you'll always be my first and only."

"And you'll always be my first and forever." He replies softly, eyes glistening with tears.

With a final, lingering look of love and heartache, he steps back, his hands reluctantly falling away from mine.

"Goodbye, Tiffany Weathers."

Through the sobs wracking my chest, I summon the strength to whisper, "Goodbye, Mason Boom."

Chapter 22

Ends of the Earth – Tiffany

"Ladies and gentlemen! It's halftime, so you know what that means. Get up out of your seats and put your hands together for the powerhouse of sound and soul, the Morehouse Tigers Marching Band."

The sun dips low, casting long shadows across the field as the announcer's voice booms through the speakers. Cheers erupt around the stadium in a thunderous roar that seems to shake the air. I'm at the edge of the field, my heart is pounding in sync with the heavy beats reverberating from the band. They're a wall of sound, blaring a mix of neo-soul and old-school funk that seeps into the ground beneath my feet, urging me to move, to dance.

When the drum major gives the high-stepping cue, my team takes our position at center field. Our sequined uniforms catch every flicker of light and shimmer like stars against dusk. The soles of my jazz shoes grip the turf, and all at once, we explode into motion. My body feels like a live wire, every movement charged with power—a symphony of high kicks, sharp turns, and body rolls.

I hear voices across the stadium chanting my name, "That's right, Tiffany! Get it, girl!"

But I'm caught in my flow, executing a series of eight-counts, arms slices, toe touches, splits, and powerful snaps.

When the final notes end, our routine culminates in a dramatic formation. Breathless, I stand there, chest heaving, as applause washes over us like a rainstorm. This is my safe place. This field has brought me peace for the past eight months. This field is where I belong.

After the football game, Mel and our roommate, Monica, rush over to me. "Damn, Tiff! You killed it out there!" Monica gushes. "Like, we literally couldn't keep our eyes off you. You're the most talked about girl in Howard-Harreld Hall."

I dismiss her compliments with a roll of my eyes. Monica is so sweet. When we first met during orientation, she barely made eye contact, and she flinched at the slightest touch. I knew she'd been through hell. She needed a group of women who'd support her, hype her up, and assure her she'd never be alone again. She found her safe place with us at Spelman.

"I just mind the business that pays me, so why in the world am I always being talked about?" I ask, half amused, half bewildered.

"Tiff, please! You can't expect to look that damn fine on the field every week and *not* be talked about. Just look at Donny over there. He can't take his eyes off you. Give the boy some play. He is too fine—looking like Blair Underwood's son on a hot summer day!" Mel laughs.

We all laugh. Mel knows good and well that I'm not entertaining any of these thirsty footballers. When would I even find the time? As soon as my performance on the field ends, it's time for me to head straight to Aunt Dora's to see my little man, well, my growing big man, Drew.

Aunt Dora recently moved out of her old home in College Park. Thankfully, she lives less than ten minutes away, and she's always hosting me and the girls for dinner on the weekends.

And tonight's no different. As soon as we arrive, the smell of her delicious lasagna seeps up my nostrils.

"Umm, it smells like it's time to eat!" I announce.

"Oh, no, it isn't! Don't you come in this house walkin' to my table when you see all these toys layin' around my floor. This little boy is messy, just like you and your sister. Always getting into everything, and he's barely been walking a week."

I laugh at Aunt Dora's fussing. Drew does keep her busy but he's so dang on cute. "Oh, Drew!" I playfully call out his name. "Where's my Drew?"

We hear his adorable giggle from the playroom, and he comes running straight into my arms. "Oh, I missed you so much! I hate going all day without seeing you."

"It's crazy how much he looks like you." Mel says.

I laugh. "He looks like his mom, but nowadays, Tiny and I practically look like twins."

We all sit down for dinner, where I tell Aunt Dora about our new stands and formations. Watching her face light up when I talk about dance is exciting, especially since she temporarily closed her dance studio to take care of Drew. I'm working at a new job that pays a lot of money, so hopefully, I can alleviate some of the burden. Aunt Dora's got spunk and energy for days, but she's getting old, and she shouldn't have to raise kids all over again.

Our conversation is interrupted by Mel's phone. It's Mase, who I haven't spoken to in eight months. But he sure as hell doesn't mind calling Drew damn near every day. How disrespectful is that?

"Hi, Mase!" Mel answers via video chat.

"Sup, Mel. Just calling to see my boy. What's he up to?"

"He's busy making a huge mess! Lasagna and mashed peas." Mel angles the phone towards Drew. "Isn't he cute?"

Mase coos at him. "He sure is." Mase's tone shifts when he asks, "Is Tiffany there?"

I immediately start shaking my head and signal Mel to cover for me.

"Uh, no, but she'll be here soon. I think she got caught up after the game, talking to one of the players. You know how that goes. All the guys want a piece of Tiff." She teases to purposely piss Mase off.

"Who was she talking to? Donny?" I sense the irritation in his voice. "Does she like him? He's been all over her posts flirtin.' His lame ass ain't even her type."

Mel waves him off. "Boy, you got some nerve! Word travels, you know. I shouldn't know how big my best friend's ding-a-ling is." I silently clap for Mel as she chews Mase out in my defense. "You and Tiff had a mutual break-up. She didn't break your heart. Yet, you flaunt an assembly line of girls all over your socials, *and* you brought a girl home during fall break!"

"That was *after* she ghosted me all summer. *After* she blocked me. And *after* she followed Donny online." His voice begins to soften. "It was after I got the message loud and clear that she didn't want me anymore."

"Well, if you're calling to tell me you have a girlfriend then I already know. Rafe told me, and I'm gonna tell Tiff."

Mel's news is new to me. The shock on my face doesn't even compare to my breaking heart, but Monica gently squeezes my hand to soften the blow

In a teasing, somewhat unbelieving tone, Mase asks, "Hmm, you sure she isn't there? I – I just wanted to give her the heads up before she saw any pics online. My girl is the flashy type, you know?"

"No, I don't know, nor do I care to know. Now, I gotta go tell my best friend that her ex has moved on, and so should she." Mel hangs up in Mase's face and mouths, *I'm sorry.*

I manage a shaky smile and shrug. "It's fine."

I don't have time to focus on love, which is why I had to let him go. If there's ever a chance for us to be together again, I need to take care of my responsibilities first. My weekdays are booked with classes, practices, and helping Aunt Dora take care of Drew, and my weekends consist of games,

Drew, visiting Tiny, and work—the latter of which is where I need to be right now.

"I'll be home around 3 a.m." I tell Monica and Mel, who selflessly watch Drew when I'm at work.

Mel frowns. "How long do you plan to work at Lure? That place is a police sting waiting to happen! You're not even 21! How are you a bartender?"

"Bartender in training. I'll stay as long as they keep the doors open. I'm making good money—made two grand in tips last weekend alone. That money's going toward my apartment next year, so Drew can live with me, and Aunt Dora can finally take a break."

"Child, I ain't taking a break no time soon. I can't let you raise this little speed racer all by yourself. You're too young to be so dang on serious."

"She's right," Monica adds. "You need to take a break from that club, Tiff. I can't imagine being around all those men. They only want one thing, and they usually take it by any means necessary."

Poor Monica. She's from our sister city, Beverly Mills, and she reminds me so much of Tiny—once mistreated and abused. This is why I can't even think about dating right now. My focus is on the people who need me: raising Drew, protecting Monica, and keeping an eye on Mel, whose fragile mind feels like it could shatter at any moment.

"I'll unwind at Drew's first birthday next month."

Mel gently probes. "But are you ready to see Mase?"

With a heavy sigh, I muster a facade of indifference. "I have to be. I'm not 'bout to trip over a *boy* who's been doin' everyone he can to get over the *woman* he can't have."

Aunt Dora offers a knowing smile, her words wrapping around me like a warm blanket. "That's my girl!"

After bathing and putting Drew to bed, I head to work. Working at Lure is like being in another world. As usual, several men vie for my attention with outrageous offers.

One businessman, leaning too close, proposes, "Nicole, I'll pay you $10,000 just to have a drink with me."

His competition, a flashy baller, ups the ante. "Make it $50,000 to spend the night with me."

I dismiss them with a practiced smile. "How about I serve you a double shot of drinks on the house instead?" They're dissatisfied, of course, but they're used to being turned down by me.

These men remind me of Pop—predators. I shake off my disgust and focus on mixing drinks, flashing smiles, and avoiding unwanted advances.

Then, in walks Donny Baines, Morehouse's star running back. He's cocky and loves to win, games and women. Donny turns heads, but his efforts to catch my attention always feel too forced, rendering me uninterested and absolutely turned off.

After closing up, I step outside to head home, but Donny catches me off guard.

"Tiffany!" He calls out.

Startled, my reflexes kick in, and I spray him with my pepper spray. He howls in pain, but I unapologetically stand my ground.

"Holy shit! You good?" I ask in a detached tone.

"Damn, what was that for? I can't believe you pepper sprayed me." He grumbles, rubbing his eyes.

"You better be glad that all I did! You got me fucked up if you think I'd be impressed with you waiting for me after work. Do you know how crazy that is? Leave me alone, Donny."

"I don't understand why you don't like me. Is it because of your baby daddy?" He asks, slightly irritated.

Confused, I ask, "Baby daddy?"

"Yeah, everybody knows you and Mason got a son – the baby that the old lady brings to the games. Plus, ya boy sent me a message..." He trails off, showing me the messages on his phone.

Leave my family alone.

A surge of irritation floods through me. "Unbelievable! Didn't he just tell Mel he has a girlfriend now?" I mumble under my breath.

"So… How about we get some payback? Let me take you out to lunch tomorrow?"

His boldness is impressive, but still I decline. "No."

"Fine, but have you at least seen his new girl yet?"

He's baiting me, and I desperately want to bite. "You're gonna show me, anyway, aren't you?"

Donny smiles and shows me a picture of Mase's new girlfriend. She's drop-dead gorgeous, and in the last five minutes, she's posted nearly ten photos of them together.

Feeling petty and provoked, I grab Donny's phone, snap a flirty selfie with him, then type the caption 'The Football Player and His Dancer.'

"Post it." I challenge with a reckless smirk playing on my lips.

"Tiffany Nicole, you are somethin' else." Donny's smirk lingers as he uploads the photo. There's a spark of mischief in his eyes, and I suddenly find him a bit more attractive.

Within minutes, the photo circulates, and garners likes and comments that fuel an untamable fire. However, the next morning, Mase retaliates with his own series of posts, cozying up to his new girlfriend

Over the next few weeks, social media becomes our battlefield, with likes and comments being our weapons of choice. But despite the thrill of the game, a part of me feels hollow. It's as if we're communicating through these shared glimpses into our lives, each trying to outdo the other while displaying our longing. I find myself checking his profile more often than I'd like to admit, analyzing every photo, his smile, his body language—

anything that might reveal that he's faking it–that he misses me as much as I miss him.

I mean – he has to or else he wouldn't have made rounds of calls to Mel, Rafe, and even Aunt Dora, seeking scraps of information about me and Donny's 'relationship.'

Nevertheless, I'll know the truth today because it's Drew's first birthday. I'm nervous to be in the same room as him, let alone breathe the same air. He torments me in the most tantalizing way, and there's no way we can ignore our unresolved feelings when we're face-to-face.

Drew's party is an intimate celebration with just our families–the Booms and Bakers. The thought of seeing Mase stirs a mix of dread and anticipation within me. When he finally arrives, he bears an armful of gifts and toys. Drew instantly recognizes him and squeals as he reaches for him. When Mase scoops him up and embraces him, I nearly shed a tear. I watch, torn between happiness for Drew and a deep-seated longing for what could have been

As the party winds down, Mrs. Sherri unexpectedly approaches me outside.

"Oh! Mrs. Sherri, you scared me. How have you been? It feels like forever since we've all been together."

What I really meant is that she hasn't talked to me since she covered up a whole murder I committed!

She manages a faint smile. "Oh, Tiff, you just keep getting more beautiful. I hear you're juggling a lot—dance, school, work, and caring for a baby. My goodness, you don't think it's too much?"

"It's all worth it for Drew." I respond, hoping my voice sounds more confident than I feel.

"He's so precious. I think we've all fallen in love with him. You want custody of him, right? I can help you with that."

Her offer catches me off guard. "Really? You'd do that for me?"

Sherri nods. "Yes, but I need something from you in return. It's about Mase—he," she hesitates. "He recently made a terrible decision. I often question the choices he makes, but in the end, I know everything he does is because of you."

Confusion clouds my thoughts, and I quickly reply, "Mrs. Sherri, I have no idea what you're talking about. Mase and I don't communicate at all. He's dating someone, and so am I."

With a piercing look, Sherri's eyes meet mine. "Tiff, what'd you call this silly back and forth on social media? Making one another jealous, driving each other insane. I really don't understand the connection you two have, but it's dangerous. It literally ends lives. I've lost a husband, a best friend, and two goddaughters. I can't lose a son, too. Please stay away from him. Your bond is toxic."

Feeling insulted, I clarify, "You mean—you think I'm toxic? You think I'll destroy his life."

Sherri doesn't immediately respond, but her silence speaks volumes. I struggle to keep my composure, but the reward of her proposal is what I desire the most. "So, if I promise to stay away from Mase, you'll ensure Drew stays with me?"

"Exactly," Sherri affirms. "Let Mase find his happiness. In return, I'll ensure that you, Drew, and Ms. Dora are taken care of—forever."

I can go eight months without talking to Mase but forever? I only wanted time to heal from the damage I caused in our lives, not to close the door entirely, but if that's the sacrifice I have to make to be with the little boy who has become my world, then so be it.

I return inside, but the lightness of the party clashes with the heaviness in my heart. Rafe wraps his arms around Mel and Mase and proposes a night out for old time's sake.

"We can go to my club." I say with a sigh, only addressing Rafe and Mel.

"And maybe I'll get to meet the guy who's been blowing up your phone for the past two hours?" Mase asks, his tone laced in jealousy.

"Yes. Perhaps, you'll meet Donny."

"And perhaps you'll meet my girl, too." He winks then he and Rafe depart back to the lake house.

Mase and Rafe depart to the lake house while Mel and I head back to our dorms, where we beg Monica to come with us and let loose.

"I really wish you'd come out with us tonight. You'd absolutely love Mase and Rafe." I say, trying to hide my disappointment as I lean against the doorframe of Monica's room. "And you gotta get off campus at some point."

Monica smiles with firm resolve. "And I will," She insists, her voice threaded with a newfound confidence I attribute to the counseling sessions she's been attending. "But tonight is game night in the student center, and I'd much rather be here, safe and sound with my Spelmanites. Besides, I'm not quite ready yet, okay? But I will be soon." Her enthusiasm grows as she shares her plans. "Tomorrow, my mom, best friend Avery, and I are going to my brother Deacon's art show. See? I'm gonna have fun this weekend, too. Don't worry about me. I'll catch up with y'all tomorrow night at the freshman stroll-off. Just go out, have fun, and be safe!"

Reassured but still a tad concerned, I head back to my room to get ready. I decide to put on my most alluring outfit—a deep gold velvet dress with a thigh-high slit that clings to my every curve. I pull my hair into a high bun, leaving a few natural curls artfully framing my face, and slip into a pair of towering heels.

"Whoa!" Mel gasps as she walks in. "Mase is gonna lose his mind when he sees you."

At the club entrance, the bouncer, who literally sees me every weekend, does a double take. "Damn, Ma, you're definitely going to VIP tonight." He remarks, his eyes wide in appreciation.

I playfully slap his arm. "Slim, it's me, Tiffany Nicole, the bartender."

"Oh, shit! Damn, girl, you clean up nice!"

I laugh off his shock, and we make our way inside. Heads turn, eyes follow, but only one set of eyes matter.

I know I swore to Mrs. Sherri I'd stay away from Mase at all costs, but we're magnetically attracted to one another. I can even feel him in the room.

Mel leans in with a lowered voice. "Mase is to your left—don't look yet. He's gawking at you. Let's walk to the bar and make him come to you." We giggle, weaving through the crowd, but I can't help but take a quick peek.

"Damn, Mel, he's looking Reggie Bush fine tonight."

As we reach the bar, my co-workers gather around, all echoing the same sentiment. "You must be on a mission, Nicole."

Then, a deep, familiar voice cuts through the noise, sending shivers down my spine. "Only I can call you Nicole."

"Donny, is that you?" I tease, turning my head slightly to catch his reaction.

Mase leans in, his breath a whisper against my ear. "So, Donny's the man that makes the hairs on your arm rise?" He murmurs while playfully running his finger down my arm.

My knees almost give way—thank God for the strength of these heels. Slowly, I face Mase, who's looking every bit of tall, dark, strong, and handsome.

"Where's your girlfriend, Mase? Why are your eyes burning through my dress instead of hers?" I challenge, meeting his eyes with a defiant stare.

He avoids my questions with a low, firm demand. "Dance with me, Tiffany Nicole."

Taking a breath, I place my hand in his, pushing away the murmurs about me and the Golden Boy, focusing instead on the man in front of me as we make our way to the dance floor, where I loop my arms around his neck.

"So, this fake dating stunt of yours?" I raise an eyebrow.

"Did it grab your attention?" He grins, knowing the answer.

I nod.

"Good," He says with a touch of seriousness. "Now you can tell Donny to fuck off."

I turn around so my back presses against him, feeling the shift as I move my body sensually. He breathes hard, and his hands explore my body.

"You know we can't be together, right? I'm a distraction, Mase." I murmur, allowing the music to fill the spaces between my words.

But he ignores my rejection and roams my body. "Fuck, Tiff. I haven't seen you dance in nearly a year. Show me what I've been missing. Dance for me and for me only." He begs.

A sensual demon is unleashed inside me. I slowly wind my hips and twerk my ass on him until I feel his dick flinch through his pants, and my juices slowly drip down my thigh.

"Mase," I breathily exhale as his hands inch higher up my dress.

"Come back to the lake house with me."

I hesitate. "What about Mel and Rafe? We can't just leave them."

"They already have plans," Mase assures me. "They knew that my only intention tonight was to make you mine again."

That damned Mason Boom. It's impossible to deny my desire to be loved by Mason again. After a few more songs, we leave the club and drive to the lake house. Mase wastes no time popping open a bottle of champagne. He pours each of us a glass, and we clink them in a toast to rekindling what we can no longer deny.

I slowly enter the bedroom, my body reeling him in. He softly kisses my bare shoulder, my neck then my lips. But while his kiss is soft and meaningful, mine is passionate and desperate. His mouth inhales my moans, and I surrender to his dominance.

Mase unzips the back of my dress, allowing it to fall to my feet. I stand nearly naked with only my white lace lingerie between our bodies and breathe hard and heavy in anticipation of what's to come.

After he admires me with his eyes, he takes off his Lacoste polo to reveal his perfectly cut chest and a tattoo that I've never seen before—a heart with the words "1st" and "4ever" written in it.

Mase is my first and only. The first only man I'll ever trust with my mind, heart, and body. But I've heard the rumors. Am I still his forever? Has he kept his promise like I've kept mine?

"I know what you're thinking, Tiffany," He lifts my chin. "You're my first love, and you're still the only woman I'd ever want to spend forever with."

Relief washes over me, and in excitement, our lips into a searing kiss while I unbuckle his belt, and he unclasps my bra. Our bodies finally meet after nearly a year of being deprived of each other.

I lie down, naked on the bed, my body inviting him in. Mase hovers his mouth above my navel, gently blowing his breath to tickle my skin. A giggle escapes my lips, and I playfully tell him to stop, but he doesn't.

He alternates between hot breaths and kisses from my navel to my inner thighs to the center of my everything.

My giggles quickly turn to heavy pants, and my heavy pants turn to moans.

"Mase," I whisper, but he ignores me, too occupied with his tongue deep inside me.

He methodically rolls against my clit like a vibrating wave. His hungry groans mix so perfectly with my moans, and when he hooks his finger deep inside me, I cry out in a symphony of desire.

"Mase, it feels so good! Don't stop, please!" I scream.

And he doesn't. He licks me to the heavens and finger fucks me on a cloud of overwhelming sensation until my body bursts in orgasmic pleasure.

"I wanna eat you all night. I wanna eat you for the rest of our lives." He says in between devouring me.

My legs shake uncontrollably, but he steadies me with his strength and continues to lick me until I come again.

"I can't – I can't come anymore!" I confess.

"But you can, Tiffany Nicole. You can come all night long, can't you? Won't you?" He smiles devilishly and gives me a long, teasing lick.

"Umm," I moan. "Yes, Mase. I can. I will."

"That's my girl. That's my dancer."

He proceeds to tightly suck my pearl. Then, five minutes later, I come again. This time, however, I don't shake; my body remains still as if it's welcoming safety, happiness, and love with open arms.

He slowly moves from between my legs and hovers over me. His eyes are lost in mine, and my hard nipples graze his chest. I've been waiting for this. My body's been craving this.

With our lips connected, he asks, "How do you want it?"

I move my hand down Mase's body to wrap my fingers around his thick, long erection.

"Make love to me like you can't live without me and fuck me like you'll never see me again." I say as I stroke him.

He plunges so deep inside me that I scream, "Oh, fuck!"

For a moment, we're stuck in paralyzing pleasure, uttering words that only our bodies can fully comprehend. "Shit, Tiff. Keep squeezing my dick. You feel so good. So fuckin' good. I can't live without this. I can't live without you." He mumbles under his breath, attempting to move. Mase lifts my leg and finds his rhythm moving in and out of me as deeply as possible.

He hits every wall, both destroying and restoring me as tears freely flow down my face. "I love you. I love you so much, Mason Boom!"

He licks my tears, then kisses me deep while drilling faster and faster until I come all over him, and he comes inside of me.

Exhausted. Spent. And madly in love. Mase lies beside me until our breaths are in a calm sync.

Caught in the warmth of the moment, I find the courage to voice the fears gnawing at my heart. "We don't lie to each other, right?" I murmur.

"Never." He replies in a steady voice.

I hesitate, then press on. "Your mom—"

He exhales, then groans. "That damn Governor Carter. What'd she do, now? Threaten you? Tell you to stay away from me?"

I nod. "She told me you made a bad choice and that it's my fault. What'd you do, Mase? Is everything okay?"

He manages a breathy laugh, then gently adjusts my body so he can sit up and rummage through his duffle bag. He pulls out a t-shirt emblazoned with 'Morehouse Football.'

Confusion gives way to shock as the implication dawns on me. Why would he leave UGA? Why would he ever jeopardize his shot at the NFL?

"Mase, please, please, please don't tell me you did this for me? This isn't romantic at all!" Then, my guilt turns to anger. "You seriously make the dumbest decisions sometimes!"

He throws himself back on the bed, wrapping me in his comfort. "You done fussin' yet?" He kisses my cheek before explaining. "Unless the first-*and* second-string QBs gets hurt or transfer, I won't be starting until Junior year. I'd rather start next year, and I have a chance to do that at Morehouse."

"So, your choice has absolutely nothing to do with me?" I press, desperate to assuage my guilt.

"Oh, it definitely has *everything* to do with you." He casually admits.

I groan in frustration. "Mase!"

"What?! C'mon, Tiff," He pulls me even closer. "Life is pretty shitty not having you around. I'd follow the woman I love to the ends of the earth, and I know I made the right choice because I'm happy again. I wanna be with you. I wanna raise Drew with you. I want a future with you. I want everything with you."

"And what about your mom? Aunt Dora's getting old, and she's tired. Thankfully, they keep extending her temporary custody, but you know how broken the system is. I feel like I have no choice but to do what she says."

"At the end of the day, my mom loves me, and she won't admit it, but she loves you too. She just operates in fear. Together or not, she's gonna follow through." He assures me.

I hope so, Mase," I wrap his arm tighter around my body. "I hope everything falls into place starting tonight because I haven't felt this at peace in so long."

We fall asleep, enveloped in love. We may be two fools in love, but navigating through darkness together is better than wandering through life alone. Mase's unyielding love comforts me. When we're together, my worries dissipate. I find myself believing that everything *will* be okay because the man beside me is ready to follow me to the ends of the earth.

Chapter 23

Our Little Family – Tiffany

Keeping secrets from overbearing parents is easier said than done. Keeping a secret from a Governor and a Judge, well, that's impossible, especially when their son can't keep his mouth shut. Mase loves out loud, *very* loud, just like his dad. We managed to keep our relationship under wraps for the remainder of freshman year, but summer turned our secret to shit. Mase returned to Greer for a few weeks while Mel and I moved into our first apartment together, where we made a baby-proofed, cute little home for Drew.

But imagine my surprise when I met our new neighbors – my idiot boyfriend, Mase, and his biggest enabler, Rafe.

Mrs. Sherri nearly burned down the complex when she saw me. *That* was Strike one.

Then, during the Tuskeegee-Morehouse Classic halftime show, Mase's coach slapped him across the head for watching me dance instead of being in the locker room with his team. *That* was strike two.

Later in the season, when Mase led his team to the SIAC championship, he ended his MVP speech with, "I'd like to thank Coach, my teammates, and my family. I love you, Tiff, and Drew." *That* was strike three.

Despite these slip-ups, we somehow found a way to soften the Boom's stance on our relationship. The key? Drew Weathers.

They agreed to watch him while we went on a 'break-up' date. Three hours later, we enter Mase's apartment, littered with junk food, cartoons blasting on the television, and a pile of blankets on the floor where Sherri and Charles were snuggling Drew to sleep.

Before we bid them goodbye for the evening, Drew sealed the deal with a "Bye, Nee-nah. Bye, Pop Pop."

Let's just say Mase and I officially have weekend babysitters.

By junior year, like déjà vu, Mase is Captain of the football team and I'm captain of the dance team. He's a business major, while my sole focus is a career in dance. Mel is finally putting those cute selfie skills to use as a photography major. She's so talented and captures the most beautiful moments of life every chance she gets, which has helped her combat the dark, inexplicable thoughts that have always haunted her.

Then, there's Rafe...

"No, Rafe, absolutely not! That shirt ain't workin.' Try something else. You need to look your best for Monica. She's the best thing that's ever happened to you." Mel playfully chides.

Somehow, he and Monica found their way to each other, but I guess it makes sense. Monica is kind, caring, and quietly firm, and Rafe may be a joker but he's patient, good, and loyal, which is why he's going to make an amazing psychiatrist one day. They're a perfect match, and when I say that girl made Rafe work for her love?! She is exactly who he needed, especially after the Pop incident. His mind couldn't take what we did, what *I* did. He quit football and became a recluse. My actions cast a gloom over his natural sunshine until Monica's emergence in his life. They've been talking, literally *just* talking on the phone and texting, for a year now, but tonight, they're going on their first date.

"I don't have anything red to wear, and red is Monica's favorite color. I'm gonna look stupid standing next to her. She's a goddess. She deserves better than this!" Rafe panics while Sherri and Charles try to calm him down over video chat.

"Son, from what you told us, this young woman would appreciate you at your worst. Just enjoy yourself and build on the solid year you've already spent getting to know each other. She's a sweet girl from a nice family. I can't believe her folks live just up the road in Beverly Mills. I think I'm gonna ask them out for a coffee." Charles suggests.

"Charles, do you ever check your calendar?" Sherri gently chides. "We have a coffee date with them next week."

Rafe groans. "Hold on, what? Seriously! You're gonna run 'em away. Y'all are flashy, rich, and often morally gray politicians. Monica and her family aren't like that at all. Her dad's a pastor, for goodness sake! Tone it down when you meet them, please. I don't want them thinking I'm some rich, spoiled brat."

With deadpan humor, Mel interjects, "But you are." Rafe grunts in response as Mel continues. "You're literally taking her to the most expensive restaurant in the city and driving a brand-new Mercedes your parents just bought you last week. You're *are* spoiled...*but* you're also humble and kind, Rafe. The quicker you accept who you are, the easier you'll get over your parents embarrassing you when they meet your future in-laws."

Laughter erupts, and even Sherri and Charles join in the fun.

"Aw, damn. I thought we did such a good job with the boys. So, y'all are saying I should leave my security detail at home?" Sherri jokes.

"And I suppose I shouldn't wear my Rolex and Armani shoes?" Charles adds with a wink.

Rafe begins to look even more anxious, but his phone buzzes with a text from Monica.

Monz, my love: I'm so nervous, but I can't wait to see you. I love you so much, Rafe, and I'm excited for our first date—well, double date. Are you sure you're okay with this? I know it's a bit unconventional.

Rafe: Of course, Monz. I'll jump at the chance to be with you any time, all the time, and every day for the rest of our lives. No matter who's around.

Yeah, about that. Monica's bringing her brother, Deacon, and her best friend, Avery, who transferred here from UGA last semester. The latter two are definitely getting married one day. Monica relies on them for comfort because this isn't just her first date with Rafe. It's her first date *ever*.

"See, Rafe. You got nothin' to worry about. You make Monica feel safe, and you adore each other. Stop freaking out!" I encourage Rafe, then playfully nudge Mase.

Mase chuckles and plays with Drew, who's sprawled across his lap. "Hey Drew, your Uncle Rafe is crying."

Drew frowns and says, "Oh no! It's okay, Uncle Rafe."

"If Drew says it, then it's true." Mrs. Sherri calls from the phone. "We love you, son. Enjoy your date. We can't wait to meet our future daughter-in-law."

As Rafe finally departs, Mel places Drew on her hip. "Alright, big man! Let's give your auntie two to three hours to herself."

"Ice cream!" My three-year-old nephew cheers.

In perfect sync, Mase and I respond, "No ice cream!"

Mel wags a stern finger at him. "That's right, no ice cream!" But as she leans in to kiss Drew's cheek, she whispers something that makes him giggle.

"Okay, but I want chocolate." He whispers loudly as they leave.

There's a playful twinkle in Mason's eyes as he motions for me to straddle his lap. I loop my arms around his neck and allow him to drink me up with his gaze. I already know what he wants, but it also doesn't hurt to ask.

"What's up, Mr. Boom?" I ask flirtatiously while slowly grinding my hips against his body.

He smiles then looks down. "I'm pretty sure you can feel what's up right now."

I bite my lip and grind hard but accidentally place pressure on his abdomen.

"Ow, shit." Mase winces. His voice is pained, and his body tenses beneath me.

I immediately stop. "Mase, are you okay?"

"I'm fine. Just keep going," He grits his teeth and tries to shrug, but I can see the discomfort etched on his face, no matter how hard he tries to hide it.

"Mason Boom! You wouldn't have gotten tackled yesterday if you weren't staring at me in the bleachers. That linebacker almost took you out!" My voice comes out sharper than I intended, but the thought of him getting hurt because of me makes me sick to my stomach.

He huffs in annoyance, rolling his eyes like I'm making too big a deal of it. "I'll be fine! You know how many hits I've taken over the years?" He gives me that cocky grin, equal parts charming and infuriating. "Besides, that bodysuit was lookin' so damn good on you, I couldn't help but stare. Worth every bruise."

I laugh at how ridiculous he is. "You've seen me in a million bodysuits."

"You know what yesterday reminded me of? The first time I saw you. City Scrimmage. I was ten years old." His smile deepens, his gaze holding mine in that way that makes everything else disappear. "I haven't been able to take my eyes off you ever since."

My breath catches at the memory, and I feel my heart flutter, just like it did back then. He pulls me in, his lips pressing gently against mine in a kiss so soft and sweet. When he pulls back, I rest my forehead against his and groan breathlessly while slowly winding my hips. "Mase, I shouldn't be on top of you while you're in pain."

"Or," he smirks and tightens his grip around my waist, "You can ride me until my pain goes away. What'd you say, Captain Weathers? Will you dance on my dick for me?" He asks with his eyes piercing through me. I accept his challenge and turn on "It's Yours" by J. Holiday.

I stand in front of him with mischief in my eyes, then slowly do a seductive, sultry dance, swaying my hips to the rhythm of the music. My hands softly trace over my curves as I start to peel away each layer of clothing. His eyes never leave me. They're full of desire, as I move closer, teasing him with every step.

When I get ready to take Mase's jersey off, he reaches out to pull me forward. "I want to fuck you like this – with my jersey on, with my name on you." He says with a hungry lick of his lips.

He quickly takes off his shirt and then slides off his shorts to reveal his massive girth. It doesn't matter how many times I've seen him naked, I'll always be pleasantly surprised and instantly overcome with desire and wetness.

I chuckle in response to his fantasy, then proceed to straddle his lap. "Hold on, tight 'cause I'm gonna ride you 'til you come." I playfully caution, guiding his hands to my thighs.

I slowly descend on him, driving as painfully deep as my body allows. I cry out his name while he groans mine. The more I rise and fall, the tighter his hands grip my waist, dictating the speed and power by which my body slams against his. The harder the pound, the wetter I get, the louder I moan, the more he swells inside me.

"Mase," I scream and tilt my head, feeling my walls cave in. "I need to stop. I'm 'bout to–"

"Breath." He commands. "Breathe with me, baby. Breathe and fuck me good until we come together. It's all yours. I'm all yours, Tiffany Nicole."

Mase slides his right hand from my waist to my throat and gently squeezes while placing the tip of his thumb in my mouth. He holds me securely in place while moving his left hand to my clit, where he massages me nice and slow. I continue to ride until he rubs me into a state of euphoria.

My voice cracks, my legs tremble, and my body falls on Mase's chest, but he holds me tight, still pumping. This time slower, more sensual, and focused. I kiss him passionately as he drives deeper from every angle.

"Where do you want it, Tiff? Where do you want me to come?"

Mase traces his thumb over my lips, and I whisper, "Inside me."

We come together—powerfully, intensely, and passionately, clinging to each other with my legs wrapped tightly around his waist and his arms tightly wrapped around me.

"I'll never stop wanting you. Every time I see you, it's like the first time."

I rest my head on his chest and smile, content with our sweet appreciation for one another.

Breaking the comfortable silence and preventing me from dozing off, Mase gives my butt a playful pat. "Go get dressed. We got somewhere to be in thirty minutes."

"Thirty minutes! That's hardly enough time to get ready. Where the heck are we going?"

His eyes twinkle with excitement, and he flashes a reassuring smile. "We've been running non-stop lately — school, dance, football, and Drew. We deserve a night out, just the two of us."

I'm taken aback but excited to be a carefree couple for the night. I pull together a sexy-enough casual outfit. I redo my curly bun and swipe a dark brown lipstick across my lips. When I step out, Mase's reaction is instantaneous. His eyes widen, a soft 'wow' escaping him.

I grab his outstretched hand, and together we head out. Mase drives us to TWO Urban Licks, a swanky warehouse-style restaurant with a vibrant atmosphere and stunning city views. It's beautiful! I've been dropping hints about this place for months, but we never have time to go on actual dates anymore.

When we settle into our seats with the shimmering skyline as our backdrop, our conversation takes a serious turn. Mase reaches across the table and my hand with his. "So, you ready to be Drew's legal guardian?"

I nod, well aware of the massive responsibility. "I just hope I don't fail him. I don't want to be like my mom."

Mase squeezes my hand reassuringly. "You won't. You're nothing like her. You're everything good, Tiff. You're perfect."

His affirmation grounds me but also sparks a gnawing question. "What about you? Are *you* ready for me to be Drew's legal guardian? Sometimes, I feel guilty for thrusting you into mock fatherhood."

"I wish I could be more than just *Mase* to Drew. I see him as my son, Tiff. I love you both so much—you're my family."

Mason and I never talk about *starting* a family because we kind of already are one. The truth is, I don't know any college-aged future NFL stars who would willingly desire to take on my baggage – trauma, dark secrets, and parenthood. But he isn't just *anyone*; he's *everything*.

He places a sweet kiss on the top of my hand. It's times like this when Mase's absolute adoration of me serves as a reminder that I'm more than my upbringing, more than my mistakes, more than my choices, and more than deserving of love and adoration.

After dinner, Mase surprises me further by taking me to the Fox Theatre. The outside announcement board reads, "Alvin Ailey Celebrates the Best of 20 Years."

My heart skips. "*The* Alvin Ailey, Mase? They've been sold out for months. It's my dream to see them perform."

Pride stretches across his face. "Well, my dream is to see you smile. Considered this a night of dreams come true."

The moment we step inside, the grandeur of the venue sweeps over me—the ornate details, the plush red seats, and the gentle hum of anticipation from the audience. Mase even managed to secure front-row seats.

The lights dim, and the curtain rises, revealing the Alvin Ailey Dance Company poised on stage, ready to convey rich history, unshakeable pride, and unapologetic blackness. The performance starts with a powerful ballet number, the dancers' movements fluid and precise, telling stories of struggle and triumph without a single spoken word. They transition into African dance. The stage bursts with energy and almost primal intensity. The rhythms of the drums fill the theatre, and I find myself completely enamored. Their graceful movement captivates me, and the rest of the world fades away.

Mase watches me more than the performance, a soft smile playing on his lips as he observes my awestruck expressions. During a particularly stirring piece, where dancers depict a narrative of liberation and joy, I feel tears prick my eyes. The beauty of their artistry, the depth of their expression—and how it all resonates with my life.

As the final applause echoes through the theatre, Mase leans over and whispers, "I knew you'd love this."

We leave the theatre hand in hand with the night air crisp against our faces. Back home, as we quietly step into our apartment, my phone vibrates with a text.

Mel: Drew is sleep. Rafe and Monica had the best date ever. Now, we're all having a sleepover next door. Enjoy your night of freedom. You two deserve it.

With a content sigh, Mase and I collapse on the bed. For the remainder of the night, we enjoy being close friends, passionate lovers, and true partners. I fall asleep in his arms, feeling safe, loved, adored, and lulled to the sound of his soothing voice, "I love you, Tiffany. I love this life you've given me. It'll always be me, you, and this beautiful world around us."

~ ~ ~

My Sundays are dedicated to Tiny. She's serving life for a terrible choice I made, and I'll never forgive myself for it. She's the real victim, but no one cared. The police didn't care about the bruises on her body. No one cared she had no home. No one cared about her story. They read her rap sheet and saw a drug-addicted criminal and prostitute rather than looking deeper to try to understand how she got to that point. Her life was ripped away by those who should've cared for her, but somehow she continues to smile.

"Tiny, I don't get it. Why are you so damn happy?"

Her excitement is through the roof, but she holds back her words. "It's a secret for now, but Mrs. Wilkins is helping me with something big."

"You and Mrs. Wilkins, huh?" I respond, warmed by the thought.

"She's kind of like my fairy godmother. Like how Ms. Dora is to you. Speaking of Ms. Dora, is she back from her cruise yet? That woman has been livin' her best life for months since she's kid-free now."

"Girl, I think she even has a boyfriend too." I joke, joining in her laughter.

We dive into our weekly catch-up, where I share stories about Drew and how big he's getting.

"Okay, the pics you sent me of Drew and Mase during Halloween were the most adorable thing I've ever seen, but your Christmas photos? Girl, y'all should be on a magazine cover. Seriously!" Tiny gushes.

"Yeah, they are pretty cute. I sometimes feel like the odd one out they're so inseparable." I admit with a light-hearted shrug.

Tiny pauses in deep thought before asking a question that I haven't really considered before. "Since you're now Drew's legal guardian," she hesitates. "Have you thought about adopting him? Officially becoming his mom?"

I hadn't even thought of something so crazy. Tiny is Drew's mom. I could never take that title away from her, especially when she's been stripped of nearly everything else. There's no way I could take her motherhood away.

"Tiny, I can't believe you'd even ask me something like that. Drew is your son. One day he'll be able to meet you, and we can all live happily ever after."

"As much as I'd love that fantasy, it's just not realistic, Tiff. Drew not only deserves to be taken care of and loved, he deserves to call someone mommy and daddy. Who better than you? Who better than Mase? I love the family you created together. It's so beautiful, and sometimes –" She pauses, nearly choked up by her words. "Sometimes I lie in my cell looking at the family pics you send and wonder, maybe, if Mama and Pop loved us the way you and Mase love Drew, our lives would be completely different. Maybe I'd be in college with you." The tear finally falls, and Tiffany places her hand over mine. "Please, just consider it. You'd be an amazing mother, Tiff. You already are."

Her tears break me. "I'll consider it, Tiny," I promise softly, my heart twisting with conflict. "But in the meantime, I'll remain the aunt to the busiest kid on the planet. I'm gonna have to move into a bigger apartment soon. His toys are everywhere! Mase says he's gonna buy a house for us as soon as he gets drafted, but we'll see." I shrug, avoiding a sensitive topic of discussion.

"We'll see?" Tiny repeats. "Oh, Tiff. Please tell me you spoke to Mase about taking over Ms. Dora's dance studio after graduation?"

My silence and the pain etched on my face reveal my internal strife.

"Tiffany Nicole Weathers, are you really willing to be separated from the love of your life?" Tiny presses.

"If it means being close to you, the other love of my life, then yes. You're my sister. You were my family first, and I'll be damned if I ever take Drew away from where his mother is."

"I'm fine, Tiff. I'm clearly not going anywhere anytime soon. For once, you don't need to worry about me. I'm safe. I'm clean. And I'm building a life I'd be proud to live outside these walls. Don't imprison your heart by staying here."

I place my hand on top of hers. "It'll be okay, Tiny. Mase and I will just have to do long distance. He'll understand."

Tiny shakes her head. "That's the problem. Mase will always find a way to understand your point of view, even when you're wrong. He puts you first, and he'll always rearrange his priorities for you, including his career. What's gonna happen when the long distance becomes too much? What would he choose then? Or *who,* rather?"

Her words leave a heavy silence between us. "Me. He'd choose me. He'd leave everything behind – the money, the fame, the NFL – just to be with me. Mase will follow me to the ends of the earth."

"Exactly," Tiny says. "But are you willing to do the same?"

Our time comes to an end, and as we hug goodbye, Tiny's parting words linger. "Not that you need it, but you have my permission to be happy. If Mase asks you and Drew to leave with him, please go, Tiffany. I'm okay now, and it's okay for you to follow your heart."

We always end my visits on a high note, but not today. Now, I feel so much gloom. I feel heavy and nearly sick to my stomach at the thought of Mase choosing me over everything when I'm unwilling to do the same. I'm *unable* to do the same. No matter what Tiny says, I can't be away from her again. So, if I have to sacrifice the beautiful possibility of a family I know I can have with Mase over keeping my existing family together, then so be it.

As the weeks go by, I wrestle with the conversations we need to have. If Mase had his way, we'd marry right after college, and I'd step into the role of a football wife—a title I already half-hold, given the attention he's brought to the school. He never misses a chance to mention me in post-game interviews, and while he's not big on social media, when he does post, it's always about us or the family we've built.

But as beautiful as our relationship is, it's equally exhausting. Being Mason Boom's girlfriend means carrying a weight I never asked for. When he has a bad game, I'm somehow blamed. He skips practice when Drew's sick, even though I tell him not to, and he took on the extra stress of coaching Drew's little league team entirely on his own—but somehow, I'm always the one everyone blames. People see me as his distraction, but Mase makes his own choices—driven by his loyalty to me and Drew. Still, the whispers persist—his coaches, the media, gossip sites, and even strangers at school vying for his attention. And now, with summer before senior year upon us, our beautiful little family is about to change.

Chapter 24

Everything Changes – Tiffany

"Come home with me, Tiff. We don't have to be back at school until June. Let's get away for a few weeks–be around friends and family, maybe take a trip to Beverly Mills Beach, I miss seeing you in a bikini. Plus, mom's going home to strategize for her reelection campaign, so we'll have a babysitter nearly every day."

"You mean, we'd *actually* have a break?"

He smiles. "Yes, a much-needed break."

I want to say yes, but we need to get used to spending time apart. To live without one another. I need to prepare to break the news to him, and I will, after his game opener in the fall. Right now, I need to plan for the reopening of Aunt Dora's dance studio…behind his back.

There's so much work to do to get the building up to code again. It's practically abandoned, but there's a need for dance in the community. It saves lives. It certainly saved mine.

"I'm gonna be working at the club again this summer." I tell him, bracing myself for his reaction.

Mase's face darkens, his brow furrowing in disapproval. "The hell you are! That place is nothing but trouble. Why would you want to go back there? If you need money, you know I got you. We have plenty of money in our accounts. You don't need to work at that damn club."

"But I want to. This is something I need to do for myself. I lean on you for everything. I need to learn to lean on myself, to be more independent."

Mase runs a hand through his hair, visibly frustrated. "I support your independence, but you also overwork yourself. And Donny works there now too? You know I can't stand him."

I sigh, feeling the tension rise between us. "Ain't nobody stuntin' Donny. Since when don't we trust each other?"

Mase's jaw clenches, his concern evident. "I trust you, but I'm trying to figure out why you aren't trusting me enough to tell me what's really going on. Besides, I promised Drew we'd work on his throws. We've never been away from each other that long. I – It doesn't make any sense, and I'm not lettin' up 'til you tell me the truth."

Our argument escalates quickly, and before I know it, I yell. "I've made my decision! I'm working back at the club. Monica and Avery are gonna help out with Drew in the evenings. It's just for a month. Distance makes the heart grow fonder, right?"

Mase tries to accept my decision with a curt nod, but the remainder of the evening feels dark. In fact, the rest of May passes with a chilly distance growing between us. I'm too busy to answer calls during the day, and our texts are few and far between. Meanwhile, Aunt Dora teaches me the inner workings of running a business and helps me forge connections with influential members of the community. They serve as sponsors for kids in need who receive free dance classes. I had no idea how kind-hearted Ms. Dora and all of these people were. They entire neighborhood really did save kids like me, and it's my time to pay it forward.

At the club, I work tirelessly to pay contractors to fix up the dance studio, trying to get permits, and catching up on the back rent that I refuse to allow Aunt Dora to pay.

Donny, despite Mase's warnings, has become a decent friend, someone who makes the long nights bearable with his jokes.

"You and these damn diaries. You ever gonna let me read any of them? I wanna know what's in your head, Ms. Weathers." Donny playfully reaches for my journal.

"Nope, you'll never know." I tease while locking my belongings away behind the bar.

"I still can't believe the future W.A.G herself is back to working in the club."

"W.A.G?" I ask, confused by the reference.

"Wife or girlfriend of a ball player." He explains.

I scoff, thinking of how I'm often perceived. "Despite what everyone thinks, I'm much more than that!"

"Well, I know that, but they don't. Everything about you is always associated with Mase. I hate how they talk about you, Tiff. I know you ignore the lies, but I see the frustration in your eyes. It's gonna get worse when he gets drafted. I hope you don't have any secrets because you're gonna get ripped apart."

I freeze in horror as I consider every part of my life that could be affected by Mase's stardom–the progress Tiny's made, Drew's innocence, the truth about Pop. A future with Mase could destroy everything.

"Hello, earth to Tiff!" He snaps his fingers in front of my eyes. "You okay? I hope I didn't scare you. I just meant I know you're lowkey, and Mase is a cocky, flashy, high-profile future NFL star. His dreams don't fit with yours."

"I appreciate your concern, Donny, but Mase and I are fine. We'll find a way to work it out."

Unconvinced, he nods. "I bet you will. You know, we've come a long way from you using me to make your boy jealous."

"Yeah, about that," I laugh. "I'm sorry. What I did wasn't fair to you. Sometimes Mase and I can be so –"

"Childish." He quickly rebuts.

I playfully slap his chest. "Definitely not the word I was thinking but fair."

However, one careless moment—an innocent touch and thoughtless laughter is caught in a snapshot—sending every media outlet spiraling, especially social media. Donny's point rings true now more than ever. These are the consequences of being Mason Boom's 'woman.'

Gossip Page #1: #1 Draft Pick Gets Played by Girlfriend and Teammate

Gossip Page #2: Mason and Drew Deserve a Better Woman in their Lives!

I stare at the picture of Drew displayed across pages for the entire world to see and thousands of strangers to tag and judge me.

Troll #1: Welp! She just lost her meal ticket.

Troll #2: How you cheat with the teammate tho? #thesehoesaintloyal

Troll #3: I hope our Golden Boy gets custody of their son. She's clearly a jump-off.

As soon as I arrive home, I spot Rafe, alert, on the couch, holding a bat and ready to pounce. Then, I rush to Drew's room, where I see him fast asleep with Avery in a rocking chair and Mel and Monica snuggling him in the bed.

"Was it bad?" I ask, aware of how intrusive and downright scary fans could be.

Mel nods. "They were knocking on the door at midnight, Tiff. This is getting out of hand."

"I may not be an attorney, yet, but I'm gonna find a way to put these people in jail. Drew cried himself to sleep. He only wanted you and Mase. Where is he?"

"Probably somewhere losing his damn mind over those photos." Rafe yells from the living room.

He hasn't answered my calls either, nor has he tried to temper the online harassment.

Tiffany: Answer your phone! People came to the house while Drew was home. This isn't right, Mase! I can't continue to deal with the gossip and lies. Do something. Say something. Why aren't you protecting us? If this is how it's gonna be when you go to the pros then we can't be together anymore.

The next morning, he shows up at my place instead of reporting to the first day of summer training. It's the first time we've seen each other in weeks, and I see nothing but fury and hurt in his eyes until Drew runs into his arms.

They've never been separated for this long, and I didn't realize how much Drew loves him until he says, "I missed you, Daddy."

We were ready to argue—about the social media chaos, his failure to shield us, and the secrecy on my part that set it all in motion. But Drew's raw emotion, the way he clings to Mase, stops us in our tracks. It's a sobering reminder of what truly matters. Instead of words, we share a look that acknowledges the love and stability Mase brings to Drew's life. After playing with Drew for a while, Mase gently puts him down for his nap, and I get ready for dance practice.

I'm standing in front of the mirror, adjusting the straps of my bodysuit, when the door creaks softly as he enters. He doesn't speak, but his reflection meets mine in the mirror—a silent conversation in our gazes. Mase steps closer, and the heat from his body is a stark contrast to the cool air of the room. He reaches out to zip up the back of my outfit, his fingers brushing against my skin and sparking a current that travels down my spine.

Mase's hands linger on the small of my back. He traces the contours of my body, a familiar path he knows by heart. I catch his eye in the mirror, seeing the mix of longing and pain in his gaze. We've both missed this — his touch and my response.

He places his left hand between my thighs while his other hand travels up to my neck, gently squeezing. I tilt my head back and rest against his shoulder, giving in to the moment. Mase finds the most tender spot on my neck and kisses it softly, each touch speaking in the unspoken language that's ours alone. The intimacy of his hold, the deliberate yet tender way he claims me, even in our quiet discord, speaks volumes. The room fades away, and for a moment, it's just the two of us, reconnected in our silent dance of longing and love. Distance hasn't made our hearts fonder, it's made our hearts break.

"Tiffany Fuckin' Nicole," he whispers in my ear. "I sped three hours from Greer to Atlanta." He admits, with his erection against my back and his fingertips near my wet core.

"And why is that Mase? What were you gonna do? Tell me." I egg him on, completely turned on by his insanity.

He nibbles on my ear. "Beat the shit out of Donny, then fuck the shit out of you."

FUCK!

"Mase," I whimper. "I can't go this long without you again."

His fingers massage my body through my clothing, nearly bringing me to the edge while he whispers, "I'll give you everything you need. You know I'm yours, baby, but first –"

He stops. Mase stops as I near my orgasm!

"First," He repeats, the urgency in his voice unmistakable. "You're going to be honest with me. Why the hell are you pushing me away? What the fuck is going on with you and Donny Baines? What aren't you telling me?"

I turn to Mase and lead him to the bed. Sitting beside him, I decide it's time to confront our issues head-on.

"Nothing's going on between me and Donny. But I do need to know what's going to happen to us when you get drafted. What does our future look like to you, Mase? Me and Drew getting harassed and talked about while you play happily ever after in the NFL?"

Mase meets my gaze, his confidence undiminished. "Well, if we're together, no one would ever hurt y'all. I'm sorry about last night. I was so fucked up, thinking of a million scenarios as to why you'd be rubbing on another man. But as soon as I got my shit together, I commented on every negative post and threatened legal action if they didn't delete it. When I get drafted though, you'll never have to worry about your safety or online trolls, no matter where we end up."

"We?" I repeat in a skeptical tone, still bothered by last night's scare.

He chuckles softly, sensing my surprise. "Uh, yeah? Me, you, and Drew. I know we haven't really discussed it, but I couldn't go anywhere without y'all. When he hugged me and called me Daddy, I nearly broke. You and Drew are my everything. Outside the two of you, nothing else matters."

"Not even football?" I probe, seeking to understand the depth of his commitment to us.

He shakes his head and locks his eyes with mine. "It doesn't even compare."

This is exactly what I feared—Mase's willingness to put us before his dreams, possibly sacrificing his career for a life with Drew and me, as well as making us a target of even more public scrutiny. This makes telling him the truth even harder than ever before.

"Mase," I begin, my voice faltering as I search for the words. "I love you, and I love the life we have together, but you're right to feel like I've been holding back"

He watches me, confusion and concern clouding his face.

"I *do* want to open up a dance studio, but it has to be here in Atlanta. I'm gonna take over Ms. Dora's studio. That's why I've been working. I'm saving up for renovations and rent. Drew and I can't leave with you." I pause, struggling to gather the courage to explain further. "I can't leave Tiny here by herself. Not now. Not when I just got her back. I want to be with you, but here is where my dream of opening a dance studio will come true."

Mase's face hardens. "Why didn't you trust me enough to tell me this before? We could have figured something out together!"

I sigh, my frustration matching his. "Because, Mase, look at how you're reacting to one little post. How can we handle long distance next year if a simple picture sets you off? You say Drew and I are your everything, but that's not healthy. You need to have a life beyond us. And we need to be safe when you're not around. Last night can never happen again."

He looks wounded as he cups my face. "God, you, and Drew. Nothing else matters, Tiff. That's how much I love you. If you have to stay here, we'll find a way to make it work. I could, maybe defer a year from the draft until you get the studio up and running."

I immediately reject his ideas. "Mase, you sound crazy! I'd never let you ruin your future for us!"

"My future is with you. I know you hate long distance, and I hate the idea of not being with you."

Before I can respond, his phone starts ringing incessantly. Sherri's name flashes on the screen over and over. Then, our group chat lights up with a message from Rafe.

SpelHouse Crew

Rafe: *WTF bro, where are you? Turn on ESPN.*

Mase grabs the remote and flips through sports channels.

Headline #1: Mason Boom Misses the First Day of Practice.
Headline #2: Mason Boom Spotted at Girlfriend's Home Instead of Practice.
Headline #3: Is Mason Boom Mature Enough to be the Face of the NFL?

A wave of realization crashes over me, echoing Sherri's warnings, and Tiny's concerns. Mase's world revolves around me. My presence, my needs, my crises...they distract him from his potential. I can't allow him to destroy his life while inadvertently interrupting ours.

"Mase," I start, my voice steady despite the turmoil inside, "This... us... it's dangerous. We're consumed with each other in a way that's unhealthy for both of us. It's irresponsible. Our love is irresponsible."

He reels with pain evident in his eyes. "Don't say that, Tiff. I love you the way I'm supposed to – with every part of my being. Please don't tell me you want to break up."

I stand firm, even as my heart aches. "You know that's not what I want, but if we can't set boundaries, we'll have to separate for good. We need to detach from one another. We need distance."

Agreeing through clenched teeth, Mase nods. "Distance. Cool. If this is how you want it, then fine, it's whatever."

Equally frustrated, I confirm. "I'm just trying to make this work, okay?"

So, with collect exhales, we lay down ground rules:

1. Immediately respond to negative statements about me and Drew

2. No more missing practices for our relationship drama
3. No more posting pictures of us online
4. No more fits of jealousy
5. Protect us and or secret at all costs
6. Limit the amount of time we spend together
   And the hardest, most devastating boundary of all...
7. Explain to Drew that Mase isn't his father

We agree to *cool things off*, but a part of me mourns the fiery intensity we're setting aside while the logical part of me knows this is necessary. For Mase's career, for my dreams, and for Drew's safety and understanding of his unique world. We need to find a balance. Only then can our love survive the challenges ahead.

~ ~ ~

Tiffany: You didn't call me last night. How long were you at the party?

My 1st and Only: I'm sorry. It was pretty late and I didn't wanna wake you.

Tiffany: You could've easily come over, neighbor!

My 1st and Only: Lol. I'm trying to respect this boundary thing you started.

Tiffany: I guess…I just miss you. Are you gonna win for me today?

My 1st and Only: Only if you promise to dance for me, on and off the field 😊

Tiffany: If you win, I promise to do more than just dance

My 1st and Only: Done. Let me get this W so I can come home to U!

Tiffany: Corny. Cute. And all mine. I love you, Mason Boom.

"Mason Boom does it again! He's on fire today! Let's go, Tigers!" The announcer's voice echoes through the stadium, electrifying the crowd. "I don't know what's gotten into Boom this year, but we've never seen him play like this. He's always been a star, but this season, he's outdone himself. NFL, here we come!"

He's right. Mase's performance this season has been phenomenal, and I can't help but feel that our troubles have somehow fueled his success. It's painful to admit, but there seems to be a connection between our heartbreak and his achievements.

I used to think Mase was the only one caught in the web of our intensity, but my obsession with him became clear the moment we no longer slept in the same bed every night, when his good morning texts slowly stopped, and our daily calls became nothing more than hurried check-ins. It hit the hardest when we failed to explain to Drew that Mase isn't his father and that I'm only his auntie, not his mother. The silence in my life now seems louder than the cheers in the stands.

Days often pass without us seeing each other. Mase is consumed by practices and a press tour for the NFL draft, while I'm overwhelmed with extra work at the club and the studio. We're drifting apart, and it seems Drew is the only one holding us together.

Watching Mase now, playing in our last homecoming game, each play, each throw he makes is bittersweet. It's like watching a star burn brightest just as it's about to fade from my own sky.

I'm addicted to him, and it's deeper than just a craving. My addiction is a painful dependency. I need Mase. I need the fix of his affection and adoration. I need my man back, which is why I know this relationship will end the way all untreated addictions do – in destruction.

After the final whistle blows and the crowd surges onto the field, I weave through the chaos, eager to share a victory hug and kiss with Mase. But as I approach, a flock of cheerleaders surround him. Their celebration lingers uncomfortably long, so I hang back and wait with our family and friends.

"Is everything okay between you two, Tiff? You know the streets are talking." Charles asks.

I shrug and avoid eye contact. "We're fine. And Mase is *definitely* okay. Look at him, he's enjoying all the attention."

"But it's obvious he isn't happy." Charles insists.

I don't see what they see. I see Mase basking in his joy while I sulk in my misery, and I wonder if it's time for Drew and me to find a path of our own, one that allows us to be happy, too, without Mase.

I look at Mase's parents, who glance back and forth between me and Mase.

Sherri leans close to Charles, her voice barely a whisper. "Oh no, what if they've broken up? These kids are gonna unravel."

"Mase and I haven't broken up, but even if we did, it's no one's business."

Laughter erupts from behind me, and Rafe steps forward. "Tiff, you and Mase are everybody's business around here. You have separation anxiety, and he's got extreme attachment disorder. It's why you two are so intense together."

"Well done, Son," Charles pats Rafe on the back. "You're gonna be the best shrink Greer's ever seen!"

"Well, sorry to burst your bubble, but you're wrong. Mase and I could easily break up and be completely fine!" I bluff.

"Keep lyin' to yourself," Rafe interrupts. "It's been hell having Mase as a roommate lately—listening to sad songs, watching depressing movies, and constantly scrolling through pics of you on his phone. After he put Drew to bed last night, I had to fight him for his keys just to stop him from visiting you at the club. Mase is a big dude, Tiff! I'm in pain. At this point, just stop playing games and tell him you don't want to be together anymore. You've already shattered his dreams when you told him you weren't going to move away with him after the draft."

Sherri gasps, "Y'all aren't moving together? But why? What about Drew? He needs his fath—" Like everyone else, Sherri, for a moment, forgets who Mase is to Drew, or who he *isn't* rather. "I mean, he and Drew are going to miss each other. They're so close."

Frustrated, I snap back, "We'll figure it out, okay? Everything's become so complicated—being Drew's guardian, but feeling like his mother, his love for Mase, being in the spotlight, constantly being nitpicked, the studio, Tiny...there's just so much happening! I just don't know what to do anymore."

My outburst sparks silence, maybe even pity, but as the crowd thins and our friends and family leave the field, Drew and I linger, waiting in the stands for Mase to return from the locker room. He usually comes out much sooner, but today, he doesn't show at all, and I struggle to shield Drew from the tears threatening to stream down my face.

Tightly clutching his football to his chest, a tired Drew asks, "When is Daddy coming?"

No matter how many times I remind him of the conversation we had months ago, I think the damage is done. Mase's imprint is in Drew's heart which has now made him susceptible to disappointment.

With a heavy heart, I call Mase. "Hey, Babe. What's up?" Mase answers, his voice almost drowned by the noisy background.

"Uh, Mase? Where are you? Drew and I are waiting for you, and it's getting cold. How much longer will you be?" I press, my patience wearing thin.

"Oh, shit, babe. I'm sorry. We popped a few bottles, and I got caught up in the celebration. Wanna join? Some of your majorettes are here. Did you know about these post-game parties? Where have I been all these years? I've been missing out." He says, his tone light and carefree.

My heart shatters from Mase's comment and the snide laughter in the background.

Finally having fun, huh?
Ditching daddy duty?

You better answer before she runs to Donny.

"Kids aren't allowed in there, and I need to rest for work later. I'll let you get back to enjoying yourself. By the way, you missed out on the *fun* because you've spent every post-homecoming win with me and Drew. Bye, Mase." I say, my voice cracking as I end the call.

He repeatedly tries to call back, but I let his calls go unanswered, leaving him to revel in his newfound freedom—freedom from the family life I imposed on him.

A few hours later, I head to work dressed to impress in a sleek white and gold ensemble to celebrate our homecoming victory. The club is going to be packed, which means I could make upwards of five thousand tonight.

Donny is the new floor manager, and I must say, it suits him. He's always been handsome, but dominance and authority look really good on him. We've become so close that he senses when something isn't right with me. So, before the night gets crazy, he pulls me aside to express his concern.

"Tiff, you've been moping for the last few weeks. Go home and fix whatever's going on with you and Mase." He advises.

"Oh hush, I've been moping because I'm tired! Can you believe the landlord raised the prices again? I haven't even opened yet. He's bleeding me dry, Don."

He nods sympathetically. "Damn, I'm sorry. You spoke to Mase about it? You know he'll help."

I shake my head. "I want to help myself. Mase already pays for Drew's fancy private school, and he paid a year of my rent so I could put all the money I saved into the studio. I need to do this on my own," My voice softens. "Besides, he's been on his A-game all season, and it's because I've removed myself from his focus. He's thriving now. He's happier than he's ever been."

Donny empathizes. "But you're not. You're overworked and need some relief. There's nothing wrong with admitting that. I just want to see you smile again. Your smile is beautiful, and…it helps generate more sales for the club, of course." He jokes though his sincerity shines through.

I roll my eyes. "Whatever, Don. Tonight, we're going to kill it—Magic City style! I hate you can't have a good time and celebrate your win with the team. I know I don't say this enough, but you're an amazing football player. I'm sorry Mase gives you hell."

"It's fine," Donny says. "Honestly, I value my friendship with you more than getting the ball on the field. So, don't worry about me. I'm happy, and I want you to be happy — with or without Mase." He brushes his fingers against mine in a brief, comforting touch that resonates deeper than expected.

Flustered, I pull my hand back and muster a playful response. "We should get back to work. We got money to make."

Although Donny's still likely to be picked in the second round of the draft, he remains humble, diligently working to support his family. I find it hard to share Mase's disdain for him when Donny and I communicate more than I do with my own boyfriend these days.

Once the club doors swing open, the crowd swells to full capacity, and so does my cash pouch from the generous tips.

"Tiffany Nicole, fill me up, please!" a patron calls out, his glass raised in anticipation.

"Tiff, two Bob Marleys, and keep the change." Another customer shouts from across the bar.

Then, a familiar voice cuts through the noise. "I'd love it if you'd answer your damn phone."

Despite the cold distance between us, Mase's voice sends a rush of warmth through me, and my heart pounds as I turn to face him.

"If I don't pick up, it means I'm giving you space—to be happy without me. You aren't missing out anymore. This is what you want, Mase."

Mase's chuckle is tinged with disbelief. "What I want? Tiffany, you're all I want." His voice is thick with emotion as he leans over the bar to tenderly caress my face. "I'm sorry about the last few months. I should've never agreed to stay away, and I'm so sorry about today. I let you and Drew down. I'll never disappoint you again."

His apology sends a shiver down my spine, and I stiffen, pulling away slightly. My response is cold, a shield against the vulnerability he stirs within me. "You shouldn't feel sorry. It's not like he's your son anyway."

Mase's expression crumples as the hurt flashes across his face. "C'mon, don't do that. Y'all are my everything. Don't shut me out, Tiff." He pleads.

"Like you've shut me out, Mase?" I counter sharply as the ache in my heart seeps through my words.

Just then, a rude customer approaches, startling me and demanding a drink.

"Fuck, let me get in on that after you're done, bruh."

"Excuse me?" Mase snaps, anger flaring in his eyes. "Show some fuckin' respect."

"Ignore him, Mase. It's a bar, this happens all the time. Just let it go."

"That's right, Golden Boy. Listen to your bitch. I see who who's the captain in this relationship."

Crap, there's no backing down now.

Mase's fists clench at his sides but instead of a fist to his face, Mase grabs the back of the man's head, forcing it down on the bar. The man's scream slices through the noisy club, drawing gasps and the flickers of phone cameras.

"Mase, stop, please—you're gonna get us both in trouble!" I plead, my voice lost in the sudden uproar of the crowd.

With a menacing calm, Mase leans closer to the man's ear and hisses, "Apologize to her. Now!"

The guy's apology is strained, through gritted teeth, "I'm sorry. I'm sorry for disrespecting you, Tiffany."

Mase's grip tightens, his voice a dangerous whisper. "Naw, don't call her Tiff. Call her captain."

"Captain! I'm sorry, Captain!" The man chokes out, his face pressed uncomfortably against the cold surface of the bar.

"That's enough, Mase!" In my agitation, I slam the shot glass I'm holding down too hard, shattering it. A sharp pain shoots through my hand, and I cry out.

Instantly, Mase turns to me, and Donny rushes over as well, his eyes wide with alarm. "Tiff, are you okay?"

Mase's concern competes with Donny's, but I'm too rattled to notice the awkward tension that fills the air as they hover over me.

Mase watches as Donny gently bandages my hand. "Thanks, Donny," I murmur, then stand with his help.

Donny gives me a sympathetic look. "I'm glad you're okay, and I know you didn't do anything wrong, but, unfortunately, you can't continue working tonight. You know the club's policy about injuries and open wounds."

"You're kidding me, right? You know I can't afford not to work right now." I protest, frustration mounting.

"I'm sorry, but there's nothing I can do. Mase attacking a customer only makes things worse." Donny says firmly, his tone reflecting his new role as floor manager and underscoring both his authority and Mase's recklessness.

However, I immediately find myself saying, "Mase was just trying to defend me. It's not like he started it."

Donny's eyes widen, slightly surprised at my defense. "It doesn't matter who started it. What matters is who got hurt." He says while looking down at my bleeding, bandaged hand. "Go home, Tiff. Take the night off.

And stay off your phone. You don't deserve the things that'll be said about you over the next few days."

Crap, I didn't think about the repercussions of being the Golden Boy's girlfriend. Everything is always my fault.

Resigned, I nod and turn to leave. Mase reaches out to me, but I glare at him and sidestep his attempt to touch me. "I'm going home, Mase. Don't follow me."

Mase's reply comes with a sarcastic edge, "That's kind of impossible. We live right next door to each other."

I snap back, "Then sleep somewhere else!"

"Your place it is, then." His smirk only fuels my anger.

At our apartment complex, Mase asks if he can come in. Despite my anger, the part of me that craves his presence relents.

"What the hell was that? You could've gotten me fired. You could've really hurt that guy! You could've gotten arrested!"

Mase's attempt at humor falls flat. "I was just trying to—"

"Stop, Mase!" I interrupt, my frustration boiling over. "You can't just do whatever you want. It affects me. It affects Drew. I'm tired of being dragged into the headlines as if I'm the problem!"

I pull out my phone, showing him the constant notifications. "Look! We're already trending!" I read aloud the headlines painting our lives as a soap opera for public consumption.

Headline #1: Mason Boom's Girlfriend Gets Caught Cheating Again.

Headline #2: Mason Boom's Baby Mama Drama.

Headline #3: In Tonight's Saga of the Greer Rich Kid Gang…Tiffany Does It Again!

Tears brim in my eyes as the weight of the public scrutiny crashes down on me. "Is this what you want for us, Mase? I can't do this anymore." I whisper, my voice breaking.

Mase's demeanor softens, and he wraps his arms around me from behind, his breath warm against my neck. "I'm sorry. I do stupid shit sometimes. I didn't realize how much this was hurting you. Tiff, I love you. Let me make this right."

"That's the problem, Mase," I say, pulling away just enough to look at him. "You're just being you—a young, college superstar living life. But I can't afford to live like that. I can't afford to be with you. You're destined for the spotlight, but I need peace and privacy. It's the only way I can keep the people I love safe, including you."

In the quiet of my living room, with Mase's arms around me, a realization dawns—love, young, all-consuming love, is both a blessing and a curse. We've become everything to each other, which has stifled our individual growth. As I rest against Mase, feeling the steady rise and fall of his chest, I think about how being someone's entire world isn't always the gift it's romanticized to be. It's a heavy load, one that carries the responsibility of another's happiness and dreams.

Mase and I, we're fire and gasoline; brilliant in our blaze, yet always at risk of burning everything around us, including ourselves. Each headline, each scandalous whisper, each yearning for him, each reference from Drew as 'daddy,' each disappointment, and each increased level of intensity has chipped away at my resolve, treading the lines between support and dependency, between loving and smothering. We are each other's everything, and that very totality threatens to undo us.

My tears dampen his arm before he turns me to face him. His eyes search mine with a raw intensity. Tenderly, he presses his forehead against mine, the gesture bridging the distance our hearts had allowed.

"I've made you cry more in the last four months than you have in the last nine years," He confesses, his voice cracking with emotion. "I hate putting you in harm's way. I hate that I've done this to you."

Our tears blend together in a symphony of sorrow and regret. I meet his gaze, my voice a whisper, heavy with truth. "And I hate what I've done to you. Our love is too overwhelming. It feels older than us, and we're too young to handle it. We're a mess, Mase, but I think we've always been a mess. Our infatuation just covered it up—until now."

He nods, understanding the truth in my words. His grip loosens slightly as if acknowledging the need for space even within our embrace.

"So, we take a break," He murmurs, his voice hoarse with emotion. "Not because I love you any less but because I love you too much, in a way that's not healthy for either of us."

I take a deep breath in shared heartache. "Yeah, we just need to find ourselves, that's all, become our own people."

He kisses the tears from my cheeks, a gesture so tender it fractures my heart a little more. "Then, we come back together as whole, not halves."

With our foreheads pressed together, sharing the warmth and the sadness of our decision, I whisper back, "As a family. Me, you, and Drew. I'm going to adopt him. He deserves a mother, and someday you'll be his dad. Just not now, Mase. We need to learn to love ourselves just a little bit more than we love each other."

Mase's voice cracks through his tears. "I love you, Tiffany Nicole Weathers."

I breathe out softly, "I love you, too, Mason Boom."

We make love one final time before we depart from being one another's end all be all, savoring the bittersweetness of our love, a last dance of unity before embarking on our journeys apart.

Chapter 25

Never Settle – Mason

Sitting across from my new therapist, I can't help but crack a smile. "You know, you ain't that bad, Dr. G. Dr. Lee told me I'd like you."

He smiles back, his tone amused yet firm. "You aren't so bad yourself, Mase. Now, it's been seven months since your breakup; you have two weeks until graduation, and three weeks before your move to Seattle. Are you ready?"

I lean back while the chair creaks slightly under the shift of my weight. "Ready for what exactly? To be on the biggest stage of my life? To win a championship? To leave Tiffany for good? To abandon Drew?"

His eyes meet mine, not missing a beat. "Ah, the latter two, of course. We both know you're going to perform your best on that field, but it's going to take a lot more work to navigate your complex emotions about your relationship. First and foremost, you aren't *leaving* Tiffany. Secondly, you aren't *abandoning* Drew. Sometimes, being in someone's life from a distance is just as nurturing as being there physically. Did you suggest a visiting schedule like we discussed?"

I let out a deep sigh. "Yeah, we set up a schedule. I'll see Drew during the holidays. He'll stay with me during my little league training camps over the summer and for a couple of weeks in the off-season. I can also call anytime."

"That doesn't sound like abandonment to me." Dr. G. points out with a reassuring smile.

"I guess…" I shift uncomfortably in my seat. "But what if things change? What if Tiffany moves on? What if Drew starts calling someone else dad? What if I lose them? I feel like I need to hold on as tight as I can, Doc."

"Holding on too tightly can sometimes push people away, Mase. It's normal to fear loss, especially given your history, but it's also important to learn how to manage that fear without it controlling you. Letting go doesn't mean you stop caring—it means you're allowing yourself and your loved ones the space to grow. This doesn't just apply to Tiffany and Drew but to you as well. You're stepping into a huge new chapter in Seattle, and it's essential you embrace it fully."

I nod, slowly absorbing his words. The idea of balance, of nurturing relationships from a distance, seems difficult but necessary, especially if I want to be with Tiff again. "You're right, Dr. G. I need to focus on being healthy, not just for them but for myself."

Dr. G. offers an encouraging smile. "Exactly. You're building a life that honors your needs and theirs. It's about creating a sustainable way of loving and living. Remember, you're not alone. We'll navigate this together. I'll see you next week. Enjoy the remaining time you have left with your friends and family, Tiff and Drew included."

I leave Dr. G's office with a new confidence. I'm evolving into the man I was meant to be, but I'll always hope that I'm still the man that was meant to be with Tiffany.

For now, I'm headed to Fulton Women's Penitentiary. Tiny sent me a special invitation, but when I arrive, so do my parents, Rafe, the Bakers, and Tiff.

"Uh, any idea why we're here?" Mel whispers, glancing around.

We all look at Tiffany, awaiting an answer. Perhaps I stare longer because I haven't seen her in a while. It's been a few weeks, but she still takes my breath away. Her vanilla scent floats over to me, and I notice her quick, cautious glances in my direction. It takes all my willpower to respect the boundaries we've set and not pull her into my arms.

"I'm just as lost as y'all, but c'mon, follow me. Let's check in." She shrugs.

Tiffany leads us through the security checkpoints with practiced ease. None of us knows why Tiny has called this gathering, but the weight of the unknown pulls at our steps. When the doors of the private chapel swing open, we see about twenty inmates gathered inside, with Tiny standing proudly at the front.

"Ah, it's 'bout time you slow pokes get here!" Ms. Dora exclaims. Her eyes catch mine, and she nods with a smile that seems to know more than she lets on.

Nearby, a woman I don't recognize catches Tiffany's eye, and they embrace warmly. "Mrs. Wilkins! It's so good to see you. So, this is what Tiny's been hinting at?"

"Sure is," Mrs. Wilkins responds, gesturing towards a row of chairs. "Have a seat. I placed some tissues next to your chair."

As everyone finds their places, Tiffany and I are left to sit next to each other, where our shoulders gently brush against one another. "You smell delicious." I murmur.

She turns to me with her sparkling eyes. "And you look so handsome, Mase."

We both ask, *"How are you?"* at the same time, but before either of us can answer, Mrs. Wilkins steps to the front.

"Hello, friends and family. Today, you've been invited to Fulton Women's Penitentiary's first GED graduation." She announces. "These ladies have worked long and hard to reach this milestone, and it's my honor to present to you, our valedictorian. She's someone I've known since she was a little girl. Someone I love with all my heart—Ms. Tiny Weathers."

Tiffany's hand finds mine, gripping it tightly as a gasp escapes her lips.

As Tiny steps forward to a round of applause, tears stream down Tiffany's cheeks. I squeeze her hand, trying to offer comfort while she watches her sister take the microphone. Tiny looks out over the crowd, but her eyes lock with Tiffany's.

"Wow, I didn't think I'd be up here crying over earning my GED, but here I am," Tiny pauses, blinking back tears. "To some, this might not seem like a big deal, but to me, it's a blessing. This moment is something I never thought I'd experience—the chance to earn something for myself. Something most kids take for granted, something I had to fight hard for. This is just one moment, but it's part of something bigger. I'm slowly reclaiming everything that was taken from me—my body, my dignity, my hope, my future, my life. For so long, I didn't believe love and happiness were possible for me. Not until a few years ago."

Tiny pauses, her gaze sweeping the crowd before settling back on Tiffany. "But I have more now than ever before, and I'm happier than I could have ever imagined. I'm sober, I'm safe, and I'm loved. None of that would've been possible without my little sister and the incredible people she brought into my life. You and Drew… y'all are my world. You saved me, and I love you more than words can say." She then turns to the other inmates. "These ladies and I, we all have different stories, but they all end in triumph. We have a long way to go, but today, we celebrate a great milestone. We've done what so many people told us was impossible, and all we need was encouragement and belief. Thank you to our family and friends here today. Thank you for believing in us. We did it, y'all. We earned our GEDs!"

The room erupts in cheers, and Tiny and Tiffany rush into each other's arms for a hug that seems to last an eternity. Watching them, the clarity of their bond and the importance of their connection hit me with force. This is why Tiffany needs to stay in Atlanta. They need each other, and I'll just have to learn to live without my most basic need—the love of my life.

When I step out of the chapel, the frustration of the past few months begins to lift. I understand everything now, and I'm ready to move forward.

Letting go isn't the end of us, it's just a new beginning for us, separately but forever connected by the love we share. We'll come back together someday, and someday we'll be the family I know we're meant to be.

～～～

I sink into the plush seat across from the sports journalist. Her bright eyes gleam with curiosity and a hint of determination, which suggests she's after more than just game talk. A brief silence hangs between us before the camera light blinks on, and her voice cuts through, starting the interview.

"Mason Boom, you've had a record-breaking season. 38 touchdown passes, 975 rushing yards, and 15 rushing touchdowns," She begins, ticking off the stats. "I mean—wow! You've really redefined what it means to be a rookie and now, you're heading to the Super Bowl. How does that feel?"

"It feels incredible, honestly," I reply, my voice steady as I lean forward, hands clasped and focused despite the flutter of nerves. "Every athlete dreams of this moment, and to be here in my rookie year—it's surreal. I'm just focused on delivering my best game and staying grounded."

She nods, jotting something down on her notepad before she looks back up. "That focus has definitely paid off on the field. But let's talk a bit about life off the field. You've become somewhat of an enigma since entering the league, very private, despite your high-profile family and past relationship. What's driving that decision?"

I pause, choosing my words carefully. "Well, it's all about keeping my priorities in order, and the only public priorities in my life are football and mentorship. After I win the championship, my summer little league program begins," I explain. "Every other aspect of my life is my business only. Respecting the privacy of my family and friends is paramount to me."

"Speaking of family, there have been rumors that your tabloid-worthy ex-girlfriend, Tiffany Weathers, is *allegedly* dating your former teammate and Super Bowl challenger, Donny Baines. Any comment on that?"

The mention of Tiffany's name tightens my jaw, a reaction I hoped wouldn't be so visible. Maintaining composure, I straighten up, but the warmth drains from my tone. "I believe we agreed *not* to discuss my personal life. I'd appreciate it if we keep this conversation about the game and my performance on the field."

Her eyes flicker. "Of course, Mason. Let's get back to football then—"

But the damage is done. My focus has shifted to unwanted images of Tiffany with someone else. "Actually, I think we've covered enough for today," I interrupt, standing abruptly. "Thank you for your time."

The interview ends as swiftly as it began. I'm two weeks away from the most important game in my life, but I'm not as excited as I was because the most important person in my life won't be there to celebrate. Or perhaps she will be, cheering from the other side.

I guess I'll find out the truth before my big day which would help clear my mind, especially since the Super Bowl will be in Atlanta.

Mase: Yo! I'm leaving out in a few days.

Bash: Okay…and?

Rafe: Lol. Bash is a savage!

Jay: But he's secretly excited to see you. We all are. Especially Drew. He spent last weekend with Mom and Dad at the Governor's mansion. I love my little nephew, but he's kind of terrible.

Bash: Terrible ain't the word. He literally told me if I didn't give him $200 he'd kick my butt. And he said he could beat me in basketball!

Mase: Lol. That's my boy! I can't wait to see him. Tiff sent me a video of his long range throws.

Rafe: Ah…Tiffany…just ask us what you really wanna know.

Mase: Fine! Is it true? She and Donny? Are they really a thing?

Rafe: No! Not at all. They're just friends.

Bash: Dude's a joke. Tiff friend zoned him but he keeps trying. Everyone knows you and Tiff are meant to be.

Rafe: Whoa! Is Bash getting sentimental?

Bash: Tiff's fam. I'm not gonna let her get swept up by a cornball. See you soon, bro. Focus on the championship.

I feel a sense of relief after talking with my brothers. Tiffany and I both know it's impossible to cut each other off completely, but we've set clear boundaries. I still fly to Atlanta throughout the year to spend time with Drew, but after a few slip-ups, we decided it's best for my parents to facilitate the handoffs. Whenever Tiffany and I see each other, it's like we're two lovestruck fools all over again. To avoid that, it's better if we act like there's a protective order keeping us apart.

Since I've started to discover who I am on my own, I'm often swamped with my business investments, charity work, and mentoring young athletes. It's liberating and daunting, but every step forward is a step toward understanding my purpose.

Yet, even with my newfound independence, I still want to share my successes with Tiffany, but I'm learning to accept that it might not happen.

My phone buzzes beside me; it's Kira from the cheer squad, who's been openly interested in me since my draft day. She's cute, but she ain't Tiffany. No one is.

"Hey, what's up, Kira?" I answer, keeping my tone friendly but reserved.

"You have any plans for your off day when we get to Atlanta?" She asks, her voice casual and hopeful.

"Yeah, I'm catching up with family." I reply, sidestepping her underlying intention.

She laughs, a sound that's become familiar over the season. "So, I assume when you say family, you mean your ex?

I stiffen slightly, a reflex. "No, hence why she's my ex," I say, a bit more sharply than intended. Kira's forwardness is usually refreshing, but today it feels intrusive.

"I've seen your ex. I mean...she's alright, I guess. But you can do so much better."

My jaw tightens, and I can feel a protective fire igniting within me. "Bullshit. Why settle for better when she's the best." I counter, my tone edged with a warning not to tread further.

She pauses, sensing the shift and my visible irritation. "I get it. I overstepped," she says quickly, backpedaling with a flirtatious chuckle. "I'll leave you be for now, but if we win the big game, I'm expecting a big kiss from you."

I roll my eyes and respond in jest, "I hear you, Kira." My humor masks my annoyance, but internally, I'm firm—nobody talks down on Tiffany.

The call ends with a laugh, but as I pack for my flight to Atlanta, I can't help but think about the possibility of being with someone else. I've had opportunities to be in a relationship, to have sex, but my heart won't allow me to.

When I arrive at Hartsfield-Jackson Airport, the clamor of fans greets us, but it's the sight of Drew running towards me that anchors me back to reality. I scoop him up in a spin and momentarily forget about the cameras flashing around us.

"Where's Tiffany?" I ask Monica and Rafe as I set Drew down.

"With big-headed Donny!" Drew pipes up.

I chuckle, but my heart sinks a little. "He does have a big head, doesn't he? Is he nice to you?" I probe gently.

Drew shrugs. "I don't know. Never met him. Mom's always saying no when he asks to come over. He always asks to practice drills with me, but she says, *'That's Mase's job.'* It's annoying when he calls her babe! She's not a baby. She's old."

We all laugh at Drew's five-year-old rationale. It stings to hear her referenced by any idiom from another man. It hurts to know that she's moving forward in life and love, especially with an old teammate. The Tiffany I know would never betray me like that, but it's reassuring to know she hasn't let anyone take my place in Drew's life.

"Your mom's the best." I say, feeling a surge of respect for Tiffany's protective nature.

Drew hugs me tight and says, "You are too, Mase."

Though I'm happy back in Seattle, nothing feels more complete than this—having my boy back in my life.

~ ~ ~

After practice, a long session of reviewing plays, and planning my upcoming little league camp, there's a gentle knock at my hotel room door. I pull it open to find Kira standing there, draped in nothing but a thin gold silk teddy with her long, dark hair barely covering her hard nipples.

"Hey, Mase," She purrs, stepping into the soft light of my room. The fabric of her lingerie clings to her like paint. "Thought you could use some... relaxation before the big game."

I can't deny my immediate reaction to her boldness. But as she steps closer and the scent of her perfume hits me, it's not excitement that fills me—it's a longing for a different smell, vanilla, and for a different presence, Tiffany Weathers.

"Kira, you look incredible," I start, holding up a hand to maintain some distance between us. "But I'm really not in the right headspace for this. I need to focus. I can't be distracted right now."

Her pout is playful, but there's a sharpness in her eyes that speaks of more than just casual flirtation. "Come on, Mase. You deserve to have some fun. You're always so serious. I've seen the way you look at me. Let me give you a little Super Bowl boost." She inches close enough to grab my growing erection, but I immediately move back.

"As tempting and, I'm sure, pleasing as it sounds, not tonight. Okay?" I try to gently reject her.

Kira pouts but smiles, "Fine! *But*, don't forget, if you win the Super Bowl, I get a kiss."

I chuckle, shaking my head. "Yeah, whatever you say, Kira." I manage to smile, trying to keep the mood light. "Thanks for understanding."

Once she's gone, the silence of the room feels heavier. I try to return to my playbook, but my focus is shot.

On impulse, I pull up Tiffany's social media. There's a new post—a video of her promoting one of her dance competitions. "The Super Bowl is in ATL, but so is the Winter Grand Slam Championship. Come out and support my College Park Diamonds!" She says with her infectious smile.

I watch it twice, then a third time, each view softening the sharp edges of my loneliness. My thumb hovers, then double-taps the screen. It's a small interaction, a momentary connection across the divide that used to be our life together.

Leaning back, I close my eyes and listen to her voice echoing in my mind until I drift off to sleep, holding onto thoughts of her smile, her beauty, her strength, and our shared memories that no distance or time can erase.

Chapter 26

Vanilla – Tiffany

Life as a dance studio owner is as rewarding as it is exhausting, and adding the role of mom only multiplies the chaos. Six months ago, I made the decision to officially adopt Drew. With Tiny and Sherri's support, the process was surprisingly swift. He now officially calls me *mom*, a title I cherish deeply.

We've always been a family, but it's official, though to Drew, Mase has shifted from being *dad* to just Mase. He's somewhat aware enough to understand that Mase isn't his biological father, yet he loves him as such. Mase continues to be an incredible presence in his life, and that's something I wouldn't change for the world.

Though we've taken a step back from our relationship, I keep up with his life from afar. I've watched every game this season and even spotted the *football player and his dancer* patch I gave him in high school sewn on his jersey. That keeps my hope alive that one day, we might find our way back to each other, when we become who we need to be, when life slows down, and when his lifestyle can lend us the privacy we need to live happily ever after.

The studio's growth has been explosive; we started with eleven dancers and now have forty-two. It's exciting, but I'm already outgrowing the current space. The College Park Diamonds are the best majorette dance team in the South, and the attention they receive is surreal. It's well-deserved, but sometimes, my attachment to certain names does bring unwanted attention.

Being known as Mase's *ex*-girlfriend can be just as overwhelming as being his actual girlfriend. I'm still heavily scrutinized, especially because of my friendship with Donny. We are *just* friends. Mase would never betray me, nor would I betray him. I've friend-zoned Donny, and he's accepted it, but now that they're facing each other in the Super Bowl, my loyalties are split between my new best friend and the love of my life.

"So, I've been thinking," Donny says, folding costumes for my upcoming competition. "If I win the championship, then I get to take you out on a real date–me and you out in public."

I immediately laugh, waving off the idea with a flutter of my hand. "A date? Don, no! It's already bad enough everyone thinks we're together."

"And why is that so bad, Tiff?" Don gently probes, taking my hands in his. "We're attracted to each other. We enjoy spending time together. Are you seriously gonna let your loyalty to Mase stop you from falling in love again?"

I gently pull my hands back, keeping the mood light. "Falling in love? Boy, I'm not in love with you. And no one said anything about Mase."

"You didn't have to," he insists. "He's always the elephant in the room. There are rumors about him and that cheerleader, you know? I think her name's Kira. Just watch them at the game. You're being loyal for no reason. He's moved on, and you should too."

An awkward silence ensues as I wonder if Mase really has moved on, but then Donny shifts to an equally uncomfortable topic.

"So, you gonna cheer for me in the box with my family on Sunday?" He asks, voice full of hope.

I sigh. "I'm still thinking about it. My entire family is gonna be in Mase's box. Drew also wants to be with them. He doesn't even know your family."

"He doesn't know them because you keep me at arm's length," Donny presses, his voice softening. He reaches up to caress my cheek, and for a moment, I lean into the warmth of his touch, only to catch myself and lean back. "I want to be part of Drew's life too, not just yours."

"We're just friends, Don. That's all we'll ever be." My voice cracks slightly, betraying the conflict inside. "My heart, it—"

"I know. It belongs to Mase, but mine belongs to you. And I don't mind waiting a little longer until you feel the same about me."

Brushing off the moment, I gesture towards the pile of boxes. "Thank you. Now, let's get these loaded up. We've both got championships to win, remember?"

"You got it, Coach T." He responds with a smile, and helps me prep for my big day.

~ ~ ~

My junior majorette dance team is here at Banneker High School for the big competition, the Winter Grand Slam Championship. We've fought hard to get to this point.

As the gym quickly fills to the brim, the air vibrates with anticipation, and my dancers, dressed in glittering costumes, line up as their category and wait for their name to be announced.

I take my place at the edge of the stage, my heart pounding with excitement while faint voices yell, 'Alright, Coach T! Do your thang!' 'C'mon, Diamonds! Show 'em how College Park gets down!'

The music kicks in, and my girls launch into a routine I meticulously choreographed. Their movements are sharp yet fluid, perfectly in sync with the beats that resonate through the gym. Each pop, lock, and pirouette is executed flawlessly, drawing cheers from the crowd.

But then, the energy shifts dramatically—the cheers swell to a deafening roar. Through the main entrance strides the one and only Mason Boom, hand in hand with Drew. His presence causes a stir unlike any other.

Drew breaks away from Mase and dashes toward me, his little arms wide open. "Good luck, Mom!" He beams, wrapping his arms around me in a fierce hug.

I gather him close and look over his shoulder to meet Mase's gaze. He walks up to us, his expression tender. Then, he leans in and gently kisses my forehead.

"Knock 'em dead, Tiff." He whispers before he and Drew take a seat next to Aunt Dora in the stands.

Reinvigorated by their support, I turn back to my team, signaling them to focus. The competition is fierce, but the girls rise to the occasion. Their energy is infectious, and their execution is impeccable.

As the competition comes to a close and the announcer takes the stage, envelope in hand, everyone in the gym holds their breath.

"And first place at the Winter Grand Slam Championship goes to... Coach Tiffany's Dance Team, The College Park Diamonds!"

The crowd erupts in cheers, and my team rushes to me, engulfing me in a group hug filled with laughter and tears.

"We did it, Coach T!" A dancer cries.

"I can't believe we won! I've never won anything before." Another cries.

I cry too, because many of these girls are just like me. We don't come from much but we have so much to give, and they deserve this win and so many more to come.

"I'm so proud of you, Tiffany." Aunt Dora pulls me into a tight embrace then winks at Drew. "Come on, let's make your mom mad and go eat lots of cupcakes!" She leads a giggling Drew away, leaving Mase and me alone.

The gym slowly empties, and the noise fades into a quiet hum. "I guess it's just me and you, huh?" Mase quips with a crooked smile that tugs at my heartstrings.

"Mase, you're not supposed to be here. Tomorrow is the biggest day of your life. I shouldn't be on your mind."

He brushes a stray hair from my face with a touch that sends shivers down my spine. "Yet, you're always on my mind, Tiff."

"Mase," I whisper, my resolve quickly melting.

"Let me take you on a date." His voice is earnest, his eyes searching mine for a sign of acquiescence.

This time, with sense, I yell, "Mason Boom! You play in the Super Bowl tomorrow!"

"I've cleared it, I promise. I have seven hours till curfew, and I want to spend every minute with you. It's been too long. Every football player needs his dancer." He declares, his gaze holding mine captive.

Biting my lip, I think it over before relenting. "Okay, but just for a few hours. You need to be sharp tomorrow, and I refuse to be the reason you're not."

He kisses my hand gently, his lips warm against my skin. "Thank you, Tiff. I'll see you in a bit."

As he turns to leave, panic sets in. "Wait! What am I supposed to wear?"

He throws a mischievous grin over his shoulder. "Wear something comfortable...maybe something short and silky." His wink sends a flush across my cheeks.

Later, after settling an excited but anxious Drew into bed, I slip into a simple gold silk dress and matching heels. Then, I straighten my hair. I'd be the perfect package if only I had more of the vanilla fragrance Tiny once created.

"Mommy, why can't I go? I wanna spend time with Mase, too."

"I know, but you'll be with him for a week during Spring break and the whole month of May for camp!" I explain.

Drew, nearly on the brink of a tantrum, complains. "I wish he lived here. I wish we all lived together."

"Me too, Drew." I sigh. "Get some sleep, okay? Tomorrow, you get to see Nee-nah, Pop Pop, Nana, and Papa Baker, plus all your crazy aunts and uncles at Mase's big game. It's gonna be so much fun."

"I can't wait. I love you, Mommy."

"I love you, too, Son."

Monica and Rafe arrive just as I'm ready to leave, their eyes widening in appreciation.

"Tiffany, you look stunning. Have you seen the photos of you and Mase at your competition? You're all over the internet." Monica exclaims, her tone a mix of awe and concern.

I shake my head, unwilling to let the whispers tarnish this night. "I've been avoiding social media today. I've been working like crazy all year. I haven't been on a date since – well, college. I refuse to let anyone or any rumors ruin tonight. I just want to enjoy myself."

Not only have I not looked online, but I'm also avoiding Donny. He's called me over and over again, but I've been caught up with today's competition and Mase's unexpected arrival. I feel guilty, but I also don't owe him anything, especially as it pertains to my feelings for Mase.

"Any idea what Mase has planned for me?" I ask, turning to Rafe.

Rafe presses his lips together, trying to contain a smile. "Nope, I got no idea."

Monica nudges him. "Oh, c'mon, babe. Give her a little hint. I know it's killing you not to say anything."

Rafe easily relents, "Okay, okay! Vanilla. But that's all I'm giving you. Now, enjoy yourself. My brother's excited to see you."

I hug my friends and take one last peek at my sleeping Prince then head to the address Mase texted me. It isn't far from my home, but I was definitely expecting a restaurant or something. Instead, I pull up to Atlanta's

Midtown Florals. I don't know much about flowers, so I'm curious to know what Mase has up his sleeve.

He swings the door open, looking devastatingly handsome in tailored khaki pants and a burgundy polo that clings to his sculpted frame. His gaze sweeps over me with an intensity that sends anticipation through my veins. Our eyes lock, charged with a heat that seems to scorch the very air between us. But before we can succumb to our magnetic pull, Mase takes my hand and guides me into the floral shop.

The air is thick with a recognizable scent. I draw in a deep breath, letting the familiar fragrance fill my senses, and exhale slowly. "Vanilla."

He slides his arms around me from behind, a gesture as familiar as the rhythm of my own heartbeat. Mason leads me to a long table cluttered with an assortment of glass beakers, distillation apparatuses, and small vials of essential oils. My curiosity peaks as I survey the array of honeysuckles, magnolia flowers, and vanilla orchids.

"What's all this?" I ask, my voice tinged with amusement.

Mason grins, his eyes twinkling with excitement. "Tiny told me you ran out of your special fragrance and gave me a list of ingredients," he explains, his voice softening. "Then, I called my Aunt Crystal—you know, the chemist turned perfume billionaire—here we are, about to recreate the smell that represents home to you and love to me."

His words warm my heart. Overwhelmed by his gesture, I wrap my arms around him in a tight hug. As we slowly pull away, the air is charged with our suppressed feelings.

Mase is meticulous, explaining each step as we mix and measure, creating bottle after bottle of the precious fragrance. Our laughter fills the space, natural and free, while we flirt through our tasks, and our hands occasionally brush against one another, reigniting familiar sparks.

An hour slips by unnoticed, and by the time we've bottled enough fragrance to last through next year, the deep connection we've always shared is renewed.

Afterward, Mason leads me to a corner of the floral shop that's been transformed into a romantic dining nook. The table is elegantly set among the blooms, adorned with soft candlelight that flickers gently next to our gourmet meal.

"I can't believe you did all this," I say, my voice thick with emotion as I take in every detail, every thoughtful touch. "This is amazing. You're amazing. Thank you."

As we dine, our conversation flows as easily as the wine. But as the last of it lingers in our glasses, Mason's expression shifts to one of hesitancy. "Tiff, I have to ask...about Don. Is there anything between you two? I know I have no right to ask, but I just need to know."

I shake my head. "No, Mase. I promise, there's nothing there. He's been a great friend, nothing more." I pause, then add with soft sincerity, "You're still my one and only, Mason Boom."

Mason looks relieved. "And you, Tiffany Weathers, are still my first and forever. Always have been, always will be." He extends his hand across the table, our fingers intertwining in a familiar clasp that feels like coming home.

As we lean across the table, the moment feels suspended in time. Our faces draw closer, and the distance finally closes—the kiss we've both been waiting for is sweet, deep, and passionate.

When we finally pull away, Mase presses a button on his phone, initiating the soulful melody of Dru Hill's "Beauty."

Mason extends his hand and draws me into his arms. His hold is firm, guiding us through each step and turn with a grace that reminds me just how well we move together. As the song winds down, he gently spins me under his arm, then pulls me back against him, where his lips find the curve of my shoulder, pressing against my bare skin.

"I've missed the taste of you." He murmurs against my ear, the vibrations sending tingles through me.

I close my eyes and relish in his craving for me. "I'm yours to taste, yours to eat, and yours to love, for as long as you want, especially tonight."

We stop moving, and I slowly turn to him. Mase gently lifts my head to level our gaze, leaning in until our lips meet in unbridled passion. His hand slowly dances up my thigh, evoking moans I hadn't released in a year.

"Mase," I pant, with near tears falling from my eyes.

Mase slows down and caresses my cheek. "If you tell me to stop, I will."

I exhale deeply, with a hint of insecurity peeking through. "Do you still love me?"

He chuckles under his breath. "Was I ever supposed to stop?"

With tears in my eyes, I shake my head. "No, Mase. Don't ever stop loving me."

He kisses me again and rubs his fingers against the lining of my panties, moving back and forth until I feel myself escalating into a sensual frenzy. He effortlessly lifts me and places me on the counter, where flowers surround my body as if I'm being laid on an altar to be worshipped by him.

"Mine to taste, mine to eat, and mine to love." He places his head between my legs, where his tongue flickers inside me.

Before I could warn him, I release so wildly, so beautifully on his tongue. He responds with kisses to my inner thigh, traveling upwards to my navel, my breast, my neck, then my lips.

Mase unbuckles his pants and pulls off his shirt while I pull my thin dress over my head. Mase's eyes immediately dart to something new, something just for him. A small heart tattoo under my right breast with an inscription that says *1st and Only.*

I can *feel* the emotions on his face as I sit up, wrap my legs tightly around his waist, and whisper, "I love you, Mason Boom."

"And I love—" His declaration is interrupted by his plunge inside me. "Fuck! I love all of you—every single—" He thrusts again. "Wet—" He groans. "Tight—" He pumps. "Perfect love—"

He continues to drive deeper and deeper than I can ever imagine.

"Oh, God! I'm 'bout to come!" I cry, limp and weak.

"Me too, but wait for me."

Mase tightens his grip around my waist and pounds the sense out of me in a swift, uncontrollable fury while circling my clit with his thumb. I feel him everywhere, and I can't help but scream. We cry out in unison as we release fierce shivers and collapse on the counter.

I needed this. We needed this. He fills me up in ways that surpass physical sensation. Our bodies mold together, creating the most beautiful type of love one can ever experience—fate.

"I'm gonna win the Super Bowl for you and Drew tomorrow. Every pass, every touchdown, everything I do is for you. I love you, Tiffany, and tomorrow, we'll be together again."

Chapter 27

Super Bowl I – Tiffany

It's Super Bowl Sunday, and my emotions couldn't be any more mixed. The energy in the stadium is electric but even more invigorating is the warmth that lingers from last night. My date with Mase was everything I didn't realize I needed. For the first time in a while, I'm hopeful about us. I can imagine a future where the pieces finally fit together.

The premier box is filled with laughter from all of our family and friends. Drew is practically bouncing with excitement, barely able to sit still while soaking up the attention from his doting pseudo-grandparents. His little eyes are wide as he peers down at the field. Charles leans down to adjust Drew's jersey, a tiny version of Mase's, while Sherri fastens his hat.

"Isn't he the cutest little fan?" She gushes, her pride evident in every word.

Then, Mel nudges me with her eyebrow raised and a mischievous grin spreading across her face. "So, are you going to admit that you're in love again, or do we have to drag it out of you?"

"You see that smile? That's the 'I-just-had-the-best-date-ever' smile. Haven't seen that since college." Rafe joins in.

Mel starts singing in a playfully exaggerated voice, "Mase and Tiff, sitting in a tree, K-I-S-S-I-N-G..."

"First comes love, then comes Super Bowl rings!" Monica picks up Mel's verse with a laugh.

The three of them erupt into laughter while I shake my head, pretending to be annoyed. But I can't hide the smile plastered on my face. "Y'all are ridiculous," I mutter, but they're right. I haven't felt this giddy in a long time.

As I reach for my phone to check the time, a text message pops up from Donny and my heart sinks, knowing he must be hurt.

Donny: I saw the pictures, Tiff. I know you were with Mase last night, and I get it. He's your first love, and it's hard to move on from that, but I need to know where I stand with you. I've been here, and I'll still be here, even if it's hard for you to see. If I win today, I don't want to just win the trophy. I want to win you. I can give you the peaceful, private life you want, he can't. I just need you to give me a chance to show you how happy we can be together.

I stare at the message with a flurry of guilt and confusion swirling in my chest, but before I can process Donny's words, my phone buzzes again—this time, it's Mase.

Mase: It's always been me, you, and the beautiful family we've built. Today is the beginning of our happily ever after

The teasing from my friends fades into the background while I read Mase's words over and over again. I care about Donny, but Mase's message fills me with long-awaited peace. He is my home. He is love. I know where my heart truly lies, and the future I've imagined with Mase, Drew, and our family—it feels more possible than ever.

Suddenly, the box falls into hushed silence as two unexpected figures step through the door.

A collective gasp fills the room, but the loudest is from Sherri. "Crystal and Terry, you made it!"

Charles looks stunned, unable to find words as he takes in the sight of his best friends, the Lynns. "Oh my God, it's been too long, brother."

Sherri rushes forward, embracing Crystal tightly. "Way too long. I hope you don't mind. Mase invited us." Crystal mutters.

The rest of us watch, overcome by the raw emotion of the reunion. It's been years since Sherri and Charles have seen Crystal and Terry.

Even Drew senses the weight of the emergence, clinging to my side and whispering, "Mom, who's that lady that looks like you?"

I laugh and correct Drew. "She's good friends with Nee-nah and Pop Pop. She's pretty, isn't she?"

"Because she looks like you!" He reiterates.

Crystal wipes her eyes and releases Sherri from her tight embrace, then turns and smiles at me from across the room. I feel an almost ethereal connection between the two of us. My childhood memories are so spotty, but there's a faint memory of seeing the beautiful Crystal Lynn on a TV screen.

"Mommy," Drew tugs. "Your twin is walking over here." I laugh and tell him to go look out for Mase.

Crystal approaches me with a curiosity in her eyes that mirrors my own. It's as if she's trying to place where she knows me from. When she nears, the resemblance between us isn't lost on me, and the murmurs around us grow louder.

"Do you like the fragrance?" Crystal asks, her voice cutting through the tension. It's a simple question, yet it feels weighted.

"Yes," I respond, my voice steadier than I feel. "It smells just like the fragrance my sister and I grew up smelling—vanilla orchids, honeysuckle, and magnolia. It's like... home."

Crystal's eyes gloss over with emotion, her lips parting slightly. "Sister? Where is she? I'd love to—" But her words are cut off by the announcer's introduction of the Seattle Wolves, with Mason's name echoing through the stadium, pulling our attention away.

"I'm sorry. It's time to cheer on the star of the evening. Thank you, Mrs. Lynn. This may sound creepy, but I've always wanted to meet you." I manage to say, feeling the chaos of emotions our brief encounter has stirred within me.

Crystal nods, her gaze lingering on me with a mixture of confusion and recognition. "Same here. I've looked through so many photos of you and Mase over the years. I'd really like to continue our conversation later." She suggests, her tone hopeful yet cautious.

I nod, my mind racing with questions about this unexpected connection. "Absolutely, we'll talk later." I agree.

Drew tugs at my hand, his voice filled with excitement. "Mom! Look, it's Mase!" He shouts, pointing towards the field. My heart leaps as I see my man jogging into view, his presence electrifying the crowd. He waves energetically at us and gestures towards the patches on his jersey.

As the camera zooms in on him, the Jumbotron broadcasts his image across the stadium, then pans to me and Drew, proclaiming that Mason Boom's family and friends are here cheering him on. But then, it shifts to the Wolves cheerleaders, and one in particular who's holding a sign that reads, "Kiss Me, Mase. I'm all yours!"

Frustrated and feeling a bit insecure, I lean over to Rafe. "Hey, who's that girl over there holding the sign?" I inquire, trying to keep my tone casual.

Bash waves off my concern with a nonchalant shrug. "Kira Stellano, just a groupie. She's known for being...friendly with the team."

"Even with Mase?" The question slips out before I can stop it.

Bash softens his response, "No, not Mase. He's all yours, Tiff."

I feel a bit better, but I can't help but notice his smile toward her. I also remember Donny mentioning her name. How could I compete with someone who sees him all the time? Why would I want to compete at all? Mase and I haven't been together in nearly a year, so I shouldn't be worried or jealous, but I am.

Then, the announcer calls out the Atlanta Warriors, with their star receiver, Donny Baines, leading the way. Donny strides onto the field with confidence radiating from him. And when he spots our box, he gestures a heart towards me. The Jumbotron catches the moment, broadcasting my embarrassed expression to the entire stadium.

Bash grumbles under his breath, "I hate that guy."

And beside him, Sherri disapprovingly shakes her head. "Tiffany, I hope you stop stringing that piece of crap along. What type of man goes after his former teammate's soulmate?"

Feeling the frustration of friends and family, I announce, "I know y'all are tired of the tabloid mess but I promise Don and I are *just* friends. Though, after today, I'm ending my friendship with him. More importantly, Mase and I are getting back together!" Cheers erupt around me. Then, our focus returns to the game.

The first half unfolds with a bang. Mase throws a precise touchdown pass out of the gate. His agility and vision are on full display. Yet, Donny matches his intensity by racking up rushing yards and back-to-back game-changing catches. By halftime, the score is tied, and the energy in the stadium is exhilarating.

Amid the halftime bustle, my hand nervously clinches my dress. Crystal offers me a glass of wine to calm my nerves, but I decline with a smile. "Thanks, but the only food that calms me down is Mase's homemade biscuits."

Terry laughs as a look of surprise crosses his face. "Actually, that's my recipe."

Drew wanders over with curiosity bright in his eyes. "Why do you look like my mommy? And you smell like her, too."

"He has a point." The conversation shifts as Terry probes deeper. "I know the Bakers are your long-term foster parents, but where are you from, Tiffany?"

"Savannah but raised right here in Atlanta," I respond with a hint of caution in my voice. "But trust me, you don't want to know my story. I'd like to think that Greer is my actual home. It's where I found love and peace for the first time."

The game resumes, and my new friends, the Lynns, join us in cheering for Mase. The final quarter is a nail-biter. With ten seconds left, Mase faces a critical decision: settle for a field goal to tie the game or go for a touchdown to win. Opting for glory, he snaps the ball, dodges a tackle, and launches a perfect pass into the end zone as the clock ticks down. The crowd erupts as the receiver catches it, securing a Super Bowl win!

Ecstatic, I step onto the field with my family and friends. The electrifying cheer of the crowd meets my ears, but all the joy is sucked out of the moment when I see Kira with her arms thrown around Mase and her lips pressed against his in a scene that shatters my heart into silent pieces. The stadium around me fades into a blur, and the cheers sound distant, as if I'm underwater. My breath hitches, and the air thins around me as pain relentlessly grips my tight chest.

The cameras don't miss a beat, zooming in on their kiss. Kira's voice then rings clear over the microphone, triumphant and cutting, "Every football player needs his dancer!"

Mase stares at her as I stare at them.

She just echoed *our* words, which feels like a dagger in my already aching heart. Though Mase peels her away, the seed of betrayal is already sown, blossoming into a cold, hard lump in my throat. And what hurts more is the shocked, confused look on Drew's face. Though he knows Mase and I aren't together anymore, he sees us as a family, as his mom and dad.

Mel grips my hand tight and whispers, "Smile now, cry later. Don't give that chick the satisfaction."

Crystal Lynn, new to my life but familiar to my heart, centers me, whispering, "Maintain the grace that's within you."

The image of that kiss replays over and over on the jumbotron and in my mind, a loop that stokes the fires of hurt and insecurities that don't exist when he isn't in my life.

Caught up in the excitement, as if what we all just saw didn't happen, Mase approaches me with his face alight with victory. It's taking everything to hold back my tears and smile for the cameras.

But this is Mase's day so I force the corners of my mouth into a semblance of a smile. "Congratulations, Mason. You're a champion once again," I say, my voice steady despite the storm raging inside me. Then, leaning in so only he can hear, I whisper with painful sincerity, "You've won the hearts of all of America. Now, I'm begging you, please, give me my heart back." The words are both a plea and a goodbye, the closure I need to hold onto the peace I found away from his spotlight.

"I'm sorry," he whispers. "I didn't know she was gonna do that. I promise you. She means nothing to me."

I glance up, pointing to the jumbotron, replaying the gut-wrenching kiss. "I know you didn't want to hurt me, but it still doesn't ease the pain."

His eyes desperately search mine. "What're you saying? Please don't do this again. We want to be together. I don't want to go another season without you."

I muster a professional smile, one I've practiced for years. "I can't do this. You're bigger now than ever before. We'll smile for the cameras, then we'll return to the separate lives we've built."

"But this win is for you, Tiff. This win is for our family. It's me, you, Drew, and the world around us." His voice cracks with every hint of emotions breaking through his words.

"If it's meant to be, we'll try again." I concede. "But for now, I can't live in the glare of your stardom. You can't shield me from the hurt I'm feeling, nor can you protect Drew from the confusion that surrounds him. I need peace, Mase. Peace protects us from *everything*. Go and enjoy your victory. I'm always gonna be your biggest fan."

Outsiders easily mistake the tears that blur our vision for tears of joy amidst the celebration. Only those closest to us understand the true ache in our hearts. Today is his day. Tomorrow, I'll return to a life that no longer revolves around him. The exhilarating highs of Mase's world always come with crushing lows, a rollercoaster I can no longer ride.

After the on-field celebrations, the fans and cameras begin to drift away. Sherri and Charles take Drew with them, but not without an exchange of 'I love you' between him and Mase.

Mase's teammates, Kira, and other women surround him with a joy that I can't muster or fake, so I quietly make my exit to the opposite side of the stadium tunnel, where I see a familiar face. The face of someone who has been nothing but kind, honest, calm, supportive, and present.

I stand in front of him from a short distance watching as he walks with his shoulders slumped in defeat.

"That was one helluva game you played out there, Donny Baines." I call out as he approaches.

Donny quickly looks up, managing a half-hearted smile. "It doesn't matter how I played. I lost. I lost what I wanted the most."

"You'll have another shot to win a championship. You're bound to win one."

When he reaches me, he gazes into my eyes and gently touches my cheek. "I'm not talking about a championship, Tiff. I'm talking about you.

All I ever wanted was to win your heart, but I always come up short against him, and I always will."

I place my hand over his. "Yet, here I am, with you. I'm leaving with you. Maybe I can grow to love you the way you love me. Just give me some time, okay?"

Donny's expression shifts and he nods. "All I ever wanted was a chance, Tiffany, and now, you just made me feel like the real champion."

It's time I envision a new future—simpler, quieter—away from the relentless scrutiny that follows Mason Boom. With Donny, I see a possibility of a life centered on peace and stability and maybe even love someday.

We walk away from the stadium together, hand in hand, but my heart is left out on the field with the first and only man I ever loved.

Chapter 28

Protect Her – Mason

4 Months Post- Super Bowl Win

"Mason Boom, you're on a hot streak. You're currently the highest-paid NFL player off endorsements alone, and you just completed your Little League tour with your son. What's next for you?"

"Another championship, of course," I chuckle, trying to keep the mood light. "Seriously though, I'm just getting started. We've got some excellent new additions to the team this season, and with the coach's new gameplan, I'm aiming for a two-peat, then a three-peat, maybe even four."

The talk show host nods, her smile plastered on as she segues into more personal territory. "I love your confidence, Mason. Now, let's touch on something a bit more personal, if you don't mind. Your recent break-up with your high-school sweetheart, Tiffany Weathers, hit you hard. Would you care to address any of your post-breakup behavior?"

"No," I state firmly. "I don't discuss my personal life. Tiffany and Drew are off-limits. I'd appreciate it if we could respect their privacy."

But the host pushes, veering off-script. "Well, it seems your current girlfriend, Seattle Wolves cheerleader, Kira Stellano, doesn't share your concerns about privacy. In fact, she just posted this video three hours ago." She gestures at the screen behind her.

My heart sinks as the video rolls and Kira's crocodile tear-stained face theatrically addresses her millions of followers. "I just want my boyfriend to be happy, but he can't do that when he's being held captive by a cheating baby mama and a kid that isn't even his!"

A truth the world never should've known has just been revealed in the most assaulting way. While the video plays, a heavy silence descends. The room spins as I process the enormity of what's just been unleashed—a bombshell that could interrupt the peaceful life Tiffany and Drew deserve. If there was ever a chance for me to gain favor in her heart again, it's certainly gone now.

Tiff, My Love: Why Mase? What'd I ever do to make you hate me so much that you'd hurt Drew? You will never be allowed around my son ever again! Please leave us alone. I hate you, Mason Boom!

〜 〜 〜

2 Years Later…

The TV screen lights up with Tiffany's interview on a local news segment, and I'm amazed at how much she's accomplished.

"Tiffany Weathers, you've become quite the community advocate over the years. Your dance studio has transformed into a sanctuary for local dancers. What inspired you to open up your studio?"

"Well, my sister and I were raised in this very same community. I honestly don't know how my life would've turned out if it weren't for College Park and the amazing people who live here. It's my responsibility to invest in this city like its invested in me. Our second facility will be a state-of-the-art facility that offers free dance classes to low-income families and an after-school dance program for non-tuition students. I'm so sorry, but I have to get going. I'm headed off to my second home, Greer, Georgia, to attend the Lynn's Welcome Home Benefit. They're huge supporters of the arts. I hope to see you there."

"You sure will. Speaking of appearances, I've heard a little birdy say that a certain Super Bowl champion, Donny Baines, might be making an appearance at the benefit this weekend. Can you confirm?" She probes.

Tiffany confirms, "Yes, though he's not one for the spotlight, Donny will be there to support me. So, try to catch him while you can."

The anchor smiles. "I sure will. It's been a pleasure speaking with you, Tiffany. I'm Arlene Austin from Good Day, Atlanta. Have a lovely week!"

I've replayed Tiffany's interview over and over again for a week straight, not out of nostalgia but as a reminder of what I lost and what she's found. Donny, the Super Bowl champion—that was my title two years ago. Tiffany's man—that was my title nearly four years ago.

"Son, turn the tv off and stop moping. You've been home for two weeks and have barely stepped foot out of the house." My mom's voice slices through the silence while yanking the blanket off me. "Your dad and I have given you enough grace after that Super Bowl kiss between Tiffany and Donny."

My dad, lounging across from me, adds his own frustration to the mix. "We were mad, too, but you screwed up first with that Kira girl!"

Mom rolls her eyes at the mention of Kira. "Don't even say her name," She scoffs, curling into my dad's embrace. "We barely ever see Drew anymore. That damn Kira had no right to comment on Tiffany or Drew! She's an amazing mom. And even after that, Tiff waited on you to get your shit together before finally giving Donny a chance. If I may be honest, Donny treats Tiffany like how you *used* to treat her. Like she's his everything. Like how your dad treats me. After everything she been through, all she wants is a quiet, peaceful life. Why couldn't you just give her that? Your foolishness caused all of us to lose them both."

My dad shakes his head while comforting Mom. "Crystal and Callie told us he still gets bullied in school sometimes, and the older kids even call Tiffany all types of terrible names."

A lump forms in my throat as my parents get visibly emotional, their thoughts bringing tears to their eyes. They love them just as much as I do, and my actions are the cause of everyone's pain.

"So," I twiddle my fingers and allow a tear to fall. "Should I skip the benefit this weekend?"

"Absolutely not! How else do you think you're going to win them back?" Mom's response is instant and firm.

"Huh? But you just said I screwed up and don't deserve them."

"You don't," Dad cuts in, his voice is stern yet hopeful. "But slow and steady wins the race, Son. Start by redeeming yourself. Remind her of the friend you were before everything else, and make her forget how much of a spoiled, entitled, damn near twenty-six-year-old idiot you are. And please, for the love of God, break up with Kira. She's nothing but trouble. I never hated anyone in my life as much as her."

I wish I could tell my parents the truth. I'm tethered to this woman who has become my karma. Ever since that Super Bowl disaster, where I humiliated Tiffany with a public kiss to a woman I despise, my life hasn't seen a winning season. She's the exact opposite of Tiffany, but she's who I deserve for hurting the woman I truly love.

Kira: My plane lands tonight. Will you pick me up?

Mase: No because I told you not to come.

Kira: Please Mase! I really want to meet your family. I want to offer a proper apology. I'll be on my best behavior. I won't even talk to Tiffany.

Mase: Don't even say her name. I'll send a car to get you.

Tonight is going to be interesting. I'll be in the same room as Tiffany and Donny, who's just had the best season of his career—no doubt because he has the best woman by his side. I don't give a damn how 'good' he treats the love of my life. Any man who lurks in the shadows, waiting to take what isn't his, can't be trusted and definitely doesn't have my respect.

The Lynns have come back home after nearly twenty years of searching for their daughters. You'd think they've given up, but it seems they've simply found replacements to fill the void of what was once lost. They found Tiffany and Drew. Who doesn't love them? The Weathers, even Tiny, are infectious. They embody good. They are good. And I need good back in my life. I should've shielded them from public scrutiny, protected them from Kira, and most importantly, from myself. I should've stayed away until I was ready to stop being the NFL's selfish Golden Boy because all my actions have done is drive Tiffany away.

But thankfully, there are a few people who still believe in me. Mel and Rafe help me get my shit together: clean shave, crisp tuxedo, new shoes, fresh haircut, and a mindset focused on redemption.

"Don't fuck this up, Mase! You've literally blown through nine lives." Mel warns as she adjusts my gold lapel.

"Mel, let's be real. Tiff hates him!" Rafe retorts.

She scoffs, shaking her head. "Rafe, you've been dating Monica forever, and you still can't read women! Tiffany has been to nearly a dozen galas with Donny and has *never* smelled like vanilla, but she does tonight. She knows you're in town, Mase. I know my sister, and she may hate you, but she loves you even more."

Rafe nods. "Damn, you're right. She's also wearing gold tonight, bro. Your favorite color. Look, just like Mel knows Tiff, I know you. You'd never do anything to hurt her, so what is it that Kira's got on you? Why the hell won't you just drop this chick?"

I contemplate telling the truth, but we're interrupted by our parents, letting us know it's time to leave for the benefit. Our car ride is short since the Lynns live just a few blocks away. Their estate stretches across acres, the largest in Greer, and when we arrive, we're greeted by manicured gardens bathed in the soft glow of twilight. This gala's going to be over the top, but all I can think about is how nervous Tiff must be. She may be used to the cameras now, but I know she prefers the background. I know she's nervous tonight, and I want to show her that I'm still her best friend and that I'll always put her needs first.

So, I make a quick call to Terry and ask him for a huge favor. My parents are on edge too. Screw blood ties and screw Kira and the chaos she's caused. Drew is their grandson, and their painstaking desire to see him is all-consuming.

When we step into Lynn's grand foyer, Crystal is waiting with Drew by her side. The moment my parents see him, they rush forward and lift Drew into a heartfelt embrace, and their tears of joy mingle with their laughter.

"Oh my goodness! There's no way you're eight years old. You're a giant! I've missed you so much, Drew." Mom gushes through her tears.

Drew laughs and wraps his arms around them. "I missed you, too, Nee-nah and Pop Pop!"

Drew's laughter fills the foyer until his gaze finally finds mine. There's a hesitation in his eyes, a mix of fear and sadness that cuts through me like a knife. It's the look of a child who feels lost, and it sends a wave of guilt coursing through me. I've missed so much, lost so much time that I can't get back.

My parents gently set Drew down, and I watch him fiddle with his thumbs—an anxious tick he picked up from me. It's a stark reminder that no one could ever convince me he isn't my son.

"Hey, Drew," I manage, my voice thick with emotions.

He looks up and whispers, "Hi, Mase... I'm sorry if I ever bothered you. I didn't mean to..."

Confusion furrows my brow. "What? Drew, why would you think you'd ever be bothering me?"

"It's just..." He hesitates, his voice small. "That's what the kids at school say. That I'm annoying, and that's why you hate me now. It's why I don't see you anymore."

A surge of anger and self-hate washes over me as tears stream down my face.

"Drew, look at me," I say, kneeling to be at eye level with him. "You're my best friend, big man. Don't ever think you're annoying me, okay? You're the coolest person I ever met. I love you, and I miss you like crazy."

"Really?" His wide eyes search mine, looking for assurance.

"Absolutely!" I nod.

"Mom was right! Mom told me you'd always love me," He finally smiles. "But she also says we can't hang out anymore."

"Just for now, but we will again soon. I promise, okay?"

Drew wipes a tear from his cheek, a small laugh escaping him. "Good, 'cause Donny sucks at throwing."

We both laugh and share a light moment in the heaviness of our reunion. Embracing him, I feel a completeness I haven't experienced in far too long.

"Where's your mom?" I ask as we pull apart.

"With big head Donny," Drew replies, and we share another chuckle.

He runs off with my parents, Callie, and Crystal while I scan the room until I finally spot Tiffany. My God, that woman! She's perfect, but goofy-ass Donny is close by her side. I don't blame him, though. Tiffany is so damn sexy. Yet, I notice she's clenching the fabric of her dress. Her nerves are getting the best of her.

When he finally slips away to speak to a guest, I cautiously approach from behind and lean in as close as I possibly can, so close that I inhale her beautifully intoxicating scent of vanilla, honeysuckle, and magnolia. "Come with me." I whisper into her ear.

"Leave me alone, Mason." She snaps, her voice low and breathy.

"If only it were that easy, Tiffany Weathers," I reply, my tone gentle. "Now, close your eyes and take a deep breath."

She reluctantly complies, and I watch as the stiffness leaves her shoulders and her clenched fists slowly relax.

"Meet me in the kitchen." I say with a soft smile, turning to lead the way.

When we enter the kitchen, Terry stands before us with a warm smile.

"Terry, did Mase put you up to this?" Tiffany tries to hide her smile.

"We just want you to be as relaxed and comfortable as possible." He says, revealing a plate of his homemade biscuits.

"You're a nervous wreck, Tiff." I pick up the biscuit and insist, "Eat."

Biting her lip and fighting her stubbornness, she relents and takes a big bite of the biscuit, immediately releasing a content sigh. "Oh my God! I needed this!"

Terry and I exchange amused glances while she quickly takes another bite, her earlier poise giving way to relaxation.

"I'm losing my mind out there talking to all these people about I don't even know what. Like, just write a check already!" She's adorable as she rambles on and on.

After her third biscuit and a glass of orange juice, she gives Terry a *thank you* and an appreciative hug. "You're welcome, Tiffany, but this is all Mase's doing. He called me before he even arrived."

Tiffany's gaze shifts to me with surprise and something deeper in her eyes. She lowers her head in a bashful smile. "Thank you, Mase. I should've known."

Tiffany and I are caught mid-gaze, our eyes hungrily tracing each other, a silent acknowledgment of the magnetic pull that's never waned. Her smile is curious and knowing but slightly shifts when dumbass Donny interrupts our reconnection and pulls us back to reality.

"Is everything okay in here?" He says, instantly cooling the heat between us with his arm around her waist.

Be mature, Mase. Don't say fuck you. Don't tell him that nothing's okay until I get my woman back. Don't tell him that Tiffany doesn't even like that ugly ass white tuxedo he's wearing. Don't slip up and punch him in the face.

"Don! Hey, baby. We're just in here eating, is all." Tiffany overcompensates with a cheerful reaction, her voice high-pitched and almost flustered by his timing.

"Biscuits in the evening? That's odd." Donny picks one up and bites into it without waiting for an invitation. "Wow, these are amazing!"

Terry keenly observes, then says, "They're Tiffany's favorite. Mase made them."

Okay, Unc! We fist bump under the counter, but Tiffany turns around and glares at the both of us while Donny's chewing comes to a halt, processing Terry's words.

He then straightens his ill-fitted tuxedo. "Mason, may I have a word?"

I shake my head, choosing the more enjoyable path. "Actually, Don, I'd rather talk to Tiffany," I say, extending my hand toward her. The simple gesture disrupts whatever authority Donny *thought* he had.

He shakes his head sharply, a clear no directed at Tiffany, but I ignore him. Terry, standing a bit to the side, gives me a subtle nod and murmurs just low enough for me to catch, "That amazing woman is gonna be your wife someday, Mase. Earn her back."

Tiffany, perhaps sensing the sincerity behind my actions, gently presses her hand against Donny's chest, "I promise I'm going to sort this out. You got nothing to worry about. I love *you*, Don." Her declaration hurts me to the core, but it also doesn't seem to soothe Donny much because his face contorts with frustration then pulls out his phone and storms away.

"Run along, Donny boy." I can't help but taunt his retreating figure.

"Mase, stop!" Tiffany immediately quips.

I relent, and we step outside for some air, leaving the strained atmosphere of the kitchen behind.

"Why are you so damn childish?" She asks, half amused, half exasperated.

"Because I'm a spoiled, entitled, damn near twenty-six-year-old idiot who does dumb shit, duh." I respond with a grin, trying to lighten the mood.

She laughs, acknowledging the truth in my self-deprecation.

"So, Donny Baines, huh?" I shake my head as I glance over at her.

"Mase, don't start," She sighs, her tone tired. "You already have half the country hating me. Donny treats me well. He respects my privacy. I can be normal without having to worry about cameras everywhere and my life being picked apart or secrets coming out."

"Of course, you don't have to worry 'bout that," I retort with a smirk. "'Cause nobody gives a damn about Donny, including you. He's nice, but he ain't me. You look at him with appreciation, but you look at me with passion and desire. Even your body–it doesn't melt in his arms like it does with mine. You like him, but you damn sure don't love him, Tiff."

She doesn't confirm, but she also doesn't deny it. Instead, she deflects.

"And there's no way you love Kira!" She shoots back, her voice sharp. "Why are you here, Mase? What do you want?"

I pause to weigh the gravity of my next words. "I want you back, but I'll start slow with forgiveness, then friendship, and eventually forever," I confess, my voice thick with sincerity. "I know it'll take time, but I'm ready to put in the work, no matter how long it takes."

She searches my eyes and holds back her response but continues walking, swiftly changing the subject. "You know, I saw you earlier with Drew," she starts, her voice slightly quivering. "His world was torn apart for a long time. It'll probably never be the same again, but we're journaling together now. He isn't going too deep, but it helps when he's feeling lonely, abandoned, or like he isn't good enough to be loved by you anymore."

Guilt gnaws at me. "I'll always love Drew. I'll never forgive myself for him feeling this way. Y'all will always come first to me. I should've done more to keep Kira in her place."

"That's the problem, Mase, you didn't do anything at all. You allowed that awful woman to violate us. Why are you even with her? She hurt an innocent boy. *Our* boy." Tiffany's question is laced with pain.

"I didn't allow her to do anything, Tiff! If anything, I'm trying to protect you at all costs." I plead. "Everything I do is for you. Trust me on this, please."

She looks at me in skepticism. "I want to believe you, I do...but it's hard. You even play with a guilty conscience. Whatever she has on you, you'll survive. Just stop punishing yourself and end things with her."

Confusion wrinkles my brow. "What do you mean?"

She takes a deep breath. "In the last two seasons, you stayed in the pocket too long nearly every game. You botched nine plays and purposely fumbled six times. You could've been a three-time champion by now, Mase. I know you better than anyone else; I see what you're doing to yourself."

The realization that she's been watching so closely, despite our circumstances, leaves me speechless.

"When you're ready to tell me the truth, I'll be here," Tiff continues, her tone firm but open. "Until then, I can't be."

Her words hang in the air as we face each other, a moment filled with unspoken words and pent-up emotions. "I'll tell you everything one day, I promise." I respond earnestly, and she replies with a nod.

Lightening the mood, I reveal some of my intel also. "Your team was A1 at the Octoberfest Competition. It was like watching a bunch of mini-Tiffanys out on the field."

She laughs aloud. "Are you stalking me, Mason Boom?"

I grin. "No more than you stalking me."

She nudges me. "Your games are on TV. My competitions aren't."

"Then yes, I'm definitely stalking you." I confess with a chuckle.

Her laughter rings out, light and intoxicating, as she playfully taps my chest. Her hand lingers, a moment too long, igniting something raw between us. Our eyes lock, and before I can stop myself, my hand lifts to her face, my fingers tracing the curve of her cheek. The words spill out, unguarded and desperate.

"Tell me, Tiff. Do you still love me?"

Her breath catches, and she leans into my touch, her eyes fluttering closed as if bracing herself. She hesitates, the silence heavy, before finally whispering, "Was I ever supposed to stop?"

A consuming desire flares inside me, but before we can proceed, an unwelcome interruption shatters the evening.

We notice a frantic Donny rushing from the side of the house towards the limo Kira steps out of. Their argument is loud, even from a distance. Tiffany's brow furrows in confusion as Donny's tone shifts dramatically when he notices us approaching. I had no idea they knew each other.

"Oh, hey, Babe," Donny nervously greets Tiff, kissing her cheek quickly before hastily explaining, "I uh – I was just kicking out our uninvited guest. There's no way I'd ever allow this woman to hurt you or Drew *again*."

Tiff simply nods, albeit with a strained smile, unwilling to disrupt the peace of her meticulously structured life. But beneath her calm exterior, I can sense her discomfort—something about this encounter isn't sitting right with either of us.

"Come on, you don't want to keep your guests waiting," Donny says with his arm tightening around her waist in a possessive manner. Tiffany reluctantly turns to follow him. But before they can disappear into the party, I remember the real reason I came tonight.

"Tiff, wait up!" I call out, and she turns.

I pull out a check from my jacket and step forward to hand it to her, purposely brushing my thumbs against hers to remind her of our connection. Her eyes widen as she unfolds the check, taking in the amount.

"Mase, five million dollars? What's this for?" She says in awe and curiosity.

It's my donation to your 'state-of-the-art facility that offers free dance classes to low-income family homes and an after-school dance program for non-tuition students,'" I repeat her exact words from her recent interview, emphasizing each detail with a pointed look that conveys my admiration, intentions, and respect for her.

The smile that spreads across her face is worth more than the check itself.

Donny, on the other hand, is visibly irritated by my gesture, and his glare at Kira only intensifies the awkwardness of the situation.

"As much as *we* appreciate this, Mase, my woman and I gotta get going. You and *your woman* should leave." Donny interjects, his voice strained as he tries to usher Tiffany away. "Move along, now." He teases.

But I can't resist one final jab to assert my presence. "I'm gonna work hard as hell, Tiffany Weathers—forgiveness, friendship, and forever! No matter how long it takes!" I loudly declare, confidently, into the night air.

Tiffany pauses, turning to look back at me. I can't read her face, but I do feel her heart beating for me as mine beats for her.

They resume their night while I dread mine by slamming the door as I get into the car with Kira. The high from my encounter with Tiff evaporates under her venomous gaze.

"If you ever embarrass me like that again," Kira hisses, her threat slicing through the remnants of my happiness," I'll make sure your pretty little girlfriend goes to prison for killing her stepfather all those years ago.

Don't fuck with me, Mase. I will ruin her and everyone connected to her, especially that wannabe son of yours, Drew."

Kira's words are a cold reminder of the dark secret that binds me to her—a secret that, if exposed, could destroy everything I hold dear.

I grit my teeth and force away the urge to snap back at her. She holds all the cards, and she reminds me of it every time I get the courage to walk away, every time I get the courage to follow my heart and pursue the only woman I'll ever love. I'm trapped, but I'd rather be trapped in this nightmare with Kira than Tiffany having to experience one all over again. I'll do anything to protect her, even if it means sacrificing my own heart's desire to experience the joy and peace of her love again.

Chapter 29

Best Friend – Tiffany

Drew's 10th Birthday Party

Juggling two men at once is a delicate balance. I sometimes feel like I'm torn between my blooming *re*-friendship with Mason and my relationship with Donny.

How in the world did I get here?

Well, it's simple. Mase has worked his ass off over the last two years to earn my forgiveness, slowly and steadily making his way back into my life, one kind act and earnest intention at a time.

He's also an indomitable force on the field again, and that damn Kira is having a field day, claiming to be his lucky charm. However, I see him point to the patch on his jersey after every touchdown pass, and so does Donny, which has increased the tension within our relationship.

But today isn't about them. It's about my boy, and it only makes sense to have Drew's birthday at the Lynn's estate. He loves going to Greer, especially since Sherri and Charles no longer live in the Governor's mansion. He gets to see the Booms and Bakers all at once and the Lynns, too. I don't know what it is about Drew, but he's a charmer, just like that damn Mason Boom.

It's taken time for Mase to build trust with Drew again. It started with weekly phone calls. Then came video calls, which escalated to a visit where

I got to see the smile of a boy who missed the only father figure he ever had. Donny is great with Drew, but it just isn't the same. Donny's sweet, but sometimes he tries so hard to connect that it causes a *disconnect*.

"This is the best birthday ever!" Drew's voice carries across the Lynn estate as he dashes from one ninja obstacle course to the next.

"Crystal, you've really outdone yourself. Drew's having a blast out here and thank you for flying out a few of his friends and their families. The last few years have been so rough for him." I tell her, grateful for her generosity.

Crystal smiles. "It's the least we could do. The two of you have brought so much joy to our lives. Terry and I regret leaving Greer and not being able to get to know you sooner. Sherri would always tell me about you, the girl Mase believed was my daughter."

I laugh. "Yeah, I remember that. Mase always had quite the imagination," Then, leaning against Crystal, I quietly ask, "Do you still think about them? Your daughters?"

"Every day," She replies softly. "Our pictures of them may have been burned in the fire, but their faces are burned in my memories forever. Oh, what I'd give to be their mother again."

My hand slides over the scars where a razor blade once cut deep and down to her hand where our fingers interlock. "And oh, what my sister and I would've given to have a mother like you, Crystal."

We smile then Callie, Maurice, Sherri, and Charles all surround us to watch Drew play with his friends.

"Tiff," Charles casually says. "My devilishly handsome son has arrived."

Sherri giggles along with the other parents, and I can't help but roll my eyes. "Y'all are just as bad as your children! Mase and I will only ever be friends. I'm fine with Don."

"Fine? Who wants fine when you can have fun, be in love, and be happy?" The charmingly smooth voice rings from behind me. It's Mase, with a bright smile and a bundle of gifts in his hand. "Where is dumbbell Donny, anyway?"

Hmm, I actually haven't seen him in nearly an hour. "He's around. Where's your straggler?" I ask.

Mase's expression tightens at the mention of Kira, and he shrugs. "She's around here somewhere. Thank you for allowing her to come, by the way."

I nod, somewhat reluctantly. "She better behave." With that, I leave to find Donny and soothe his ego before it's bruised by Mase's enigmatic presence.

Roaming the estate, I finally spot Donny through the partly open door of a garden shed, where he's engaged in what seems to be a heated conversation with Kira. My heart skips a beat. *Why would Donny be alone with, let alone talking to Kira, of all people?* Her hand rests against his chest in a way that suggests a familiarity that shouldn't exist.

Straining to hear their hushed voices, I only catch snippets of Kira's frustration. "Why her and not me, Don? You never used to deny me before. The moment you became official, you dropped me. Why does everyone want Tiffany? I'm tired of making threats. I'm just gonna reveal everything. Then, all of this can be over, then Mase will be mine for good. And so will you."

My breath hitches in my throat, and the implications of her words send a chill down my spine. Then, to my shock, Donny's voice rises slightly, laced with a threat of his own, "If you ever hurt Tiffany or Drew ever again, I promise you'll regret it. Stay away from them and get Mase in line. He's back in her life, and I'm losing her." Their conversation leaves me confused and sick to my stomach.

"The burgers are ready!" Terry's voice snaps me back to reality. I hurry back to the party and push the exchange to the back of my mind to focus on Drew.

Under the tent, the aroma of Terry's barbeque fills the air. Donny takes a seat next to me. His presence is now a source of discomfort, yet I mask my unease for the sake of the celebration. Post-meal, the atmosphere shifts when Mase and Drew prepare to make an announcement.

Drew's excitement is infectious as he exclaims, "So, Mom, you know how I said I only wanted to be around our family for my birthday this year?"

I nod, intrigued.

"Well, I lied," He grins, sparking laughter around the table. "It isn't the only thing I wanted. I also want something big, and you have to promise not to say no."

Amused, I reply, "I need to know what the ask is first."

"Well, I want you to dance at the Super Bowl." He says, fiddling his fingers.

"What?" I laugh aloud. "Drew, you sure all you had to drink was soda?" I joke.

Mase takes over, "I laughed too when he first told me, but he was onto something." He pauses, letting the suspense build. "So, we called this season's Super Bowl performer, Gabrielle Sedona."

Mel gasps, "*The* Gabrielle Sedona?! I love her music!"

"And Gabrielle loves Mom's choreography." Drew adds proudly.

Mase continues, "That's right! Gabrielle is actually a big fan. Check it out."

He cues a video on his phone, and suddenly, Gabrielle Sedona herself fills the screen.

Hi Tiffany, I'm Gabrielle Sedona, and I just wanted to take a moment to tell you how much I've admired your work from afar. I've been following your journey and the success of your dance studios, and I must say, you're doing incredible things. So, I would be honored if you would be the lead choreographer for my performance at the Super Bowl halftime show. And I would love for you and your competition dance team to join us on stage. It would be a fantastic experience for all of us. I really hope you'll consider the opportunity! I can't wait to see your signature Southern, sassy majorette flair in action!

The news shocks me to my core. I'm in a whirlwind of disbelief and excitement until Drew's voice brings me back to reality. "So, Mom, what'd you say? For my birthday, will you perform at the Super Bowl halftime show?"

Laughing through tears, I vigorously nod. "Yes! Abso-freakin-lutely! OMG, choreography, dancers! Y'all, I have so much work to do!"

The table erupts in excitement. Rising from my seat, I hug Drew tight and tell him how much I love him. Then, there's Mase, who embraces me so tenderly. My body melts into his arms, and I allow his hand to go as low as possible on my back, blurring the lines between friendship and desire.

"You seriously are the best friend ever." I declare for all to hear.

He whispers in my ear, "I told you I'm gonna work hard to earn you back—forgiveness, friendship, and forever."

The intensity of our connection places us on cloud nine, but reality intrudes as Kira screams out in anger.

"Fuck this!" Donny exclaims. "Tiff, there's no way you're gonna accept this offer."

Donny and Kira's feelings cast a shadow over a once-in-a-lifetime opportunity. Donny's eyes beg me to retract my yes, but I don't live for his satisfaction, nor would I ever be stupid enough to put his feelings over my career.

"You'd really want me to say no just to appease your ego?" I softly whisper to avoid a scene. "Donny, this would be huge for me and my dancers."

Donny chuckles and rolls his eyes. "Tiff, he's just trying to win you back. He's disrespecting the shit out of me!"

Mase snaps back. "About as disrespectful as you pursuing your former teammate's woman?"

"Or as disrespectful as you claiming your ex is *just* your best friend." Kira snarks.

Sherri chimes in, "Oh, Kira, baby. Mase and Tiff are more than best friends. They're soulmates. You're just here filling space until they're ready to get back together. Don't worry though; your time is comin' to an end." She politely smiles.

Charles Boom smiles. "Damn, Sherri. You look so good when you're tellin' it like it is."

This is a disaster.

"Babe," I take Donny's hand. "Let's talk about this later, as well as some other disturbing revelations, too. But not now. This is Drew's birthday, and you're ruining it."

Mase tells Drew to go play with his friends, shielding him from any more inappropriate conversation.

In disbelief, Donny shakes his head and places his hand in his pocket. "It's always me in the wrong, huh? He calls you all times of the night. You text him all day. You smile at the mention of his name. You talk about him, write about him, and even moaned his name during sex! I mean, damn, does him shittin' on you turn you on? How many times does he have to embarrass you until you get the hint? He doesn't love you!"

"Donny, that's enough!" I yell, shocked that he carelessly revealed our private life to my family.

They stare at us in fear of speaking, but Mase stands behind me and gently wraps his arms around my waist. I inwardly release a sigh of relief. Everyone knows I hate confrontation, and I try to avoid being the center of negative attention. Right now, I just feel embarrassed and ashamed, but seeing Mase by my side or perhaps how I allow him to be the man by my side further angers Donny.

"You know what?" Donny smiles at Mase and then, in front of my entire family, says, "Fuck it. I'm not even gonna trip. I got the girl. I won, Mason Boom. She can scream your name all day long, but it's me inside her, and you'll never get to experience how good Tiffany feels ever again."

I immediately gasp in disgust and embarrassment. Mason clinches his jaw and punches Donny with a force that causes him to lose his balance and fall to the ground.

"Stay down," Mase squats down to warn him. "If you ever disrespect Tiffany or our family again, you'll have a lot more than a busted lip. Now, my dad and Terry are gonna respectfully escort you out of here to avoid embarrassment, but remember how you feel right now because next time, it'll be ten times worse."

Charles and Terry escort Donny off the property while I tearfully hang my head low in shame. "I'm so sorry, y'all. Donny's never behaved this way. I've never been so embarrassed in my life!"

Sherri, Callie, and Crystal assure me everything's fine while Mase holds me until my heartbeat syncs with his.

"Thank you, Mase." I say, with my head buried in his chest.

He lifts my chin, and we stare into each other's eyes, fighting back the urge to embrace in other ways.

"I got you, Tiff. I always got you." He says tenderly.

"Unbelievable!" Kira throws her napkin on the table.

"Oh, you're still here?" Mel laughs.

Kira dramatically stands up from the table. "I sure as fuck am! While you stay and tend to your precious Tiffany, I'm going to check on Donny. You don't deserve him. Mase, if you really cared for your *best friend* then you'd be following me out of here...right now!"

But Mase stays. He stays until the end of the party and doesn't leave until after the photographer gathers us for a family photo–just me, Mase, and Drew.

Chapter 30

My Time to Shine – Tiffany

Super Bowl Eve

L as Vegas is buzzing with the anticipation of the game. It's not just any game, it's the rematch everyone's been talking about - Mason Boom versus Donny Baines, a clash of titans on the field.

But for me, this day holds an even greater significance. I'm here to lead a halftime show that could define my career. My team of dancers have worked tirelessly over the past three months. We've transformed every ounce of pressure into motivation, perfecting our five-minute set. This journey has been a whirlwind, propelling my dance studio into the spotlight and being recognized as the best in the nation. I'm already planning to expand and open a third location as soon as I get back to Atlanta.

This morning during breakfast with Mel, Monica, and Avery is a celebration of personal victory. These women aren't just my friends; they're my family, always reminding me of how far I've come.

"Can you believe how famous you are?" Avery exclaims, her wide-eyed excitement infectious.

"It's surreal," I admit, stirring my coffee as the steam rises, mingling with the cool desert air. "But I just wish I could share all of this with Tiny."

Mel reaches across the table, giving my hand a reassuring squeeze. "She's so proud of you, Tiff. When I saw her last week, she and a few others already had posters made for you. How'd she take the news, by the way?"

"She cried like a baby!" I laugh, the sound filled with gratitude. "Sherri's working so hard to get her out. She says Tiny's conviction should be appealed in no time. There's a bit of resistance, maybe from Tiny's former rich, powerful abusers, but Callie and Sherri are fighting tooth and nail to undo the injustice against her. I'm tearing up just thinking about it."

The girls gather around me, their comfort steady and reassuring as we bask in the shared hope of Tiny's journey back home to me and Drew, where she belongs.

Just as a sense of peace settles over me, my phone vibrates against the café table, breaking the moment. I glance down to see a text from Mase.

Mase: I'm glad we're all in Vegas because we need to have a family meeting. Meet me at my hotel suite at 5. It's an emergency.

Despite the unsettling message, I push through the day. My last rehearsal goes smoothly. My dancers are sharp and ready, but my mind keeps drifting to Mase's message, so much so that I end up missing my date with Donny.

When he finally gets ahold of me, he sounds anxious and regretful. "Tiff, I messed up big time. I need to explain something to you. I need you to know I never meant to hurt you. I need to see you, please!"

Confused but too preoccupied, I dismiss his worries. "I'm sorry, Donny, but there's something urgent I need to handle with my family. It's not something I can explain right now, but I promise to fill you in when I can."

When I arrive at Mason's suite, everyone's present and looking as anxious as I feel. Mase leads me by my hand to the empty chair across from his.

"Mase," I hesitate, grounding myself before sitting down. I reach out to touch his cheek and he kisses my palm softly, his eyes filled with regret.

"I'm so sorry, Tiff. I thought I was protecting you and Drew."

His words send a chill down my spine, and a knot forms in my stomach. Now, I'm not just worried—I'm terrified. What has he done now?

"I broke up with Kira this morning."

Rafe looks around and then echoes our thoughts. "Okay... and? Is that the emergency?"

Mase shakes his head slowly and locks eyes with mine. "No, there's more," He continues. "Every football player needs his dancer."

My heart skips a beat. The phrase dances through my mind and conjures the painful memory of Mase's first Super Bowl, one of his most infamous betrayals.

"I never said those words to Kira," He confesses. "You've always been the only dancer I ever needed, Tiff." His words stir a whirlpool of emotions within me. The room falls silent, and my only response is the tears that escape my eyes.

"That stunt at the Super Bowl, the kiss, the phrase...it had to have been planned, and Kira isn't smart enough to pull off something like that on her own. The only other people who knew about our phrase were my college teammates like Donny, for instance. And remember Drew's birthday? He mentioned something about you writing about me. Why would Donny say you were *writing* about me...as if he read your journals? There was so much happening that I didn't think about it at the moment. But it's all connected. Donny and Kira have been trying to separate us for years."

My mind races, but I shake my head, denying the possibility he's suggesting. "No, Donny would never do that to me. He wouldn't hurt me like that. He loves me. He wouldn't hurt Drew." I argue, though doubt quickly creeps in.

"Think about it, Tiff," Mase urges. "He's been obsessed with you since freshman year. He tried every angle—the sweet-talking hotshot, the friendly coworker, the rebound. He'd do anything to make you love him. I know you've felt something's been off, haven't you?"

The memory of Donny's conversation with Kira at Drew's birthday floods my thoughts. Callie and Mel squeeze my hands, offering silent support as I grapple with the blitz of revelations.

"I'm so confused," I mumble, feeling naive and foolish.

"And I think...I think he's been trying to keep us apart by giving Kira information. She said she'd expose you for killing Pop if I ever left her."

Gasps fill the room, and my heart sinks. My breath is nearly taken away, and I find myself hyperventilating in panic.

Callie hugs me tight. "It's okay. Just breathe. Everything's gonna be okay."

"I've stayed with her for as long as I could. But this morning, something in me just snapped. I told her it was over, and now she's threatening to go to the press. She's vowed to 'expose everything in my journals.'" He pauses, then looks into my eyes. "What made everything click is that I never wrote about that night in my journal, but I know you did. Your entire life is on those pages, and aside me and Drew, the only other person with access to you is —"

"Donny." I say quietly, the name slipping from my lips as the weight of betrayal crashes over me.

My world spins as the implication sinks in. Donny, the man I trusted, has been manipulating us both, playing a long game with my deepest pain. The thought of going to prison, of losing Drew, of destroying the lives of my friends and their families overwhelms me. Then I stare at Mase, the man who willingly accepted years of unhappiness to protect me. I've blamed him for my pain for so long, but it was always my fault.

Charles places his hand on Mase's shoulders. "We'll take it from here, Son. It's time for the parents to step in."

Mel glances at Mama Callie, recognizing the resolve on her face. "Mom, are you gonna make Kira disappear?"

Callie hesitates, then gives a noncommittal shrug. "I don't know yet, but I do know we're gonna do what we do best."

"Which is to protect our kids and our grandbaby," Sherri adds firmly. "We promise no disappearances, but I assure you, you'll *never* hear from Kira again."

Rafe mumbles, "Sounds like a disappearance to me."

The tension in the room slightly lifts as our parents lay out their plan with resolute authority. Callie is already on her phone, coordinating with contacts to erase Kira's digital footprint and ensure her apartment is cleared out. Then, she discreetly mentions draining her bank account to cut off her resources. Charles, with his extensive legal connections, prepares to leverage information against Kira's relatives. Sherri, always the most direct, demands for someone to find her immediately. While Maurice Baker, the most innocent of all, orders dinner.

Relieved, Mel, Rafe, Mase, and I step out of the room. "Are our parents smooth criminals or what?" Mel lightens the mood with a laugh.

Rafe replies with a grin, "I don't know, but they're pretty fuckin' dope."

"Crap, Donny's probably in my hotel room. He has a key." The mention of Donny tightens Mase's jaw, and his hands curl into fists at his sides.

"Let me come with you." Mase says, his voice firm but gentle.

Our car ride is quiet but filled with appreciative glances and fingers intertwined as tight as our hearts. When we reach my room, I brace myself and unlock the door.

Donny is there, sitting on the edge of my bed, his expression remorseful, but the moment Mase steps in behind me, his demeanor shifts to defensive anger.

He scoffs. "So, you were always gonna run back to him, weren't you?" He accuses me in a bitter tone as he stands up to confront us.

Mase leans against the doorframe with his arms folded, ready to step in if needed.

I shake my head in disgust. "Shut up, Donny!" I fight to hold back my tears. "So, it's true, huh? You read my journals. You violated my trust. You invaded my privacy. You played mind games with me from the very beginning. Was this your goal all along? To hurt me?"

Donny shakes his head. "No! I never meant to hurt you or Drew. I just – I just wanted to know more about you. You're so guarded with me. I needed to understand why Mase and not me. You just won't stop loving him after I've proven myself to you, so I thought I'd find something out about him."

"But instead, you found out the truth about me, and you told the worst person in the world – the person who made my son's life a living hell. You hurt Drew. You watched him cry himself to sleep every night because of the terrible things people said about him. You gave a loaded gun to a psychopath! How could you?"

He shakes his head, his voice soft with regret. "It wasn't supposed to go that far. She was just supposed to threaten Mase. I love you, Tiffany. I just needed to keep him away so you could grow to love me, too."

"You never loved me, Donny. You only wanted to *win* me. You weaponized the most devastating day of my life. I gave you so much of me, and you didn't deserve any of it. I *never* loved you."

With tearful eyes, he reaches out to me, but I pull away. "You don't mean that, Tiff. I know you love me. I know we can work through this. It's Mase. Everything was fine until he came back into your life."

A laugh escapes me. "I don't want *fine* anymore! I want honesty. I want fun, passion, intensity, and happiness. I want love. I want Mason. He's the only one who earned my forgiveness, worked for my friendship, and he deserves forever with me. If you ever try to come near me or my son again, I *will* kill you. And as you know, that's a promise, not a threat. Now, get the fuck out, Donny Baines."

The color drains from his face as I glance back at Mase, his half-smile telling me he knows my confession is for both of them. My heart belongs to Mase now—and forever.

Donny slowly walks toward the door, hesitating as if he's about to say a final goodbye. But before he can get the words out, Mase slams the door in his face.

"I'm so sorry," I whisper, my voice breaking. "I let him break us."

Mase strokes my hair and softly chuckles. "Break? Last I checked, we were on our way to forever."

He gently leads me to the bed and helps me lie down, brushing a strand of hair from my face. I lay my head on his chest, and the steady rhythm of his heartbeat slowly eases my turmoil.

"I can't believe I trusted him. All these damn years, we could've been together. We should've been together. We lost so much time."

"We got all the time in the world, Tiff. You know I'm a patient man," he whispers. "Don't worry about us. Just get some rest. You have a big day tomorrow. The entire world will get to see you dance. It's your time to shine, and it's my time to be the support you've always been for me."

~ ~ ~

Super Bowl Sunday arrives with a mixture of nerves and excitement, but after last night's emotional storm, I feel calm. I slept peacefully on

Mase's chest, like nothing in the world could touch me while I was wrapped in his arms.

Now, as my team and I finish our last rehearsal in the stadium, I give my girls and their families a pep talk, but I can't help but notice they seem a little too enthusiastic. Even Gabrielle is smiling wider than usual.

"Okay, what's goin' on? What's got y'all so giddy?" I ask, laughing softly.

One of my dancers' eyes sparkles as she bounces up and down. "Oh my God, we finally get to see them together!"

I arch an eyebrow and slowly smile. "Is Mason Boom behind me?" I ask, already knowing the answer.

They all nod excitedly, and before I can turn, I feel his arms wrap around me, pulling me into his chest. His familiar scent and warmth wash over me, and I lean back, feeling that undeniable connection surge between us.

"I just came to say good morning." Mase murmurs into my ear, his voice low and smooth.

I turn in his arms and give him a playful look. "You could've texted me that, you know?"

He shrugs, then grins. "But I wouldn't be me if I weren't a little extra. Besides," he adds, "You'll be couped up in the tunnel until halftime, so this is the only time I could see you before then. And you know the football player needs to see his dancer."

I blush. Heat rises to my cheeks despite the sea of people around us. "Well, now you see me," I tease, then gently turn him around to face the exit. "And now you don't. Go focus on your game, Mason Boom! And win for me today." I call after him.

He looks back over his shoulder, winks, and yells for my entire team to hear. "You already know. This win is all for you, Tiffany Weathers! It's all for you, baby!"

~~~

My big moment arrives much sooner than expected, with only three minutes left before halftime. I'm supposed to be in formation with my dancers, but I've been near the tunnel entrance clutching my side for two quarters. I can't tear my eyes away from the field.

Whatever Mase told his defense to do to Donny worked because they're all over him. Every time he tries to make a play, Mase's defense either denies him or brutally tackles him.

And Mase? He's perfect. A surgeon on the field, threading the ball between defenders with ease, finding his receivers every time. The Seattle Wolves are up by a touchdown, and the championship is theirs to win. But now, it's time for me to shine.

I take a deep breath as I step back into formation with my girls. My hand instinctively reaches for my thigh, squeezing lightly—my little habit whenever my nerves hit. But just as my anxiety starts to creep in, I glance toward the tunnel and see them.

Mase and Drew.

They're supposed to be elsewhere—Mase in the locker room and Drew up in the box—but there they are, standing together, watching me with matching looks of pride. My heart swells, and suddenly, all my nerves vanish.

The music starts, and Gabrielle's voice rings out over the speakers, powerful and full of emotion. The energy surges through me, and with every beat, my dancers and I hit our marks—every sharp move, every sultry body roll, and every stunt is executed flawlessly. The crowd roars. Their energy feeds into us, making each move feel bigger, bolder, and more invigorating than ever. We just made history right here, right now—bringing majorette dance, our culture, and our life to the world's biggest stage.

My team seamlessly transitions off the field as Gabrielle takes center stage to finish her performance. With my heart still racing and adrenaline coursing through my veins, I rush toward the tunnel, and as soon as I reach my boys, Drew throws his arms around me.

"You did it, Mom!" He shouts, his face lit up with joy.

Mase is right behind him, pulling me into his arms. His lips brush against my cheek as he whispers, "I couldn't take my eyes off you."

I smile, breathless and exhilarated. "You're supposed to be getting ready for the second half." I tease, but I can't hide how much his words mean to me.

Before he can respond, his coach appears, clapping him on the back. "Alright, Boom, you got your wish. Now get your ass in the locker room and get your head back in the game!"

Mase winks at me one last time before jogging away, and Mel takes Drew back to the box. By the time I congratulate my dancers, get changed, and head up, the second half is well underway, and Mase is dominating. I stand at the edge of the box, watching him command the field with grace and precision that leaves no room for error.

When the final whistle blows, the scoreboard confirms the Seattle Wolves have obliterated their opponents, and Mason Boom has just secured his second Super Bowl ring.

As the confetti rains down, my heart races as we're escorted onto the field. The energy is overwhelming, but my focus is entirely on Mason.

He's there, front and center, and when he grabs the mic, his voice booms over the stadium. "Every football player needs his dancer!"

The crowd erupts, and before I know it, he's pulling me into his arms and into a fiery kiss. It's more than just a celebration of his win. It's a moment that's been years in the making—one filled with all the love, pain, and triumph we've experienced together.

We share our first Super Bowl kiss. The one we were always meant to have.

Chapter 31

At Peace – Mason

"Bro, it's my wedding day!" Rafe says, shaking his head but grinning. He's trying to keep the mood light, but I can see the excitement and nerves flickering in his eyes.

I should be focused on celebrating my brother, but my mind is stuck on the woman I haven't been able to get out of my head.

"My bad, man. It's just... I haven't seen Tiffany in three months. She's been so damn busy with that dance tour, and now they're offering her some kind of reality show. Plus, competition season is starting up in a few weeks." I sigh, running a hand over the back of my neck. "We ain't ever getting back together, are we?"

"Probably not!" Bash interrupts with his usual bluntness, walking into the conversation like he owns the place.

Jay shakes his head. "Classic Bash."

Bash rolls his eyes. "Oh, y'all want me to tell a lie? Bruh, Tiff dropped everything to take care of you when you sprained your shoulder and tore your ACL. She even moved you into her house so y'all could be a happy family during your recovery. *But* you just couldn't chill. You had the audacity to give her an ultimatum—'be together in Seattle or else.'"

"I was just playing! She takes everything so seriously." I joke, trying to laugh it off.

Bash raises an eyebrow, unimpressed. "Because you *were* serious, dummy. You literally bought a big-ass house in Seattle and prematurely snagged a building for a new studio, thinking she'd follow you. You always doing dumb shit."

I sigh and take his jab. "Apparently, I always do dumb shit when it comes to Tiff."

Jay chuckles. "You don't say."

My brothers and I laugh and tease one another while getting dressed for Rafe's big day. He and Monica are finally tying the knot, a moment that's been years in the making—one that almost didn't happen. From college to now, we've seen Monica transform, growing stronger, more open, and slowly allowing herself to embrace the unwavering love Rafe has always offered her.

We may have lost a parent when we were young, but Monica lost both. Raised by her aunt and uncle in Beverly Mills, she endured trauma that left deep scars, shaping much of her life. Through it all, Rafe stood by her side, supporting her healing with steadfast love. What Monica may not realize is that she brought Rafe back to life too. He loves her fiercely, with his whole heart, and his protectiveness stems from their shared understanding of pain and the resilience they've both had to find. When she broke up with him out of fear of being happy, Rafe thought he'd lost everything.

Thankfully, Mom and Callie stepped in to bring Monica's abuser to justice—*their kind of justice*, which brought Monica a sense of peace, and maybe even closure. It inspired her to believe that life is always worth living because pain isn't permanent, but happiness is, if you allow it to be.

My parents' backyard has been transformed into an intimate wedding escape. The grass is perfectly trimmed and lined with elegant white chairs and delicate floral arrangements. It's the kind of day that makes you stop and breathe in the beauty of life. But my chest tightens because I know any minute now, I'm going to see Tiffany, and she's going to take my breath away.

Her flight to Greer was delayed last night, so I didn't get to see her at rehearsal, which means I'm going to either do or say some dumb shit the moment we walk down the aisle together.

Then, I see her.

She's wearing a stunning gold silk dress that clings to her skin. The sight of her makes my pulse quicken. The moment I take a whiff of my favorite scent, I'm suffocated by my desire for her. What gets me most excited is her hair—she's cut it to her shoulders. The sleek look fits her perfectly. Her beauty is unreal, and I'm completely in awe. My mouth goes dry as I try to hold it together.

We reach one another, and I offer my arm when she takes her place by my side. The warmth of her touch sends a shock through me.

Tiff tries to keep a straight face but fails, letting a small smile slip. "Mase, I see your knee is holding up." She casually emits, glancing up at me through her lashes.

I smirk, trying to play it cool, but my heart is hammering through my chest. "No thanks to my sexy nurse who abandoned me, of course. You should've warned me you were gonna look this good, Tiffany Nicole. New hairstyle, huh?"

She softly laughs and shakes her head. "Mase, you're ridiculous, but thanks. I wanted to try something new heading into my thirties. What'd you think?"

I nod, still taking in the sight of her. "If you wanna know what I think, then just look down and find out."

Tiffany looks down and sees my growing erection.

"Mase!" She whines. "When're you gonna grow up?"

We both laugh and then look up to Rafe, who silently fusses at us through his tight face.

But she leans in closer and teases, "So, you missed me, huh? Have you learned your lesson yet? To stop being so damn extra?"

I chuckle, feeling relaxed as we've now fallen back into our natural rhythm. "Yeah, I've learned my lesson. No more antics. No more ultimatums. No more impulsive behavior. I promise."

"Good," she says with a grin. "I'm having Drew's 13th birthday at my house this year. It's just going to be the three of us – me, you and Drew. I want him to read my journals. I think it's time we tell him the truth about who his birth mother is. Can you fly in for the day?"

I feel honored and so damn grateful that Tiff trusts me to be part of a moment so special. I nod, and we fall silent for the ceremony to begin.

"We're moving back home to Greer." Rafe declares at the reception. "And we're hoping our friends will join us, too."

Moving back home... it's something I've thought about more than once, and now that Rafe is returning, it feels like the time is right. But not without Tiffany. She waited for me when my life was moving 100 miles per hour, so I'll wait for her to slow down as well. Then, we'll make our way back home and into one another's hearts.

~ ~ ~

It's Drew's 13th birthday. I just made their favorite meal – my homemade biscuits, and now I'm sitting on Tiffany's couch, where we're about to tell him everything—the truth about his Aunt Tiny, the parts of his life he's never known, Tiffany's life story. She calms her nerves with a bite while Drew lounges across from us, flipping through page after page. As he reads Tiffany's words, written in her most vulnerable moments, he uncovers her trauma, her journey, and the truth about Tiny. He even smiles at the bits of humor she wove in about me and the beautiful chaos of our lives together.

Finally, he looks up, his voice quiet but steady. "So... Aunt Tiny's my birth mom?"

Tiffany nods slowly. "Yes."

Drew processes it for a moment, then asks, "And she went through all of that?"

Tiffany nods again. "Yes, she did."

Drew's face softens, and he shakes his head. "I'm sorry y'all had such a terrible mom. And I'm glad Pop is burning in hell." Tiff and I exchange a look, and I swallow hard as Drew continues, "I can't wait to meet Aunt Tiny. When is Grandma Sherri getting her out?"

Tiffany places her hand over Drew's. "Any day now, Son." She responds softly.

Drew has a million questions, and we answer them all. But one stands out— "Me, you, and the world around us—what does that mean?"

I smile, remembering the day me and Tiff *officially* met at my parents' wedding. "Well, I first heard it when I was a baby. Crystal Lynn came up with that phrase. She used to read us bedtime stories—me, Rafe, and the Lynn twins—and she'd always end with that to remind us that no one is more important than family. Then, when I met your mom, I told her the phrase, and we've been saying it ever since."

Tiffany looks muddled and surprises me by interjecting, "Uh, that's not entirely true. Tiny and I used to say that to each other all the time."

I blink, confused. "Huh? Why didn't you ever tell me that?"

Tiffany shrugs, a far-off look in her eyes. "I don't know. Mama always drugged us back then, moved us from town to town, and told us lies. I don't mention my childhood much because we never knew what was real or fake. My life didn't really begin until I met Aunt Dora. And it didn't get better until I moved to Greer. Everything's a blur, but that phrase is something I'll never forget."

She pauses, trying to remember more. Tiff has never dug this deep into her past. "You know what? There was also a blanket… it had the phrase on it. I think that's when we first smelled our fragrance! It used to remind us of Mama before she became so…evil."

Tiffany trails off into random streams of consciousness, mentioning something about a house fire and a woman named Harriet, but her memories are too fragmented for anything to make sense. I feel a pull deep inside me. I don't want to alarm Tiffany or Drew, but I need to figure out how all of this connects—our phrase, the blanket, the fire. It all feels tied to my childhood, but I stay calm while she dives into untapped memories.

Later, when Tiffany walks me out, I ask her, "Have you thought any more about moving back to Greer?"

She hesitates, looking up at the stars. "It would be nice, you know...to be back home."

I nod and further make my case. "The Lynns have practically rebuilt the city. With Mel still there and Rafe opening his private practice. Sports teams are rolling in, including the Renegades. I only got one season left on my contract. It'll be the icing on the cake to end my career in Greer. It makes sense, Tiff. The only thing that's missing is a dance studio owned by the world-famous choreographer Tiffany Weathers."

Tiffany smiles, but there's caution in her eyes. "It's tempting, Mase, but I'm not making any promises. And I don't want to get your hopes up. You take maybes and just run with it. I'll think about it, okay?"

I grin, then lean down to kiss her forehead. "You thinkin' about it is good enough for me."

After saying goodbye, I head straight to the tarmac to catch my flight back to Seattle. I'm ready to dive back into football after my 10-month injury. But, of course, football will have to come second to my first priority— figuring out who this incredible woman I've loved my entire life truly is.

Chapter 32

Revelations – Mason

Now that football season's over, I can do what I do best—focus all of my attention on my future wife and the son I hope to one day call mine. My season didn't go as planned after reinjuring my knee. But in truth, it went exactly how it was meant to.

I'm not the Golden Boy of the NFL anymore. I'm still the most handsome man on the field, of course, but I ain't the youngest. I'm pushing thirty-one, and honestly, I couldn't care less about keeping up with the 21-year-old quarterbacks chasing rings. I'm chasing something different nowadays—peace. And my peace is rooted in Greer, Georgia. After months of research and replaying decades of my life over and over again, I'm convinced that everything I ever held dear started in my hometown.

So, today, I've made a life-changing decision, one that I desperately hope I don't regret. I take a deep breath as I stand on the podium, looking out at the crowd of reporters for the last-minute press conference my publicist and sister-in-law, Monica, arranged.

"Thank you for being here. I wanted to address an urgent matter today, and I figured it was best to say it directly rather than let rumors fly. I know the season begins in just a few weeks, but after immense prayer and discussions with my loved ones, I've made an extremely important decision. After ten incredible years with the Seattle Wolves, I've requested an early release from my contract. I want to take a moment to thank the entire organization—my coaches, teammates, the staff, and the fans. Leading this team for the past decade has been one of the greatest honors of my life. But I need time to focus on myself and to prioritize my family. Football has been my life for a long time, but it's not everything. Not anymore. I'll be taking this season off with the hope of returning to the league as a free agent. I'm not saying goodbye forever, just...goodbye for now. In the meantime, there are personal matters that may come to light in the coming months, and I ask that you respect my privacy and the privacy of those involved. Thank you for your support, both on and off the field. It's meant everything to me."

With that, I nod, step away from the podium, and move quickly through the crowd. I can hear snippets of questions, the urgency in their voices as they try to get a statement, a headline, a smidgin of truth to turn into gossip. But I'm done talking. I make my way to the car and ride until I pull up to the tarmac, where my private jet awaits. It's time to say goodbye to Seattle and time to say hello to the next chapter of my life.

I board my jet, ignore the barrage of phone notifications, and focus on my next destination—Atlanta. During my flight, I observe the file on the seat beside me, the one I've been obsessing over for weeks. It's full of research, notes, and half-buried memories that feel like puzzle pieces I can't quite fit together.

Everything I've discovered so far about Tiffany's past, her trauma and fragmented memories, leads back to my original belief that Tiffany Nicole Weathers is Nicole Lynn.

As soon as I land at the private airfield, I drive straight to College Park to meet up with the one person who knows Tiffany better than I do.

"Alright, boy," Ms. Dora says, standing at the entrance of one of her old homes, arms crossed like she's been waiting for me all day. "You ready to get to work? Pack up these boxes. I've got decades' worth of information on our girls."

I don't waste any time. I load box after box from her attic into the car. They're heavy, filled with old photos, records, and documents—a lifetime of history tucked away for far too long. Then, we drive to her condo downtown, where our families are already waiting—Mom, Dad, the Bakers, Mel, Rafe, and Monica.

As soon as we pull up, we're bombarded with questions, starting with Rafe, who's already wound up and pacing before I can even get out of the car.

"Mase, you better have a damn good reason for dragging all of us to Atlanta! Look how distressed my beautiful pregnant wife is! What if she goes into labor?"

Mel and Monica laugh and shake their heads. Monica rubs her belly, all calm and collected. "Babe, I'm fine. We got a whole month before she arrives."

"Exactly," I chime in. "Which means we've got one week to solve this case."

Mel crosses her arms and plants her feet on the ground. "Okay, but what about Tiffany? Why isn't she here? She's been blowing up our phones since that press conference stunt you pulled. This better not be about her."

Dad squints his eyes as if he's trying to read my mind. "What're you up to now, Son?"

Before I can respond, Ms. Dora barrels past everyone to unlock the door to her home. "Quit with all the questions and get inside so y'all can find out."

"But wait," I pause before everyone enters. "No offense, Monica, but it probably isn't a good idea for you to be here. There are secrets about our past." I state, trying to avoid revealing the truth about Pop's murder.

"I already know what happened to Pop." She shrugs nonchalantly. "Rafe told me during our second phone conversation back in college."

Everyone groans, and Mom yells, "Rafe!"

Monica smiles and grabs an unapologetic Rafe's hand. "Y'all know my husband can't keep a secret."

Rafe shrugs. "I knew this woman was the one from the moment I saw her, and Dad told me never to keep secrets from the love of my life. So…Monica's in this now."

"I did a damn good job with you boys." Dad smiles proudly.

I signal to Rafe, and he follows me back to the car to help me unload the boxes while Ms. Dora starts preparing the family for what's coming.

The air in Ms. Dora's living room feels heavy, and my family waits for me to explain why I've dragged them all here today. I set up the whiteboard, tacking up notes, photos, and documents to convey the puzzle that's stuck in my head.

Mel watches me, half-amused, arms crossed, leaning against the back of a chair. "Mase, this is like Inspector Gadget times ten. What exactly are we solving here?"

I take a deep breath and pray they take me seriously. "We're going to solve the mystery of the Greer House Fires." My voice feels stronger than I expected while picking up a picture of Tiny and Tiffany and pinning it to the board. "And I'm going to prove that Tiffany and Tiny Weathers are actually Nicole and Taylor Lynn."

The room erupts in chaos. Rafe groans and throws his hands up in disbelief.

Mom exhales deeply and asks, "Mase, you've got way too much time on your hands."

"And way too much space in your head." Mel chimes in, shaking her head with a grin.

Dad sighs, giving me that concerned, fatherly look. "Does this have anything to do with Tiffany moving back to Greer?"

My head snaps up. Dad's news sends a jolt of excitement through me. "Wait, what? Tiff's moving back?" But I shake my head and get back on track. "No, this isn't about that. Just...hear me out."

I begin with the house fire—Tiffany's vague, fragmented memory of escaping it. Her memory lines up too perfectly with the fires that ruined our lives. Then, there's her middle name—*Nicole*. She never thought much of it, but I did. And then there's the phrase, '*Me, you, and the world around us.*' How could Tiffany know it if she didn't hear it from me? And the physical resemblance between Tiffany and Tiny—Rafe noticed years ago—they look like twins. And finally, both Crystal and Tiffany's fragrances are practically the same.

I go through all these details, and I can feel the emotions in the room. My parents had no idea that Tiffany survived a house fire, let alone somehow knew of Crystal's phrase. They listen quietly, but their eyes tell me they're beginning to understand. Every connection, every detail, each coincidence—they all lead back to the same place, the truth. I know, deep in my gut, that I'm right.

"I know it sounds insane," I say in a steady tone. "But if we can piece together what happened back then and pull from the conversations and moments we've had with the Weathers and Lynns over the years, we might be able to solve this."

They all fall silent and exchange unreadable glances. But then, one by one, they nod.

"Alright," Rafe finally says, his voice more serious than I expected. "Let's figure this out."

For the next few hours, the room turns into a makeshift investigation headquarters. We spread out the old boxes that Ms. Dora had stored away and rummage through random documents, flip through files, and piece together fragments of Tiffany's past.

After a while, Rafe finally breaks the silence and asks, "Shouldn't we call Crystal and Terry? I'm sure they collected a helluva lot of information over the years."

Everyone seems to agree, but Mom is particularly uneasy. "No," she says firmly, though there's a hint of fear in her voice. "Y'all don't understand the pain Crystal and Terry went through. They weren't just traveling the country looking for their daughters all these years. They were in the deepest pits of their grief, and they barely made it out. We need to be absolutely sure before we drag them into this."

My dad, usually so composed, breaks his silence. His voice is low and almost remorseful. "Crystal and Terry used a surrogate for the twins. Her name was Kayla Drexler. She was the estranged daughter of a family we locked away, and she was also a drug addict. Crystal and Terry didn't know who her family was—hell, they didn't even know about her addiction until they caught her using late in her pregnancy with the twins. We had her committed on a *somewhat* legal psych hold until she could deliver the girls. She hated us for it and threatened to kill us all, but we didn't think anything of it because word got out she died of an overdose shortly after. The only person left in her circle was Ricky Preston, who happened to be the man Tiffany knew as Pop."

My heart thuds painfully in my chest, his words sinking in like stones. I didn't see that coming. Pop, the man who raised Tiffany and Tiny. The man who tried to destroy them.

With his hands clenched in a fist and trembling with regret, Dad admits, "We should've told Terry and Crys about Ricky's death that same night, Sherri!"

Mom straightens up. Her jaw is tight, and her eyes are filled with frustration and pain. "We didn't know, Charles! Crys literally tried to kill herself the week before. I was just trying to protect them," she says in defense. Then, her tone hardens, turning cold and unforgiving while staring down at the floor. "What we should've done was killed them all. If we would've killed Kayla and Ricky, the fires probably would've never happened."

Everyone reels as the revelation sinks in, but it's still all speculation. So, the Bakers use their network of contacts to dig into the previous addresses listed in their CPS and foster agency files. They find nothing at first—no rental records, no official history matching their names or their mother's aliases.

Then Callie calls out, "There was a case in Macon, Georgia, over twenty years ago. A woman named Harriet was killed in a house fire. The police wanted to question her tenant, who had two daughters, but they were never found. Turns out, the tenant had a forwarding address from a PO Box in Greer. The original detective on the case is dead, but apparently, he was known for taking bribes. He closed the case right after the fire. I'm waiting to get the records of who owned, or maybe *still* owns that PO box."

Rafe and Monica continue rummaging through boxes when Monica suddenly freezes and then holds up an old, grainy photo. "Hey guys… doesn't Tiffany always say she's from Savannah?"

I nod, unsure where she's going with this. "Yeah, why?"

Monica squints at the photo and then hands it to Rafe. "I grew up in Beverly Mills, and I know my town like the back of my hand. Avery, Deacon, and I used to hang out at the pier all the time. This is Beverly Mills Beach, *not* Savannah's Tybee Island. Rafe, look! We just had our maternity shoot there last weekend."

I grab the photo and stare at two toddlers who look just alike, trying to understand why it looks so familiar. And then it hits me. I've seen a similar picture like this before. We hardly had any photos left after the fire, but there was one family photo we took at the beach. All of our families have a copy of it.

"Mom." I say, nearly breathless, but she's already one step ahead of me.

"On it." She says, pulling out Dad's wallet. Inside, folded and worn from years of being carried around, is the photo I used to stare at nearly every day. She lays it out on the table beside the one Monica found.

Tiffany and Tiny are wearing the exact same bathing suits as the Lynn twins in the old photo.

And *now* we *know* the truth.

Mom gasps, covering her mouth as the reality of it sinks in. "Oh my God," she whispers. "It's them. It's them, Charles! It's the Lynn twins."

She collapses into Dad's arms and cries hysterically as the room falls into an emotional whirlwind. We all stand still, taking in the truth and finally understanding what happened to all of us on the day that changed our lives forever.

For decades, my parents accepted a false narrative in order to move on with their lives, but in this moment, we're grieving all over again. Monica comforts a broken Rafe, who now has to accept that his dad was murdered. And though Sherri's been the best mom to me, I'll never know what it's like to experience the love that my mother had to give. There's so much pain, so much dark history unraveling around us.

As I find myself suffocating from the darkness I thought I had overcome, Mel sits beside me and wraps me in a tight, reassuring hug.

"Fate never fails, Mase. We'll never know why, but life is as it should be. And this unconventional family you've been blessed with? It's beautiful. And what's even more beautiful is that you always knew. You knew who your Tiffany Nicole was, and it's because of you that she's remained in your lives. Your mother would be so proud of the amazing man you are, crazy and all."

We all comfort one another the best we can.

Then, Dad kisses Mom's forehead, his eyes red and tearful. With quiet determination, he says, "Now, we call the Lynns—Terry, Crystal...and Tiffany."

Chapter 33

The Truth – Tiffany

I don't consider myself a prideful woman, but I'm so proud of the life I've managed to build over the years. From college dance teams to Juilliard to Alvin Ailey, my students have thrived under my guidance. Girls dream of joining my dance company, and I've traveled the country choreographing performances for some of the world's greatest entertainers. Yet, nothing compares to the feeling I get when a little girl tells me she wants to be just like me when she grows up. *Those* moments remind me why I started dancing in the first place—because Aunt Dora saw something in me that I hadn't seen in myself. Now, I help other young dancers see their potential—not just as good or even great dancers, but as the best. I still can't believe the impact I've made in so many lives.

But lately, I wonder—am I wrong for wanting more? Is it selfish to think the life I've built isn't good enough? Am I ungrateful for feeling like this life, as fulfilling as it is, could be even better?

I'm ready to slow down, but I'm not ready to settle. I need some spontaneity to balance the stability I've worked so hard for. I need unpredictability to break through my well-ordered lifestyle. I need to have some fun to offset my unforgiving work schedule. I need optimism to counterbalance my realist nature. I need unbridled passion to break through the logic that rules my life.

I need Mason Boom. I need all his silliness, his carefree attitude, his confidence, his unapologetic desire for me, and his ability to irk my nerves and turn me on all at once.

It's time, and I think we're both ready to take the next step in our friendship. I think we're ready for forever because he's my first everything, and he's still the only man I've ever truly loved.

We've thrived on our own for ten years, constantly alternating between hating and loving one another but never getting back together. This time will be different.

We once promised that we'd find our way back to each other, and over the years, we have. Even when we were apart, we supported one another. Mase has always chosen me, and now, I'm choosing us.

I actually think his optimism has finally rubbed off on me, and I have so much planned for our future – starting with home.

"Finally!" Tiny tells me during our Sunday visit. "I still can't believe you had that man waiting for a decade. I would've been left your stubborn ass."

I roll my eyes. "Mase was *not* waiting on me. We needed to get our shit together. It was bad, Tiny. He couldn't breathe without me."

She smirks. "Girl, you were suffocating when that man gave you space! Now, look at the both of you breathing on your own yet still obsessed with each other."

"Ain't nobody obsessed over no damn Mason Boom!" I laugh, shaking my head. "Anyway, how're you doing? Did you get Drew's article I printed? It's kind of scary that the world is raving about a kid who hasn't even begun high school. They're already calling him the future of the NFL. Mase has done an outstanding job as his trainer and mentor."

"Whoa!" Tiny's eyes light up. "He's *that* good?"

I nod, smiling with pride. "The absolute best, Sis. But what's even better is that he's a genius—just like you."

Tiny gasps. "So, he did it? He won first place in the science fair?"

"He sure did!"

"Oh my God, that's amazing!" Tiny exclaims, her voice filled with joy. "I can't wait to meet him one day."

"And he's excited to meet you, too. I still can't believe this is our last Sunday visit. You sure you don't want me to stay?"

"Girl, if you stay one more week, I'm gonna tell the guards to turn your ass away." Tiny jokes.

I sigh, still shocked that I'm making such an impulsive decision to just up and leave Atlanta.

"Okay, fine. I won't change my mind. But I'll miss you, Tiny. Your appeal may have gotten denied this time, but I swear we're gonna get you out. We're gonna bring you home where you belong, with us, in Greer."

Tiny places her hand on mine, and we share sweet sentiments before I head home to call Mase and share the news I've been sitting for a few weeks.

First, I have to unblock him. He just kept bothering me last night! I told him to stop texting me unfunny memes, but he didn't listen, so I had to teach him a lesson. But damn, I can't wait to hear his sexy voice, let alone see his handsome face.

I really can't wait to tell him that I've decided to move back to Greer. It makes total sense. Drew is a teenager now, which means he has no problem voicing his opinion. So, when he told me he wanted to play for the best football program in Georgia, I already knew what he meant, Greer High School. He also apparently met some girl at a party, Lea, who happens to live in Greer. He claims it's fate, and I couldn't help but laugh because Mase and I met around the same age.

It's hard to ignore when the stars start to align. Mel's back home, Rafe's practice is expanding faster than any of us could've imagined, and Monica—well, her career has completely taken off since she became Mase's publicist. It's like everything's falling into place for everyone.

And Drew? He's so over the moon to be closer to his grandparents. The Booms and the Bakers stepped in as family from the very beginning, and because of them, Drew has never had to want for love. They've always been there, and he's never questioned how deeply he's cared for. They've been more than grandparents; they've been a lifeline.

The Lynns have transformed the city, spurring incredible economic growth. It's one of the top emerging cities to live in now, and not just because it's beautiful. It's become an epicenter for professional sports teams. Mase's contract is almost up, and I can't help but want—no, I *need* him to explore his options. And by options, I mean me. I can't deny it anymore. He once promised he'd follow me to the ends of the earth, but I don't need him to follow me across the globe. I just want him to come back home.

We've both grown so much. I no longer need him out of dependence or to feel whole but because his love enhances my own and allows us to grow stronger together. Our thoughts are intertwined, and our hearts fit together like puzzle pieces. We're just meant to be together.

I no longer care about his intrusive lifestyle, and I don't fear being exposed. I just care about him and the way that he loves me and Drew endlessly.

I've been scouring the area, looking at possible locations for a third dance studio for weeks now. We were initially going to wait until the spring semester, but Drew wants to play football for Greer High his freshman year. Therefore, we're relocating sooner rather than later.

And I can't wait to tell Mase.

I smile to myself and grab my phone. Mase is going to be over the moon when he hears the news. Knowing him, he'll probably start looking for a new building for me within the hour. That's just who he is—always ready to make sure I have everything I need, even before I realize I need it.

I can already picture his grin when I tell him. Seeing me happy makes him happy, and knowing he'll be happy when I finally give in to what we both want brings me so much joy.

But when I call him, he doesn't pick up.

Mase *always* answers my calls, especially now that we've been talking about serious things—us, home, the future. I wait a minute, then try again. No answer. Not even a text back.

I try not to panic, but my mind is already racing. What if something happened? What if he's hurt? What if something went wrong with the team? It's as if every worst-case scenario starts flooding my head all at once, drowning out the rational part of me that's trying to remain calm.

Just as I'm about to dial his number for the sixth time, Drew texts me from school.

Drew: Turn on ESPN.

I don't even stop to question it. I rush to the tv, grab the remote, and flip to ESPN.

There he is—Mase, standing at a podium He looks calm, too calm, like he's rehearsed whatever he's about to say a hundred times. My heart pounds, and my stomach sinks as I watch the screen. Something feels wrong. His face is serious, and his usual playful spark is nowhere to be found.

Then I hear him say it.

"I'll be taking a year off with the hope of returning to the league as a free agent after this break. I'm not saying goodbye forever, just...goodbye for now."

The words hit me like a punch to the gut. My heart skips a beat. I stare at the tv, stunned, trying to process what I'm hearing. Why would Mase do this? It's because of me. It has to be because of me...it better not be because of anyone else.

Panic sets in, and my thoughts spiral into a deep, dark rabbit hole. Did something happen that he hasn't told me about? Why didn't he call me first?

I grab my phone, my hands trembling, and text him again.

Tiffany: Mase, what are you doing? Why didn't you tell me? Call me, please.

No response.

I try to call Mel next. No answer. Then Callie. Nothing. Maurice? Voicemail. It's like they've all gone radio silent, and now I'm really freaking out.

So, I dial the one person who I know will tell me what's going on—Rafe.

He picks up after the second ring, his voice unusually chipper and forcefully fake. "Hey, Tiff! What's up?"

"Rafe Carter Boom," I practically growl. "Where is Mason?"

There's a long pause, and I can practically hear him sweating through the phone. "Uh... Mase? I mean, he's—uh, you know, busy. Really busy. Doing stuff. Like looking at papers and whatnot."

"Rafe, I swear to God, if you don't tell me—"

Before he can stutter out another lie, I hear Mel's voice in the background, clear as day. "Hang up the damn phone, Rafe!"

I narrow my eyes, my blood boiling. "Rafe, don't you dare hang up on me!"

But all I hear is *beep,* letting me know he did indeed hang up the phone.

Something is definitely going on, and now I'm even more anxious. I know Mase is always up to something, but why would Mel and Rafe keep anything from me?

Needing to distract myself from the growing pit in my stomach, I decide to move forward with my day. I spend the next few hours searching for homes in Greer online, clicking through listings that could potentially be the future I've been dreaming of. Then, I read up on the new football team that the Lynns are bankrolling, the Greer Renegades. It's exciting to think about. I can already picture Mase getting picked up and our dreams finally becoming reality—a life together in Greer.

But even as I try to immerse myself in the possibilities of our future, a looming darkness hangs over me. We've spent so long hoping, waiting for the right moment to come back together, but life always seems to find a way to tear us apart. What if this time is no different? What if, after all this time, we're destined to keep missing each other?

By the time I finish teaching my classes at the studio, I still haven't heard back from Mase. But I do have a few missed calls from Crystal Lynn.

I immediately dial her back, my heart in my throat. Crystal sounds worried the moment she picks up.

"Crystal, what's going on?" I ask, my voice trembling slightly.

"Tiff," she says quietly. "Can you pick us up from the airstrip to head to Ms. Dora's? Our jet lands in an hour."

Her words send a chill down my spine. "Wait, why? What's happening?"

There's a pause, and then she says, "The Booms called. It's an emergency."

Panic tightens around my chest. "What kind of emergency? Is Mase—"

"I don't know, Tiff," Crystal gently interrupts, trying to keep her own voice steady. "Just... just be ready. Okay?"

I quickly make arrangements for Drew to stay at a friend's house and head to pick Crystal and Terry up from the private airstrip. My nerves are on edge the entire drive, and the quiet car ride only amplifies my growing sense of dread. When I finally reach the strip and see them, I greet Crystal and Terry with a warm hug, trying to ground myself in the familiarity of their presence.

Despite the tension in the air, there's always been a level of comfort between us. Still, as we drive towards Ms. Dora's house, that unshakable feeling of dread hangs over me like a storm cloud ready to break.

Crystal turns to me, her voice soft but full of concern. "How's Tiny doing?"

"We're optimistic," I say, trying to focus on something good. "Especially since y'all have stepped in to help with Tiny's appeal. I can't thank you enough for everything you've done."

Though Crystal and Terry don't know the full extent of Tiny and my history, they've been fierce advocates for her release. They believe in her, and that's meant more to me than I could ever express.

Terry speaks up, his tone thoughtful. "How's Mase doing?"

I hesitate for a second. "I... I'm not sure. I'm worried. Mase and I have a connection I can't explain, and I just know when something's wrong."

Terry gives me a sad smile. "You know, when Mase was a baby, he and our daughter Nicole were inseparable. They'd even scoot across the crib just to be near each other, always finding a way to lock fingers. They were like magnets. No matter how far apart we put them, they'd end up side by side."

His words hit me in a strange way, stirring something deep in my chest. That magnetic pull—it's exactly how Mase and I have always been. Always drawn back to each other, no matter how far apart life tries to pull us.

As soon as we pull up to Aunt Dora's house, I force myself to readjust and compose my swirling emotions. Crystal and Terry are on each side of me, their hands holding mine and grounding me in the moment. But as we reach the steps, I barely have time to knock before the door swings open.

It's Mase.

Before I can think, I'm lunging toward him with my arms wrapped around his neck, clinging to him like he's the only thing keeping me from falling apart.

"Oh my God, Mase! Are you okay?" I grab his face and check for bruises before clinging to him again. "I've been calling you over and over again."

But he doesn't respond. Instead, he pulls me in tighter with an almost desperate grip. I can feel the tension in his body, like he's holding onto me for dear life. He's never hugged me like this before—like this is the first time he's ever held me, or maybe like he's afraid it'll be the last.

Crystal and Terry quietly close the door behind us, then Mase and I finally release each other. I step back and search his face, but his expression is unreadable. His eyes are bloodshot red and filled with brokenness, distress, but somehow relief. It's like he's carrying the weight of something heavy, something I don't yet understand.

I notice the others; they all share the same expression: sadness, sorrow, regret, and something else I can't quite place. A growing sense of fear tightens in my chest, making it harder to breathe as I follow Terry and Crystal into Aunt Dora's living room.

My eyes land on a large board cluttered with pictures, thumbtacks, and string connecting various points. It looks like some kind of investigation, the kind you see on detective shows, but it makes no sense to me. What could they possibly be investigating?

Terry and Crystal are focused on the board, but my attention drifts to the dining room, where I spot boxes filled with my old things. I gravitate towards them with a strange mix of nostalgia and unease. My fingers brush against the edge of a pink, dusty, ragged blanket hanging out of one of the boxes. The smell is awful, but I don't care. The comfort of my memories overpowers its haggard state, and for a moment, I let it transport me back to a time when Tiny and I sought comfort in its warmth and smell of home.

"Aunt Dora, I can't believe you kept this." My voice comes out as a whisper, barely audible. I hold the blanket like a relic from another life, something that shouldn't exist anymore but somehow still does. I turn toward the others, my heart pounding in my chest. "I haven't seen this blanket in years."

I stand there, cradling my old blanket in my hands while faint voices drift from the living room, almost like they're speaking in the distance but just loud enough to hear.

"It's true, Crys. It's her." I hear Sherri murmur through her trembling voice.

Terry's voice cracks, struggling to keep it together. "I knew it. I swear, I knew it."

Their words float in the air like a cloud. My heart races faster as I walk back into the living room, but the second I step in, silence falls. Everyone is staring at me, tears welling in their eyes—especially Terry and Crystal.

There's something heavy in the air now. It's like I'm standing on the edge of a cliff, and all it'll take is one word, one truth, to send me plummeting into a world I can't escape.

"This was once my mother's blanket," Crystal says softly, her voice thick with emotion. "Then, it became mine when I was born."

I blink, confused. This blanket is *mine*.

"And then," Terry chokes out, tears streaming down his face, "We gave it to you and Taylor... the day you were born, Nicole."

Nicole?

The name slams into me like a tidal wave, knocking the breath out of my lungs. My chest tightens. My heart pounds erratically. I want to say something, to demand an explanation, but my voice is caught in my throat.

I glance at Mase, hoping for some kind of explanation, something to anchor me, but all I see is the same broken expression on his face—the one that matches everyone else in the room.

"Um, y'all know my name is Tiffany. Nicole is just some fake name that stuck." I stammer, tears prickling the corners of my eyes. "What's happening? Why's everyone acting so weird? Why's everyone staring at me? Mase? Aunt Dora?"

Aunt Dora looks at me with soft eyes and gestures toward the board. Mase gently pulls me over, and I stare at the old photos tacked up there, barely recognizing the pieces of my past.

One photo catches my eye—me and Tiny on Tybee Island in Savannah. "Where'd you find this picture?" I ask, confused. "I haven't seen it in forever."

Crystal cries harder, which only confuses me more.

Mase points to another photo. "This is me," he says softly. "This is my mom, and this is Rafe's dad. And these..." He swallows hard, pointing to two baby girls. "These are the Lynn twins."

He points to the two girls. I stare back and forth between the two pictures. "Their bathing suits...they're the same as ours. Why do they look like me and Tiny?"

The truth is here, staring me in the face, but I can't bring myself to accept it. My entire body trembles as tears stream down my face.

"Mase, what's happening?" My voice cracks as panic sets in.

His hand gently lifts my chin so our eyes meet. "You've always been my Nicole," He whispers, his voice breaking. "You're Nicole Lynn, Tiffany. You're Crystal and Terry's daughter."

The air leaves my lungs in a rush, and I feel dizzy, like the ground has been ripped out from under me. I can't breathe. I can't think. My past, my life, everything I've ever known feels like a lie.

"But this means... my life... it was all fake. I can't—"

I stumble backward, my legs shaking, but Crystal steps toward me, reaching out for my hand. "Nicole, please sit—"

I yank my hand back as panic floods through me. "That's not my name! My name is Tiffany!"

The words tear out of me, but they don't feel like enough. My chest tightens. I can't get enough air, my breaths come in short, frantic bursts. The world around me blurs as I feel myself slipping, grasping for something… anything to hold onto. Something that makes sense. The childhood I never wanted but accepted as mine is unraveling before me, and I'm terrified—terrified of what it means, terrified of losing everything I've known.

Suddenly, a memory crashes into me with painful clarity—Mama's voice, sharp and cold, slicing through my thoughts like a whip. Her belt cracking down on my hands, forcing me to remember who I am. Forcing me to never forget.

I glance down at my palms, the faint marks of her punishments still etched in my skin.

"I'm sorry, Mama," I mumble, the words trembling from my lips as I collapse to the floor, my knees giving out beneath me. "I won't forget my name. Just don't beat me again. Please. My name is Tiffany. Tiffany Nicole Weathers. My name is Tiffany. Tiffany Nicole Weathers. My name is Tiffany. Tiffany Nicole Weathers. My name is —"

I chant it like a lifeline, over and over, rocking back and forth. My voice is frantic, desperate, as if the words alone can anchor me to the reality I've clung to for so long. But that reality is slipping away, dissolving in the flood of memories and truths I'm not ready to face.

Suddenly, I feel two sets of arms wrap around me, pulling me in and holding me close.

Crystal's voice comes next, soft and gentle in my ear, like a balm for the wounds that are tearing me apart. "Okay, your name is Tiffany Nicole Weathers. We'll call you whatever you want us to call you. But you *are* our daughter, and we love you with all our hearts. We've always loved you, Tiffany. We love you, Tiny, and Drew. We'll never let you go. Never again."

Her words wash over me, wrapping me in a warmth I didn't know I needed. Terry's voice follows, thick with emotion but steady. "We're going to bring Tiny home, too. We love you both so much. We're yours, and you're ours."

I blink through my tears, looking up at them, my voice trembling, broken. "But I don't have a mom and dad?"

Crystal wipes away my tears with a tenderness that makes my heart ache. Her eyes, full of warmth and love, meet mine. "Yes, you do, baby. You have a room full of parents, including us now. We're all going to love you for the rest of our lives and beyond. It's me, you, and the world around us."

Her words—the phrase—hit me like a shock of familiarity. The scent of vanilla radiating from Crystal fills my senses, and suddenly, it connects with the voice I remember. The voice that Tiny and I clung to as children, a voice that brought us peace when everything else was chaos. It was never Mama's voice—it was Crystal Lynn's. It was always her. It was her smell. It was her voice that gave us hope that better days were sure to come.

The realization breaks something inside me, and for the first time, I allow myself to let go. To let the truth in.

In this moment, I lean into the embrace of the two people I never imagined calling out for, my voice trembling with vulnerability and raw emotion. "Mom...Dad?"

We cry together on the floor, holding each other until every last tear is drained from me, leaving me empty but somehow full at the same time.

"What do we do now?" I ask, my voice barely above a whisper as I look up at Crystal and Terry. There's so much confusion swirling around in my mind.

Crystal presses a soft kiss to my forehead, her touch gentle but filled with a depth of emotion I'm just beginning to understand. Her voice is calm and steady, but beneath it, I can hear the strength of a woman who has waited years for this moment.

"We get your sister out, and we find the woman who stole you from us. We get justice for both of you. And we get justice for the Booms. We have so much time to make up for Tiffany, and so much healing to do, but we'll get there. We're together now, and we'll get there."

Her words wrap around me, and I can feel the weight of what's to come. This road ahead is long, filled with pain, anger, and memories I don't want to face. I hold onto the Lynns, letting their presence calm the storm inside me so I feel at ease—like a part of me has finally come home. But there's something missing. Someone. I slightly pull back, wipe my face, and look around the room.

"Where's Mase?" I ask, my voice soft, almost tentative.

Mel steps forward, her face etched with empathy. She lays a gentle hand on my arm. "He needs time, Tiff. He's so happy for you, for what you've gained today. He did all this for you. But," she pauses, her eyes clouding with something deeper, something sad. "He has to process the truth of how he lost his mother."

Her words hit me like a punch to the gut, and suddenly, the joy I felt is overshadowed by reality. Mase did all of this—for me. He uncovered truths that shattered his own world just to bring mine together. I've gained two parents, but in doing so, Rafe and Mase have learned how they lost theirs.

"Oh my God," I murmur while glancing over at Monica, who consoles Rafe. "I need to find him."

I pull out my phone to call him, but he already texted me.

Mase: Seeing you happy brings me so much joy. I knew I'd find you someday. I always knew who you were in my heart. Get Tiny back. Get to know who you are and where you came from. Most importantly, heal. You, Drew, Tiny, Crystal, and Terry are the most beautiful family I've ever met. Right now isn't our time, but I promise we'll come back to each other and be a family one day. I love you, Tiffany Nicole Weathers.

Chapter 34

Life's a Cockblock – Tiffany

Two weeks have passed since that day at Aunt Dora's, and life has been moving faster than ever; like a runaway train, I can't slow down. The DNA test confirmed it—I'm Nicole Lynn. Those words feel strange in my mouth, like they don't quite belong to me. I'm a grown woman, but in the face of this truth, I feel like a stranger to myself.

And Drew? He's handled it like the teenager he is, totally unbothered and more excited about the perks than the heaviness of what it all means. His reaction — *"Holy crap! I got three sets of grandparents? And they're billionaires?"*

Can you believe it? That's all he had to say. His focus right now is on football. I want his life to remain as normal as possible, especially before the media finds out who we really are. So, I shipped half of everything I own back home and enrolled Drew at Greer High School. He's barely begun school, but he loves it already. Apparently, it's a *flex* to have his grandad as his principal. And he enjoys being spoiled by our family. Drew is *definitely* a Greer kid.

Meanwhile, my head's been spinning with the enormity of it all—the implications, the history, the past I never knew was mine. Mostly, my thoughts have been consumed with Mase—his face, his voice, the way he always stood by me, even when he didn't know everything. I wouldn't be here without him. He's the reason I found my way back to my real family.

Which leads me here today, boarding a flight to Seattle.

"Are you sure you're going to be okay? We can delay the press conference. We know how important Mase is to you, to all of us. Please send him our love. We're forever grateful he brought you home to us." Crystal's words echo in my head as she sees me off.

"Mom, bring him back, please." Drew adds, his eyes wide and hopeful as he hugs me goodbye.

I nod and board the jet with a heavy heart. I'm going to Seattle to get my man and bring him back, to remind him that he's just as important to me as the truth he uncovered, and I'll always be there for him as he's been there for me.

As the jet hums beneath me, I sift through the documents Callie and Sherri pulled together over the past few days. They've been trying to track down Kayla Drexler, the woman who tried to break me and Tiny in every way imaginable.

I should've known she was an imposter. I should've sensed it. But how could I when she played so many twisted games with our minds and warped our reality, making it impossible for Tiny and me to believe we could ever deserve a mother like Crystal Lynn. We were always just the Weathers— two poor girls surviving by clinging to each other until we couldn't anymore.

Mama and Pop shattered Tiny's innocence, and in the process, they shattered so much of the life we could've had. A life filled with love, warmth, peace, safety, and happiness.

Tiny deserves better. She's always deserved better. When I told her the truth about our family, I felt like I broke her all over again. She's reclaimed so much of herself from behind those bars, but knowing what we were supposed to have—the life we were meant to live—it was like opening a fresh wound. We have our real mother now. A mother who has love and positivity pouring from her heart, who has been searching for us, praying for us. Yet still, Tiny refuses to see her.

As I drift off to sleep, my thoughts carry me back to last weekend when I told Tiny the truth. I remember the way her face shifted, the devastation mixed with a flicker of hope, a hope she's too scared to hold on to.

"Not yet," She whispered, shaking her head as tears welled up in her eyes. "I don't want to meet them yet. Not like this, Tiffany. If this is true—like you say, like I believe it is—then I don't want our first time meeting to be in a prison. Please, don't let them come. I don't want them to see the daughter they've prayed for like this. I know I'm better than I used to be, but I'm not where I want to be. Not yet."

I grabbed her hand, squeezing it, wanting her to feel the strength she's always had. "But Tiny, you're perfect. You've always been perfect. They'll love us regardless. Crystal and Terry are incredible. And you look just like him—just like our dad."

Tiny started to cry then, her voice breaking as she said, "Dad... Oh my God, we have a dad!"

"We do," I whispered, tears filling my own eyes. "We have a family, Tiny. We're going to get you out, and we're going to be together."

"I love you, Sis," she said through her tears.

"I love you, too... twin."

I wake to the gentle motion of the plane descending as the wheels touch down on the tarmac with a soft thud. I'm in Seattle now, the cool air creeping in through the cracks of my doubt, but it's not enough to stop me. Mase left so abruptly, and I know he's hurting. He's the type of man who takes care of everyone else even while his own world falls apart. Now, it's time I take care of him.

The drive to his place feels surreal, each mile making my heart beat a little faster. By the time I reach the gates of his mansion, my hands are trembling, but I punch in the code for the gates—my birthday—and they slowly swing open.

I drag my suitcase behind me, the wheels bumping along the cobblestones as I make my way to his front door. I'm nervous, and my stomach twists, but there's no turning back now. I lift my hand to knock, but before my fist can connect with the wood, the door swings open.

And there he is. My Mase.

Shirtless, his body is all hard lines and skin as smooth as planes. His sculpted perfection leaves me breathless, temporarily paralyzed and caught between lust and love. His sweatpants leave no room for my imagination to exist.

But it's his eyes that hit me the hardest. Red, tired, and hollow. It's like looking into a soul that's been scraped raw.

And before I can think, my hands are on his face, cupping his cheek. "Oh, Mase," I whisper, my voice trembling with emotion. The sadness in his eyes shakes me to my core.

He leans into my touch, turning his head just enough so his lips brush against the inside of my palm. It's soft, barely a kiss, but it feels like the most intimate moment we've shared in years. "My Tiffany Nicole," he murmurs, his voice raspy and low. "What're you doing here?"

I manage a small smile. "What do you think? I'm checking on my family." The word hangs between us, heavy with meaning.

His arms wrap around me, pulling me close, and we hug like we haven't seen each other in years. It's more than a hug—it's a reunion of the souls of two people who were meant to grow up together and fall in love. But then, as quickly as the tenderness fills me, my frustration takes over.

I slap his chest, hard enough to make a point but soft enough not to hurt. "If you ever leave like that again, Mason Boom, I swear I'm gonna kick you in that recovered knee!"

He laughs, that deep, familiar sound I've missed so much, and it makes something inside me click back into place.

I pull back and glance around his house. The place feels... morbid. There's a heaviness in the air, like grief has settled into every corner.

"How long have you been cooped up in here?" I ask, my voice softer now.

Mase shrugs, his gaze dropping. "Since I got back. She deserved justice. She deserved a son who could've figured out the truth a decade ago. It's like I'm mourning all over again, but how do you mourn someone you don't even remember? I can't remember her laugh, her voice. I don't know what she smelled like or what she sounded like when she told me goodnight. I've got nothing but a picture, and that's not enough. It's never going to be enough, Tiff."

"I know it feels like a piece of you is missing, like you'll never get back what was taken, but you haven't been without love. Your dad. And Sherri loves you like her own. Callie, Aunt Dora, Crystal—they've all poured love into you, which has allowed you to love yourself, me, and Drew so deeply. You, Mason Boom, are a son any mother would pray to have, and your mother lives in you. You're a good man, and I'll never let you think otherwise."

He releases a deep sigh of relief and kisses my shoulder. "Thank you, Tiff." Then, he looks at my suitcase and asks, "When're you leaving?"

"Well," I say, trying to keep my tone light. "Drew's getting settled into Greer and being doted on by our parents and friends—so I'm staying at least a week. Maybe longer if you need me. You've supported me my entire life, now it's my turn."

Mase meets my eyes, and something shifts behind his exhaustion. There's a faint smile as his lips part to speak, but I cut him off. "As much as I enjoy being wrapped in your arms, you stink, Mase. Go take a shower."

He chuckles, and it feels like the air lightens just a little. "Aye, aye, Captain." He says, his voice teasing with a glint of gratefulness in his eyes.

He leans in and press his lips to my forehead before disappearing down the hallway toward the bathroom.

As soon as he's gone, I glance around the kitchen and shake my head. The fridge is practically empty. There are just some old takeout containers and a half-empty carton of ice cream.

"Pitiful," I mutter to myself. "Absolutely pitiful. Guess I'll have to order something to get us through the night."

I tidy up, trying to make sense of the space that feels like a stranger's home despite how well I know it. I'm halfway through planning out a food delivery when I hear him re-enter the room.

"Okay, I'm thinking we'll order from—" I start, but my words trail off when I turn around and see him.

Mason is standing there, fresh out of the shower, with nothing but a towel slung around his waist. His skin glistens with droplets of water, and I feel my breath catch in my throat. For a moment, I'm stunned, frozen in place, and every word I was about to say is completely forgotten. He looks like a god standing there, and my body reacts instantly.

"Oh... hello." I manage to say, my voice coming out in a whisper that's far sultrier than I intended.

Mase smirks, that cocky, confident grin that always gets under my skin. "You were saying?"

His tone is playful, but I can see something else simmering behind his eyes. Something darker, something that mirrors the desire pulsing through me.

I bite my lip, trying to pull myself together as my mind races. "Food," I mutter, more to myself than to him. "We need food."

But Mase steps closer, closing the gap between us. I feel the heat radiating off him. There's this undeniable energy between us, charged with something electric. It makes the air feel thicker, and my heart beat harder.

"You know I love to eat." He murmurs, his voice lower and deeper. His eyes hold mine, pulling me in and dragging me into a place I'm not sure I can resist.

My breath hitches, but I fight to stay grounded. "Mase!" I begin, my voice skipping between exasperation, desire, and amusement. "You were just crying in my arms thirty minutes ago! And now you're flirting with me?

He shrugs, completely unapologetic. "I had a good cry in the arms of my woman. Then took a hot shower. I feel better already. You have no idea how damn good you make me feel. *And* I have you all to myself for an entire week?"

His grin is crooked, a little mischievous, and God help me, it's doing all types of things to me, especially when I look down to see his swelling dick print nearly slipping through his towel. I try to stay composed, though my pulse is racing.

"Well, you won't feel good for long if we don't get some food in this house," I say, trying to push through the sexual tension building between us. "Lemon pepper wings and onion rings?"

"Oof," he groans, placing his hand across his chest. "A woman after my own heart."

While I order, he picks up my suitcase and carries it to the guest room, but I stop him. "So," I begin slowly, cautiously. "I was thinking...maybe I could sleep in your room, if that's okay with you," I swallow hard, meeting his gaze with uncertainty. "I figured you might want company this week. *My* company."

His eyes darken, and a slow smile creeps across his face. He doesn't say anything right away, but he reaches for me and pulls me close, this time with something raw, something primal, and something thick resting against my leg.

"You sure you want that? You sure you want this?" He whispers, his breath warm against my temple.

My hands find their way to his chest, then slowly travel down to lightly rub against the outside of his towel.

I let out a long breath, minced with a sensual moan. "I'm sure, Mase. I'm so damn sure."

With a smile, Mase lifts my chin and kisses my forehead. "Then it's settled. I'm gonna hold you in my arms every night right after I finish fucking the shit out of you…every night."

While waiting for the food delivery, I take a shower. I need to clear my mind and ease the tension running through my body. Every moment between Mase and me is damn near sinful, and it's only the beginning of what promises to be a long week.

Under the hot spray of water, I let my hands glide over my skin, washing away the day's exhaustion and lust. But no amount of water can wash away the electricity running through me. Mase and I have been dancing around this line for what feels like forever, and now? Now it feels like we're ready to cross it again.

When I step out of the shower, I grab one of Mase's oversized T-shirts and slip it over my damp skin. It hangs loose on me, falling just above my thighs. I keep my panties on, but the feeling of his shirt against my body, the lingering scent of him, feels intimate, like I'm wrapped in his presence, even when he's not in the room.

When I walk back into the living room, Mase is already settled on the couch, and the glow of the TV casts shadows across his handsome face. His eyes lock onto me the moment I enter the room. His gaze is intensely heated, and it roams over me like he's trying to reacquaint himself with every inch of my body. I can feel his thoughts running wild, and it sends a shiver down my spine.

I pretend not to notice and sit next to him, teasingly swinging my legs over his lap. We fall into a cozy rhythm of eating wings and watching football.

"How does it feel to be on this side of things?" I ask, gesturing to the tv. "Watching instead of playing?"

Mase takes a moment to think, his eyes never leaving the screen. "Honestly?" He glances at me, his hand gently resting on my thigh. "It feels... good."

I blink, surprised by his answer. "Good?"

He nods, then slowly moves his fingers up and down my thighs, sending sparks through me with each stroke. "Yeah. I mean, don't get me wrong, I love the game and always have. I think I've even got maybe five more years left in me, but..." He pauses, a small smile tugging at his lips. "I only want to play one more. Back home."

My heart leaps in my chest. "For the Renegades?"

He nods, his eyes softening as he looks at me. "Yeah. One more season. In Greer. I'd love to play back home, where you are, where we can be together."

For the first time in forever, our desires are perfectly aligned. My heart swells with joy, with the overwhelming sense of hope that maybe, just maybe, everything we've ever wanted is finally falling into place.

"Mase," I breathe, hardly able to contain the excitement building inside me. "That'd be amazing. But what about after?" I ask quietly, turning to look at him. "What happens after you retire?"

He leans in and brushes his lips against my temple while his hand trails further up my thigh, a comforting warmth that makes my entire body hum with anticipation.

There's something raw and honest in his expression. "I want to grow our family. I want marriage, a home, kids, everything with you. Do you want that with me?"

His question hits me like a soft wave. We've never spoken about marriage or kids before, not seriously, at least, but the vulnerability in his voice emboldens me to reciprocate my feelings.

"Of course," I whisper. "I want everything with you."

His hand squeezes my thigh, and the tenderness in his touch tells me everything I need to know. This is real. This is us. This is Tiffany and Mason, forever.

I lean my head on his shoulder, and we finish the game in peaceful silence. The weight of his arm around me feels like home, and before I know it, my eyes grow heavy, and I drift off to sleep to the steady rise and fall of his chest.

Sometime later, I feel myself being lifted. Mase's strong arms are cradling me as he carries me to his room. He gently lays me on his bed, where I feel the mattress dip as he settles beside me. Mase's lips brush my shoulder, and his hand rests lightly on my waist.

"Goodnight, Tiff," He whispers, his voice barely audible in the darkness.

Half asleep, I turn to face him, my eyes fluttering open just enough to meet his. "Mase, I never got the chance to say thank you."

He smiles, his hand coming up to cup my cheek. "We've got the rest of our lives for thank you's."

I shake my head, my voice sleepy but full of emotion. "No, this is a special one. You brought me back to who I am, and I'll never be able to thank you enough for that."

Without waiting for his response, I press my lips to his, and the kiss that follows is slow, deep, and filled with everything we've held back for so long.

The moment we touch, every nerve in my body ignites. There's a tenderness in the way he kisses me, but it's layered with pent-up desire. He moves his hand from my cheek and up my shirt, emitting moans and groans as his hand finds my hard nipples. My breaths increase, our kiss deepens, and I feel the wetness between my thighs as the heat between us rises. His mouth is warm, his touch is intoxicating, and I feel myself melting into him, losing myself in the moment. He moves from my mouth to my neck and from my neck to my breast, slowly and methodically making his way downward between my wet entrance.

"It feels so good to be home." He whispers before diving headfirst inside me.

I gasp at the skilled flick of his tongue and grab his head tight.

"I love the way you taste," he groans. "I can live here forever—my face between your legs."

The way he licks me—deliberately and with every intention to satisfy me, increases my pleasure. He devours me with an insatiable hunger that has long been suppressed then slides a finger inside me, evoking a sensual moan.

"More!" I beg him to fill me up.

He inserts another and licks me until my moans turn into cries and my cries into hoarse pants. I soak his tongue with my sweet juices, and he slides upward to meet my lips, where we exchange a succulent kiss.

"Umm, umm, umm, the sweetest love I've ever known." He whispers, then stands to reveal his naked body and his thick, erect nine inches of glory. "Now, tell me, Tiffany Nicole, you gonna keep testing my patience? Or give both of us what we need?"

My mouth waters at the sight of him, and without a word, I bend over with my ass positioned perfectly in the air for me to experience what we both need—a homecoming.

Mase firmly grips my waist and slowly enters me from behind, but his caution steadily dwindles with each movement in and out of me. His thickness fills me up in ways that could only be explained through feeling, and he makes me feel so damn good.

He's overcome with ravenous desire. The sting of his hand on my ass is painfully pleasing, sending my body into a wild frenzy.

He slaps my ass again, then groans out loud. "Fuck, Tiff, did you just get even wetter?" He asks, while simultaneously pounding my aching, sensitive body and massaging my clit.

"Mase, you make me feel so fuckin' good!" I scream, voice hoarse and cracking.

"And your pussy wrapped around my dick feels so fuckin' good. Now, come for me, long and hard," He urges. "I know you're ready, and I'm ready to start round two."

So many sensations run through me, and I tremble, coming long and hard on his command.

"Umm," I moan in a state of euphoria as my body goes limp, but Mase pulls out and gently places me on my back.

"Mase, I want you to come." I whine, still completely out of breath.

He kisses me soft and sweet. "And I will. I just want to look into your eyes when I do."

He lifts my leg and drives deep into the depths of my soul. It's like he's pouring all of his emotions into me. I feel his grief and anger, his love, his fear, and his hope all at once. Our tears fall, and our hearts are opened once more.

"This is where I belong–with you, inside you, and by your side."

We come together so beautifully and so damn sweet. Falling asleep in his arms tonight is just a glimpse of the peace I look forward to every night for the rest of our lives.

~ ~ ~

Every day for the rest of the week feels like a dream filled with passionate lovemaking, packing, goofing around, and deep conversations planning our future. It's everything I could ever imagine a relationship with Mason would be.

But when the morning comes for us to leave Seattle and start our lives together in Greer, something changes. The brightness in Mason's eyes is gone, dimmed by something heavy weighing him down. The charming smile I adore fades as we get closer to our departure time.

"Mase, what's wrong?" He hasn't said a word in the last hour, and that's not like him. This man talks my head off.

He sighs deeply, rubbing his hand over his face, and it's like the weight of the world is sitting on his shoulders. "Promise me you won't be mad at me?"

I raise an eyebrow, already knowing I'm not going to like whatever he's about to say. "No, I don't promise 'cause now I'm sure you're about to piss me off."

He lets out a small laugh, but it's empty, strained. "I've been thinking… You've been hit with a lot over the last few weeks. Finding out about Crystal and Terry is a huge deal that I don't think you've quite processed. Then, you have this press conference coming up where you're going to reveal who you really are to the world. Our parents might've found your kidnapper, who also might be the person who murdered my mother. It's a lot for you and for me, Tiff. "

I nod, my heart pounding. We've been preparing for this moment, for the weight of the truth to finally come out. "I know it is, but as always, we'll be there for each other."

"Well, that's the thing…I can't be there for this." His voice is now quiet, almost fragile. "I know you want me by your side, Tiff. And God knows I want to be there. But I can't," He pauses, swallowing hard, his eyes closing for a brief moment as if he's trying to find the right words. "Grappling with my mother's death all over again has put me in the darkest headspace of my life. I can't handle the cameras and intrusion. I'm so fuckin' tired. I feel like I'm standing on the edge of a cliff, and I don't know how much longer I can stand without falling off. My mind's constantly racing. I'm emotionally drained. You being here with me this week—it's what I wanted more than anything, but it's not what I *need*. I don't want you to be my band-aid. I want you to be my wife, my partner, the mother of my kids, but I have to be whole first, not half, not tired, not broken, but whole."

My tears for him spill over, and though I can't fix how he feels, I do try to offer him assurance.

"Oh, Mase," I begin, my voice thick with emotion, each word heavy with care. "I've learned a lot over the years, and I've realized that we don't need to be whole to be loved, and I promise I'll love you through this. I'm scared too, but we'll be home and with each other through it all. We're all we need."

Mason sharply exhales and slumps his shoulders, then rubs the back of his neck. He's weary, but even more than that, he's terrified. Looking up, his eyes meet mine, clouded with turmoil that tugs at my heart.

"I need more than that. We need more than just each other. I gotta get away, Tiff. There's a wellness facility nearby. It'll just be a few months. I need to find my center again."

My eyes widen, and a rush of panic tightens my chest as his words sink in. I shake my head and struggle to hold back my fury of emotions.

"No! No, Mase. Not again. We're not doing this anymore! I'm sick of the separation. I'm sick of the distance. We've wasted enough time apart, and I won't go another second without you. Whatever you're going through, we're gonna get through it together. No more running. We grow together. We heal together. We belong together. We need to go home...together. Please, Mase." My desperation beats through my heart as I beg and plead for him to allow me to love him as he is.

But his eyes, red and heavy with emotion, hold steady.

"I can't," He says quietly, his voice cracking at the edges. "I need time. I can't act like I'm not broken, and I refuse to let my brokenness break us. You got what you need. Let me get what I need. Please, just wait for me."

"I won't." My reply is short, sharp, and almost cold, but it's not anger. It's fear. Fear that waiting means losing him, forever this time. We're not kids anymore. We aren't trying to find ourselves. So, why do we have to keep deferring our happiness?

He lets out a heavy breath, sucking his teeth in frustration. His jaw tightens, but he holds back whatever he's feeling. He doesn't argue with me. He just nods, like he expected this. Like he knew I wouldn't understand. Like he knew I wouldn't compromise.

When my car pulls up, the silence between us feels suffocating as he walks me to the door. And before I step out, he stops me and locks his eyes on mine with an intensity that steals the air from my lungs.

"I've followed you to the ends of the earth. I've done everything your way. I wasted years of my life with Kira. I waited for you to get rid of Donny. I stood by your side. I've given you my all, and at times, still punished myself for not giving enough. And all I've asked is for you to allow me to be the best man I can be for you. Maybe I'm not the only one who needs help. Goodbye, Tiffany."

The drive to the airstrip is a blur of emotion. I need Mase with me at home, but he also needs to heal. We're both right in our own ways but stand firm in what we need, and again, it feels like life just won't let us be together. Every time we get close to peace, something tears us apart. It's like we're caught in an infinite loop of *almost* and *never enough*. Maybe that's just how it is for us—two people who love each other but can't seem to find a way to hold on. The thought that this might be where the road ends for us sits like a stone in my chest, a pain that's sharp and dull all at once.

After takeoff, I break down and allow myself to sob the ugliest tears I've ever cried over the loss of the most beautiful love I ever had. They come harder when I think about all the years we've spent together *and* apart. The love that's never been enough to keep the world from pulling us apart.

Then, my phone buzzes with a text, and the words on the screen leave me breathless.

Crystal: We found her. We found Shirley Weathers aka Kayla Drexler.

Chapter 35

Reckoning – Tiffany

When I return to the Lynn estate, I'm greeted by the people who anchor me to my new reality—Crystal, Terry, and Drew. It's comforting but also painful. Mase should be here with me, but he's not.

Crystal opens her arms wide, and I fall into her embrace while Terry joins in, wrapping his strong arms around both of us. This makes me feel secure, even if everything in my life feels like it's spinning out of control.

"We heard about you and Mase." Terry says gently.

Crystal pulls back just enough to meet my eyes, her gaze filled with empathy. "I'm so sorry, sweetheart. I know how much you love him."

Her words nearly undo me. I love Mase with every part of me, and leaving him behind felt like tearing a piece of myself away. I've barely been able to hold it together since I walked out of his door.

Drew steps forward and leans his head on my shoulder. "We're gonna be okay, Mom. Mase is a superhero, you know that." His voice is soft, but there's a certainty in his words that makes me pause. "He always comes back, better, stronger, and ready to fight for us."

Drew's right. Mase always comes back. He's hit low points before, and each time, he's learned how to step back and find a way to reset. He doesn't let his pain take over his life. Mase knows how to steady his emotions, how to rebuild himself so he can be whole for us, not half. It's one of the things I admire most about him. It's why he's the most amazing man I know.

I begin to wonder—maybe I should do the same. If Mase can take a step back to heal and come back better, why can't I? If he's working on becoming the best man he can be for me, then I need to be the best woman for him. I need to reset, to make sure I'm strong enough to handle everything coming our way, especially with what's about to unfold.

"So, you found Shirley Weathers?" I ask, pushing through my swirling emotions.

Terry nods solemnly, and we all move inside to the living room. I sit on the edge of the couch, my heart racing as Terry begins to explain what they've uncovered.

"The forwarding address from the P.O. box we found only received mail once after you left. It was registered under a fake name—Margaret Joseph. We didn't know who that was at first, so we started digging through anything we could find. We got nothing until one of Callie's hacker friends located digital mail records, Marge Joseph *Drexler*, signed for a certified letter."

My stomach twists at the name. I don't know a Drexler, but if she's connected to her, she has to be a monster, too.

Terry continues, "We dug deeper and found that Kayla Drexler had an aunt—the only Drexler who slipped through the cracks when Sherri and Charles locked the rest of them away. Her middle name was Margaret."

They begin to connect the dots, but it feels like the room is spinning. "So, this Margaret...is she still alive? Does she know where Mama—" I pause. The word *mama* gets stuck in my throat.

I see Crystal and Terry exchange a glance, their faces softening at my slip-up. Crystal's expression is filled with understanding, but the pain is there too. It's like I can't separate myself from the woman who raised me, who manipulated and tortured me—it's hard to let go of the only reality I've ever known.

"If we can find Margaret, we might be able to track down Kayla. She could be the key to finally getting the answers we've been searching for." Terry says softly.

Crystal reaches for my hand, squeezing it gently. "Tomorrow, we'll show up unannounced. We'll catch them off guard. And we'll finally get justice for what she did to you and Tiny."

Anger swells in my chest, hot and fierce. "For you and Terry, too. And the Booms," I add, my voice tight with emotion. "She needs to pay for what she did to all of us."

Even in my fury, I feel the emotional toll of it all pressing down on me like a tidal wave. I sink into the couch and release a long, shaky breath, trying to steady myself, but I finally feel the emotional and mental exhaustion of the past few weeks catch up to me all at once. I understand how Mase feels. I feel...like I'm not okay.

"I need help," I whisper. "I've been on autopilot since discovering the truth, and now I'm just...overwhelmed and scared. I don't think I'm prepared or even strong enough to see *her* again...or to get through any of this. I want to move forward, Crystal. I want to call you *Mom* and Terry *Dad*. But I... I need help getting there, and if I don't get it, I think I might break. I need to go back to therapy, now more than ever."

Crystal wraps her arms around me and pulls me close. Her embrace is warm, steady, and filled with the kind of love I've only ever dreamed about. "That's a great idea, Tiff. I think all of us could use some healing."

～～～

A long night's rest, surrounded by Crystal and Terry was just what I needed to help me get to the next day. Warm, buttery, freshly baked biscuits are just what I need to start my day. The aroma is in my nostrils, and I can taste the perfect flaky layers that melt in my mouth. But then it hits me hard... Mason *isn't* here. The biscuits *aren't* his. They're Terry's, and as comforting as the scent is, it only amplifies the ache of missing him, so I decide to send a text.

Me: I'm sure you already know, but we're chasing a lead today. Hopefully, we'll find Kayla. I miss you, Mase, but I'm taking a page from your playbook and taking care of myself for once. I'll have to put my dance studio search on pause while I deal with everything else. I hope to see you soon. Hopefully, when you return, we'll have everything we want, including each other.

After a hot shower, I pull myself together and head to the kitchen, where the clatter of plates and the sound of laughter greets me as I walk in. Everyone I know and love is gathered around the table. They're all here, back in Greer, and the sight of them fills my heart in a way I can't quite put into words. This is what family looks like. This is home.

Mel spots me and immediately makes me a plate, then slides it across the table. Callie and Sherri are deep into planning, their voices low but determined as they map out the day's events. Drew is sitting between Aunt Dora and Maurice, attempting to eavesdrop.

"No disappearances, okay?" Callie and Sherri quietly discuss amongst themselves, but we all overhear.

"Uh, Gram-bams," Drew jokingly says to Callie and Sherri, his voice hesitant. Should I be in here for this?"

Everyone bursts out laughing, and Sherri shakes her head. "Why does everyone think Callie and I are some bloodthirsty assassins or somethin'?"

Aunt Dora chimes in, grinning. "Because you are, Sherri. I've learned so much about my once-sweet niece Callie and you, Booms, over the last fifteen years. I'd hate to get on your bad side."

Drew nods with a mischievous smile. "Aunt Dora's right. Y'all are like small-town mafia politicos. It's kind of dope."

I laugh, shaking my head. "Alright, Drew, you better get ready for school, and you better not be late for class again. 'Round here drooling over your little friend."

Drew blushes before heading out, but the lighthearted moment fades, and the air shifts as Callie continues to lay out the plan, her voice calm but direct.

"Sherri, remember not to go too hard—at least not in public. Charles is a judge, and you're the former governor. If you see her, keep your composure. We've sent every file we've found over the past month to the FBI and the news. We need to play this smart."

Sherri rolls her eyes but gives a small nod. "I can't make any promises, but I'll try. For now."

Breakfast wraps up with hugs and goodbyes. Rafe pulls me into a tight embrace before turning to his dad. Charles places a hand on Rafe's shoulder, his voice low but full of love. "I love you, Son. I promise we'll get justice for your father by any means necessary." Rafe nods. "I can't wait to get back to see my first granddaughter be born. You're gonna be a great father, just like Rafe Sr. was."

Rafe whispers, "And just like you are, Dad."

The ride to Atlanta is long but peaceful. Crystal and Terry tell stories of when Tiny and I were babies. Their voices are light and filled with love as they share memories they've held onto for decades. I listen intently, trying to picture myself in those early days I can't remember.

Crystal glances over at me and rests her hand on mine.

"I know how much you love the Bakers, and I'm so glad they've taken such good care of you and Drew. But I'd be lying if I didn't admit that it was nice having you and Drew sleep in our home last night. If you want, y'all are welcome to sleep over or even live with us until you get settled. I'd love another chance to live under the same roof as my children."

The words hit me in a way I didn't expect. Without hesitation, I nod. "I'd love that."

Terry grins from the driver's seat. "Soon, we'll have both our daughters home, right where they belong."

Shortly after, we pull up to a sprawling estate in Buckhead. The home is elegant and imposing with perfectly manicured lawns and a driveway that seems to stretch on forever. I stare out the window, my heart pounding as I take it all in.

"Who owns this place?" I ask, my voice barely above a whisper. "And why does this Drexler woman live here?"

Crystal and Terry exchange a glance before Terry answers. "Callie said it's owned by a wealthy surgeon, Dr. George Wheeler, his wife Andrea, and their daughter. I couldn't find any information on Andrea. She seems to be a recluse, but George is nearly everywhere on the internet. Marge Drexler has been living here for years. Maybe she's their housekeeper, and hopefully she can help us find Kayla."

Charles and Sherri pull up right behind us, but when they begin to approach the home, I stop them. "Wait," My voice is steady, but my nerves are on fire. "Let me go in first. I need to do this alone."

Crystal reaches for my hand, concern etched on her face. "No, absolutely not. You have no idea what you're walking into."

"Please," I insist. "I *need* to do this *alone.*"

Crystal and Terry share a look, the kind of silent communication that only parents can manage. Terry steps forward, then places a steady hand on my shoulder. "We'll be right here. We're ready and waiting."

"To attack." Sherri sharply cuts in from behind us.

I laugh despite the tension squeezing my chest. Turning toward the house, I take one step, then another, until my feet approach the door.

I muster all the courage and adrenaline I have left to ring the doorbell. After one long, agonizing minute, the door swings open. A cute, innocent girl, no more than thirteen or fourteen, answers.

"Hi, I'm sorry, but we're not interested in anything you're selling." She politely says.

For a moment, I'm frozen, and my nerves take over, but then I snap out of it and force myself to speak.

"Oh, no, I'm not selling anything. I was actually hoping to speak to Margaret Drexler."

She furrows her brows, confused. "Drexler?" Then her face lights up. "Oh, you mean my great-aunt Marge? She's never had a visitor before. What's your name?"

"Tiffany. Tiffany Weathers."

Her eyes widen, her curiosity clearly piqued. "And how do you know Aunt Marge?"

I take a steadying breath, trying to keep my emotions in check. "I'm an old family friend. From Greer."

Her jaw practically drops. "Greer? Oh my God, really? I have so many questions. So, you know my mom, too, right?"

I falter. "Your mom?"

"Yeah, well, technically, she's my stepmom, but she's been my mom ever since my real one died in a house fire when I was little." She divulges, completely unaware of the devastation her words bring me. "Mom met my dad shortly after the fire, and she's been taking care of us ever since. She and Aunt Marge are the greatest."

My stomach churns, and my knees almost buckle beneath me. Fire. Everything burns to ashes when Mama is involved. This girl's mother didn't die in a tragic accident—Mama burned her life to the ground, just like she did mine.

Suddenly, my head begins to spin, and I can barely breathe.

"Ma'am, are you okay?" The girl asks. I try to steady myself and weakly nod, but she turns and calls out, "Aunt Marge! Mom! There's a woman here asking for you. Her name's Tiffany Winters... or Weathers. Something like that."

The girl looks back at me with innocent eyes and a sweet smile. "Would you like to come in?"

The warmth of the home is felt immediately. It's filled with family portraits, and the walls practically glow with love and happiness. Everything this house represents is what Mama never was.

"Your home is beautiful, and your form is impeccable." I compliment her, observing her ballet photos.

The girl grins proudly. "Thanks! Hey, wait a minute..." She squints at me, and her face lights up. "Holy crap! You're Tiffany Weathers, the dancer! I've seen you perform at the Super Bowl! Oh my God, I watch your team's competitions on tv all the time! I begged my mom to enroll me in your studio, but she refused. I can't believe this. I follow your son Drew online. He's so dreamy! And his girlfriend's a dancer, just like you. It's like the story of you and Mason Boom! By the way, what's the deal with you two? I swear y'all are endgame, but my friends think otherwise. Can we take a selfie?"

She just rambles on and on, and by the time I try to answer, a familiar voice calls out. "Riley, go upstairs. Now. Don't wake your dad up, and don't come down until you finish studying!"

My heart stops, and I turn to see her. Mama. She's different. Refined. Classy. Not Crackhead Shirley from College Park. She slowly walks toward me with her eyes locked on mine, wearing an unreadable smile on her face.

"Go to your room, Riley!" She snaps, her eyes never leaving mine.

Riley hesitates, and her eyes flicker back and forth between us until she finally retreats up the stairs.

Though she coolly takes a step closer, I feel her nerves radiating from her body. "What are you doing here?"

"That's no way to speak to your daughter."

Kayla ignores the sting and softens her composure. "Hello, Tiffany. You look beautiful. I always knew you'd make something of yourself. I guess Ms. Dora's dance classes paid off, huh?"

I clench my fists at my sides. "Yeah, Aunt Dora raised me well. So did my foster parents and everyone else in my life but you."

Her expression falters, and she reaches out for me, but I quickly step back.

"Don't you dare touch me." I scowl.

She drops her hand and sighs. "You're right. I'm sorry. I'm sorry I wasn't there for you and Tiny."

A bitter laugh escapes my lips at her pitiful apology. "That's it? That's what you're sorry for? Woman, you've got a whole lot more to apologize to do, but that's a start."

She slightly shakes her head and continues. "Again, you're right, but you also gotta let that hate out your heart, Tiffany. I'm sober now. I'm twelve years sober, and I've found God."

My voice rises, and my anger begins to boil over. "Tell me—did you find God before or after you killed your husband's wife in a house fire?"

Her eyes widen in shock, and her hand flies to her chest. "Tiffany, why would you say something like that? I know your heart is hardened, but you gotta learn how to forgive. I'm not who I used to be."

My fury consumes me, and I no longer hold back. "You were never anyone to me! You weren't my mother. You're an abuser. You're a murderer. You are still a liar. And you're still evil. I will *never* forgive you for what you did to me, and I'll *always* hate you for what you did to Tiny!"

Mama's indignance holds steady. "Tiffany, please. I told you I've changed."

I can't take her performance anymore, so I scream. "Stop calling me that! You *know* it isn't my name. You are *not* my mother, and you need to say my name!"

The mask finally crumbles. "Please don't do this," she cautiously whispers. "You *are* my daughter. I carried you."

"Say my name," I demand, my voice steady, cold. "Say the name my *real* mother gave me!"

A man, tall and graying at the temples, appears at the top of the stairs. His face is kind but concerned, and he tenses when he sees me in confrontation with his wife.

"Honey, what's going on?" He asks, voice steady but wary. Then his eyes shift toward me. "Who is this woman? Do I need to call the police?"

I open my mouth, but before I can speak, Riley appears next to him. Her face is now filled with fear instead of curiosity and intrigue.

"They're already here. Dad, something's happening. My phone's blowing up. We're all over social media and on the news. People are sending me messages and saying awful things about Mom. What's going on?"

A frail, older woman, Margaret, I assume—steps into the room. "It's over, Kayla. It's been a long run, but it's time. Give the girl her peace back. Give all these people their peace back."

Redirecting the conversation, I appeal to this woman one last time, "I've never asked anything from you. But I am asking you to say my name, just this once. Tell me what I know to be true."

Realizing her tyranny is finally ending, she relents and whispers, "Nicole. Your name is Nicole Lynn, and your twin sister is Taylor Lynn."

My anger dissipates. The courage and adrenaline that rushed through my veins are gone, replaced by a wave of exhaustion. This isn't the closure I imagined. It's not the relief I thought I'd feel. It's just...pain—so much pain caused by the monster in front of me.

There's a knock on the door, and when I open it, Crystal and Terry are there.

"Oh, baby, we were so worried."

Crystal's arms tighten around me, and Terry's hand rests protectively on my back. Their warmth, their strength—it's all I need right now to steady myself.

Terry steps forward, his eyes scanning me for harm. "Did she hurt you? Are you okay?"

I nod, tears streaming down my face. "She hurt me for so long, but she can't anymore, Mom and Dad."

Sherri and Charles enter next, followed by the authorities. Sherri, who is always composed and stoic, is overcome with emotion when she comes face-to-face with Kayla.

She takes a step forward, her voice sharp as a venomous blade. "Kayla Drexler, you evil piece of shit. I should've killed you a long time ago. But you're going to spend the rest of your life in prison and an eternity rotting in hell."

The police guide her away, but even in this moment of victory, I feel the pain of the girl behind me. Riley has no idea that her mother, her so-called savior, is a monster. For decades, this woman has destroyed so many lives, her victims left to put themselves back together.

When I step outside, my family surrounds me, shielding me from the flashes of cameras and endless waves of reporters. Headlines are already being written, and questions are shouted at all of us from every direction.

Reporter #1: *Will your daughter inherit your billionaire empire?*

Reporter #2: *Is this why Mason Boom quit the league?*

Reporter #3: *Tiffany, how did you find out the truth about who you really are?*

Reporter #4: *Crystal, what about your other daughter?*

The last question stops my mom, my *real* mom, in her tracks. Any mention of Tiny breaks her heart. So, she steps forward in front of the crowd and addresses everyone with a strong, unwavering voice.

"I'm grateful to have my daughter home, but we won't rest until *both* our daughters are home. Taylor *Tiny* Weathers was abducted," Crystal says, her voice catching just slightly, but she pushes forward. "She is a victim of abuse, of forced drug addiction, of sex trafficking, of sexual violence, and an unfair justice system. She doesn't belong in prison. And my promise to everyone watching is that every single person who had a hand in her misery, in her pain, will be held accountable. I don't care if it's detectives, judges, politicians, or friends. We'll find them all, and they'll experience the wrath of parents who will do anything to avenge the pain of their children."

The press madness continues, but none of their questions matter right now. All that matters is that we're leaving behind Kayla's wreckage and stepping into a new phase of our lives—one filled with healing, rebuilding, and reclaiming everything she took from us.

~ ~ ~

8 months later

We did it! After years of heartbreak, appeals, and fighting a seemingly endless battle, Tiny's conviction was finally overturned. The victory feels surreal, but I'm savoring it. It took us a year just to get our last appeal heard, and that only ended in a denial. But this time? This time, Mom went all-in, pulling every string and moving every obstacle in our path. She managed to get the appellate court to review Tiny's case thoroughly. They found legal errors, pay-offs, and oversights that should have been caught years ago, sparking a full investigation into her sentencing. In just a few weeks, we'll know if she's headed back to trial court for a new plea hearing or if her charges will be dismissed entirely. We're sure it'll be the latter because, no matter what's on her record, Tiny never should have been locked away. Everyone failed her, including me. But I swear we're going to make it right. Every single thing she lost, she'll recover a hundred-fold.

"So, it seems you've all been adjusting well to your new lives as a family. Interviews and the amplification of business aside, how're you all feeling, especially after the big court win?" The therapist asks, her voice warm as she looks around the room at each of us, seated in a quiet circle in one of our final family therapy sessions.

Drew, my parents, and I sit together, exchanging a look of relief and gratitude. Mom's voice is the first to break the silence, full of warmth and excitement. "It feels amazing. We haven't been this happy since the twins were home with us. I'll never get tired of seeing pictures of Tiny, but I'm ready to see her in person. She looks just like you, Terry."

Dad's eyes soften, a gentle smile spreading across his face. "It'll be impossible not to hug her for hours." He murmurs.

Drew playfully nudges him. "Gramps, you think you're gonna hug her first? I got first dibs when I meet her."

Our family revels in the anticipation of meeting Tiny. They'll finally get to see the amazing gem she is.

The therapist lets the moment settle before turning her attention to me.

"And you, Tiffany?" She asks gently. "How are you doing? I know there's still a long road ahead, but now that you've taken this huge step toward a new life with your family, are *you* ready to move forward? You've purchased a home. You're planning a charity gala. Your Atlanta dance studios are thriving, but you've paused the building search here. So, what's next for you?"

I lean back on the sofa, feeling both comforted and challenged by the familiar, safe space. "Honestly," I say, taking a breath, "I think I need more time. Running the studios already takes so much out of me, and right now, my heart is with family. I want to spend as much time with them as possible, especially when Tiny comes home. Besides, I've enjoyed my side gig coaching my former dance team. I also get to keep an eye on Drew at school. He's got a flock of girls running after him. They're just distractions."

Mom laughs, and even my therapist cracks a smile. Drew just rolls his eyes and grins with that newfound confidence of being a future star quarterback. "Chill out, Mom. I'm the only athlete who's a STEM scholar, and you know I only got eyes for Lea. You don't gotta worry 'bout me."

I scoff, feeling that instinctive pang of overprotective mom energy. "Don't mention her. You're way too young to be dating."

Then, Mom raises a playful brow. "Speaking of dating, Doc, can you please convince my stubborn daughter to admit she misses my future son-in-law."

Heat rises to my cheeks. How embarrassing!

"Mom!" I blurt out. "This is a family session, not my individual."

Dad chimes in, nodding toward me with a knowing smile. "Your mother's got a point, though. I've seen you tuning into ESPN, waiting to see if a big announcement is gonna be made."

I exhale, feeling that familiar ache in my chest, and begin to ramble my feelings away. "Fine. I miss him. But I wouldn't have to stalk the headlines if y'all would just give me something solid. Even Rafe's keeping quiet. I just need to know if Mase is coming home or not. He spent three months at that mental health retreat, then went straight to physical therapy for his knee. When he came home for Kayla's sentencing, he nearly broke when he saw that monster for the first time. I just wanted to hold him, but instead, cameras were shoved in his face and ended up disappearing back to Seattle without even telling me bye."

"Tiffany, maybe we should revisit this in our one-on-one. Crystal, Terry, I love watching your family interact so naturally, but there's a lot to process here. I think Tiffany needs time to face her feelings about everything before diving into a relationship again. Wouldn't you agree, Tiffany?"

Mom lets out a dramatic sigh while Dad shakes his head with a playful eye roll, and I can't help but smile.

"Yes, Doc, I absolutely agree!" I say, flashing a triumphant look in Mom's direction.

We wrap up the session with hugs and goodbyes, then Drew and I head to school. Coaching the Greer Pipettes keeps me going, but I'd be lying if I said I didn't miss my own studio. There's something about the adrenaline of recital season, the intensity of competition days, the countless hours spent with dancers who pour their hearts onto the floor. My soul aches for it, but time is a rare commodity these days. The whirlwind of public attention hasn't made it any easier. Just a year ago, I was "d-list famous" at best. Now, my face is everywhere, and they've got all sorts of labels for me— 'dancing billionaire beauty' and 'Greer's Princess Anastasia' are two of the kinder ones, and then there are others like 'Mason Boom's billionaire ex-baby mama. It's surreal, chaotic, and so far from anything I ever imagined.

My train of thought breaks when two familiar voices drift into my office, singing in unison, "Oh, Tiffany Nicole!"

Mel and Rafe are in my doorway, grinning from ear to ear. Mel's holding a bottle of champagne in one hand and three flutes in the other.

"What the hell?" I say, laughing despite myself as I glance around to make sure no one's watching. "You can't bring alcohol onto school grounds."

"Oh, please! We used to do it all the time, remember?" Rafe reminisces.

"We, as in you, Mel, and Mase. Don't lump me in with y'all rich kid shenanigans. Mel, your dad will kill us if we get caught!"

She waves me off with a grin. "Daddy's too busy watching ESPN right now."

Her words hang in the air, and the gleam in her eyes gives away the secret they've been keeping. She fills my glass to the brim, and I quickly turn on my office tv.

And there he is—Mason Boom, looking infuriatingly handsome, standing in front of a sea of reporters. Monica and his agent flank him, but my eyes are glued to him alone as he speaks into the mic.

"Well, this feels like déjà vu, doesn't it? Thank you all for being here today. It's been a while since I've spoken publicly, yet somehow, it feels like

I've been talked about more in the past year than in my entire career. I needed to take time away from the game I love to focus on myself, but I didn't realize the extent of what my family would endure. The weight of it all nearly broke me. It took a toll on my already beaten-up body and exhausted mind. Nevertheless, I'm here today, stronger and better. I'm also here to announce my return to the NFL."

I can't help myself; a surprised and happy squeal escapes my lips.

The room quiets, and I catch Mel giving me a playful side-eye and gentle hand squeeze. "Keep listening, girl."

"The next part is for you." Rafe adds.

My heart races, and I focus on Mase as he straightens his posture and softens his tone.

"After this upcoming season, I'll be stepping away from the game for good. Retiring. But there's no better way to end my career than by going back to where it all began. This season, I'll be returning to my hometown to play for the Greer Renegades. Home is where the heart is, and my heart belongs to Tiffany Weathers. I'm coming home, baby."

Though the tv continues to play, and Mel and Rafe's voices are somewhere in the background, my heartbeat is the only sound filling my ears. Mason Boom is coming home—to me. For good.

After a celebratory toast with Mel and Rafe, I feel lighter than I have in months. My workday moves along perfectly. Just before I head out to coach the Pipettes, my phone buzzes, and I see Mase's name lighting up the screen.

"Hello, Mr. Renegade." I answer, letting a teasing tone slip into my voice.

"Coach Weathers." He replies with a hint of mischief evident even through the phone. I can practically see the grin on his face.

I act indifferent, though my heart betrays me with its eager thudding. "If you're calling to ask if I watched your press conference, yes, I did. So, what do you want?"

A low chuckle rumbles through the phone. "That's not why I called. I know you keep tabs on everything I do," He pauses, letting his words linger before continuing. "I called because I need you to sign the deed for your new dance studio."

I blink, caught off guard. "What studio? I put my search on hold months ago."

"I know, which is why I went ahead and purchased that building Crystal and Terry said you've been eyeing for months." He replies smoothly and unbothered.

"You did what?" I exclaim, half-shocked and half-excited. "What the hell, Mase? You shouldn't have done that. That building costs over a million dollars! I could've bought it on my own. You know I'm rich now, right?"

He bursts into laughter. "But you're still the cheapest person I know. And you're an overthinker. Besides, I wanted to do this. Greer needs a dance studio run by a passionate teacher who inspires her students every day. I know you miss it, Tiff. So, you gonna sign the deed or not?"

I sigh, letting my guard down a bit. "Yes, okay? I miss it more than I can say. So, I'll sign the damn deed, but only if you promise to take care of yourself and give your football season everything you've got. For example, you should be handling interviews and training, not calling me, let alone buying me a damn building!"

He pauses and, in a softening voice, declares, "Interviews and training can wait. Right now, all I care about is our future."

I let his words settle and lean into his energy, but I can't give in that easily. "Mason Boom, just because you claimed me on tv *again* and forced me to pursue my passion doesn't mean I'm going to throw myself in your arms."

He releases a deep, genuine laugh that makes my stomach do a little flip. "I don't expect you to, Tiff, but I know you. You're stubborn and keep pushing your happiness aside. I know Tiny's return is your sole focus right now. So, let's make a deal. After Drew's 16th birthday, once Tiny's home and settled...*then, and only then*, will we finally be together. No interruptions. Just me, you, and the world around us."

Mase is beyond understanding. He knows me better than I sometimes know myself. He appreciates the way I pour all of myself into my family, just as he's poured his love into me, steady and unrelenting, for years.

"Deal. After Drew's 16th birthday, we'll be together. For good," I say, my voice steady, carrying all the history and hope that's brought us to this moment.

For years, life placed one roadblock after another, keeping happiness, family, and love just out of reach. But now, for the first time, I'm standing on the edge of finally having it all without compromise. The idea of a life with Mase, without barriers or doubts, fills me with dizzying anticipation.

It's no longer about cautiously holding onto moments of joy; it's about embracing everything all at once. My new sense of family, my son, Tiny's return, Mase coming home. All of my happiness is here, finally within my grasp, and it doesn't feel borrowed or fleeting. This is the life I've waited for, one that's mine, steady and true, with Mase by my side and room to build even more.

PART 4

FOURTH QUARTER VICTORY

Present Day

Chapter 36

Ready for Love – Tiffany

It's Drew's 16th birthday, and his surprise gift has just been revealed—not just to him but to me, too. We'd kept Tiny's release date from him for months, waiting for this perfect moment. Seeing my sister and Drew together feels like a long-lost dream come true. And when I feel Tiny's embrace again, it's the answered prayer I've whispered to myself over and over.

The warmth inside my home is almost overwhelming. Drew and Tiny cling to each other and share endless affection to make up for years stolen from them. There's laughter, tears, and the familiar voices of family filling the air. Aunt Dora, the Booms, the Bakers, everyone we love is here in a room filled with anticipation. But two people are still missing—our parents. And my heart beats anxiously as I wait for them to arrive.

They've been limited to staring at pictures of Tiny for a year because she wanted their first meeting to be special. She wanted to meet on her own terms. She wants them to meet her like this—free, whole, and filled with unmistakable joy.

And finally, there's a knock on the door. As soon as I swing it open, I'm greeted by two faces that express decades of pain and thousands of prayers.

Mom frets and clutches Dad's hand as they stand on the doorstep, already on the verge of tears. "We're so sorry we're late! The cleaners took forever with your blanket, and Terry burned the biscuits—three times! And then we—"

I gently cut her off, trying to calm her nerves. "It's okay. The only thing that matters is that you're here. You two alone are everything she needs right now."

I take Mom's hand, and she takes Dad's. They trail behind me, tentative but hopeful, as we enter the living room. As soon as they see Tiny, all conversation ceases, and the room falls into a reverent silence. Tiny's smile tightens, and her face reveals the depth of her longing as she takes in the sight of them. She takes one step, but our parents take two. They embrace her tightly with the kind of grip that only comes after years of waiting and loss.

"Daddy." She chokes out, her voice trembling and tears streaking down her face.

Dad's voice breaks as he wipes her tears. "I never thought I'd hear you call me that again," he says, his words soft and full of love. "Oh, Taylor, I love you so much."

They laugh through their tears, and Tiny leans into Mom, breathing deeply. "You smell like home."

Mom hugs her tighter, her voice warm and steady. "And that's exactly where you are. Welcome home, Taylor."

"We're sorry. We know it's Tiny, not Taylor." Dad chimes in softly.

But Tiny pulls back and shakes her head. "I always hated that name. Please...call me Taylor. My name is Taylor Lynn."

They happily nod, and we spend the rest of the evening enjoying Drew's 16th birthday and Taylor's homecoming, wrapped in the kind of happiness that once felt impossible.

~~~

"So, you're telling me I bought a beautiful home for us to live in after we've been separated for decades, only for you to stay with Mom and Dad?! We're twins! We aren't supposed to be separated." I give Taylor a pointed look. My tone is playful yet genuinely exasperated.

Taylor laughs, brushing off me off as usual. "Tiff, you're being extra. I've practically lived at your place for the past month! I've disrupted y'all's life enough. You gotta get back to normal."

Drew chimes in, laughing. "But Aunt Mom, we're not exactly a normal family."

Taylor's face lights up with laughter. "Okay, that's it—you've got to come up with a new name for me! How about 'Aunt T'?"

Drew rolls his eyes with a sigh. "Fine, I guess Aunt T works."

I look at Taylor with a touch of concern. "Are you sure you'll be okay without us?"

"Of course, Tiff! Moving in with our parents is honestly a dream come true. Life's moving forward, and I'll find my place in your lives—not the other way around. Besides, my schedule's filling up fast. I've got tv interviews, NA meetings, and my new sponsor? She's amazing! Therapy has been surprisingly helpful, too. I'm not looking to work any time soon, but there's so much I want to do! School, for one—I'm thinking of enrolling in the community college and maybe even working for the family business someday."

Mom's smile is wide and filled with pride. "Oh Taylor, you're gonna *run* the family business someday."

Taylor beams, and her eyes glisten with the happiness she's only beginning to believe she deserves.

"But enough about me," Taylor says. "You have a big day ahead, and you're avoiding talking 'bout it. A whole-day date with Mason? This is huge, Tiff!" She claps her hands in excitement.

Dad shakes his head, chuckling. "You've been on edge all week, and now here you are, eating biscuits like it's your last meal."

"Tiff, honey, just breathe," Mom says. "Your date's gonna be wonderful. Mase has something special planned for you, and I know you've got something special planned for him, too."

"But nothing ever goes according to plan with us! And a day-long date? So much could go wrong in twelve hours. I'm so nervous." I admit.

Taylor throws a biscuit at me with a laugh. "Scarf down that biscuit, girl, and pull yourself together! We're not letting you back out now. You and Mase deserve this."

We finish breakfast and enjoy a morning filled with laughter and the warmth of family. I feel lighter as Drew heads off to school in his new car while I, on the other hand, return home to prepare for my date with Mase.

I stand in front of the mirror, observing my outfit. Mase said to keep it casual and sporty, but I'm still bringing my A-game. I choose high-waisted joggers that hug my curves perfectly, paired with a cropped zip-up hoodie that reveals a hint of my midriff and a teasing peek of my black sports bra.

Then, I pack my overnight bag with a swimsuit, my leotard, and lingerie. But more than anything, I pack with the hope that tonight ends the way I've dreamed of—wrapped in the safety and love of his arms.

On cue, the doorbell rings, sending a thrill through me. I take a deep breath, steady myself, and walk over to open the door. When I do, Mason stands before me, holding a bouquet of flowers and looking better than I could have imagined in a simple dry-fit shirt and ball shorts. My eyes trace the way his shirt clings to his sculpted frame. He's here, and it's really happening.

For a moment, we just take each other in. His gaze drinks me up, and I can feel his stare like a warm wave rolling over me. The intensity in his eyes leaves me breathless, hot, and filled with desire.

"You see something you like?" I tease, raising an eyebrow, hoping to snap him out of the trance.

He laughs, finally breaking the tension. "No, Tiff. I see everything I love."

His words spark a fire in me, and I blush despite myself. His admiration is so genuine, so raw, it's like we're on our first date all over again, butterflies and all.

Mase takes a step closer with the flowers still in his hand. "You ready for our forever to begin?"

The sincerity in his voice makes my heart skip. I nod, unable to keep the smile from spreading across my face. "Yes, I'm ready. I'm ready, Mason Boom."

Chapter 37

Forever Date Pt. 1 – Tiffany

Forever Date – Part 1

Mase is going all out for our date. He pulls up to my house in his favorite car, a sleek gold Lamborghini Veneno, and lets the top down as we glide through the familiar streets of Greer. There's an ease between us that's impossible to ignore, and I catch him glancing over at me with that knowing smile of his. We reach for each other's hand, and our fingers intertwine effortlessly. I feel a comforting warmth wash over me, like we're exactly where we're supposed to be.

"Mase, where the heck are you taking me?" I ask, giving him a teasing look.

He smirks, his eyes twinkle with excitement. "Just sit back and relax. I'm taking you on a journey."

As we cruise through the town, I notice the beautifully restored buildings that once stood vacant and neglected. This town has seen so much darkness, but there's also a spirit of resilience here—transforming, recovering, and finding new life in what was once broken—much like my own life. As we near our destination, I smile, now knowing where Mase is taking me.

He pulls into the old community football field, the very place we *kind of* met when we were nearly ten years old. Nothing about it has changed. It feels frozen in time, holding the memory that started it all. We walk hand in hand across the field and allow the cool morning air to settle around us.

He stops me in our tracks and turns to me with his hand, lifting my chin, then glances down at me with a soft smile. "I still remember the moment I saw you. I knew you at first glance. No one could tell me you weren't Nicole Lynn."

I laugh, nudging him playfully. "And you freaked me out right away." Then, my smile softens, and the memory tugs at my heart. "But I couldn't stop thinking about you after that. It was like we were…meant to find each other. You were meant to find me."

Mase softly kisses my forehead, and we move toward the benches on the sidelines, where he gestures for me to look closer. There's a small plaque gleaming in the sunlight. I bend down to read it, and the words take my breath away: *This bench is dedicated to Tiffany Weathers. No fire could ever burn her spirit.*

My hand trembles slightly as I touch the plaque. Overwhelmed by his thoughtfulness, I look up at him and murmur, "Mase, this is so sweet. Thank you."

Without thinking, I throw my arms around him, holding him tightly and feeling every word he doesn't have to say. We share a quiet moment, just the two of us in the place where our love story began. When we finally pull apart, Mase reaches under the bleacher and pulls out a thick photo album.

As we flip through the pages, I see pieces of our life together captured in snapshots I didn't even know existed. Dance practices, birthdays, homecomings, prom, graduation, my face in the stands at games, competitions, Super Bowl pics, candid photos he took when I wasn't looking. There are pictures of Drew as a baby, late nights and early mornings of us trying to figure out how to be parents, moments I forgot we captured. But what chokes me up are the photos from Aunt Dora's boxes, images of me and Taylor, two little girls lost in a world of our own.

Then, Mase turns to me and wipes the tear I hadn't realized I shed. "You may not remember every moment of your past, Tiff, but life can begin where you choose. For me, my life began the day I met you. These are your memories. This is your story."

We sit, wrapped in each other's arms on the bleachers for nearly half an hour, reminiscing about our life together. We laugh over his antics to win me over in high school and have a blast teasing each other about our wild college days. As we observe every photo and recount each story, we realize that Mase's life is mine, and mine is his.

When we get to the last page, there's a note that says, *'more memories pending.'* And he's right because our story is never ending.

I close the album with a soft thud, savoring the memories we just relived. "C'mon." Mase reaches down and extends his hand with a warm smile. "We're headed to Beverly Mills Beach."

The beach is only a short drive away, the journey rich with nostalgia. Familiar songs from our past flood the space between us, and I can't help but join in his terrible singing, belting out lyrics with him between fits of laughter. We reminisce on weekends at the Baker's beach house when we would sneak away at night to do things we had no business doing in high school.

The scenery changes as we near Beverly Mills Beach. Tall grass, marsh water, and narrow winding roads. It's the kind of quiet that lets anticipation hum softly.

"Oh, crap! I need to change into my bathing suit." I exclaim, rummaging through my bag.

He glances over with a mischievous grin playing on his lips. "You want me to pull over on this narrow one-lane road surrounded by nothing but marshes? Tiff, just change here in the car." His eyes gleam with humor but also with a tantalizing lust.

His idea sounds both ridiculous and completely tempting. I give him a mock glare, but his grin is infectious. "You want me to strip naked? In front of you?"

"Technically, you're next to me. And I've seen every delicious part of you more times than I can count. I think it's cute that you're nervous, though." He shifts his attention back to the road and adopts an exaggerated look of virtue. "I swear, I'll keep my eyes forward. Scout's honor."

"Oh, please, you were never a scout!" I laugh and shimmy awkwardly as I attempt to change discreetly into a backless, metallic gold one-piece.

The car wobbles slightly as I struggle, and Mase glances over, biting his lip to stifle a laugh and *other* things.

He groans, his voice a low rasp. "Damn it, woman. You plus gold is a seductive combination. Why are you doin' this to me?" His eyes dart back to the road, but there's a heat simmering just under his skin that he's struggling to hold back.

I swat his arm and laugh despite myself, eventually managing to wriggle into my swimsuit.

When we pull up to the northern entry point of the beach, he leans back and casually strips off his shirt, revealing those perfectly sculpted abs I've missed way too much. Though I try to keep it cool, he catches me staring almost instantly.

"Uh, uh," he smirks. "Eyes forward."

"You're ridiculous." I scoff, rolling my eyes, but I steal another glance as he changes into his swim trunks. He catches me *again*, laughing in that deep timbre that melts every last piece of my composure.

"Fine, you can look," He says, his voice edged with something wicked. "I don't mind. You can even touch." Mase winks.

"Boy, don't nobody wanna touch you!" But indeed, I do. I want to see, touch, and explore every single throbbing inch of him, and he knows it.

When we step out of the car, hand in hand, the salty breeze wraps around us, and memories flood back—our young love phase, carefree summer days, and quiet nights under the stars. But as we walk the beach, I notice the empty stretch of sand, completely untouched by footprints except for ours.

"Mase," I whisper. "Is the beach closed today?"

He squeezes my hand and softly holds my gaze. "To us? No. To everyone else? Yeah. The beach is ours for as long as we want. We can do whatever we want. We can do *whoever* we want."

Mase's words send a thrill through me and melt away my nerves, allowing my desires to take hold. His touch is a delicate contrast to the intensity of his gaze. His eyes roam over me, slow and deliberate, from my lips to my breast, down to my stomach, and stopping at the curve of my legs. It's as if he's memorizing every inch for his mouth to explore, and I can feel the heat of his admiration like sunlight on my skin.

He leads me to a beautifully set table under a cabana, an unexpected touch of elegance framed by the sun and ocean. The spread is stunning— mini sliders with truffle aioli and thinly sliced Wagyu beef on toasted brioche, a vibrant arugula salad, and skewers of grilled vegetables, served alongside coconut rice and pineapple salsa.

My eyes go wide in excitement. "Oh my god, Mase! This is so much food! And I'm gonna eat all of it."

"As long as I get to eat you afterward." He picks up a slider and holds it just out of reach, his eyes dark with mischief.

"Open your mouth," He murmurs, brushing a finger along my cheek as I lean in to take a bite.

My pulse quickens as his touch lingers, his gaze intense and unwavering. His fingers find my chin, lifting it gently as he feeds me a piece of mango from the salsa.

I savor the taste, letting out a contented moan before sipping my champagne. "I could get used to this. Being home with you. Eating, laughing, and loving each other in peace. I've waited for this day for so long," I pause and take in the moment. "I'm happy to be here with you, but it breaks my heart a little. Look at all this beauty around us. Tiny's never experienced anything like this. And ever since I saw that photo of us as babies, I feel this ache… guilt almost, because I can't remember that day. I don't have any memories with my family."

Mase tightens his hand around mine, his gaze tender. "We've got the rest of our lives to make new memories. There's so much I want to do with you, so much we'll share with everyone we love." He shifts closer, his voice dropping to an intimate murmur. "I promise to give you everything you've dreamed of, Tiffany Weathers, and I'll give you even more than you can imagine. If you let me—if you let me love you the only way I know how, the way you deserve—endlessly, relentlessly, passionately, and fiercely."

Mase's lips trail from my hand to my wrist, then up my arm, finally stopping at my neck. His kiss ignites a fire in me that's impossible to ignore, and his loyalty to me is unmistakable.

"What do you say?" He whispers against my skin. "Will you let me love you deeper than I ever have before?"

I let the question hang in the air, savoring the intensity in his eyes, until my lips curve into a playful smile, even as my heart pounds. "Is that a promise… or a guarantee?"

His lips brush mine, and his breath heats my skin, but his firmness and assurance are all I need. "Both. He says."

My eyes flutter, and my heart nearly drops. "Yes, Mason Boom. You can love me as deep, as long, and as hard as you want, and I'll do the same. I'll love you for the rest just as I have all my life."

Mase's hand cups my cheek, and I feel my pulse racing beneath his touch. His lips brush mine with a soft kiss that contradicts the strength in his gaze. Slowly, our kiss deepens, and I melt into him. My hands find their way to the back of his neck, drawing him even closer, leaving only the rhythm of our breathing and the warmth of his mouth moving against mine. Nothing else matters. It's me, Mase, and the world around us. His fingers slip through my hair, sending shivers down my spine as he cradles my face, his touch filled with reverence.

When we finally pull back, he rests his forehead against mine, and I feel his breath warm on my skin. I open my eyes to find him staring at me with an intensity that makes my heart skip, his lips curving into a small, contented smile.

Mase then takes my hand and guides me from the table to the canopy lounger. He kneels beside me, then leans forward and traces my lips with his thumb. His lustful eyes wander my body so hungrily that a titillating thrill rushes between my legs.

"You're breathtaking, Tiff." He murmurs, his voice husky and heavy.

As I lie back, I allow him to slowly run his fingers over the thin fabric of my bathing suit, stopping on my hard nipple and flicking it back and forth.

"Mase," I moan. I feel a million sensations coursing through my veins, and they all stop at one place.

Staring into my eyes, he whispers, "I want my fingers to travel to the place they love the most. Somewhere warm. Somewhere inviting. Somewhere that's all mine. Tell me you missed me, Tiffany Nicole."

My body can't take any more of the teasing, the yearning, the touching, the months of waiting to be filled by the only man who has ever satisfied me.

I finally cry out in the open ocean air. "I missed you. Now, shut up and make me come!"

He slides my suit down and takes one long gaze before his lips meet mine, and his two fingers enter inside me. With each thrust, I scream his name, but my cries are muffled with his kisses.

"I missed the way you feel." He whispers in my ear, but I'm breathless, speechless, and too dazed to reply.

I forgot how magical his fingers are, and he makes me feel even better when his lips travel lower and lower to my sensitive clit.

"Umm," He groans. "This is exactly what I've been missing. Your delicious pussy in my mouth."

Mase licks, sucks, and fucks me with his tongue and fingers like a madman. My legs tremble and my body goes weak as I lay my head back and allow the breeze to wash over me like a high tide.

With heavy breaths and a coarse voice, I pant. "Yes! Yes, Mase! Don't stop, please. I'm 'bout to come!"

He pushes his fingers deeper inside me one last time, causing me to cry tears and thank the heavens for the most exhilarating, clit numbing orgasm I've ever felt. Then, he slowly removes his fingers and places them in my mouth for me to suck them dry.

We moan in unison, and he peppers me with his sweet kisses. My curls nearly cover my face. My exhaustion is evident, but so is my insatiable hunger. "I want more. I want all of you in me." I quietly beg.

Mase laughs, then gently tucks my hair behind my ears. "Later. I'm gonna make love to you, then fuck you to sleep. In the meantime," He stands up all jolly and obviously up to no good. "Our family just pulled up. So…you might wanna put on some clothes."

"Mase!" I scream, then hurry to cover myself up. My heart is racing. "What the hell! Why is our family here? Is this a date or a family day? And my hair! I look like I just had an orgasm!"

He's laughs, entertained by my panic. Then, he wraps his strong arms around my waist, transferring his calm energy to me.

"Throw me my clothes! Now!" I fuss.

"But you look so damn sexy, Tiff." He teases, not budging an inch.

"Mason Boom!" I huff, narrowing my eyes. "You won't be seeing any more of my sexy if you don't grab my bag."

"Okay, okay," he chuckles, reaching for my bag, still clearly amused. "Stop worrying. You're perfect. Now," With a grin, he playfully pats my butt like he's gearing up for a game. "Put on an innocent smile and act like you didn't just come all over my face."

Our families approach with faces lit with warm smiles. Everyone's happy to see us together. There's a genuine joy in their laughter, a lightheartedness I haven't seen in a long time.

And before I know it, Mel is the first to throw a suspicious look our way. She raises her brow and smirks. "So…were y'all—did y'all just have—"

I quickly cut her off, eyes wide and cheeks flushed. "Mel! The parents are right here!"

Everyone laughs, and Sherri, arms crossed and smiling, gives a little shrug. "Tiff, we know how babies are made." Her tone is warm, and she exchanges a knowing smile with Aunt Dora, who nudges her.

Rafe, cradling his baby girl in his arms, gestures toward us. "Look at Uncle Mase. He's finally happy again."

I glance over at Mase, and our eyes lock. He reaches for my hand, and it feels like we're making a declaration, finally allowing ourselves to be exactly who we are. Completely in love and healthily obsessed.

The parents exchange delighted glances, cooing and laughing, while Aunt Dora shakes her head and gives me a playful smack on the arm.

"Well, it's about damn time," she says, grinning. "I didn't know if I was gonna live long enough to see you two fools get back together."

Her laughter is contagious, and soon, the whole family is caught up in the moment, teasing and talking over one another.

Mase holds up his hand to get everyone's attention, and his smile turns serious for just a moment.

"Thank you all for coming here today." He then nods to the photographer, who's patiently waiting with a camera in his hand.

"Oh, God! Anyone but him." Mel groans and rolls her eyes.

Jay, the youngest Boom, raises his brow. "And who the hell is he, Mel?"

There's an edge in his voice, a hint of jealousy that surprises us all, and the tension in the air makes everyone pause. But it quickly fades as we all await Mase's instructions.

Mase clears his throat and gestures toward the photographer. "He's here to help us make a new family memory. We're taking the first official photo of all of us together—just like the one that survived the fire."

He looks at me, and my heart swells. It's a small gesture, but one that holds so much weight. This moment is just one of many wishes that continue to be fulfilled.

I mouth *I love you*. And with a shrug, he mouths *I know*.

Our families move into position—squeezing shoulders, slinging arms around one another, holding our loved ones close. The photographer snaps a few shots, then moves around, capturing different groupings—the Booms, the Bakers, all of us Lynns, and everyone with our beloved Aunt Dora. Then finally, a photo of me, Mase, and Drew, just the three of us. My head rests on his shoulder, his arms protectively around the family he loves with all his heart. It's the first image we'll have that shows us not just as old flames or best friends but as partners ready to embrace everything we ever wanted.

After the photos, the beach becomes a playground of laughter and fun as we throw ourselves into a game of beach volleyball. I exchange quick kisses with Mase whenever we score a point, earning groans and playful eye rolls from our family, but we couldn't care less because today, and every day after, there's no holding back.

As the sun dips lower, casting everything in a warm, golden glow, I realize it's time for my part of this date. While slow dancing around the crackling bonfire, I pull back just enough to meet Mase's gaze, tracing little circles on his back as I do. "Alright, Mr. Boom," I say, grinning up at him. "It's my turn now, and I have a surprise waiting for you."

With a mischievous glint in my eyes, I hold out my hand, motioning for his car keys. He raises an eyebrow, and his eyes light up with intrigue.

We share quick hugs with our family. Then, I slide into the driver's seat and speed off to take him on a date he'll never forget.

Chapter 38

Forever Date Pt. 2 – Mase

Sometimes I feel like life's been like a slow burning fire, but not anymore. Not when I'm on the brink of having everything I've ever wanted—this woman, forever. She's sitting in the driver's seat, and I'm doing my best to play it cool, but it's damn near impossible when she's lookin' fine as fuck. And I know her, probably better than anyone, so I'm sure as hell she's going to test every bit of patience I have tonight and tease me 'til I explode.

But that's fine because she's mine now, and I'm hers. I can't even believe I'm saying that. Tiffany and I have come a long way. I was once a love-struck young boy obsessed with a confused, guarded girl and now I'm a love-stuck grown man obsessed with a confident, successful, beautiful woman. I'm lucky to love and be loved by this woman, and I'll be damned if I lose Tiffany Weathers ever again.

She glances over, catching me in my thoughts, a playful smirk tugging at her lips. "What're you thinkin' 'bout over there?"

I can't resist her, never could. I lean back, letting my gaze linger on her. "Just wonderin' where we're headed. You gonna treat me like a king tonight?"

She meets my eyes, her smile softening. "I'm gonna treat you like a king *every* night, Mr. Boom."

The promise in her words ignites something deep inside me, a smoldering ache that makes it hard to keep my hands to myself. We've had years of missed moments and countless times life refused to let us be happy, and right now, I want to make up for every single one.

I slowly trail my fingers along her thigh. Her breath hitches, and she murmurs, "Mase."

"Eyes on the road, Tiff," I say, my voice low as I keep my hand there, kneading her thigh just enough to make her squirm. She's always tried to keep that cool exterior, but she crumbles at the slightest touch from me.

"Oh... that feels so good." She breathes, almost as if she's surprised at her own reaction.

I chuckle, feeling the power shift between us. "And you say I'm the dramatic one?"

"Oh, hush. I'm calling the shots for the rest of the night. So, stop trying to seduce me," she pauses, her gaze lingering on me. "I'm the seductress tonight."

My brows lift in anticipation as we pull into the parking lot of her new dance studio. I know her well enough to sense she's got something up her sleeve.

I step out of the car and circle around to open her door, letting my hand linger on her waist as she steps out. The connection between us crackles, even with this simple touch. "So, what's the plan? You gonna teach me how to dance?"

She gives me a sly smile, her eyes flickering with mischief. "Patience!"

I follow her inside, and as my eyes adjust to the soft, ambient lighting, I take in the full effect of her studio for the first time. It's perfect—so unmistakably Tiffany with all white everywhere. And I can't help but notice the gold accents she's scattered throughout. I know she won't admit it, but I'm pretty sure it's an ode to me.

Watching Tiffany perk up as she takes me on a tour of her new studio is adorable. "The front rooms are hip-hop and majorette. To your left is the ballet room, and to the right are jazz and tap. I just love this space. Do you like the setup? It gives a more intimate vibe than my other studios."

"It looks incredible, Tiff." I say, admiring her pride and passion.

"And it's all because of you, Mase," She whispers, her gaze warm. When she pulls back, there's a glimmer of magic in her eyes. "So, you ready to see my favorite room?"

I smirk, crossing my arms. "Hmm, why do I have a feeling it's going to be my favorite room, too?"

With a smirk, she turns and leads me down the dim hallway, each step bringing me deeper into her world. At the end of the hall, she pushes open the door to a small studio. The walls mirror our reflection from every angle, and in the center of the room sits a single chair, seemingly waiting just for me.

Tiffany, still in her swimsuit and cover-up, steps closer, then rises on her tiptoes until her breath is warm against my ear, sending a shiver down my spine.

"Sit," She whispers. "And wait for me."

Obediently, I settle into the chair, my eyes tracking her every move. She crosses the room with effortless grace as her hips sway slightly with each step. She's intoxicating, and I'm drunk off her presence alone.

The second Tiffany slips away into her office, I try to steady myself, but my hands shake, and my dick throbs as the anticipation takes over. My thoughts are drenched in my carnal desires, and every one of them only makes the heat rise under my skin.

Suddenly, Beyoncé's "Dance for You" cuts through the room, and every nerve in me lights up. I let out a low breath, already feeling the pull of her presence before she even steps back into the room. And when she does, my heart damn near stops. She's draped in a gold bodysuit that accentuates her body perfectly. It's impossible to look away.

I'm transported back to the days when I watched her from the sidelines, unable to tear my eyes away as she danced across the field. She was a vision then, but now, here, she's a force.

Tiffany glides over to me, her eyes locking onto mine with an intensity that leaves me breathless. A smirk teases her lips as she leans in, close enough for me to catch the faint scent of vanilla, and whispers, "Does the football player ever miss his dancer?"

I can barely keep the gravel out of my voice as I reply, "Every damn day."

And with that, my dancer performs for me.

She turns her body to me and slowly rolls her hips, grinding in my lap against my hard dick, almost making me come. Her movements are slow and hypnotic, sensual and erotic. She takes my hand and moves it from the middle of her chest down to her wet pussy before teasingly sliding off me to tantalize me with her sexiness.

I'm lost in her, in the way she knows exactly how to captivate me, how to command my attention without even trying. My hands grip the edges of the chair, fingers digging in as I fight the urge to pull her to me and fuck her senseless. But I stay still, paralyzed by her. It's been years, but the effect she has on me hasn't dulled; if anything, it's intensified. This is a woman who's claimed me—mind, body, and soul. There's no part of me that doesn't belong to her.

When the song winds down, her movements come to a slow sway toward me, but she stops at arm's length. For a moment, neither of us says a word. I'm too caught up in the silence that stretches between us.

But this time, I steady my breath, and with deliberate slowness, I pat my leg. My voice is low, steady, and in command. "Sit."

Tiffany takes a step towards me and slowly sits in my lap, our lips nearly an inch apart and her breathing a mix of nerves.

Ready to dominate her body, I lightly rub against her clit through her leotard.

Her eyes roll back, but I murmur, "Look at me, Tiff," she whimpers and tries to focus on my words. "Now, look down, and pull out my dick."

Tiffany slightly adjusts her straddle to pull it out, and I notice her biting her lip so I nod, and she slides down my lap to grip my dick before putting it in her needy, warm, tight mouth.

"Fuck, Tiff," I groan while gently pushing her down deeper. "You make me feel so good. That's right. Let me fuck your throat."

She nearly sucks me to the edge, but when I notice her playing with herself, a part of me gets jealous. So, I stop her and pull her up to completely undress her.

We kiss and move together until her back is against the mirrored walls.

"I want you." She mutters in between our kisses.

Tiffany's hands are tightly clasped around my neck while mine travel down to her breast and then to her waist. I can't control myself any longer, nor do I want to while she's inviting me to have my way with her.

I turn her around, and she places her hands on the mirror and then arches her back so I can view her exquisite body from every angle around the room.

"Give it to me, Mase." She whines.

Without hesitation, I enter her soaking wet pussy, and I feel her walls closing in, gripping me as tight as possible.

"Fuck! This pussy is perfect." I groan immediately upon entering.

"And it's yours, Mase. This perfect pussy is all yours."

Her declaration sets something off inside me, a feral possessiveness that drives me mad. I squeeze her ass cheeks tight and pound against her walls while she moans and screams until her voice cracks.

Feeling her grow weak, I grab hold of her waist and push her to the edge. "Look at yourself. Look how beautiful you are when you're getting fucked good." Her wetness nearly suffocates my dick.

"Fuck, Mase! I can't take it. Please." She cries amidst her orgasm.

But I keep pounding her until her legs give out. When I lift her up, she wraps her legs around my waist, our bodies are melding together while I thrust deep inside of her until she comes one last time.

Tiffany screams my name, but I place my hand around her neck and silence her with a passionate kiss as I come long and hard inside her.

"I love you, Tiffany Weathers." I whisper, breathless and sweaty, while wiping the tears from her eyes.

Restless and weak, she flashes a faint smile. "And I love you, Mason Boom. Forever."

Chapter 39

Livin' the Dream Date – Mase

2 Months Later

Waking up to the most beautiful woman in the world every day is a dream come true. Tiffany doesn't officially live here, but each week another suitcase full of her things *magically* appears in the closet or bathroom. Okay, so I might've asked her to leave a few of her belonging here—just a slight nudge toward making this place ours.

I just need to see this beautiful sight every morning. She's gorgeous even when she's snoring with her mouth wide open and body wildly tangled up in the sheets.

I can't help myself. And today's no exception. I start leaving gentle kisses along her arm, working my way up to her shoulder, hoping to wake her up to something sweet...and erect.

"Mase, let me sleep," she groans, barely opening her eyes. "The studio's been so busy, and the Pipettes have been practicing non-stop for the championship game. No kisses until I wake up and brush my teeth."

I sigh dramatically, still pressing my lips against her shoulder, my voice laced with a playful persistence. "But I want kisses now."

She laughs with her eyes still closed. "Oh, so you want to smell my morning breath?"

I reach over to the nightstand and grab one of my homemade biscuits. "Freshly baked just for you. This way, I'll only taste your sweetness."

She chuckles, then reaches for the biscuit but pauses, "Or I could just give you a morning breath kiss."

I shrug and lean down with a smirk. "Beggars can't be choosers, I guess."

I press a lingering kiss to her soft lips, and just as I'm about to deepen it, a knock on the door interrupts us.

"Y'all got clothes on?" Drew calls out from the other side.

"Come on in, Champ," I call back, still holding Tiffany close.

Drew opens the door and throws himself on the bed.

His face is lit with excitement. "Y'all ready to watch me play tonight?"

"You mean, are we ready to watch you win a state championship? Absolutely," I tell him, my pride spilling into every word. "I'm proud of you, Drew."

My sentiments land, and I see how much it means to him. "Thanks, Mase."

Then, Tiffany reaches over and gives his hand a squeeze. "The whole family will be there, cheering you on. We made even bigger posters than last time!"

Drew laughs, then hesitates before slowly getting to the real reason he's in our room. "Uh, speaking of family, I was wondering…could Lea stop by this morning? Just to wish me good luck. I won't be able to see her until after the game, and I won't even get to see her dance at halftime."

Tiffany's eyes narrow with playful suspicion. "Absolutely not! You're still grounded for throwing that party here last week when Mase and I were out of town. I can't believe Taylor and your grandparents tried to cover for you."

While she continues, I give Drew a subtle nod behind her back.

"Mason Boom, I can feel you undermining me right now." She smiles and shakes her head. "Ugh, fine! She can stop by, but only for five minutes."

Drew hugs us both before heading out. "Y'all are the best. Thanks, Mom. Thanks, Mase."

Once Drew leaves, I test my hot streak and plant a few more kisses all over Tiffany's body. To my surprise, my grumpy morning queen melts at my touch, and we make love to start our day.

After showering together and getting dressed, Tiffany runs through our family schedule.

"I wish we could have lunch together, but I'm busing to the game with the Pipettes today. So, make sure you have all the posters and noise makers. And tell Taylor and my parents to leave on time! They move so slowly, and I want y'all to have good seats. And can you double-check that Drew has everything he needs—his spare jersey, cleats…" She trails off, her nerves rising with each word.

I pull her close and kiss her gently to ease her tension. "I got this, babe. Just focus on your team and Drew. I'll corral the family and make sure everything's set."

She relaxes in my arms and releases a deep breath. "Thank you, Mase. I'm gonna leave everything with you. I can't believe both of my boys are gonna be champions in the same season! Have a great practice, okay?"

We share one last kiss, and as I head out, I feel a deep sense of peace. This life—having Tiffany by my side is all I ever wanted. Every part of my life is falling into place, which is why I know it's time to take the next step.

Tiff knows I have practice this morning, but I have to make a stop first. I pull up to my jeweler, where Taylor looks through the loupe and marvels at the 14-carat princess-cut diamond.

"I have no idea what I'm checking for, but it's beautiful! My sis is going to love this. I can't believe you designed this ring five months ago. Y'all have literally only been dating again for two months!"

I shrug, trying to hide the nervous energy thrumming beneath the surface. "I knew I wanted to marry her the moment I laid eyes on her. You think she'll say yes?"

Taylor studies me for a moment then softens her expression. "Think? I *know* she'll say yes," She smiles, both reassuring and teasing. "There's no doubt in my mind. Tiffany's stupid in love with you, Mase. You should see the girls' group chat. She's happier than I've ever seen her."

"Well, you know that's because you're home, right?"

"And you're the reason Tiff and I are *both* home, where we belong. That's all that matters," With a grin, she nudges me. "Now, I gotta get to the registrar's office. Come January, I'll officially be a college student!"

Filled with joy, I hug my future sister-in-law. "I'm so happy for you, Taylor."

"I'm happy for all of us, Mase."

Afterwards, I head to practice, only to be met by my coach, who's ready to rip me a new one. "Boom, you're late! And I'm gonna assume it's because of that video you posted on social media." He says, raising his brow.

"Boom, your girl is gonna kick your ass for posting a video of her sleeping." One of my teammates jokes.

Another chimes in. "You're 'bout to get dumped by the billionaire baddie...*again*. How do you keep fumbling that bag?"

I laugh, shaking my head. "I'm actually surprised she hasn't cussed me out yet."

Just as the words come out of my mouth, my phone buzzes.

Tiffany: Mason Boom! Delete that video now. And 'White Noise' as the caption? Why are you so childish? Lol.

Mase: ☺ Because you love it and because you love me.

Tiffany: Unfortunately, you're correct. The comments are actually funny. I used to dread your posts, but I'm getting used to them. And there are a couple of guys messaging me too...

Mase: Hmm...Let me go report their pages right quick.

Tiffany: Lol. See you in a few hours.

Easy. Our love has become so damn easy. After practice, I chat with reporters and sports analysts to discuss the upcoming playoffs. Some predict another ring for me, while others wonder if I still have what it takes.

"Mase, this season is the most confident we've ever seen you play. What's changed?"

I smile and look into the camera, knowing Tiffany watches every interview.

"Everything. I got the love of my life and my family back. Now, I gotta get going because Drew Weathers has a high school championship to win tonight. So, I'll talk to you again in a few weeks, *after* my Super Bowl win."

Chapter 40

The Final Ring – Tiffany

I've been through so many phases in my life, but this one—the one where Mase and I are back together—is my favorite. We've been solid for three months, and it's been nothing short of perfect. He warms my heart and calms my soul, and even though he drives me crazy sometimes, he's the most incredible man I've ever met. But lately, something feels off. He's been distant and secretive. I keep telling myself it's just nerves with the Super Bowl coming up, but that little nagging worry won't go away. Every time I ask, he brushes me off, saying I'm being paranoid. But I know Mase. I know when something's wrong.

After Drew won the high school state championship, we were all on cloud nine. Mase has been training him his whole life; it was a proud moment for both of us when Drew hugged him first after his big win. To celebrate, we surprised Drew and his friends with a weekend at the Booms' lake house. It was perfect. Mase was perfect...until about two weeks ago, right before his own big game—Super Bowl run number three. Now, his mind seems somewhere else, and I can't shake the feeling he's hiding something from me, which is why I've gathered my personal task force for an emergency meeting.

"Do y'all think it's just nerves?" I ask, resting my head on my mom's lap as she strokes my hair.

"Well, you know Mase has a lot on his shoulders. He's under pressure, and people have been doubting him." My mom says softly, her voice steady and reassuring.

"Exactly," Mel adds, leaning in with that knowing look. "You know how he is when he's dealing with stress. He's got to sort out his feelings in his own time."

I shake my head emphatically. "No. This isn't just stress. This morning, I overheard him on the phone with Rafe, asking, *'But what if I don't win? How should I do it?'* And it was in this weird tone. Monica," I turn to her, narrowing my eyes, "Has Rafe mentioned anything to you?"

Monica's eyes dart around, looking a little too suspicious, and I know she's hiding something. "Uh, no. Rafe's been his usual self, and so has Mase. He was at our house with Charles and your dad last night, laughing like always."

I sit up, instantly alarmed. "Wait—he told me he had a late practice! He didn't say anything about meeting up with the guys. And Dad definitely didn't mention it at breakfast."

The group exchanges looks, all of them rolling their eyes at me like I'm being over dramatic. Their lack of concern annoys me, and I feel my frustration building.

Taylor laughs. "Is this what y'all had to put up with when I was away?"

Everyone nods, and Mel adds, "This isn't even the half of it!"

I huff, crossing my arms. "Fine! Don't believe me, but I know something's up, and I'm going to find out what it is."

Mel sighs. "Enough with the dramatics! The real mystery is what you're wearing to the Super Bowl! Have you even thought about it?"

"Mase's jersey, obviously." I answer.

Monica grins. "You should dress it up, maybe pair it with heels, or wear a cute dress. You know, for photos."

I roll my eyes, but the idea does sound kind of nice. "It's cold as hell outside, and I'm not dainty and cutesy like you, Monica."

"Oh, but you are when it comes to my son," Sherri teases, chiming in with a laugh. "Your tough exterior melts away. Especially with that little whine you have—*'Mase!'*"

Aunt Dora smirks, "Or when you use his full name like you're doing roll call—*'Mason Boom!'*"

Laughter erupts, and despite myself, I join in, feeling a little ridiculous. "I just love his name, okay?"

Mom places a reassuring hand on mine. "And he loves you. You don't need to know everything, Tiff. Let it go."

"Fine. I'll drop it...*for now.*"

I surrender, but my heart's still churning with suspicion. I can't help but worry. It took us forever to get to this place, and I can't shake the feeling that something's threatening it. While they all continue laughing and talking about outfits, I decide that once I'm home, I'm going to confront him. Whatever he's hiding, it ends today.

I pull into the driveway of Mason's sprawling mansion—the home that's slowly become my own. My clothes *magically* appear in the closet every week, and though Mase pretends it's all my doing, I know he's sneaking my things over here every chance he gets. The man couldn't be less subtle if he tried.

As I step inside, the smell of something delicious travels from the kitchen. Garlic, basil, maybe a hint of rosemary...whatever it is, it's rich and inviting. My heart lifts for a second, but then I hear voices—Mase and Drew, chatting quietly. So, I move closer to listen to their soft but intense conversation.

"It's gonna be okay. Just say how you feel. She'll always love you, and so will I." Drew advises.

I freeze in my tracks. Mase has always been nervous before big games, but this conversation doesn't sound like football jitters. This sounds different.

I clear my throat, startling them. They both turn around, and I try to keep my voice casual, but I know they can see the concern in my eyes. "Is everything okay? Why the long faces?"

Mase's eyes flicker, just for a moment, before he flashes me a grin, the one he uses when he's hiding something. "Oh, nothing, babe. Just running through some Super Bowl plays with Drew. You know, mental prep and whatnot."

I raise an eyebrow, unconvinced, but I decide to play along for now. "Well, it doesn't *sound* like you're talkin' 'bout football, but if you say so."

Feeling the tension pool in my stomach, I head down the hallway, and before I can stop myself, I'm slamming the bedroom door and muffling a scream with my hands. The frustration, the anxiety, the gnawing feeling that something's slipping from my grasp all come pouring out at once.

Within seconds, Mase is at my side, wrapping his arms around me and pulling me close. He holds me tight, his breaths steady against my own frantic heartbeat, and I allow myself to lean into him.

"What aren't you telling me, Mase?" I murmur against his chest, my voice catching. "Are we…are we okay?"

Mase lets out a soft laugh. He tilts my face up to meet his gaze, tempering the storm that's been brewing inside.

"Baby, yes," he says, his voice steady and confident. "We're more than okay. You make me the happiest man in the world, Tiff. Trust me."

I want to believe him, and for a moment, the way he looks at me, so full of love and certainty, eases my fears. He places a gentle kiss on my forehead and brushes his thumb along my cheek.

"Now, go relax, alright? Your bubble bath is waiting for you," he says, giving me a little nudge toward the bathroom. "I have to head to Dallas with the team early tomorrow. So, I want us to have a family dinner. I'll see you shortly."

Although the anxiety still lingers, a soft smile plays on my lips, and his touch, as always, brings me back to solid ground.

After a long soak, I find him and Drew in the dining room setting up for dinner. They've put together an incredible spread—grilled salmon, roasted vegetables, a salad with walnuts and cranberries, and creamy mashed potatoes.

Drew grins when he sees me and pulls out my chair like the perfect gentleman. "You look relaxed."

"Thank you. It helps to have two amazing men in the house taking care of me." I say before I sit.

Mase takes his place beside me and reaches for my hand under the table, his thumb gently tracing circles along my knuckles.

We laugh and talk as we eat. It feels right—so right that for a moment, I forget about the anxiety of losing it all.

After dinner, Drew heads to his room, and we head to bed. Mase pulls me into his arms, and we just breathe together.

"So...now that you're calm, and since we won't see each other until Super Bowl Sunday, any chance I could get some good luck sex?"

I laugh, completely unsurprised, but my heart skips a beat at the touch of his lips. I adjust myself and slide onto him so I can look straight into his eyes, my fingers tracing his jaw and cheek. "You don't need luck, Mase. You're going to win your third ring. You got this."

With his smirk still present, he nods. "Okay then... may I just have some good sex?"

I shake my head and chuckle, leaning down to press a slow, lingering kiss to his lips, savoring the taste of him. "How about great sex instead?"

His eyes darken, and his hands move to my waist. In this moment, I feel safe—no nerves, no doubts, just us. I give in to every sensation he stirs in me, and we sink into each other, filling the night with whispered promises, laughter, and lovemaking. With Mase, I know that no matter where life takes us, I'll always have a place where I'm cherished, where I'm loved completely, and where I'm finally deeply at peace.

~ ~ ~

Today is the day—Super Bowl Sunday. The last game of Mason Boom's career. Decades of grit, passion, and relentless focus all lead to this moment. He's built a legacy not only as a formidable player but as a man with heart and integrity.

Tiny bounces in her seat, her excitement barely contained. "It's game time! Are you excited? I've never been to a Super Bowl before! This is so cool!" Her voice is practically a squeal, her energy contagious.

I smile, glancing around the box filled with family and friends who've supported Mase every step of the way. Every face here reflects the same anticipation, the same thrill.

The stadium lights dim. The roar of the crowd peaks, and my heart feels like it's about to burst as the announcer's voice echoes through the air. Mason's name reverberates around the stadium, filling every corner of the massive arena. He runs onto the field, and the crowd erupts, a roar that shakes the air and vibrates through my chest. Even from up here, I feel his presence like a heartbeat—steady, strong, and entirely focused.

Then, just before kickoff, he glances up toward our box, his gaze fiercely intense as he points to the patches stitched on his jersey.

Taylor nudges me, her eyes bright with admiration. "He's looking at you, Tiff. I just love your love story." She whispers and squeezes my hand.

"But there's nothing more beautiful than our family's love story." I smile back as we watch with pure joy.

My heart races with every snap, every tackle, and every yard gained. Mase is a force on the field, and he's still one of the best in the game. However, he isn't as quick as he used to be, and he's getting pretty banged up out there. For every perfectly thrown pass, there's a brutal tackle waiting.

I see the wince he tries to hide, and he's been slow to get on his feet. Each hit cuts through me, and my hands ball into fists.

"Aw, c'mon, Ref! That was a late hit!" I shout, unable to hold back. The entire box erupts with groans and shouts of protest. My mom lets out an exasperated sigh beside me, and Sherri stands, shaking her head in disbelief.

We're all riding the tension, and by halftime, the Renegades are down by two touchdowns. I can see it on Mase's face from up here; he's deep in his head, off his rhythm, and that fire in his eyes is dimming. He's pressing too hard, trying to force a perfect play instead of letting his instincts lead.

Desperate for a bright idea, I scan the room until my gaze lands on Jay and Bash. If anyone can help me pull off a halftime pep talk, it's them.

I slide over with determination in my voice. "Alright, I need you two to be the greatest distractions of your lives so I can talk some sense into your brother. Think you can pull that off?"

Jay raises a brow, catching on with a smirk. "You want us to help you get into the tunnel?"

Bash grins, cracking his knuckles. "Tiff, we got you."

With that, they lead the way as we weave through the bustling crowd in the stadium corridors. Jay's infectious energy draws the attention of fans, reporters, and even the security staff. He's all smiles and swagger, signing autographs, posing for selfies, flirting, and making promises to the guards— anything to pull focus. Bash, with his natural intensity, steps in close behind, shielding me as we slip into the tunnel.

As we head closer to restricted territory, the roar of the crowd is replaced by the pounding of my heart echoing in my ears. Just ahead, I catch sight of Mase emerging from the locker room. His head is bowed, and he's surrounded by a huddle of teammates and coaches. But when he looks up, our eyes meet, and his surprise shifts into something softer.

"Tiff, what the hell?" He breathes, his eyes roaming over me. "Damn, you look good. But wait—how did you even get in here? What're you doing?"

I wrap my arms around his neck, allowing the vanilla to overtake him. "I'm here to remind you of the champion you are. I don't know what's going through your mind right now, but it sure as hell isn't about winning. Clear your head, Mase. I love you. You're the greatest to ever play this game, and I refuse to let you walk away without a ring tonight. Get it done."

I pull him into a deep, fierce kiss. For a brief, stolen moment, it's just me, Mase, and the world around us—wrapped in each other, in a universe that exists solely between his heartbeat and mine.

A voice crackles from behind us, security sternly reminding me it's time to go, but as I pull back, I see the fire back in Mase's eyes. His focus is renewed, and determination is etched across his face. He doesn't need to say anything. I know that he's ready to win.

I slip back into the stands with Jay and Bash, and when we reach the box, Charles and Sherri are waiting, their smiles wide and knowing.

Sherri leans over. "So, you went and kissed some sense into our boy, didn't you?"

I give a bashful smile, but my heart swells with pride and certainty as we all turn our attention back to the field. Mase strides onto the field, fully in control and orchestrating his offense with unwavering confidence. Every play is near perfect as he brings his team back from two touchdowns.

"Damn, Tiff! Did you give him a quickie down there? I knew it was a good idea for you to dress up. You got Mase playin' like he's twenty-two again." Mel teases.

Our spirits are high, and laughter bubbles around the box, but as the fourth quarter winds down, a tense silence settles over us. The game is tied with less than a minute on the clock, and every second feels like an eternity.

My hands grip the side of my clothing as I watch Mase in the huddle. His face is intense, and his eyes are locked in. He glances toward the sideline, and though the distance between us is vast, I swear he's looking right at me. It's like he can feel my heart beating in sync with his, rooting for him with everything I have.

The ball snaps, he steps back, and scans the field with laser-focused intensity. He's in complete control, calm and commanding, dodging defenders left and right. Time slows as he launches the pass—a perfect spiral slicing through the air, hurtling toward the end zone.

For a split second, the entire stadium holds its breath. The receiver stretches out, fingertips just grazing the ball before securing it and crossing the line.

TOUCHDOWN!

That's all we hear! That's all we see. He did it! Mason Boom just won the Super Bowl, again!

In the box, we burst into tears, hugging one another in pure joy. The final whistle blows, and the stadium explodes in exuberant chaos. We're caught between shock, relief, and elation as security quickly escorts us down to the field. We push through the throngs of people, and when I finally spot Mase amidst the celebration, he turns, and he only sees me.

With determined strides, he moves toward me, weaving effortlessly through the cameras, the crowd, and the barrage of questions. When he reaches me, he doesn't hesitate—his arms envelop me in one fluid motion, lifting me off the ground. He spins me, and for a moment, it's just us, lost in a kaleidoscope of confetti, cheers, and unspoken love.

Mase lowers me, his hands strong on my waist and eyes holding mine with a tenderness that makes the entire world blur around us. Without hesitation, he leans in and presses his lips to mine.

When he pulls back, he whispers, his voice low and steady, "Thank you."

I shake my head, feeling a laugh rise from my chest. "You've been in your head for weeks, Mase. I couldn't let you go home without a ring."

A grin tugs at his lips as he stifles a soft chuckle. "That's funny," He murmurs, his voice heavy. "Because I can't let you go home without a ring either."

Confusion flickers in my mind, but I see his subtle nod over my shoulder. I turn, my heart pounding, as I catch sight of our entire family standing nearby. Their faces are filled with pure joy, and their eyes are glistening with unshed tears. Reporters pivot toward us, their microphones capturing every moment.

With his voice unwavering, clear, and filled with a depth that shakes me to my core, Mase begins, "Tiffany Nicole Weathers. When I first met you, it felt like my heart finally became whole again. I loved you before I even knew you, and every moment since, you've been my reason, my anchor, and my heartbeat. There is nothing I want more than to stand by your side for every moment we have left in this life."

Mase lowers himself onto one knee and looks up at me with eyes filled with love and certainty.

My pulse quickens, and the realization hits me all at once. "Mason," his name slips out of my mouth in a whisper.

Drew steps forward and extends his hand to give Mase an elegant ring box. Mase takes it from him and nervously grins from ear to ear. He takes a breath before he opens the box and reveals a stunning ring that brilliantly catches the light.

"Tiffany Weathers, will you marry me? Will you make me the most fortunate man in the world and let me be yours forever?"

Tears spill over as I nod silently until my trembling voice finally emerges. "Yes, yes, Mase! Of course, I'll marry you!"

A roar erupts around us, but all I feel is Mase as he slips the ring onto my finger and rises up to pull me into his arms again. Our beginning started in the middle, and now it found its way to forever.

His kiss seals that promise, and in his arms, I feel our destinies finally merge into one. I feel whole as if every winding path we took was leading us right here—to this moment, to each other.

Our family surrounds us. Their faces beam with pride and love, and I feel Drew's arms wrap around us both, completing our circle. We're almost to our forever, and I'm more ready than ever to live it with Mason Boom by my side.

Chapter 41

The World Around Us – Tiffany

"So, what's on the schedule for tonight? I don't want to be out long. I'm not playin', Mel. I refuse to follow up with you and Taylor's antics. I don't even feel like being out. Mase was lovin' me down this morning. I just want to be in his arms right now. I don't want to party, and y'all will not make me late for my wedding!" I fuss, glancing around at my sisters while they stifle their laughter.

Taylor smirks at me like she knows something I don't, which makes me suspicious already. A very pregnant Monica acts innocent while Avery, who's also pregnant again, grins at me with that knowing smile only she can master.

But Mel just waves me off like I'm overreacting. "Relax, Tiff. You're about to have the night of your life. Trust me. We've planned everything down to the last detail."

"That's what I'm afraid of," I mutter, crossing my arms as I lean back in my seat. Next to me, Lottie Daniels, the co-owner of the Greer Devils and our newest addition to our friend group, chuckles softly. She's been hanging around more lately, thanks to Bash practically begging us to include her in our circle. I can't help but notice the way her cheeks flush whenever his name comes up. Something's definitely going on there.

"Look," Mel announces, gesturing dramatically as the car pulls to a stop. "We've arrived."

I glance out the window, and my jaw nearly drops. We're at the Greer Deluxe Glamping Resort, an exclusive hideaway tucked into the picturesque countryside just outside of town. We're surrounded by towering oak trees that form a natural canopy over elegant, oversized glamping pods that look like something out of a magazine.

"Okay, I'll admit," I say, stepping out of the car. "This is impressive."

"Impressive?" Taylor echoes, rolling her eyes. "Girl, this is luxury. So, thank Mel and me for sparing no expense."

We're greeted by staff who escort us to our pods, each one a miniature palace with plush bedding, gold-accented décor, and private outdoor soaking tubs. The air smells like fresh pine and lavender, and for a moment, I feel myself relax.

After settling in, we head to the onsite winery for dinner and a wine tasting. The sprawling vineyard stretches endlessly under the golden hour light, the rows of grapevines creating a breathtaking backdrop. A long, rustic table has been set up for us, adorned with candles, flowers, and the most elaborate charcuterie board I've ever seen.

We sip wine, and the conversation flows effortlessly. Taylor is the center of attention and she updates us on her college courses. "I aced my finals. It just feels good to finally be in control over my life." She says, her voice tinged with pride.

Then, Lottie jumps in, her curiosity getting the best of her. "And what about my team's assistant coach? Did you ever call him back about the prison reform benefit?"

Taylor's cheeks turn pink, sipping her non-alcoholic cider. "No," She says quickly, avoiding eye contact.

I narrow my eyes. "Taylor Lynn! You're my twin. I know when you're lying. Spill it. Now!"

With a dramatic sigh, she finally relents. "Fine! I called him back, okay? We ended up talking... for hours... about everything. He's just so... nice. And... smart. And, well... cute. So dang on cute! I've been ignoring his calls ever since, but I may answer again... at some point."

The table erupts into 'awws' and 'oohs' and playful teasing, and even Taylor can't help but smile.

Meanwhile, Monica and Avery turn their attention to Mel. "What about you?" Monica asks, winking. "Still juggling a million men?"

Mel snorts. "Hardly. Just one—a douchebag photographer who's now my sworn nemesis. And maybe someone else. We're kind of just friends, but that man and I would be a hot mess together, so it's complicated."

"Complicated?" Monica presses, her tone laced with mischief. "More like forbidden, if you ask me. I *know* who has your nose turned upside down."

Mel groans but doesn't deny it, and we all laugh as the evening continues.

Later that night, we return to the resort for a surprise that Mel has orchestrated. I should've known better than to trust her.

"Hot oil massages?" I ask, narrowing my eyes at the setup. Each of us has a private cabana, and Mel, practically vibrating with excitement, looks way too pleased with herself.

"No, ma'am. The only hands I want on me are Mase's," I declare firmly, crossing my arms.

Mel waves me off with a dismissive flick of her hand. "You're about to get married. This is your last chance to indulge before he monopolizes you for the rest of your life. Trust me, you'll thank me."

Grumbling, I step into the cabana and eye the massage table like it's some kind of trap. "I don't know about this."

"Just lie down!" Mel calls from outside, her laughter fading as she retreats to her own cabana.

Reluctantly, I lie face down on the table, letting my head rest in the opening and arms dangle below. The soft music playing in the background does little to soothe my nerves. I hear the sound of footsteps approaching and feel the faintest brush of air as someone steps inside.

"Good evening, ma'am," a low voice greets me. It's smooth but carries a strange, almost exaggerated accent. "I'll be your masseur tonight."

"Your accent is so strange. Where are you from?" I ask.

His voice falters for a moment like he's trying not to laugh. "A little Caribbean paradise called Black Summer Island."

The masseur's hands land on my shoulders, and my entire body goes still. The first press of his fingers sends a wave of relaxation coursing through me. He works his way down my back with expert precision, and I have to bite my lip to keep from moaning. The tension I didn't even know I was holding melts away with every stroke, but something feels oddly familiar about his touch.

"This is…wow," I admit, letting out a deep sigh. "You're *good.*"

"Thank you, ma'am." He replies, the accent still intact, though it sounds slightly strained now, like he's fighting against himself, and a part of me is tickled.

His hands move lower, kneading the knots in my lower back, raising my suspicion. His touch is *too* familiar, *too* precise. It's not just good—it's *perfect.* The way his thumbs press into the exact spots that always ache, the way his hands linger just a second longer than necessary. I *know* this touch. I *love* this touch.

His hands move to my arms, and the way his fingers glide over my skin sends shivers down my spine. There's no denying it now—this is my Mase.

My lips curve into a smirk. "What did you say your name is again?"

"I didn't," he says, short and curt. "My name's Kason Toom."

I snort, barely able to suppress my laughter. "Well, I'm warning you, Kason Toom, my fiancé is crazy. If he finds out you're touching me like this, he'll teleport here and whoop your ass."

He chuckles, his voice low and rich. "I'll try to behave, but Miss, your body is irresistible. So, I think I'll take my chances."

"Kason Toom, you're a bad man," I drawl, unable to keep the laughter out of my voice. "Tell me, do all your clients get this type of...special treatment?"

"I can't say they do, ma'am," he replies, his voice dropping an octave. "You're a special case. I'm drawn to you – your smooth sexy brown skin. That sultry voice. May I be so candid to admit that I want you?"

I chuckle, fully amused by Mase's effort. "You know," I say, turning my head slightly in the massage chair opening, "I love a man who goes after what he wants. You remind me of my fiancé. And your hands feel an awful lot like my fiancé's."

"Do they?" He asks, feigning innocence.

"They do," I say, my smirk widening. "And if you're not careful, I might have to tell him how good you're making me feel right now."

He leans closer, his breath warm against my ear. "Maybe you should tell him right now. I bet you'll turn him on."

I flip over, and sure enough, there he is—Mase, grinning like the Cheshire Cat, his deep brown eyes twinkling with mischief.

"You're ridiculous," I say, swatting at his chest.

"You love it." He replies, leaning down to kiss me. His lips capture mine with a playful intensity, and for a moment, we forget where we are and have a bit of *fun*.

When we finally emerge from the cabana, hand in hand, we're met with a chorus of cheers and laughter from my girls and the guys, who are gathered around the fire pit.

"Y'all think you're funny, huh?" I ask, glaring at Mel.

Rafe winks. "We were told the ladies needed some eye candy for tonight."

Monica smirks, her head lying on his shoulder. "No one said that, Rafe. Absolutely no one." She laughs while Rafe rubs her belly, sending a fair warning to us all. "*This* is the result of eye candy hanging around."

With the night winding down, Mase and I slip away to the resort's private hot springs. The water is warm and clear, and the stars above twinkle like diamonds. Steam rises around us, creating an intimate cocoon while Mase pulls me close, his arms wrapping around me from behind.

His lips graze my shoulder, and his voice is a low murmur. "You know you're getting married tomorrow, right? Are you ready?"

I lean back into him, my heart full. "Since the moment we met. Are you ready, Mr. Boom?"

He gently turns me to face him, his steady gaze brimming with love. "Since the day I was born."

I smile and stare into his eyes. "Speaking of born, how 'bout we get started on expanding our family...right here, right now."

Mase's eyes widen, and a smile stretches across his face. "Really? Are you ready for that?" He trails his fingers down the middle of my body.

"I'm ready for everything with you, Mason Boom."

We make sweet love in the soothing warm waters, working towards our shared future one thrust at a time. The moment feels so surreal, and when we come together, I see every version of myself, past, present, and future, with Mase by my side. And tomorrow is when our forever finally begins.

~ ~ ~

If anyone knows about trauma, disappointment, and hardship, it's me, but if anyone knows about hope, faith, and restoration, then it's also me. There were times in my life when I wondered when things would get better. There were moments when I questioned whether happiness was something

I could truly attain. I've been broken, bent, and almost beaten down, but somehow, even in the darkest hours, a spark kept me moving forward. A whisper of hope would always come in human form – Ms. Harriet, Aunt Dora, the Bakers, the Booms, and Drew. But the loudest whisper came in the form of a man who knew me before I even knew myself and loved me more purely than anyone else. Today, I get to marry that man. The man who has been my best friend, my truest partner, and my greatest love.

"Are y'all crying again?" I tease, glancing at my mom, Aunt Dora, Sherri, and Callie, whose eyes are brimming with tears as Mel, Taylor, and Monica add the final touches to my dress and prepare to turn me around for the big reveal.

"Of course we are!" Mom exclaims, her voice thick with emotion. "You look so beautiful! So perfect!"

"Here y'all go again," I laugh, feeling my heart swell with warmth. "You act like I'm just some ragdoll any other day."

Aunt Dora gives me a playful shush. "Because you are, little girl—always running around in joggers or workout shorts. Now hush and turn around so you can witness the miracle they've worked on you."

With a deep breath, I finally turn to face the mirror. As I take in my reflection, I nearly lose my breath. I look… like a work of art. My hair is swept up with soft curls that frame my face, and my dress—oh, my dress—fits like a glove with intricate lace and beading that hugs my every curve and flows into a soft, elegant train.

"I hope Mase likes what he sees," I quietly murmur, unable to hide the shy smile that slips through.

Monica catches my eye and grins. "Girl, he's going to love what he sees. And he's going to love on you for the rest of your lives."

I share warm, heartfelt hugs with the women who've been my foundation through so many different phases of my life. The moms take their seats first, and then my beautiful bridesmaids begin their walk down the aisle in their gold gowns, shimmering gently in the sunlight.

I take a peek out the window to see my parents' backyard transformed into an intimate sanctuary of love with soft gold-dusted roses and lanterns lining the aisle. It's finally feeling *real*. My happy ending is just a few minutes away.

At the back door, Dad awaits. When I reach him, I can see the faintest shimmer of tears in his eyes.

"Dad." I whisper, my voice thick with emotion.

He extends his arm to me, his hand steady but warm. "Daughter." It's a single word, yet it holds decades of meaning.

I lean into him with my voice low and filled with affection. "Happy much?"

Still trembling with emotion, he chuckles. "I just never thought I'd be able to walk my daughter down the aisle. This is one of the happiest days of my life. I love you."

With a tearful smile, I press my head against his shoulder. "I love you, too."

We take our first steps together with his quiet tears dotting my arm.

I lift my gaze, and there, waiting for me at the altar, is Mason. His expression says it all. His tears evoke my tears, and the love radiating from his gaze anchors me, even as my own emotions threaten to pull me under. My father's steady grip is the only thing keeping me grounded as I draw closer to the man of my dreams and, in just a few moments, my husband.

Dad places my hand in Mase's, a silent blessing passing between them. Mase's fingers wrap around mine, helping me stand before him. His eyes are wet with tears that seem unstoppable, like the endless love he holds for me.

"I wish I could kiss you right now." He whispers, gently squeezing my hand tighter.

But before he can act on it, Pastor Owens, our officiant—and Monica's father—clears his throat with a knowing grin. "Not yet, Son. Just give me a few more minutes."

Our wedding guests erupt in low laughter, breaking the tension and making us all feel the warmth and joy that fills the air around us.

Pastor Owens clears his throat and begins, a quiet reverence settles over us, the voices of our loved ones and the rustling of the wind fade into stillness. His words carry warmth and hope as he speaks about love, commitment, and the journey that has led us here. I feel my heartbeat steadily rising when he finally nods to Mase, signaling it's time for his vows.

He clears his throat and gently tightens the grip on my hand.

"When I was young, I thought I'd lost everyone I loved. I thought that my life would be spent chasing ghosts and trying to fill those empty spaces. But the moment we met, I felt something I couldn't understand, I was drawn to you. A part of me always knew you were the girl whose picture I used to stare at. You became the girl I imagined by my side in every childhood hope, every wish, and every prayer. You always say I found you, but I promise you, baby, you found me. You brought me back to life, filled every broken piece, and gave me a purpose beyond anything I ever dreamed. Fate never fails, and it's our destiny to be together. I love you, Tiffany Weathers. You're my first and my forever. And I promise, from this day forward, I'll give my all to you, to Drew, and the beautiful world around us."

His every word wraps around me and fills me with endless love. I try to steady myself, blinking away the tears that blur my vision, but there's no stopping the emotion he's stirred within me.

"Today, as I stand here in front of you, surrounded by everyone we love, I realize that every twist, every broken piece, every hard-fought battle led us here to the beginning of a life I never dreamed possible. But you did, Mase. You believed in us before we even existed. You were the first person to make me feel happy, safe, and loved. You've seen me at my worst, and somehow, you brought out my best. You're the best man a girl could ever dream of, and you're my reality. This isn't just our wedding—it's our homecoming. Mason Boom, you're not just a good man—you're my man. And from this day forward, I promise to worry myself crazy so you can calm my fears. I promise to fuss at you when you post candid photos of me online. I promise to eat your homemade biscuits every morning. I promise to emphasize your first and last name every chance I get. But I also promise to give you warmth when life treats you cold. I promise to love you as deeply and purely as you've always loved me. I promise to be the woman you need and the wife you deserve. You're my first and only love. And I promise to cherish what we have forever. I love you, Mason Boom, and I am so blessed to be your wife."

Mase wipes away my lingering tears, and Pastor Owens, with a smile on his face, looks between us. "With the power vested in me, I now pronounce you husband and wife. Mason, you may now kiss your wife."

Mase grins, and I can see the pure joy lighting up his face as he steps closer to wrap his arm around my waist and pull me against him. Our kiss is gentle but filled with the kind of passion that makes my knees weak.

Our family and friends stand in applause and cheer, but as we pull back, Mase rests his forehead against mine, his voice a soft whisper meant just for me.

"Welcome to forever, Tiffany Nicole Boom."

Our story of forever begins here in Greer, Georgia, surrounded by the family I once only dreamed of having, but now, it's real. I have everything I could ever need—the peace, happiness, and safety I once believed was out of reach. My heart is full, and I know that every step forward will be taken with Mason by my side and with the beautiful world around us as our witness. Forever, here we come!

Epilogue

Tiffany

O ur driver pulls up in front of the courthouse, and Mase is out of the car in an instant with his hand protectively placed on my back. His eyes hold a familiar, worried glow as he looks me over, searching for the slightest sign of exhaustion.

"You sure you're okay?" He asks, his voice laced with genuine concern. "Did you take your vitamins? Tiff, I'm not playin'. You've been going non-stop with your competitions. You're tired, babe."

I laugh and give his hand a reassuring squeeze. "Mase, I'm barely even showing! This is gonna be a long nine months."

Drew sidles up to us with a smirk, "Yeah, Mase, you're stressing my baby sis out already."

A laugh escapes me, and I turn to Drew. "A girl? That's your prediction?"

Mase exchanges a fist bump with Drew. "There's definitely a little Tiff in there."

We step up to the courthouse doors and spot our families waiting inside. They're all standing together to show their love and support as we finally complete our family circle.

Mel catches my eye and flashes a grin as Jay leans close to her. The two of them look annoyingly comfortable. I raise an eyebrow and shake my head, teasingly scolding them. "So, you two an item now? I saw those steamy pictures in the blogs."

Jay laughs and flashes a devilish grin. "And if we were, what's wrong with that?"

Mel rolls her eyes but smirks. "Trust me, Tiff, we are *not* together. Long story. I'll fill you in later."

We push through the doors of the courthouse and join the rest of our family while Rafe strides over to Mase and Drew.

Rafe pats Mase on the shoulder, and his face breaks into a smile, glancing between them. "You two ready for this?"

Mase's expression shifts, turning serious, and he nods. "Been wanting to do this for seventeen years."

When we step into the judge's chambers, the room is quiet, with only the judge seated before us. She smiles at us then glances at the paperwork in front of her.

She leans forward and looks first at Drew, then at Mase. "Mr. Boom, do you understand the responsibility you're undertaking as Drew's adoptive father?"

Mase's voice comes out thick with emotion. "Yes, Your Honor. He's always been my son."

"And Drew, do you accept Mason Boom as your father?"

Drew nods without hesitation, his voice steady. "Yes, ma'am. He's always been my dad."

The judge's gaze softens, and she places her pen on the paper with a final signature. "Well then, young man, it is my great honor to declare you Drew Boom. Congratulations to you and your family."

The words settle over the room like a benediction, filling every corner with profound joy. We exit the chambers to meet up with our anxiously waiting family.

Drew spreads his arms wide and announces, "Well, your boy is officially a Boom!"

Cheers and laughter ripple through our loved ones. Sherri and Charles pull Drew into a tight hug, their pride and love for their grandson exuberant. Mom and Dad follow, then Aunt Dora as she wipes away happy tears.

Taylor sidles up next to me and slides her hand into mine. "You've given him such a beautiful life, Tiff," she says, her voice slightly cracking. "Everything we never had. I knew you'd be an amazing mother."

I turn to her and squeeze her hand. "You gave him this, you gave me him, and now we get to experience all of this beauty together. We did it— me, you, and the family we created."

I look at Mase and Drew embrace one another in a way that I've never seen before. A hug from a father to his son.

He turns to Mase with his eyes glassy but clear and full of the love he's finally ready to put into words.

"I love you, Dad."

Mase's face softens, "I love you, too, Son."

I feel the completeness of the life we've built and the peace I was destined to have. Here in Greer, Georgia, I've discovered that home is truly where the heart is, and my heart has found its safe place to land in the care of the beautiful world around us.